The Courting of Alta Belle

The Courting of Alta Belle

ODYSSEY WEST QUARTET BOOK ONE

ROSE WALKER

Tuxtails Publishing, LLC

Tuxtails Publishing, LLC

www.tuxtailspublishing.com

First Tuxtails Publishing Print Edition June 2023

ISBN: 978-1-957211-10-7

eBook ISBN: 978-1-957211-11-4

Cover art by Ella Kate Dewees

To Dominic Francisco, Agent Extraordinaire

To Madeline and Liliana Francisco, endlessly patient first readers and Computer EMTs

And to Christina Malango, Research Wizard and story editor, for laughing at all the right places

Thank you.

PART ONE
The Buford Sapphire

Chapter One

JUNE 1886

"Hortense, who is that man?" I asked my friend, almost holding my breath.

"Who?" she responded, as so often lost in her own thoughts, while we wandered arm in arm along an upper path in the lovely park above the North River—just now bursting into a New York June lushness.

"The one in the white boater hat, coming in with Buzzy Buford," I indicated with my chin. Ladies do not point.

We both gazed down the gentle slope to a pleasant grassy glade where our crowd was gathering in the welcome June sunlight, all thoughts of harsh winter weather gone.

The boys had all discarded their jackets and were running around like idiots, doing flips and handstands on the grass. We girls, on the other hand, had all come out dressed in new spring regalia.

I was particularly pleased with my own appearance today. I had worried a little that my spring-green muslin, with matching parasol, was too bright in color, but as soon as I stepped among the other girls, I knew it had been the right choice. They were a lovely, mixed flowerbed of light colors. I stood out and caught the eye—like a stalk of Bells of Ireland surrounded by butterflies. The yellow-green satin streamers that tied my wide-brimmed straw hat under my chin fell all the way to the toes of my elegant tan boots and fluttered charmingly in the light breeze. I meant to be the picture of springtime.

Hortense, bless her plump little heart, was lovely in lavender-dotted swiss, and the others looked like butterflies in pink, light blue, and the palest green. I stood out like a lighthouse on a shore of pastels. Who could ask for more?

Below us to one side of the sunny lawn, servants were setting up a long table under a shady copse of leafing elm trees. On the snowy white cloth, large platters of sandwiches and little cakes were being laid out, along with a huge punch bowl for lemonade.

The young man was being introduced to Tom Jarvis, our host, who had invited us all to his "Frolic on the River" to celebrate the blooming of summer. The new man was tall and elegant, and I could see at once that he was a little older than most of us. He was dressed stylishly in a blue-striped blazer with white trousers, and he carried a cane for effect—not because he needed it. He looked quite the *man-about-town* and I at once dismissed every other male present as immature and gauche.

Hortense had spotted him now. "Oh, that's Charles Buford, Buzzy's Boston cousin," she pronounced, peering intently through her wire-rimmed spectacles. "The shipyard Bufords. He just finished law school at Yale and passed the bar. They say he will start as an apprentice at Deering, Mason, and Deering this fall."

"That's a very prestigious law firm," I noted, thinking he was the best-looking man at Tom's picnic.

Hortense slipped her little hand over my arm and pulled me down to whisper intimately, "They say his family has sent him to spend the summer here in the city with his cousins, in hopes he will find a suitable wife!"

"Do tell!" I giggled, and we hugged each other with the deliciousness of it all.

"How do you hear these things?" I exclaimed. But I knew the answer to that. Hortense's family, the Duprés, owned Éclair —an extremely popular downtown lunchroom we all frequented—along with their relatives, the LaSalles. Hortense always knew everything.

"I have very good ears," she informed me accurately. Indeed, her ears were lovely, dainty, shaped like little seashells, and adorned with a truly fine pair of pearl studs.

I bent over and whispered into the nearest one, "Hortense, I think I've just seen the man I am going to marry!"

She pealed out a charming little laugh, her second-best feature, and squeezed my arm.

"In that case, Alta Belle, I think we'd better get you down there fast. It looks to me as if the Van der Meer twins have already claimed him!"

It was true. Matching blonde corkscrew curls bobbed on either side of the new man. It was possibly Daisy clutching his left arm and Maisie his right; who knew which was which? Identical sky-blue eyes, identical dimples, identical shrill giggles —it was all too much!

Tom Jarvis was making introductions all around as Hortense and I sauntered down the path, careful to give no impression of haste.

"Ah," said Tom as we approached. "Here is Hortense, I think you know her."

"Horty!" the new man cried familiarly, and tried to reach out to her, but his clinging blonde attachments prevented that. "Buzzy said you would be here. Good to see you."

I shot Hortense a fish eye, but she jauntily ignored me—as

well as the twins—and went up on tiptoe to salute him on the cheek.

"Charles," she said. "I'd like you to meet my friend Alta Belle Carlton. Alta, this is Charles Buford."

Well, thank you, Hortense! She did come through in the end.

I smiled at him and, somehow, he slid one hand free enough to take mine in a firm handshake—a new practice I personally much preferred to the old-fashioned hand kiss. It was quite nice to meet a forward-thinking young man.

"Miss Carlton," he said. "So pleased to meet you."

"Carlton & Hughes Mercantile, on Fifth Avenue," Buzzy whispered in his ear. We could all hear him, but I didn't mind. I certainly wanted this man to know I was a member of an important merchant family, easily his equal in any social situation.

Charles winked at me—acknowledging the sideline coaching—and bowed, causing the twins to bow as well, which sent them off on another bout of annoying giggles while they tightened their grips.

"Mr. Buford," I said. "I hear we are to congratulate you on passing the bar."

"Hortense, you've been telling tales again," he pretended to scold. "Is Larry coming?"

"Yes, indeed," Hortense promised. "He'll be happy to see you."

This was a reference to Hortense's second cousin and intended fiancé, Laurence LaSalle. Her family made it clear these two were meant to wed when the time was right; that is, when she had "come out" and he was established at Éclair. The light began to dawn. Larry had also just graduated from Yale and was preparing for his second attempt to pass the bar. The little minx! Hortense already knew this man—pretty well, I guessed.

"Larry was my roommate at Yale," Charles explained. "Two years ago, we toured the continent together."

"How nice for everyone," I said somewhat tartly, feeling bamboozled. Hortense just laughed at me.

Her fiancé-to-be arrived just then; after giving her a scandalous hug and a smacking kiss on her cheek, he and Charles embraced each other so fervently the twins were dislodged—a most welcome development. I noticed that Charles took precautions so that they could not latch onto him again, taking Larry's arm with one of his and tucking his cane under the other.

Aha! I thought. *The twins are out!* I boldly engaged him in conversation.

"Mr. Buford," I said, somewhat impertinently. "You must be vastly intelligent to pass the bar on your first try, since our Larry here must try again for a second time! How can you be friends with such a laggard?"

This sent the two men off into gales of laughter and a bout of competitive arm wrestling, which Hortense ended by bearing Larry off to the refreshment table for sandwiches and cake.

"Miss Carlton, would you care to follow them?" Mr. Buford offered his arm and we walked off, thereby eliminating the twins. They trailed uselessly along behind us, listening to our conversation I suppose, but I didn't care. I had his full attention and his arm. He had handled that well.

As we approached the refreshment table, we saw old Mrs. Jarvis, Tom's grandmother and our official chaperone for this picnic, dithering among the many platters of food set out for us.

"Hello, dear Charles," she said, giving him a pat on the arm and a kiss on his cheek. "And Miss Carlton. I'm afraid these foolish servants have got everything wrong. I am sure they have forgotten the pickles!" She gazed vaguely around. "I don't know..."

"Right here, ma'am," responded Sean, one of the servants, putting down a large platter of pickled cauliflower, peppers, crab apples, and assorted cucumber delicacies.

"Oh, dear!" Mrs. Jarvis moved the platter slightly, to what she considered a more proper angle. Turning to me, she clutched my arm and further complained, "I know they have forgotten the ice for the punch!"

"Putting it in right now, ma'am," said Dicky calmly, in charge of that important item. Both he and Sean were well accustomed to Mrs. Jarvis's style of managing her servants, as were we all, from the many times she had entertained us.

"Oh, dear! I don't know…" She fluttered vaguely over to the punch bowl and back again.

I put my arm comfortably through hers and turned her away from the table. "Everything is fine, Mrs. Jarvis. You have laid out a superb feast for us. Now you must come and sit down and enjoy the picnic yourself!"

I led her to a chair and side table that had obviously been set up for her in the shade of a nearby chestnut tree on a handsome horsehair blanket: a shady retreat for our chaperone. Gratefully, she sat down, fanning herself.

"Let us bring you some punch and nibbles," I proposed.

"So kind, Miss Carlton," Mrs. Jarvis beamed approvingly as the two of us went on that errand.

Mr. Buford took a plate and began to sparingly serve it.

"You seem to know all my friends very well, indeed!" I reproached him.

"Well," he disparaged, "only through Arty and Tom."

He showed me the plate and I pretended to be horrified at his selections. He proposed to give her a plate with one tea-cut chicken finger sandwich and one small spice cake. I took it out of his hands; what an excellent opportunity to tease him even more!

"Mr. Buford, I see you don't know much about middle-aged ladies!" I proceeded to load the plate with a large mound of potato salad, two of each of the three kinds of tiny sandwiches, pickles, and one of each kind of cake. Mrs. Jarvis received this largesse, along with a glass of lemonade, with cries of delight, and we left her happily refreshing herself in the shade.

Tom chose that moment to bring over a new candidate to meet Mr. Buford: Letty Wallis. I was not pleased to see her. A tall, willowy blonde, her family was as socially prominent as mine, maybe more so. Heir to the Gold Crown Beer fortune, she was just the kind of girl Charles Buford's family would be hoping he might meet.

Freed of the clinging twins, he was able to freely shake her hand and even bow over it much more charmingly than he had over mine. Not good. I greeted her coolly and fancied Mr. Buford had a glint in his eye.

They began a conversation, but almost at once she let out a shriek and pitched herself into his arms—moaning piteously about being stung by a bee. This was absolutely indecent!

I pulled her out of Mr. Buford's arms, thrust my parasol into his hands to keep him off her, and took charge of the pathetic victim myself. She had indeed been stung on her upper left arm. I pulled out the stinger and urged Letty to bear up.

For once, I was glad to find the twins craning at my elbow to see what had happened and put them to work.

"Daisy, run and get some ice from Dicky at the punch bowl and wrap it up in a napkin. Maisie, support Letty on her other side."

Daisy came running back quickly with the ice, which we applied to Letty's poor arm to relieve the pain.

I commandeered Percy Ward, who was standing to one side, trying to be inconspicuous. He was the shyest, least confident boy in our set; nonetheless, I put him in charge of the casualty.

"Mr. Ward, please escort Miss Wallis to that bench over there, under the forsythia. She needs to sit in the shade and recover. Daisy, see that she keeps the ice pack on, and renew it when it melts. Maisie, run and get her some lemonade; something sweet to drink will help with the shock of it all."

It was amazing how obedient all four were to my commands. I'm sure each felt the star of a drama, and the role of being Florence Nightingale to Letty was especially appealing to the twins.

I retrieved my parasol from Mr. Buford with a demure smile, and we watched the little party set off for the bench per my instructions—only stopping briefly to inform Mrs. Jarvis of what had happened. For a chaperone, she did not seem to have been concerned enough about the incident to put down her plate, but I suppose she had confidence that whatever had happened, *Dear Charles* would be able to handle it.

Mr. Buford seemed amused, but he was also looking at me with admiration.

"We seem to be on our own, Miss Carlton. Would you care to walk with me? The view of the river from the top of the bluff must be very inviting."

I took his arm with a smile. "It is well worth the climb," I agreed, and we set off. Alone at last.

"I shall feel quite safe with you by my side, no matter what happens," he assured me, his brown eyes sparkling with laughter. I was quite pleased with him. He had missed nothing of what had just happened. Most of the boys in our set would have taken everything at face value. It was so pleasant to be in the company of someone older.

Our path wound pleasantly through sun and shade, made private by hedges and small groves of trees.

He spoke of Yale and some of the exploits he and Larry had gotten up to. I mentioned that I had graduated from Oakmont, a well-thought-of finishing school. He spoke of his coming apprenticeship and how he hoped he would enjoy the practice of the law. I remarked that I would very much have liked to be given some small job at my father's Mercantile, but my parents wanted me to make my debut this December at the annual Snowflake Ball, our version of the posh St. Regis Ball, at which the society debutantes were presented. Apparently, my working at the store would somehow interfere with that procedure.

He expressed sympathy. We leaned against a railing to enjoy the view. He asked if I had traveled.

I admitted I had never been outside the state of New York. He spoke brilliantly of his travels to London, Paris, and Rome, and leaned so close to me that he pressed against my side.

I slipped away, smiling, opened my parasol, and we walked on.

He asked me if I liked to dance. I said I adored it. He asked hesitantly if I knew how to waltz. I confessed that I did, but of course, had never performed that risqué dance in public—just in the privacy of my dancing class.

He confessed that the waltz was his specialty and that if I allowed him to teach me several special steps, he was sure we would be excellent dancing partners.

We found a shaded bench, well hidden among some blooming hydrangea shrubs, and I lowered my parasol. We sat down. He gazed at me ardently and declared how much he would like to take me to Paris, to attend a public ball.

"They waltz there as nowhere else. You would wear camellias and a white gown with a very full skirt, and I a tuxedo. We would dance together so perfectly, everyone would stop dancing to watch us as I swung you 'round and 'round, and they would applaud when the music ended."

I closed my eyes to picture this beguiling fantasy and felt his arm slip around my waist as he pulled me closer. Opening my eyes, I saw that his were fixated on my lips and that he was bending toward me. Instantly, I leaped to my feet and popped open my parasol. It was much too soon for such intimacy. Besides—I intended him to take me seriously.

"Mr. Buford!" I reproached him. "You are very forward!" I smiled at him sweetly, to show I wasn't really offended. In fact, his ardent approach pleased me very much. But it was important that he understand I was a well-brought-up young woman not to be trifled with.

He grinned at me ruefully and, as we began to retrace our steps back to the others, he spoke to me of his interest in the law and his hopes for his internship with Deering, Mason, and Deering.

When we rejoined the picnic, Letty was fully recovered and walking in the rose garden with Percy Ward—an interesting development. Daisy and Maisie rushed up to us and, ignoring me, noisily invited Charles to ride with them at the stables in Central Park tomorrow morning. He accepted with apparent pleasure and then turned to me.

"Miss Carlton, do you ride?"

I responded that I did, having had lessons since I was five.

"In that case, you must join us," he exclaimed. "And maybe Hortense and Larry can come, too."

Thus, he cleverly converted what had been meant as a private invitation into a group outing, to the chagrin of the Van der Meer twins, and ensured that we would see each other the next day.

I smiled at him in appreciation. It would seem we were equals in manipulation.

We did indeed ride in the park the next day. And a few days after that he turned up at Sara Sherwood's musical evening—where it was proven that we were, as predicted, excellent dancing partners. On that evening we became *Charles and Alta*.

On Sunday, I was not at all surprised to find him at services at our Presbyterian Church. Afterward, he came up to greet me and it was possible to introduce him to Father and Mother.

"What a nice young man," Mother commented. "You did say the Boston Bufords?"

A few days after that, he made an appointment to see Father in his office at Carlton & Hughes and formally requested permission to call on me, which Father gladly gave.

Charles Buford was a very eligible gentleman.

After that, we saw each other every day in one way or another. The summer passed in a dazzle of tea dances, parties, ferry rides, excursions to Long Island for the beach, and outings in Central Park. We lunched at Éclair and went in large groups to concerts, revues, and dinners in fancy restaurants.

Charles was my escort to all of these, and we were easily the "top couple" in our set. I had never had so much fun in my life.

In late August, for my eighteenth birthday, my parents gave me an elegant tea dance with a gazebo and dance floor on the lawn. As dusk fell, little colored paper lanterns holding lighted candles were hung everywhere. It was an enchanted fairyland.

At the height of the dancing, Charles pulled me away into the rose garden, where—in the shelter of a huge bushy cabbage rose—he seized me and kissed me full on the lips. In the shock of the moment, and swooning from the scent of the roses, I registered only surprise that the kiss was so wet, but it was not unpleasant. And then in the next moment, he was on one knee holding out a jeweler's velvet box.

"Alta Belle, will you marry me?"

"Oh, yes!" I said, and he put the Buford Sapphire on my finger.

Chapter Two

M y parents were not best pleased with my engagement. "Eighteen is too young, and you've barely known him for two months! Besides, you must make your debut in December. You can't be engaged!" protested Mother.

"You were eighteen when you married Father," I pointed out. "And I don't want a debut. I've told you and told you. It could never compare with the fun I've had this summer. And besides, I'd rather go to work at Carlton & Hodges."

Mother sputtered, but Father responded with logic. "We were a different generation, brought up to marry young and work. My father and I were just enlarging the Saddlery into what would become our big store. And I rescued your mother from having to become a nanny. You, on the other hand, have been raised and educated to marry well and run a large establishment. Quite a different thing."

"I'd rather work in the store," I muttered sulkily.

"Why do you give us so much trouble?" Mother reproached me. "Your sisters both loved their debuts. Look at Adelle, how well she married, and how happy she and John are! And Agnes, getting a year in Europe after her season was over."

It was true. Adelle, a lush blonde like Mother, had met and quickly married John Hudson, a young banker, the following autumn. John was doing very well at his bank; Father pronounced him *solid*, predicting he would end up a vice president—at least.

Adelle promptly produced a son and heir within the year, John Jr., and was now joyfully awaiting the arrival of baby number two, giving every sign that she adored her—in my opinion—dull spouse.

Our middle sister, Agnes, had been considered a great success as a debutante, and had her picture in the commercial newspapers several times as "Daughter of Prominent Merchant Dubbed Belle of the Year," and "Daughter of Wealthy Merchant Rides in Central Park," to name a few.

Agnes and I greatly resembled each other—both dark-haired and pale like Father's side of the family, not delicate roses like Mother and Adelle. We were both short but made up for it with animation and energy (a bit too much on Agnes's part, but that is just my opinion).

Despite all the acclaim, Agnes failed to fall in love that year, and it was a stroke of great good fortune when Mother's younger sister, Adelaide, newly widowed, decided that she could never recover in New York City but must go abroad for at least a year, and that Agnes was the perfect companion for her pilgrimage in search of health.

So much had they enjoyed their progression through Switzerland (for the waters), Italy, and especially France that they had extended their stay in Paris. We did not expect them home until September.

Although Father, always indulgent, seemed inclined to let me have my way about the debut, Mother was adamant. I should have every advantage my sisters had enjoyed, whether I wanted it or not.

The family was at an impasse, everyone equally stubborn. So, we called Charles in, hoping for a voice of reason. However, this only complicated matters. Never mind the debut, Charles pressed eagerly for an early marriage, as his parents had promised him six months in Europe for a honeymoon as a wedding present. His law firm was willing to delay his entrance to the firm, as they preferred to employ married men, but expected him by next fall at the latest. In addition, his father promised Charles a house fronting on Central Park as a final gift, upon the couple's return.

This inducement was too generous to be ignored, but my parents must also be appeased; so, after a time, we all compromised and reached something of an agreement. Charles would be made known to my family as a prospective member, but our engagement would not be announced until after I had made my debut. We would announce in January and wed in late May.

This last point was bitterly contended until the end. Mother felt a May wedding was indecently hasty, and that we should properly wait a full year—if not two. Father pointed out that we should not risk losing a wedding present that would set us up so well. Charles campaigned hard for the full six months in Europe, but Father pointed out that three months was perfectly adequate. And besides, Deering, Mason, and Deering would probably prefer it. In the end, we agreed, but I felt my personal distaste for the debut was entirely ignored.

Not for the first time, I realized how vastly different I was from my sisters. It seemed such a waste of time and money to me, the expense of a dress—indeed, a whole new wardrobe—for *the season*. The waste of time with all the fittings that would ensue, the classes on dancing and deportment, sessions with hairdressers—all of it tedious beyond bearing. I would enjoy the dancing, but the rest of it stretched boring and glum all the way until December when I could be doing something useful instead. I was not so sure what "something useful" might be, but I was sure there was a better way to spend both my time and Father's money. However, my feelings were discounted.

Charles didn't care whether I made a debut or not. He was concentrating on the trip and the house, with his apprenticeship to follow, but of course, he would be my escort at the debut.

Mother was somewhat mollified by the thought of the engagement party she would give in January. I could see that she was already planning how to make it the party of the season.

Thus, all was arranged, and Mother was willingly deflected into preparing an elaborate family dinner, at which to present Charles to our relatives and intimate friends. I looked forward to this event as if it were the official announcement of my engagement.

Charles was insistent that I should keep the Bufford Sapphire, as we both considered ourselves to be committed. So, Father bore it away to be resized for my small finger. Mother decided I could display it for just this one evening. Otherwise, I could wear it around my neck on a long velvet ribbon, so it wouldn't show.

The Buford Sapphire was a large square-cut stone of the deepest blue, surrounded by three rows of tiny—but real—seed pearls. To tell the truth, the ring trembled on the verge of vulgarity, but it was a genuine family heirloom handed down from mother to eldest son for who knew how many generations of Bufords—so that no one could say a word against it. I thought it garish but fabulous and would be proud to wear it.

I did have a moment of compassion for Mrs. Buford, however.

"Your mother was wearing this?" I asked Charles.

"Yes, of course."

"You just took it off her finger and gave it to me? Didn't she mind?"

"Of course not. It was the same for her. Old Mrs. Buford lived another thirty years after Father gave the ring to Mother. Naturally, Grandfather Buford replaced it with a two-carat canary diamond. She said she liked that even better than the sapphire."

"Oh." I saw how it worked. "And your mother?"

"She has decided on a Brazilian emerald. A suite, actually: with a pendant, earbobs, and a bracelet. Father's working on it."

That was raising the stakes quite a bit! When my time came, perhaps I would ask for diamonds!

Mother insisted that the family dinner was not to be held until Aunt Adelaide and Agnes returned from Europe. It seemed to me that Agnes was delaying her return just to irritate me! She would not be pleased that I should be engaged before her. No doubt the two would decide to stay yet another month! However, only a week later, we finally received a telegram from aboard their ocean liner, naming the day and time they were expected to dock. Mother set the date of our dinner for the very next night.

I could not believe it! I was expected to share my triumphant evening with a welcome home party for Adelaide and Agnes!

Such is my life!

Finally, they arrived—both looking and sounding so French, we hardly recognized them. Of course, it was exciting to see Agnes after a whole year and tell her my news, but we hardly had a chance to talk with all the hustle and bustle of arrival. And there was no late-night visit of sisters with their hair up in rags, as Agnes was too exhausted. She slept in so late, I had not even seen her at all on the day of our dinner.

In the late afternoon, I sat in front of my vanity, brushing my shoulder-length dark hair, and waiting for Mariah, the little Irish maid we had always shared, to finish with Agnes and come to help me.

Critically examining my face in the mirror, I was pleased enough. My dark eyes were shining and my cheeks were pink with excitement. We girls all knew how to enhance our looks, if necessary. Only fast women used paint, but who would ever suspect what could be done with a piece of damp, red blotting paper! I had done it often, being pale-skinned like Father. I would not be needing that help tonight!

My hair was much like Agnes's: long, thick, dark, and with a slight tendency to curl, which made it wave just a little. It had been pleasant to have Mariah all to myself for a year, but frankly, I had come to require very little from her. I seemed to be developing a fairly independent frame of mind. However, for tonight, Mother thought it would be appropriate for me to have a slightly more sophisticated coiffure, so Mariah it was.

I was already fully dressed up to my shift, waiting only for my hair and someone to do up the sixteen buttons on the back of my beautiful dress. I was so proud of my special gown. Mother's dressmaker had designed it specially to compliment the Buford Sapphire. Made of soft, dove-gray silk, it was printed all over with tiny, dark blue mignonettes—forget-me-nots.

I was thrilled that Mother had allowed the dress to be cut in the forward-looking style we were just beginning to see. It had a high, Chinese neck, and the sleeves were quite puffed and full at the shoulder, then tight down to my wrist, where the cuffs closed with more of the tiny, hand-carved pearl-shell buttons that marched down the back.

The most shocking feature was that the bustle pad was completely eliminated, the skirt being drawn tight and simply draped in the back, forming a sort of faux-bustle, held in place by a large bow. Bustles were definitely on the out. It was a most elegant gown, in the height of style, and I felt older and more sophisticated. I could hardly wait to put it on, whereas I cared not a fig for the other dress being made for me—a frothy white confection for my boring debut.

There was a knock on my door and, expecting Mariah, I called, "Come in."

But it was Father. "Alta," he greeted me, "I like you with your hair down, but why aren't you dressed?"

"Just waiting for Mariah to be done with Aggie, Father. I'm nearly ready."

"That's outrageous!" he exclaimed, angry on my behalf. "She's had Mariah since noon! I'll go and shoo her in here at once!"

I begged him not to make a fuss, assuring him I would be fine without help if only he would button me up. I put on the dress and he made a great production out of it, but in the end, he did manage. I couldn't help agreeing that it was an excessive number of buttons.

"Alta, you look beautiful," he complimented me, kissing me on the forehead. "My lovely girl! But what about your hair?"

"I'll do it up the way I do every other day. No need to be fancy." I sat down, and in a trice, had pinned four fat rolls on the top of my head, each anchored by one long tortoiseshell hairpin. To my mind, this simple arrangement, along with my fashionable fringe, did very well for all occasions, and Father agreed. He was not a "Fancy Dan" himself.

"Alta," he then said, pulling out the chair from my desk and sitting down. "I did come on an errand, to return your ring. Tiffany's did a great job sizing it for you, I think."

He handed me the black velvet box lined in blue satin, which I was very glad to have back, and the ring fit perfectly. The previous generations of Bufords must have had large hands and fingers, for the jeweler had to fuse in a full gold circlet to bring the ring down to my size. I flashed it around a bit, trying to get used to the heavy weight on a finger that had never worn a ring before.

"Oh Father, thank you! It's perfect with the dress, don't you think?"

He agreed but then took out from his pocket a second box. "As long as I was there, I thought, why not?" he explained, handing it to me.

I opened it with my heart in my throat... beautiful—but dainty—matching earbobs, dangling just the right amount on bits of pure gold chain, tiny square sapphires of exactly the same dark blue, surrounded by one tasteful row of seed pearls. We Carltons were holding up our side with this addition to the Buford treasure, which should now be known as the Buford *Sapphires*—plural.

"They're perfect!" I cried. "Father, you are too good to me!"

"Not half as good as you deserve, I fear," he said pensively, and I guessed he was thinking I was the only one at all like himself. It was true, and I was proud of it.

He left me then, remarking that Mother was a good fifteen minutes away from being ready. I tapped my fingers nervously on the vanity and couldn't stand to wait a minute longer. My room, which I loved, felt like a hot, little box today, and I felt shut-in. I would wait downstairs, even if it was early.

I opened the small, white florist's box waiting beside my hairbrush. Charles, in perfect fiancé form, had sent flowers for all the women of the house to wear at this festive dinner.

Mother had been left speechless by the elegant spray of white orchids he had selected for her. It was exactly right.

"What a nice young man," she cooed, for about the eleventh time.

For Agnes, he sent a box of miniature pink carnations, which made me laugh with a mean little grin. I wish I could report that my character is more elevated than that, but the truth is, I knew she hated carnations and regarded them as common. She would be compelled by good manners to wear them!

As for myself, I was still swooning with delight at the gift my intended had sent for me. Inside the little white box was a posy for me to carry, an exact replica of the ring! Deep blue mignonettes, possibly dyed to be so dark blue, were shaped in a square and surrounded with the tiniest white rosebuds. It was very clever, and I laughed with delight when I saw it. There could not be a more elegant and creative man in New York City! Charles always knew exactly the right thing to say or do, despite his family heirloom! I took the posy out of its nest almost reverently and then ran downstairs to await the coming of my beloved.

Chapter Three

In the parlor, Harrison—the butler—and several other servants were bustling efficiently about, making the final preparations. In this room, our guests would be served sherry—Father's finest Spanish Amontillado—before adjourning to dinner in the formal dining room, shining with candles and crystal and awash in the scent from vases of Mother's roses.

"Can I get you anything, Miss?" Harrison asked.

"No thank you, Harrison. I just prefer to wait for everyone down here."

"Not long to wait, Miss Alta." He bowed politely and went back to supervise the laying out of the sherry table.

Trying to stay out of everyone's way, I curled up in a corner of the main settee. Our parlor was large and amply furnished, with six couches of various types, overstuffed chairs, end tables, and kerosene lamps. The far wall was mostly window, with French doors, open to the warm evening, leading out into the rose garden. The large fireplace was still in its summer mode, filled with potted ferns.

We used this room to receive guests, but the rest of the time it was where our family gathered in the evenings, despite its size.

An especially comfortable divan and several stuffed chairs were grouped there with a careful arrangement of more potted ferns and palm trees—Harrison was adept at creating a cozy retreat for us.

This evening, in its social guise, the room was shown with candles, vases of flowers, crystal bowls of bonbons, and humidors of cigars, which Father would offer our male guests—for smoking in the garden, of course.

At last, Mother and Father appeared, coming down the great staircase. They made a most distinguished couple. Father looked aristocratic in his dark frock coat and gold and crimson brocade vest. Mother was stunning in a burgundy sateen dinner gown, revealing too much embonpoint—to my way of thinking —but then, she had it to show. On the scrap of fabric that covered her left shoulder, she wore the spray of orchids, quite elegant.

First to arrive was Mother's eldest sister, Aunt Adah, with Cousin Edgar, a favorite of mine. They brought Adelaide, the youngest, who had taken my sister Aggie to the continent. My Aunt looked well on the way to recovery, but she had come home very French, even so far gone as to have a slight French accent. But it went very well with her plump, blonde beauty.

Next came my sister Adelle, with John. She looked happy to have left John Jr. at home with his nanny and just to be out in public. A voluminous, white, lace shawl covered her interesting condition.

Charles came right on their heels. Mother broke off talking to Adelle to greet him, hugging him and thanking him for the flowers so warmly that she made it clear he was practically a member of the family. Then, there were introductions all around, before he could draw me to one side in the entry hall and greet me.

Taking the hand which wore his ring, he kissed it and then

whispered, "Alta, how lovely you are tonight, and how well this suits you!"

"And, how clever you are, Charles!" I responded. "This posy is just like the ring! I shall dry it and keep it forever!"

Pleased, he gave me a little hug, which was not missed by anyone in the hall, I am sure.

"I will always give you white roses and mignonettes," he whispered in my ear, warmly pressing my arm.

I nearly swooned with pleasure.

Then, we all turned to greet the next contingent coming in the door.

It was the Sherwoods, my parents' best friends, with their daughters Sara and Margaret, friends of mine. They were closely followed by the Warrens and the Casters, then Father's brother Basil and his little wife Dorothy. We were all assembled, except for my sister, Agnes.

Well, I thought. *She probably wants to make a grand entrance!*

And she did, running lightly down the stairs and arriving at the landing with a flourish.

I couldn't help gasping. My sister was wearing a scarlet ball gown!

Well, cerise, at least. It was the flimsiest voile, with a low, flounced neckline and hardly any sleeves at all. It was an evening gown that could only have come from some French boutique. She was a vision, the rosy incarnation of late summer.

I could have killed her! Knowing we were so alike that I would have looked just as delectable in that dress did no good at all.

Crimson Aggie blew kisses to all of us below.

"Sorry to be so late," she excused herself sweetly, "but I had to make sure these lovely carnations were perfect!"

She had piled her hair up on top of her head, much as I had, but she had dismantled her bouquet and used the pale pink blooms to highlight her curls, using the last few to thrust deep into the crevasse of her flounced neckline, which was at least as low as Mother's, if not more so.

Aggie skipped down the remaining stairs lightly, her rosy skirts sweeping from side to side, beguilingly. She must have been wearing six petticoats! She went straight to Charles and took both his hands.

"You must be the wonderful Charles Buford I've been hearing so much about! I'm Alta's sister, Agnes. Thank you for the carnations. They're my favorites," she said, then smiled sweetly at him. He appeared hypnotized.

I opened my mouth to protest this blatant lie, but she silenced me with a venomous glance.

"I love the cinnamon scent of carnations," she caroled on. "Don't you? Here, smell!"

For one awful moment, I thought she was offering him her bosom to be inhaled, but then she dipped her head and Charles inhaled her hair as if he had never smelled carnations before.

"You poor thing!" she trilled, while he looked at her with astonishment. "No one has gotten you any sherry! Come along and we'll find a place to talk. I must get to know my brother-to-be!" She took his arm and led him away, toward the parlor, chattering and smiling at him archly, while Charles, bless his heart, allowed himself to be herded like a sheep.

I started after them and then stopped. I didn't want to rail after them like Mary's Little Lamb! I didn't know what to do.

No one else seemed to have noticed except Sara and Margaret, who came to console me.

"I can't believe I just saw that!" Sarah protested. "She shanghaied him, just like some poor sailor drunk in a Boston bar!"

That was a bit fanciful for Margaret, who was more plain-spoken, but even she agreed it was a most un-sisterly act.

Everyone was trouping in for sherry now, so we got in the back of the line to await our half-glass—all Father would allow us because of our youth. If I had been with Charles, I bet he would have given me a full glass!

"Where are they?" I asked, peering around.

"In the back, there, under that greenery." Margaret pointed out a far corner. You could just see a flash of Aggie's red skirt and the curve of Charles's back. They were conversing with great animation.

I was terribly confused and hurt. Charles was supposed to be with me, being introduced to everyone and showing off my beautiful not-quite-yet engagement ring. Why was he under a palm tree talking to Aggie?

I would not allow myself to cry, and it would be equally bad form to smash sherry glasses. I was at an absolute impasse, and the sherry drinking went on and on.

Finally, Mother signaled Harrison and a few minutes later, he announced dinner. Mother moved us all along into the dining room, where people began looking for their place cards.

Charles and Aggie came up to me then. Charles greeted me enthusiastically and hugged me, offering me his arm to go into dinner. What a relief he was coming back to me.

"Alta," he cried. "Why haven't you told me about this wonderful sister of yours? I had no idea!"

I opened my mouth to protest, but Charles was offering his other arm to Aggie, who gave me a poisonous smile, and we all went in together.

Charles was seated to my left, and Aggie was to go directly across the table on the other side. But she scooped up the place card, which read Adah Abbott, and went in search of that lady.

"Auntie, you must exchange with me and go across! I need to sit beside this fascinating man. I'm just getting to know him and need much more time to talk to him!"

Aunt Adah gave her quite a look, and then slid one at me, but she nodded affably and went around the end of the table to the place meant for Aggie. Charles, beaming like a first grader who had just been awarded a gold star, seated Aggie, and then, with some confusion, realized I was still standing and seated me. I was embarrassed, but he turned at once and began a conversation with Aggie.

Seated on my right was Mr. Sherwood, who never had much to say. I turned to speak to him, as was correct, but he merely grunted at me. After a silent minute, I remarked that the weather seemed cooler these days. He responded that it usually was in September. After that, we waited to be served our soup, in silence.

On my other side, I could hear Charles and Aggie in animated conversation. They seemed to be sharing opinions about various art galleries in Paris and Rome. I was quite surprised to find that either of them was interested in art.

The soup, a mushroom puree, was hard to swallow. The white wine served with it stung my throat. I ventured a desperate remark about the stock market, but Mr. Sherwood seemed to prefer the soup. I'm sure it was very good. Our cook, Mrs. Croft, was noted for her soup.

The bowls were removed and replaced by small plates of steamed trout on lettuce. Mother mercifully signaled for the change of conversation, and everyone reversed. I turned with relief toward Charles, but he did not turn toward me. He remained deeply engrossed with Aggie. She absolutely snubbed Uncle Basil, who was somewhat miffed, as he liked to talk to pretty, young girls. However, he made up for it by trying to talk to Sara Sherwood across the table.

I was so shocked. I tried to pretend I was concerned about finding bones in my trout, but I could not eat a bite. I just pushed it around on my plate and pretended I didn't notice Aunt Adah giving me the eye from across the table.

The trout was replaced by *poule au coquille*. Mother reversed us again, but I didn't bother Mr. Sherwood this time. The dinner went on and on interminably, through the beef and the bouillon. Somewhere around the salad, Charles did turn to me.

"Your sister is amazing!" he exclaimed.

I couldn't think of any response to that, but it didn't matter, as he immediately turned back to her and did not speak to me for the rest of the meal.

I endured desert, a scrumptious chocolate souffle which is usually my favorite, merely poking at it with my spoon while Aunt Adah frowned at me across the table.

At last, Mother stood, signaling the withdrawal of the ladies back to the drawing room—as it was called on special occasions such as this. I was surprised when Charles rose and came with us, instead of remaining with the men for brandy and cigars, but absolutely dumbfounded when he and Aggie hurried across the room, out the open French doors, and vanished into the rose garden—holding hands!

This could *not* be happening!

Mother looked as shaken as I was, but she is made of steel. Taking a deep breath and pulling herself up to her full height, she took my arm and led me to the main settee, to preside with her over the pouring of the coffee and tea, a job she had meant for Aggie.

My face burning red, I took up the teapot and set it back down at once with a thump, burning my fingers.

Mother gave me a potholder and a look to stiffen my spine. We prepared to soldier on. Mother chatted easily about Adelaide's trip, but she did not urge the ladies to visit the garden to see her Jenny Lind tea rose, as I know she had meant to do.

I was unable to say much more than "lemon?" or "sugar?"

As soon as she possibly could, once the first pouring was done, Mother abandoned me and serenely left the room. I saw her cross the hall and go into the dining hall. Quite soon after, she came out with Father and they went away down the hall, no doubt to his library.

My hands began to shake and I found it hard to breathe. I'm sure every lady in the room noticed, but they politely continued to chat and sip from their delicate Haviland cups. It was a great kindness to me.

Sara and Margaret came to sit with me, one on either side. Sara gave me a little hug, and then, bless her heart, took up a silver dish of bonbons and went about the room, passing it.

Margaret patted my knee and said, "Bear up, Alta. You're doing fine. All you need to do is carry on."

She was right. I gave her a grateful smile and sat up straight, holding my head high, only to glimpse Mother hurrying past the French doors, in the direction of the garden.

I got a grip on myself as best I could and summoned Harrison for water to brew a fresh pot of tea. While I waited, I tidied and rearranged the low serving table so energetically that no one spoke to me.

Just as Harrison returned, I saw Mother pass back, with Aggie and Charles in tow behind her arm in arm. All going to the library. I should be there! I made to rise.

Margaret detained me, once again laying her hand on my knee. "No Alta. Wait here. If you leave, it will make a scene."

Ladies do not make scenes.

I stayed where I was, and by the time the new pot of tea was ready, I was able to rise and walk around the room, offering any lady who wished it a second cup.

Moving around made me feel so much better, I did the same with the coffee pot. It was tepid by now, but no one complained. Margaret nodded at me encouragingly, and I felt able to do what needed to be done.

I turned to Mother's friend, Mrs. Warren, sitting near the serving table, and inquired as to the progress of a tapestry project I had heard her mention on happier occasions.

She threaded her needle, so to speak, and plunged it garrulously into this topic, requiring little from me beyond an occasional exclamation. A year ago, she had commenced a tapestry so large she hoped it would occupy her for years. A wall hanging six by six feet, it depicted the Warren yacht *Happy Days*, berthed at a New Jersey yacht club. Behind it, many different watercraft sported in the ocean and bay. In the foreground, flower beds bloomed prolifically.

So enormous was this project that Mrs. Warren had already enlisted the help of her lady's maid to fill in the blues of sky and water, comprising at least a third of the canvas and the most boring part.

She was now trying to convince the two upstairs maids to lend a hand in their spare time.

"They cannot object!" she enthused. "Think how it will enhance their resumes to be able to add a valuable skill such as needlecraft!"

"Of course," I politely agreed with her, but I was not so sure her poor maids would.

Our conversation was in no danger of running aground, and it looked as if I were luckily in for a long voyage, requiring little response from me beyond "Oh, yes," or "Is that so?" But at this point, Mother came back. She stood in the doorway to the parlor, seemingly at her most composed. She looked so lovely, standing there with her flowers and the becoming gown, and her crown of blonde braids shining in the lamplight. How well she was handling all this! My heart swelled with pride.

Mother smiled at us calmly. "Dear friends and family, I am sure you all understand that the festivities must end for this evening. Your carriages are being summoned, and your gentlemen will join you in the entranceway."

Our guests rose at once, setting down unfinished cups of tea and coffee, hiding half Bon-Bons in napkins, and allowed themselves to be shepherded out. I stood with Mother and Father, shaking hands, and thanking them for coming.

They must have been the most polite people in New York City that evening for not one question was asked, not one comment about the sudden end of an evening, which should have lasted at least two more hours, and no question about an announcement that did not happen. The gentlemen, at least, were jollier than usual, having consumed a great deal more brandy than usual, once Father had marooned them in the dining room!

Only Margaret whispered to me as she hugged me goodbye, "Come see me, Alta, if you want to talk. My sitting room is very private, and I'll make you hibiscus tea."

I thought I might go and see her. A few years older, she would make a good confidant. She had certainly helped me tonight!

As the door closed on the last guest, Mother turned and headed for the library. I followed her, but she stopped me at once.

"Alta, wait in the parlor. We will call you when it is time."

Waves of anger washed over me.

"But this concerns me especially!" I protested.

"Not yet," Mother snapped, and went into the library, shutting the door firmly behind her and leaving me standing in the hall.

Seething, I returned to the parlor and threw myself back down on the settee while the servants moved sedately around me, removing all the detritus of after-dinner tea, and putting the room to rights once more.

When all was to Harrison's liking, he came to me and asked politely, "Can I get you anything, Miss Alta?"

"No, nothing, thank you, Harrison," I said. "I am told to wait."

He bowed and went quietly away.

I waited.

Chapter Four

It was Father who came, after what seemed like a long time but was probably only an hour. He stood in front of me, his hands behind his back and a rueful expression on his face.

"Alta, you must realize that your engagement to Charles is no longer possible. Naturally, Charles is devastated, but he is firm. He cannot go on. However, he must explain to you himself. He would like to come to you now, and we beg you to hear him out. Will you do that?"

I tried to speak but seemed to still be afflicted with the inability to think of words with which to answer irrational questions. I wanted to shout "NO!" but of course, I wanted to see Charles. Finally, I just nodded.

"Good," Father said, then left.

I waited.

Charles came down the hall and I stood, clutching my posy, now wilted and ragged, for dear life.

"Alta," he greeted me solemnly. "Shall we sit?"

We sat; knees angled toward each other. He did not look very devastated to me. Rather, coiled tight and ready to spring into action. He assumed a mask of sorrow and regret, but inside, he was brimming with excitement. I looked away.

"Alta," he pleaded, seizing my hands. "This is so unfair to you, but what can I say? The truth is, I am in love with your sister, Agnes."

Silence can only last for so long! I made an unladylike sound and snatched my hands away.

"How can that be?" I cried. "You've known her how long, all of three hours?"

"That is true in one way," he retorted, rather prissily. "But in another, I have known her since I met you. What drew me to you was the reflection of her!"

I slid him a look out of the corners of my eyes. He was in earnest! "Bosh!" I muttered once more no lady.

"You two are so alike," he persevered, "in looks as well as behavior, but in every way, she is more. Can't you see? She is more animated, more experienced, more refined, wiser. You are younger, less formed, a paler version of Agnes. She is so... so much more vivid!"

I stared at him, unable to believe my ears! I longed to throw my crushed posy at him, but that would not be "refined!"

He rhapsodized on, "We have so much in common! She has traveled, I have traveled. She has read the classics, so have I. She shares all my interests, art, music, dancing, poetry, the law; her hopes for the future are exactly mine. We were made for each other! Oh, Alta, when I met you, is it any wonder I was drawn to you? After all, I had not yet met HER!"

I stared at him, struck wordless once more. He actually seemed to believe this nonsense!

I could only gape at him.

Now, he stared at me. After a painful silence, he burst out, "Alta, please say something! I am trying to be honest with you!"

"Are you?" I asked.

After another short silence, he begged, "At least tell me you understand what I have said."

"Oh, I understand the words," I replied. "But they make no sense to me."

The mask slipped slightly, and I saw a flash of anger in his expressive brown eyes, always a window inside. "Very well, I see I must be blunt. You appreciate our predicament? I love another. The pretense of our engagement cannot go on. It is not honorable."

"Not honorable," I echoed. How could he say such words?

"So...?" He lifted his hands, palms up, in a gesture of expectancy.

I looked at them in confusion.

"So... what?" I asked, mystified.

The mask slipped completely, now, and I saw the real man. "The ring, Alta! I need the ring!"

"Oh!" I sat back, as comprehension flooded in. The entire conversation became clear to me. I lifted my presumptive left hand, still displaying the Buford Sapphire. "Of course. You want the ring so you can give it to Aggie."

This was a little too blunt, even for him. He shifted uncomfortably but held his ground. "In a word, yes." He rather glared at me.

The ring slid off my finger easily. I knew it would fit Aggie, too. I placed it gently in his hand, as a lady would, and without another word I rose, quietly mounted the stairs, and went down the hall to my room. I left them below to their curious arrangements. Whatever they might get up to, it was clear no one felt it had much to do with me.

I quietly closed my door and leaned against it for a while, trying to regain my composure, but I was shaking and felt icy cold, even though the September night was mild. I felt as bedraggled as my posy, now the symbol of nothing, although I still held onto it. After a while, I went across to my fireplace, where a fire was laid ready to be lit now that it was autumn. I struck a sulfur stick and soon had a small but brisk blaze, onto which I carefully laid the posy. I sank back into my rocking chair and watched it burn, along with all my hopes and dreams. I had nothing left.

My fire had burned to embers when there was a quiet knock on my door, and Mother finally came to me.

She joined me at the fireplace, pulling over the stool from my vanity, and shook her head at me dolefully.

"If only you had not been in such a rush to be engaged, Alta, and so stubborn about taking advice. Those two could have met in a normal way, without the whole world watching, and all this could have been avoided!"

I said nothing. It would have been nice to at least have started this interview with a little motherly comforting. I'm sure the situation was painful for her, too, but she appeared focused less on my disappointment and more on the plans she had formulated and begun to put in motion, which would now have to be changed and begun again.

It really seemed to me that this was not my fault, but still...

Mother lined out for me my future behavior. I was to accept the fact that my beau and my sister were now a couple, as politely as possible. Any recriminations I might feel were not to be expressed, especially outside this house. In public, I was to make it clear that my relationship with Charles had been a delightful summer fling and that it was wonderful that he and my sister had discovered a more serious connection. I was to go forward with my head held high so that no one would guess I had been disappointed in love.

"I imagine you feel right now that your heart is broken," Mother lectured me, "but I assure you it is not. You are very young. I think it is safe to promise that within a year you will be in love with someone else, perhaps someone you will meet at your Snowflake Ball."

"Never," I muttered defiantly. She ignored me.

"You must grow up now, Alta. This disappointment is an opportunity to develop your character. If you behave with compassion and grace, people will not pity you and you will not spoil your sister's chance of happiness. It will make a mature woman of you. Don't miss this chance to improve yourself, Alta."

With that, Mother gave me an austere kiss and a firm hug, and quietly left the room.

It was too much! I threw myself into my bed, pulled the covers over my head, and did not come out for the next three days—except to keep my fire burning and drink tea. I refused all food. I divided my hours among pacing the room, weeping, and sleeping. I saw only Mariah. Mostly, I floundered in grief and despair over the loss of Charles, the best man I had ever known and the only one I could ever love. The rest of the time I focused with growing anger on Aggie; how could she possibly justify her behavior? And what would she say to me when I saw her again? But she did not come.

At the end of the third day, Mariah brought me a note from Mother. It read: *Alta, we will expect you at breakfast in the morning, and thereafter.*

And so, the end of sanctuary.

The next morning, I appeared as ordered, and everyone behaved as if nothing had happened.

Father read the *New York Times* and commented on the stock market. I ate a few spoons of oatmeal, my first food since *the night.*

Mother said that she was planning a full round of social calls tomorrow and would expect me to accompany her, as Aggie was busy. I nodded dutifully and crumbled toast into my bowl.

Aggie chattered on and on about an appointment to ride in Central Park this afternoon, and a large group outing to Flushing Meadows tomorrow for the horse races. No doubt Charles would be her escort to both, although she didn't say so. I stirred sugar into my coffee until it was so sweet I couldn't drink it.

As far as I could tell, her left hand did not yet bear the Buford Sapphire. At least there was that.

In this way, my family took up a semblance of normal life. It was uncomfortable for me, especially going out in public, which I avoided as much as possible. But Mother was so adept at evading unwanted questions, I soon felt more at ease. Besides, Aunt Adah usually either went with us or appeared soon after we made a call, and her wry sense of humor and blunt comments amused and protected me.

It was surprising how soon Mother was able to chat easily about Agnes and "Dear Charles," and the world continued to turn on its axis.

As to my particular friends, I easily deflected their commiseration with my flippant attitude.

"It wouldn't do, you know! All that boring talk about law." Then, I would take a tragic pose and add, "I do miss the ring, of course." Causing them to collapse with laughter and make hilarious comments on good taste in jewelry. Soon enough, the whole matter faded away as new events became more interesting.

The outings with Mother were at first hateful and then became merely tedious. It was the gatherings of my set that were agony. Aggie and Charles were naturally included in every single one, and I could not bear it. Their behavior as a couple was too painful to watch.

At card parties, they could not be parted, had to be partners no matter what their hostess decreed. They must always sit together and God forbid they should converse with anyone except as a pair. They danced only with each other, except when Charles must perforce dance with his hostess, and then Aggie waited on the sidelines, tapping her foot and refusing any invitations until he was free once more.

Charles was always teaching her new steps, and even I had to admit they were wonderful partners, easily the best dancers in our set.

Watching all this was bad enough, but what I truly could not bear was the attention the new couple focused on me. They were so solicitous; I was nearly driven mad! I was nearly smothered in pillows wherever I sat, and the two fussed over me until I could have screamed.

"Did I feel a draft?" or "need a cup of punch?" or "would I rather sit in the window?" It went on like this until I wanted to beg them to leave me alone. Then they must commandeer someone, anyone, to come and talk to me. All my friends saw them fussing over me and understood my feelings perfectly. It was humiliating.

And then, there was their effort to hold hands in the carriage as we rode back and forth without my noticing.

After a few evenings such as this, I refused to go out with them again, no matter how much they urged me. It was almost pitiful to see the relief with which they were *forced* to accept one of my feeble excuses: I wanted to stay home and read tonight because I had just reached the great fire in my current novel *Jane Eyre*, or that I had not slept well the night before and needed to make it up by going to bed early tonight. Limp as these excuses were, they were absolutely true. Either was preferable to spending an evening watching the new lovers together.

Mother disapproved of my staying home, of course.

"You must not stop going out altogether Alta, or people will talk."

In any event, even if I managed to get out of going to parties with them, I could not avoid the loving couple at home. On Sunday nights and any other that they were not going out, Charles came to our house for dinner, and then they spent the evening playing duets on the piano and singing together. Sometimes they played cards with Mother. Charles had interminable conversations with Father about business and the law. They all got along so well!

I felt an intruder, and so I tried to bury myself in some novel, but they insisted on including me and my reading was constantly interrupted. I tried taking my novel to the far corner of the room, but then I was accused, rightfully, of trying to avoid them. If I took my tapestry to sit sewing beside Mother, this was deplored as equally antisocial, and would I please come and play the piano so that they could practice a new dance step?

This last was perhaps the worst, as I wanted to be the one dancing with Charles, not the piano player.

Charles never left until ten, so I took to retiring earlier and earlier until Mother lectured me again about being rude. I could not win.

As September turned into October, Mother began to harp about my debut. My expressed wish to pass it by, under the circumstances, was dismissed as "nonsense." Mother signed me up for deportment and dancing classes, to begin in November. And I had to commence a series of fittings with her dressmaker on the fancy ballgown I did not wish to wear.

The dress was multiple layers of the lightest tulle, gathered and ruffled until I feared I resembled a giant vanilla bonbon, but Mother pronounced it beautiful.

She used the occasion of another family dinner, attended by both her sisters and Cousin Edgar, to try to boost my non-existent enthusiasm.

A smaller, more informal group this night, we all withdrew to the parlor together, the men taking brandy and cigars in front of the blazing fire and we ladies having tea in the front of the room, removed from the tobacco fumes.

Mother opened her topic bluntly: "Adelaide, perhaps you can talk some sense into Alta Belle. Her debut is barely a month away, but she doesn't seem to appreciate what an important event it is. As I recall, your debut was especially beautiful and eventful."

I cringed at this ambush, but Aunt Adelaide's face grew pink with remembered pleasure. "Oh, Antoinette, it was wonderful! My dress, my flowers... oh, I have never looked better! I asked Orson to be my escort, although I hardly knew him, and that was the night we fell in love!" She clasped her hands over her heart in remembrance of her late husband. I recalled him as a balding, middle-aged man, but perhaps he had been an ardent suitor in his day.

"Oh, yes," Adah added to the reminiscing. "I remember him tripping over his shoestrings and nearly taking you down!"

"He did no such thing!" Adelaide protested, which amused Aunt Adah to no end.

Mother seized the opportunity she had created: "Can you believe it, here it is nearly November, and Alta has not yet settled on her escort!"

"Heavens above, Alta Belle, you must choose someone at once! All the good ones will be already gone!"

I tried to pacify her: "No doubt, Aunt, but we'll find someone, it's really not important." I wished we could change the subject.

"Alta Belle Carlton! Not important!" Aunt Adelaide set down her teacup with such a clink I feared for the Haviland. "A girl's debut is the most important night of her life!"

"Come, come, Addie, surely not the most important," teased Aunt Adah, ever the voice of reason. "But for most girls, certainly significant."

Naturally, Aggie had to put in her two cents: "Charles has offered to escort her time and again, but Alta always says no!" she accused.

Charles jumped up to join us and confirm that he was most willing. How could he possibly be so unaware of how I might be feeling?

I feebly demurred, yet again, "no, no, not necessary!" Anger is all that I was feeling at this point.

"Well, well," intervened Aunt Adah, bless her. "A deb must be allowed her choice." She looked around the room and raised her voice to call to her son. "Edgar, you could be Alta's escort. It would be most appropriate."

"Not on your life!" Edgar declined vehemently, getting up from the fire and walking over to us. "No offense, Alta, but I've put in my time with the debs! No one can say I haven't paid my dues. Besides, Mother, you know I am courting Eugenia Moffit now."

"Not very energetically," Aunt Adah observed.

In the general chafing of Edgar and his pursuit of the aging Miss Moffit, which followed this exchange, the subject of my debut expired, but I knew I could not put this matter off much longer.

This was the night Aggie finally chose to come to me. After everyone had retired for the night, I heard the soft knock on my door and opened it to her.

We sat in front of my dying fire, she all rosy from having just said goodnight to Charles, and we talked.

"Alta, why do you continually refuse Charles as your escort? I know you had already asked him, before."

"Aggie, are you so unable to imagine my feelings? He is your escort now, the last person I could want."

She looked at me and her smile faded. "Are you so very angry at Charles and me?" she asked.

"How can you ask that?" I cried, my anger brimming over. "I am not allowed to be angry at you! The entire family has made that quite clear."

She looked at me skeptically. "You are, aren't you?"

"Aggie," I said, as steadily as I could manage, "after much thought, I can kind of understand Charles's reasoning, although I absolutely refute it as illogical and immoral. But as to what you possibly can have been thinking is completely beyond me."

She flushed and glared at me. "No doubt you think I should have walked away from my feelings for him, my one chance for happiness, just because you had a schoolgirl crush on him! Indeed, the happiness of all three of us. How long do you think you would have been happy, had he remained with you out of a sense of obligation, knowing he would rather have been with another?"

I opened my mouth to shout accusations at her, but then I shut it again. I am not much given to taking advice, but Mother's words still rang in my ears.

There was a certain sense in what Aggie said, at least from her point of view, much as I did not want to hear it.

After a silent time, during which she stared at me like a basilisk, I said quietly, "Very well, Aggie. I wish you joy."

"I hope you do, Alta, because I intend to be very happy

indeed!" She rose, smoothed her skirts, and left with exaggerated dignity, closing the door so quietly I had to check it to make sure it was properly shut.

That was the end of it, apparently—at least for her. It left me with even more questions than I had before.

Chapter Five

T he Snowflake Ball came and went; that is the best way to describe my debut. I steeled myself to appear willing, but enthusiasm was beyond me. I would so much rather have been in my room reading *Wuthering Heights*. In a way, I did not so much "come out" as become an observer of a strange tribal social rite.

Like the posh St. Regis Ball, where the society debutantes came out, our Snowflake Ball was held in mid-December. Our pictures were presented on the Society page of the *Business News*, and we emerged to start our middle-class version of the social season.

Our ball was held—not in a fancy hotel ballroom, but the Hall of Labor and Commerce. Usually the site of lectures and campaign speeches, it did well with the addition of large mirrors and a greenhouse full of ferns. We did not have a concert orchestra, but Harry's Moonlight Band was great fun to dance to. And I believe our dresses were easily the equal of anything paraded at the St. Regis Hotel.

Trying hard to be the daughter my parents wanted, I had submitted dutifully to Mother's pre-debut regime. I attended a weekly deportment class, where I was joined by Sara Sherwood and Letty Wallis. Much like me, Letty had no visible scar to show for her mishap at that "Frolic on the River." We were joined by the Van Der Meer twins and other girls our age. Hortense was a year younger and would debut next year. I missed her, but bless her heart, she was more and more taken up with her Laurence, just as she should be.

I was curious who Letty's escort would be, remembering her interest in Percy Ward, but it turned out that I could not add "matchmaker" to my list of achievements. Letty was astonished at how out-of-touch I was and proudly told me she was now "seeing" Cadet Jared Marshall from the Academy at Annapolis, and that right after the debut he would be requesting official permission to call on her. She rhapsodized that, although it would be yet another year before he matriculated, she was sure they would be married then—"under the swords," as it was said.

I thought of warning her that a year was a great deal of time, during which a person's feelings might change, but I did not. Let her enjoy her dream. Maybe it would come true.

Meanwhile, this preparatory class was meant to teach us how to behave at a formal dinner table—which utensils to use and such. One would hope we already knew these things, but it did not hurt to brush up. We all could use a refresher course in how to make introductions and hold a polite conversation! Other items included how to enter a room, sit gracefully in a chair, descend a staircase, walk down an aisle with everyone staring at us, and—most important and difficult of all—make a perfect, full, *court curtsy.*

The day we were forced to walk about with dictionaries on our heads "to improve our posture," I almost quit the class, possibly because it was a skill I simply could not master. However, I reminded myself this was about Mother, not me, and confined myself to scowling in the background, something I was good at.

As if deportment class were not enough, we must attend special dancing classes with the boys, to learn the latest steps. Here, I re-encountered several young men in our crowd, such as Wally Cunningham and Rudolph Van Brocken, from old dancing classes, who trod on my toes and hinted that they were available for duty the night of the debut. I shuddered. Did everyone know all my business? I smiled sweetly and did not comment. Either of these young men would have assumed being asked to be my escort was tantamount to an invitation to call on me and begin a courtship. No, no, no!

It was clear I must do something about my escort problem, so I devised a strategy, which I hoped would protect me. Since Letty didn't need him, I waylaid Percy Ward, trying to hide behind the ferns in the corner, hoping to be overlooked as a dancing partner. Since Percy practically needed permission to breathe, I thought he should be safe. Besides, I had been bossing him around since our first "play parties." Percy turned scarlet, stuttered, and accepted without ever looking me in the eye. He then immediately vanished, but one problem was solved.

Mother still expected me to accompany her on her regular round of calls, as "Agnes is busy." I thought I was equally so, but Mother did not agree. After that, if I had even a minute of spare time, it was eaten up by interminable fittings for all the tea gowns and other outfits Mother felt I would need for the ensuing *season.*

During this time, I did have one consolation. I began to call on Margaret Sherwood and found her even more congenial than I had expected. By some miracle, Mother considered this to be progress on my part and excused me from duty whenever I claimed an appointment with my new friend. For this reason, I probably sought her company more frequently than I might have otherwise, and for this, I was rewarded.

Margaret was three years older than me, and I was surprised to discover that she had done her debut much as I was—to please her parents. At last, a sympathetic ear!

It took but the slightest acquaintance to discover she was not at all quiet and retiring, as I had thought, but politely hiding her distaste for what passed as "conversation" in our circle. Margaret was not in the least interested in gossip or the latest style in hats—she wished to discuss more serious topics.

Sara was rarely at home, so we survived the slight awkwardness of my calling on the elder sister rather than my age-mate. It was hard to believe they were sisters, so different were they.

Margaret was the pretty one. Sara, smaller and lighter in her coloring, overcame her basic plainness with vivacity and charming humor. She was close friends with the Van Der Meer twins and more than any other activity preferred strolling with them in Central Park, eager to see who might turn up in an open landau and offer them a ride.

On my first visit to Margaret's charming suite of rooms, overlooking the leafy greenness of Central Park, she sat with us at first, but when it proved our conversation was unlikely to touch on boys or clothing, she jumped up and was off with hardly an excuse, leaving us to our "moralizing," as she dubbed it.

Margaret and I stood at the bay window, watching Sara run across the street and into the Park, where her friends awaited her.

I let the curtain fall back, shaking my head.

"I can hardly believe I'm the same age as those girls, they are so young and scatter-brained! They are like dandelion puffs, and I'm a thistle and I feel one hundred years old."

Margaret gave me a little *tsk, tsk.* "Where is your compassion, Alta? Just give them time. They run careless and free because, unlike you, they have yet to stub their toes. Sadly, it is inevitable that they will have their turn one day, sooner rather than later."

She acknowledged my misery yet urged me to be a better person! I liked her more and more and admired her character.

"You are right. I shall try to be kinder, but with the Van der Meers it will be hard. Sara is not that bad."

Margaret laughed. "I do have hope for my little sister. It is pleasant to think that one day we might make good companions for each other. There is no friend like a sister."

Looking at my face, Margaret laughed again. She gave me an absolutely evil grin.

"Of course, that does not apply to you! Your sister is Aggie!"

Our giggles were every bit as bad as those across the street, where Wally Cunningham was now strolling off toward the lake with Sara and the twins.

I believe this was when Margaret and I began to become real friends.

As such things must, the great night arrived at last. Naturally, the weather turned on us, and by noon of that day, it began to snow heavily. By mid-afternoon, it was more falling slush mixed with rain, and blown uncomfortably sideways by a rising wind.

Mother and Father came to me together and gave me a suite of Oriental pearls. There was a two-strand necklace, stud earrings, a four-strand bracelet, a button pearl ring set in a silver mounting, and a set of silver combs banded with seed pearls. The glowing jewels came in a delicate lacquer box from Japan, with a secret opening. It was a lovely and traditional gift; each of my sisters had received the same, in their turn, so we all knew the trick of opening the box.

The wind threw sleet against our windows and the sky darkened. Mother was quite upset about the weather. I guess I was the only family member who thought it an amusing trick of fate, after all our fussing.

Mother, who had sat on the Snowflake Ball Committee ever since Adelle's debut, was not amused. I don't know why she was worrying. Weather notwithstanding, the ball was already considered a great success. A charity event, it had become what was called "oversubscribed." St. John the Baptist Orphanage would be receiving a larger check this year than ever before. Mother would be accepting congratulations all evening for a triumph.

I was late in dressing for my big event. When Mother came in to check the result, I was, again, still waiting for Mariah to button me up and do my hair.

"Why aren't you dressed?" Mother scolded in exasperation as if I were the last straw.

"Mariah will come any minute now," I said, carefully. I didn't want Mariah, who is a very nice girl, to get in trouble. It wasn't her fault.

"Inconsiderate girl!" Mother snapped, very out of character. I flushed with guilt.

"I'm sorry," I hastened to appease. "You are right, I should just have gone ahead myself. I can do my own hair, but Mother, I really can't button up the back of the dress..."

Mother gave me a weary look as if I were mocking her— which I was not.

"Alta, how can you possibly think that I meant you? I meant Aggie. On this night, she should have sent Mariah to you first, if her hair was going to take so long." She shook her head at me, as if in despair, and left the room.

It was nice to hear that Mother might find any fault with Aggie, but why, then, was she angry with me?

I attempted to begin putting up my hair, but we had decided on a style that was not easy to do myself: half my hair hanging down, and the rest piled on top in six coils. I'm afraid I had made quite a mess of it by the time Mother returned with Doris, her own maid.

"Mariah is still busy with Agnes. It can't be helped," Mother said calmly, herself again. "Doris will help you."

Doris put me in my dress and did up the twenty little faux pearl buttons up my back, and then sat me down and redid my hair, crowning the curls with a circlet of white rosebuds. Mother looked me over and pronounced me ready.

She then produced the square, white florist box containing the bouquet I would carry. By tradition, one's escort sends this small gift, after inquiring as to what would be appropriate. Mother informed me that, once again, Charles had asked for the privilege, and sent flowers for us all.

I opened it with some trepidation and took out a lovely cluster of white roses mixed with baby's breath, long satin ribbons hanging down. I sighed. Charles was almost true to his word. He had promised roses. At least he had the good sense to leave out the forget-me-nots.

Mother loved the bouquet.

"So like Charles," she murmured, with fond appreciation.

Yes, indeed.

The weather had, if anything, worsened. Father had the great carriage brought up for the two of us, as we had to be there early. I prepared to face the elements by pulling on my heavy boots and carrying my satin slippers in a bag. Holding up my skirts in a most unladylike manner, I ran for the carriage with Simmons trying to shelter me with a huge black umbrella, Father coming along behind, getting wet. We all three got wet but headed for the hall in high spirits from the exhilarating dash for cover.

The gaslights lining the streets all had halos from the storm, and colored lights from the other carriages going to-and-fro looked so festive. I surprised myself and began to get the Christmas spirit. I had not expected to enjoy this evening, but if there was any pleasure to be had, I would not say "no!"

Simmons soon got us safely to the hall. I had to laugh, another thing I had not expected to do tonight. A double row of umbrellas formed a passage up the two flights of stairs to the entrance, protecting arriving debs from the rain. Looking closely, I recognized some of the escorts, Percy Ward among them, doing double duty for us on this night of rain and wind.

Simmons dropped us off and returned to the house. He would bring the others while Father and I attended the dress rehearsal.

A debut required a father or father figure, called "the presenter," to bring the girl to the stage and hand her off to the escort. The escort brought her to the head of the steps, where her name was announced, and the dreaded curtsy took place. The father then retired, and the escort led the deb down ten steps to form a row at the bottom. One would not think this was difficult, but apparently, it was fraught with perils, thus the dress rehearsal.

A two-time veteran of the *debutante wars*, Father knew the drill and led me to the backstage holding room where most of the others were already waiting. He greeted Mr. Sherwood and they relaxed on chairs lined against the back wall, no doubt going on about how fast little girls grow up.

I moved a little closer to hear them, as I'm a terrible eavesdropper. They were discussing the stock market! Served me right. The sentimentalist here tonight must be me.

All the girls were repairing their hair and adjusting their

gowns, gabbling at the top of their voices. The din grew louder and shriller with each new arrival. I took no part in it; it hurt my ears.

We had our rehearsal, and then returned backstage to wait as the hall filled with our families. The din grew even louder—if that were possible. I don't know about the other girls, but the main thing that was achieved by the rehearsal was to make me nervous, whereas before I had not been. Now, I knew all about the calamities that could befall us and grew more worried by the minute. What if the announcer called the wrong name? What if my rose wreath fell off during the curtsy? What if I wobbled or tripped on the stairs? I did not think I could rely on Percy to catch me if I did.

One of the girls was having hysterics because her escort had not yet arrived. At least Percy was there. Be grateful for small blessings!

We had been told not to gape through the stage curtains, as it was unmannerly and vulgar, but I did anyway, making a little gap near one far end of the proscenium.

I spotted my family near the entrance. Adelle and John had just arrived. My heart swelled with pride, for they were all fine-looking people.

Father, chatting away behind me, was an imposing man in black tie and tails, with a silver brocade vest, in keeping with the "snowflake" theme. He had a head of silver hair, a well-kempt, white beard, and snapping dark eyes that seemed to see everything. Father was an extremely successful and well-thought-of businessman and was providing us with a comfortable life, which I fear I sometimes took for granted.

Mother, greeting Adelle's husband, John, was still beautiful, despite being surrounded by grown daughters. She was so blonde that the gray growing into her shining hair was hardly noticeable. She wore a gorgeous emerald satin gown, with a low neckline, of course, but tonight the attention was drawn away to the magnificent spray of orchids Charles had sent her. They were white, as before, but had deep scarlet throats, quite spectacular.

John was solidly handsome in his tailcoat. Father was right to be proud of his son-in-law.

Adelle was well draped in morning-glory-blue taffeta and wearing her debut pearls. Her abundant hair was as blonde as Mother's. She wore it up in a corona of braids and carried a posy of red roses from John. She glowed with excitement and looked determined to wring every ounce of joy out of this evening, probably her last public appearance for the next four months, before the birth of the second Hudson heir.

I speculated briefly on the coming child. Her first, John Jr., was a rosy, blond boy of dismaying energy. The new baby, if a boy, could be named whatever, I was only really interested in the possibility of it being a girl and needing a name starting with A. Auralia might be nice, or Aura Lee, like the college song, especially if she were blonde—very likely.

If I ever had a little girl, I planned to name her Betsy! Wouldn't that cause a stir in the family! This naughty thought made me laugh for the second time that night.

Now I could see my middle sister fussing about Adelle's gown and I had to admit, as much as I currently disliked her, Aggie did the family proud. Tonight, she did wear scarlet, an appropriate pre-Christmas color, I conceded. Charles had quite smothered her in white carnations, and this made me chortle right out loud, imagining a scene in which she disabused this romantic man of his cherished idea that carnations were *their* flower. I am sure such a discussion would have to take place at some point and wondered how long Aggie would be able to bear it. I looked at Charles with, for the first time, just a hint of pity. Poor lamb, he had no idea!

He was perfection, as always, in black with a carnation in his lapel. I had to look away as he put his arm around Aggie's waist, and she turned to smile at him. I stepped back from the curtain with a jerk. I didn't want to see them anymore.

Anyway, the presentations were about to start. Father and I took our place in line, near the front, as we girls were to be called alphabetically. Each girl would be announced with her full name and, as Margaret would say, her pedigree.

Our turn came. Father gave me his arm, walked me out, and handed me to Percy. The announcer's voice boomed: "Alta Belle Carlton, daughter of Horace and Antoinette Carlton, of New York City, escorted by Percy Heston Ward Jr., New York City."

Percy walked me forward. I made my full court curtsy—without a wobble—to light applause.

I have heard that girls in Texas do not make the court curtsy, but rather something called "The Texas Dip." I surely wished I knew what that was, but even if I knew, I would never have actually done it. I preferred to be noticed as little as possible on this night of nights, not attract attention.

Leave that to girls like Letty, who dropped her handkerchief, leaving her father and her escort, the Cadet, to wrestle over who should pick it up! Finally, her father did and handed it to the Cadet, who gallantly kissed it and gave it back to her. She gave him a luminous smile and tucked it into the front of her dress near her heart. What a silly little show! But the audience loved it.

I merely took Percy's arm to descend the steps. Scarlet and perspiring, he fell over both of his own feet and managed to step on one of mine, but I was able to steady him, and we did arrive safely at the bottom and then lined up with the other couples in front of the stage.

Father returned to the holding room, shaking his head, and went out from there to join the family.

When the last couple went down, the lights were lowered, the band struck up a foxtrot, and our escorts took us out onto the dance floor. It must have been a beautiful sight: the girls all in their white ball gowns, the chandeliers glowing, the flowers, the brightly garbed on-lookers, the sparkling jewels. An unforgettable moment.

However magical, it was wasted on me, as I was doing the box step with Percy and trying to be polite. Compassion was what was called for.

Percy's conversation consisted of: "Sorry, Alta."

Each time he trod on my foot, or the hem of my dress, or got off on the wrong foot, he apologized. My back and waist, wherever he touched me, were damp with his perspiration, and only the deportment class kept me from snatching my hand out of his wet grasp so that I could dry it on my skirt! He was sorry about that as well.

"Percy, just stop apologizing!" I demanded at last. "It's all right, everything is fine. You are fine. All we have to do is just get through this one dance and then we can sit down!"

This did seem to settle him enough to finish the set and we sat down with relief.

"Alta, I'm sorry! You are very kind to me, and all I do is step on you and tear your dress," he said gloomily.

"It's all right, really, Percy," I insisted. "I don't care about the dress. I won't be wearing it again."

"I'm sorry, Alta. I know I'm not a very good dancer, o-or anything, but I am really proud to be your escort. I was so surprised when you asked me! There are so many other chaps—"

"Please, Percy!" I cut him off. "I am the one who is grateful to you for seeing me through this ordeal. So, I should be thanking you."

"Really?" he asked, looking surprised. "Alta, do you think..."

"Do I think what, Percy?"

"Do you think that, after this is over, I might call on you?"

Oh, for heaven's sake! But I steeled myself to be a lady.

"No, Percy. Absolutely not!" I replied, firmly but as nicely as possible, and patted his hand. "I am forever grateful to you, but no."

"I didn't think so."

He looked so crestfallen; I almost took it back.

Fortunately, at this moment, my family came up to congratulate me. The band started a set of popular melodies and general dancing commenced. This was one night no girl sat in the wallflower chairs, and I did not lack for partners. I danced with Father and then with John, and then, inevitably, with Charles. It could not be avoided.

"Well, Alta, this is your night to shine," he cried, twirling me expertly. "So, tell me, which one of these young men will come calling now? Or, perhaps, more than one? Give them a good race, Alta!"

Sparing me any need to respond to this hurtful sally, Charles suddenly spun into a set of dance steps so intricate I tripped over his feet and almost caused us both to fall!

"Oops!" he laughed, keeping us both upright by brute strength alone. "Forgot who I was dancing with! Aggie and I have that one all worked out." Peering around the dance floor, he spotted Cousin Edgar taking a glass of punch and foxtrotted me to a stop in front of him.

"Edgar, your turn to dance with the deb of the evening!" Charles thrust me at Edgar and dashed off to return to his regular partner—who knew the steps.

Edgar put down his cup and trotted me dutifully around the floor, mercifully not committed to any fancy maneuvers.

"Alta, you look very nice this evening."

"Thank you, Edgar."

We waved to Adelle and John, dancing by, and then to Father and Mother.

Edgar grinned at me. "Altogether, we're not a bad-looking family, don't you think?"

I had to agree. But I couldn't help asking, "But do you think good looks is everything?"

Never at a loss for words, my cousin spun me out and pulled me back. "Handsome is as handsome does, Alta. Don't worry, someone even better will come knocking on your door. Meanwhile, this is a great party!"

I had to laugh, yet again. "Well said, cousin! And aren't I lucky, to have a cousin who is both good-looking and wise!"

That made him guffaw, and we both enjoyed the rest of the set.

Truth is, by the time the midnight supper of oyster stew and hot buttered rolls was served, I found I had enjoyed the whole evening. I had danced almost every dance and laughed any number of times. My debut turned out not to be an ordeal, after all.

It was fully two in the morning when we finally got back home to take off our wet boots and wrinkled garments, put away our jewels, and toss our wilted flowers on the dying fire.

At least that is what I did with mine. Mother kept her gorgeous orchids until they expired of old age. What Aggie did with her carnations, I do not know.

Two weeks after the ball, Aggie and Charles announced their engagement at a splendid reception at The Palms Hotel. The striking couple would wed in May. Aggie's ivory silk tea gown was a stunning background for the Buford Sapphire.

Of course, I gave her the earrings. It was the right thing to do.

Chapter Six

"Father, you have got to do something about Alta!"

I was coming down the stairs, only three steps from the bottom, when I heard Agnes's strident voice issuing from the library, then the low rumble of Father's reply.

"I am calm," Agnes retorted, barely lowering her tone, "but it just can't go on! She's always somewhere lurking in the background, like some dark cloud looming over everyone! Last night I came home so happy, just dying to tell you all about our dinner at Fanny's, and what fun we had. But there she was, hovering behind the piano, her mouth such a tight line and looking so judgmental as if I were being inappropriate! I can't stand it anymore!"

My father's voice rose to her level. "You're not wrong, Aggie, but I wish you could show more compassion. Alta has suffered a disappointment. We must remember that."

"Am I to be punished for that forever? You know it bothers everyone, not just me. And as for disappointment, spare me! It's been months! She's so young; she should have got over that long ago."

There was a quiet murmur in response. I turned to flee, one hand on the banister.

"Nonsense, Father! Why do you allow her to confine herself so? There are half a dozen young men who would love to squire her with the slightest encouragement. But no, she refuses every invitation and just stays home doing that endless needlework, and you let her! People are starting to notice and ask me questions!"

I fled, breathless, to my room, and I did not come down again until dinnertime.

Charles was dining with us tonight, as he now usually did. As ever, he was overly solicitous of me: holding my chair, calling for my water glass to be refilled, urging me to have another helping of roast—as he did not feel I was eating enough. I wished he would just ignore me, but strangely, he seemed to think I should appreciate these attentions.

When the meal was over, Charles and Father remained at the table while Mother, Agnes, and I retired to the drawing room. I made sure to sit beside Mother on the great divan by the fire, not in my preferred retreat under the potted palm beyond the grand piano, and took up the offending tapestry; there was really nothing else to do after dinner.

Mother was also involved in a needlepoint project; she was making a small purse, which she would eventually line with silk and sew onto a lovely, silver-plated frame. It would doubtless become a gift for one of her friends. I speculated on which one —perhaps Mrs. Warren. She appreciated tapestry.

Agnes paced restlessly about, finally perching on the arm of a chair beside Mother and me.

"Ah," she said, looking at my work. "The endless needle-point! So much blue."

I looked down at my sewing. It delighted me, and nothing was more pleasurable and calming than to work at it. My own design for a pillow was simply a mass of flowers in every shade of blue I could find at Father's store, from the palest baby tint to dark indigo. It was surely the best thing I had done yet.

"And which room is this masterpiece to grace, if you ever do finish it?" Agnes went on, rather bitterly, I thought.

"Perhaps the morning room," I mumbled. Aggie had never taken to handwork; she could not sit still long enough to thread a needle.

"Oh, it will do marvelously there, with all the green drapes!"

"Girls, stop fussing," Mother admonished, mildly. "Alta may put the pillow wherever she likes."

Agnes would not put down the topic. "I don't see how you can spend so much time just sitting there, poking your needle in and out. I should die of boredom!"

"No doubt," I replied.

Aggie jumped up clapping her hands. "Here they are, at last!"

Father and Charles came in from the dining room, trailing smoke and brandy fumes. Charles's face brightened to see Aggie, like lighting a lamp, and he rushed to her side. She practically ran into his arms. After all, they had been parted for nearly half an hour.

"Charles, come and let's play duets! I have a new one I got from Peggy. You'll love it!" She leaned into him and said, confidentially, "It requires us to cross hands!"

"Brilliant! I can hardly wait!!" Charles enthused, and off they went to the piano.

Mother looked at me over the top of the glasses she used for close work. "Alta, why don't you join them?"

"Mother, it's a duet."

"You could be the admiring audience. That always makes music more fun."

"Somehow I doubt that," I muttered, and stitched on.

Mother frowned at me and let it pass, but not for long, I guessed. I sighed.

The next day after breakfast, Mother asked me to join her in the morning room. She sat at the desk where she did all her correspondence but left me to stand beside it. A serious talk, then.

"Alta, it is regrettably necessary for me to speak to you about your behavior." she looked at me with disapproval. "You are far too old to go about glowering at everyone. I must ask you to learn to govern your countenance, and your remarks."

I flushed with anger, but said nothing, lowering my head.

"We all realize this is a difficult time for you. However, allowances cannot be made forever. You must pick up your life and get on with it. Your Father and I both thought that your debut and the fun and excitement of your first season would be a nice distraction for you. We are astounded that you refuse to take part. You are not even trying to help yourself. We must insist that you go to *some* of these parties if you won't go to all."

"But Mother, I don't enjoy them! The girls are so silly; all they do is giggle and show off for the boys. And the boys are worse!" It was true. I felt years older than them now, they seemed children to me.

"Nevertheless, I must insist you begin accepting some of your invitations. You need a social life. This constant isolation has been a bad influence on your moodiness and given you a most disagreeable disposition."

"I visit with Margaret!" I protested.

"Well and good," Mother replied. "Margaret is a very suitable friend for you; a fine, sensible girl. But you know that is not what I mean. We are discussing your lack of a social life."

She paused to see if I had anything to say. I did not.

Mother went on: "I can see that you might find the evening events requiring an escort less pleasant, for a while. But at least you must go to the afternoons, which you can attend with a group of friends. Are there no other girls you can go with? You used to spend time with the Dupre girl, what about her?" Mother reflected a moment and then answered herself. "Oh, she is not yet out. Well, then, Sara Sherwood, can you not go to the teas and musicals with her?"

"I thought you needed me to go with you on your calls," I prevaricated, sounding limp even to myself.

"Really, Alta, I got on very well without you before!" Mother retorted. "Will you make this compromise? Your Father and I are willing to excuse the dinners and other evening outings if you will go willingly to the afternoon gatherings."

The silence grew. I had to say something. "Very well," I muttered, but I was not well pleased.

Mother was relentless. "I believe there is a tea dance tomorrow afternoon, is it the Birmingham's?"

"Yes, ma'am."

"And you will go? Perhaps with Sara?"

I sighed deeply. I knew Sara would agree, I had only to send a note. But that also meant the twins!

"All right."

"I have your promise?"

Another sigh. "Yes, ma'am."

"Very well, then." Mother smiled at me encouragingly. "And we shall expect to see a noticeable change. Next month we must give some entertainment ourselves. Perhaps an afternoon tea with a theatrical reading afterward? Your group used to enjoy that." She looked at me expectantly.

"Yes, Mother," I sighed.

"A word to the wise. Those sighs are exactly what I was talking about. You must learn to restrain them. They are too expressive of negative feelings." She smiled wryly and shook her head at my recalcitrance.

I said nothing but did manage not to sigh just then.

"Very well, Alta. I consider that I have your promise. You may go." She dismissed me and began to write a letter. Mother is not much of a disciplinarian.

Father was more severe on me. He required a visit to the library, late in the afternoon: "I presume your mother has spoken to you?"

"Yes, Father."

"And?"

"I am to smile more, stop sighing, and go out, at least in the afternoons."

"So?"

"This afternoon is over; I believe it is officially evening." I tried a light tone, hoping to amuse him.

"Alta, this is not funny," Father said, sternly. "What's done is done. You are eighteen now. You must learn to govern your feelings, as all adults must do, for the peace of this family. Do you understand?"

"Yes, Father. I will try."

Father frowned. "At least, you can stop being reproachful."

Is that truly how I appear? I was taken aback; I had thought that was merely Aggie's spite, and that I had Father's sympathy, at least. This was how they all regarded me? As a child having a tantrum, too young to have real emotions, incapable of grief?

"Father, I don't know how to act the opposite of what I feel," I protested. Indeed, it was a plea.

"That is exactly the problem. You must learn not to inflict your feelings on others." Father was adamant.

I just looked at him.

He seemed to try at patience. "Instead of dwelling on unhappy things, you must practice guiding your thoughts to more productive things. You must begin to behave as you did before all this happened. We shall expect you to resume going about with your friends. If you can't share their interests right now, set your feelings aside and try to be more companionable for their sake. You are much too old to sulk like this."

Sulk! What an ugly word. Grieving, to be seen as a sulk! I could not speak.

Finally, Father sighed, and said, "Well, Alta, think about it. If you cannot discipline yourself to move forward, at least stop punishing everyone else. I expect an observable difference in your behavior, immediately."

I was dismissed. I left. I was bitter. I deliberately *sulked* in my room until dinnertime but was too much the coward not to go down at all. Besides, I was hungry.

I truly did not understand how to change; holding my tongue was not enough. The only thing that was clear was that the small solace of allowing myself to sit apart was now denied to me. I should have to join in with the family and participate in general conversation. In the end, I would have to pretend, however badly. It was asking a great deal; there was little recourse but to try. I could not think of a way out of this unbearable predicament.

I sighed many times, then changed and went down to dinner.

I was in a tricky position. If I suddenly became all sweetness and light, they would think I was mocking them, or else I had gone completely insane. I paused in front of the hall mirror and tried to school my face into a pleasant expression. I hoped it would be acceptable. I was resolved to say something pleasant but unremarkable to each of them.

"Good evening, Mother. What's for dinner tonight?"

"Sorry, Alta, it's salt cod and cabbage. I know it's not your favorite, but your father does enjoy it so."

"That's fine Mother. I will eat it and enjoy watching Father."

"That's very sweet, dear," Mother said, giving me a nod of approval.

"Aggie, what a pretty dress," I said next. "Is it new?"

My compliment deserved more than the suspicious look it got.

"So, what if it is?" Aggie practically spat at me. "I can't have a new dress without you being jealous?"

"I'm not jealous," I protested, trying for a light tone. "You look especially nice in puce; I've not seen you wear that color before."

"Mother, make Alta stop making fun of me. She is just mean!" Aggie cried.

Mother frowned. "Alta," she reproved meaningfully.

"All right, then, I *don't* like your dress!" I cried, losing my temper. All my good intentions were ruined, nothing did any good. I fled to my room and didn't come out again.

Mariah brought me a chicken sandwich on a tray, with a little note from Father: *Try again*, it read.

The next afternoon, I did go to the tea dance, since Mother had forced the promise, but I left it early. I had not particularly enjoyed it, but I had not suffered, either. I even danced a few sets, and the Birminghams did serve quite an opulent tea.

That night I went down to dinner with a new strategy, quietly unsmiling but not scowling, either. I did not initiate any conversation, but when spoken to, I replied pleasantly.

Mother at once asked me about the tea dance.

"It was very nice," I answered truthfully. "I danced with Tom Jarvis, and also Percy." Ugh! Percy's dancing had not improved, but he was so pathetic I could not refuse when he asked me to dance.

"Very good, dear," Mother whispered, always the optimist.

"So, you had a good afternoon?" asked Charles, who had

himself put in long, dull hours at the law firm, filing and doing research for the partners.

"Yes, very nice, thank you, Charles. On the way home I walked in the Park, even though it's cold."

He said he liked a walk, too, but preferred it on the harbor down at the Battery, with a view of the new statue raised on a tiny island there.

I thought I was doing well, but Aggie interrupted Charles just as he was describing the new structure.

"Why in the world did you dance with Percy Ward, Alta? Are you trying to encourage him? That's the railroad Wards, isn't it? Next thing you know, he'll be asking to call on you!"

"No, Aggie, I don't mean to encourage Percy Ward. Just being polite. We were taught in dance class that a lady does not refuse an invitation to dance from a gentleman—weren't you?" That was a mistake, I shouldn't have said that. This was hard!

Aggie bristled at what she must have seen as a reproach. "You may accuse me of not being polite, but I would never raise the expectations of some poor boy I had no intention of seeing!" She shot a triumphant glance at me while Charles patted her hand in appreciation of her superior virtue.

I sighed, never mind that Mother noticed and frowned. In a supreme act of will I remarked, "Well, lucky you, you wouldn't have got your toes stepped on then, as I did. Percy is a terrible dancer."

Graduation with honors! Mother smiled her approval, Father nodded his, even Aggie was appeased.

"So right, I would have refused in no uncertain words! He would not be asking me a second time; you can be sure."

We let it go at that.

"Here, Alta, have a new napkin. You seem to have lost yours." Charles must have thought of it as a peace offering, I don't know, it was idiotic.

"Thank you, Charles, but I do have mine, right here," I said very, very carefully.

The moment passed, but only because Harrison brought in the saddle of mutton just then and began to serve our plates.

It is said: *A mild manner turneth away wrath.*

I wasn't at all sure how long I could keep this up.

Chapter Seven

"Father, may I speak with you?" I requested, accosting him in his library.

Father was busy with a crossword puzzle and did not look up.

"What is it, Alta?" He wrote down a word.

"I hope you are satisfied with my behavior?" I asked.

He looked up blankly. "What?"

"Since last we talked. I hope you can see I'm trying to be better?"

I had his attention, now. He looked at me questioningly.

"Yes, I can see you are trying," he allowed. "Your Mother says you are going out more. You always seem busy."

I shrugged. "Reading and sewing and practicing the piano are fine, but I find myself wanting something more important to do, something real. Father, I'm trying to do as you and Mother asked, now give me something that will make me happier, a little reward."

Father looked perplexed. "What is it that you want, Alta?" he asked.

"Could I not come into the store with you and be useful there? Could you not find me some small sort of job?"

Father was astonished. "The store, Alta? You're too young! You should be out and about with your friends!"

"We talked about this," I retorted, a bit impatiently. "Those girls only care about beaux, shopping, and traipsing about the park in large groups, rushing off to someone's house to have tea. The young men are just as bad—all tennis and horses and shoving each other... and lacing the punch with rum! I am trying to be good company, but they bore me to tears."

"Rum in the punch!" Father said reflectively, then came back to the point. "Well, Alta, you've not been brought up for trade, and I will have to speak to your Mother, but if it's really what you want, I don't see the harm, a few hours a week for a while. We're starting Inventory on Monday, and usually put on a few hands then." He chuckled. "Heads, too. We always need more of those! I could put you in Findings. You do enough sewing; you should recognize those. Of course, you wouldn't be up to waiting on customers, but we could keep you busy enough."

Why not customers? I thought waspishly. I have been one myself long enough! How hard could it be to help another woman buy what she needed?

Father eyed me speculatively. "I don't suppose you'd want to get up early enough to go in with me in the mornings?"

"Father, I've been having breakfast with you and Mother for years! I would prefer mornings." Fewer calls with Mother!

"Well, Alta! Imagine one of my daughters being interested in the store! All right, how about two mornings a week? I will speak to your mother, and we will see."

If I had been a boy, you would have expected it, I thought sourly.

"But you must still go to the parties," Father admonished me.

"Very well. And thank you." In keeping with my promised reform, I smiled in what I hoped was a pleasant manner and went quietly away, rather than leaping about and proclaiming my satisfaction, as I might have liked.

Mother frowned but did not refuse permission. I think she felt I did deserve some reward, although it was not one she would have chosen. I was to go with Father in the carriage at eight in the morning and work until one in the afternoon. Then, I was to call a cab to take me home, where Mother would be waiting with lunch. I was to receive a small salary and Father would reimburse me for the cab.

It was a real job! I would have worked for nothing.

Aggie thought me ridiculous, but I was spared much of her scorn, as we rarely saw her at breakfast; she preferred to sleep in and usually did not get up before noon. No doubt she would be having breakfast in bed when Mother and I had lunch.

Aggie went out most afternoons, often with Mother, and her evenings, naturally, were spent with Charles.

I was spared having to spend much time with her, but frankly, I didn't care what her opinion was; I had received a gift from my parents and appreciated it.

Mother's only request was that I should sometimes accompany her on her calls when Aggie was busy. I willingly agreed—anything to spend mornings in the fairyland of my dreams: Carlton & Hodges.

Women like my mother made calls several days a week. Dressed in their finest, they would take their carriages to the homes of their friends, making two or three calls a day, between ten and eleven in the morning, or from two to four in the afternoon. They would "drop in" for visits that could last from fifteen minutes to more than an hour.

There, they would find mutual friends, also dropping in, and be offered refreshments. According to some unwritten book of rules I was not privy to, at some houses, refreshments would politely be refused. The ladies would chat briefly about the latest news, then the guest would leave with affectionate goodbyes and go on to the next call.

At other houses, unspecified refreshments would be accepted, wraps taken away, and high tea would be served all afternoon along with delightful gossip and speculation. Mutual friends would be constantly coming and going and all was as festive and exciting as any French salon could ever have been.

After an unpredictable length of time, it was on to the next house, where the lady might not even leave her carriage but instead send her driver to the door to leave her card.

I understood enough to know that Mother was at *home* the last Thursday of the month. There would be a great house cleaning and Mrs. Croft would put her crew to turning out cookies, ices, and little cakes and sandwiches.

Friends would arrive in droves, and Harrison would be hard put to manage all the wraps and carriages.

Expected to be on hand—to represent the family, I suppose —I was surprised to find I enjoyed talking to some of Mother's friends. They were ladies who put on a show of idle frivolity, but who managed large estates and houses filled with servants. They mediated between feuding relatives, dealt with unreliable tradesmen, handled crises among the servants, and quelled disasters with unfailing calm and dispatch. Yet they still had time to work for various worthy charities—orphanages, hospitals, and settlement houses—patronize the arts—galleries, the opera, and the theater—and excel at demanding hobbies, such as needlepoint or gardening. Sadly, some of them were saddled for life with disagreeable, critical husbands, yet they maintained a cheerful demeanor and, for the most part, kept their troubles to themselves. I came to admire them greatly. I thought they could be excused for sometimes taking an overly enthusiastic interest in the troubles of others.

At lunch, Mother asked me to accompany her on calls this afternoon, as Aggie had a dressmaker's appointment and then was planning tea at the Plaza Hotel with friends. I was pleased to find we were calling on Myra Sherwood, and that gave me the chance to chat with Margaret. I was bursting to tell her my news.

"Good for you!" she enthused. "As surprising as your choice of activity may be, it cannot but do you good. You spend too much time at home. Actually, I envy you a little."

"You want to work in a store, Margaret?" I was surprised.

"The equivalent, perhaps. Something more than this endless round of socializing."

"You feel that, too?" I thought a moment. "Actually, I'm not really surprised. I always feel we have much in common, yet you are so much older."

"Not that much older, Alta," she laughed. "Only a few years. But yes, I have little in common with the party crowd. I long for some real work to do. Of course, I have my volunteering. I go to Presbyterian Hospital three mornings a week, but one understands they can't give me anything serious to do; usually I just take around the library cart. Not very gratifying."

"Can you not get a real job? Go to a secretarial course, perhaps, or even to nursing school? I know, of course, that is not usual for girls like us, but one does hear of more and more women taking actual, paying jobs."

"You are lucky, Alta. Your father is a merchandiser and sees nothing wrong with taking you into his store. My lawyer father has delusions of grandeur, I fear. Both my parents forbid me to take any such training as you mention. They say I was brought up to be a lady. Marriage is the only option for me. And I doubt your parents feel much differently. Your father indulges you, for a while."

"Perhaps you are right. So, that is why you still go to the parties?"

"Yes, dear Alta," she replied ruefully.

We sat there, both of us, I am sure, reviewing the uninspiring roster of available young men we knew, and growing more and more depressed.

"Oh, Margaret," I whispered, grasping her hand in despair.

"So, you see, Alta, Percy Ward was not necessarily such a bad choice of escort for your debut as you seem to have thought!"

I did see. Or at least I was beginning to see. Percy was respectable and kind and his background was substantial. He was painfully shy and inept, but he was not silly!

I had never thought of marriage in this context before.

Working at the store sounded much more inviting.

On Monday, attired in a black skirt and white blouse with sensible shoes and my hair in a neat bun, I was handed over to a Miss Bailey in Findings and introduced to Carlton & Hodges, and the world of commerce, at the worst possible time.

Inventory week was not business as usual, I soon came to understand, but business plus a great deal of confusion, noise, interruption, and running around. I loved every minute of it.

I loved the store. It was so huge—two stories taking up an entire block; so modern and elegant, with what seemed miles of carpeted aisles, glass counters, shelving, and striking displays. I loved the great vases of fresh flowers, the grand staircase going up to the second floor, and the enormous chandeliers, glittering in the sun rays from the skylights. I had always loved the store. As a child, I thought it full of wonders, even more so now.

The work Miss Bailey gave me was easy to understand and enjoyable: counting out each stack of goods, neatly writing the amount down on a temporary list, and restoring any mistaken items to the proper placement. This meant that one had to then change that total, of course. Only when inventory was done would the final figures be entered into the official ledger. Miss Bailey seemed surprised to find that I understood this basic function; her surprise was surprising to me!

I loved handling the rolls of trimmings, the soutache, the piping, the tatting, the lace and ribbons of every kind, the yards and yards of beads on strings, the appliqués of jet or seed pearls, the big cushions full of extravagant hat pins, the glass case of silk flowers that looked so real, the combs and clasps, and bolts of at least twenty different kinds of veiling.

Then, there was the button section, with variety beyond description. On to sewing boxes and all the necessary fittings: measuring tapes, scissors, needles of all sizes, tracing papers, patterns, supplies for knitting and the other fine handcrafts, and anything one could possibly need to practice these arts.

There were small displays scattered everywhere of completely unnecessary, but delightful, items one could only call fripperies—but what pleasure they might add to chores and drudgeries! Why not use an alabaster egg for darning stockings, instead of a boring wooden one? Why not enjoy the endless miles of seams, knowing one was using needles tipped in real gold and wearing a solid silver thimble! Why not have a small globe of brightly colored Venetian glass florets, into which one could stare for hours? There was even a small, stunning display of little tortoiseshell pots holding waxy essences of perfumes— perhaps from France? It was all fascinating beyond words.

The most astonishing modernity of all was the great system of pneumatic tubes descending from the ceiling to deliver a cylindrical container to each main departmental counter. Detaching this cylinder, the clerk inserted the bill of sale with the payment and slipped it back into the tube. With a delicious *whup* the tube was sucked back up to the business office on the second floor. In a few minutes, the cylinder would *whup* back down, now containing the customer receipt and change, if any. Wonder of wonders! I could have watched it all day long.

To make any sort of final inventory count impossible, stock boys kept bringing us boxes of new arrivals, which had to be examined, priced, and put into stock. I loved writing the price tags, coin-sized rounds of cardboard rimmed in tin with a hole for string with which to attach them. I was delighted to hear this would be one of my *permanent* jobs. I liked these tags so much; I surreptitiously made myself a little bracelet of them, with a piece of thrown-away string.

Miss Bailey shocked me when Father came to see how I was doing by complimenting him on my handwriting, showing him one of the tags.

"A legible hand, sir! May I say, a true Carlton hand?"

I thought that was a bit much, but nonetheless, I blushed down to my toes at the praise, and I could see that Father was pleased, although all he said was "Harrumph."

It was easy to convince Father that I needed to go in every morning during inventory, to be of any real help. Afterward, it would be back to business as usual. But I liked going in every day. It was nice to get up with something important to do, much as going to school had been, yet I was reluctant to open the topic of a real job again with Father, for fear he would say no.

So, perhaps deviously, I simply came down every morning ready to go, and, somehow, Father didn't object. I became a fixture Monday through Friday, never on Saturday, and was quite pleased with this arrangement.

The other clerks in Findings regarded me askance. I was "family" and had received "preferred treatment." Many needy young women would have loved my job, but I was not about to apologize. If one has an advantage, it is only good sense to use it —keeping it is up to individual merit. This was not my livelihood, but at the moment it was saving my life!

There was plenty of work for me to do as a stock girl. Boxes of new merchandise were constantly arriving at my special counter. I opened them and examined the items for any irregularities as I had been taught. If anything was marred, or if the count was wrong, I reported it to Miss Bailey, who settled the matter in the shipping department. I longed to explore the mysteries of shipping, but my job did not require that I go there. Rather, it came to me.

When the box was unpacked, I compared the shipping bill with our pricing "Bible" and then wrote out and attached a dear little tag to each item, putting them away in their proper place on the shelves, *in stock*.

Miss Bailey noticed one of my impromptu bracelets and laughed. "Alta, you are a child! But no harm. I love them, too. And, Lord knows, we have millions of them."

I quickly learned where everything was kept. All was logical and perfectly organized. When the stocking was done, I roamed the whole department, tidying up, removing empty boxes and trash to the waste bins in the back, and wiping and cleaning the counters.

If the other girls resented me, they could hardly say anything to my face. I was sure my work was good; I was competent and knew better than ever to appear idle, unlike some of them.

I watched the clerks and how they interacted with customers and presented the merchandise. Whenever asked, I ran errands very willingly.

We were all women in Findings, although there were several men clerks in the large Fabrics section next to us, which was run by Mr. Jonas Demming, a longtime houseman of Carlton &

Hodges. Miss Bailey also reported to him as he was in charge of our entire department, Dry Goods.

The clerks of Findings continued to be civil to my face and were helpful if Miss Bailey asked them to be. However, my departure every day at one o'clock increased the barrier; I was not one of them.

I would gather my things and exit the store through the front doors—not something the other employees were allowed to do—where the doorman would hail a horse-drawn cab and see me off with a jovial wave of his top hat.

Mother would give me lunch in the morning room. I would regale her with stories of my adventures at Carlton & Hodges, designed to make her laugh, and she would shake her head.

One day, she said, "Alta, I never supposed you would take to the trade. You are not at all the shop girl type, one would think. I am still not sure it's entirely appropriate for our daughter......."

"Mother, I assure you we are all quite refined at Carlton & Hodges. We shall just tell everyone it is my little amusement for the time being."

"Well, I dare say all our friends think it very odd." Mother was implacable, but she did not forbid me.

In the middle of my fourth week at the store, an event occurred that changed much. We were unusually busy that day and all the clerks were involved in lengthy transactions. Miss Bailey was handling two customers at the same time, a skill which no one else seemed able to manage.

I had been observing her with awe while restocking the glove drawers when I noticed a matron standing impatiently just down the counter from me. I realized that I knew her and that she would not be willing to wait very much longer. I looked about, then thought: *Why not, they can only reprimand me!* I put down the gloves and went to her.

"Good morning, Mrs. Everly. Do you remember me? I'm Alta Carlton."

She peered at me, then nodded. "Yes, Alta, I remember you. I'm just surprised to see you here!" Then, she grew flustered. "Of course, it's your store! I mean..."

I rescued her from her embarrassment. "Father lets me come in sometimes, just for fun. I love the store so much. Can I help you with anything?"

"Well, yes you can. I came in for some gray veiling. You know, the kind with black dots."

I knew, quickly produced what she wanted, and chatted while measuring off the yardage. "I was working in the glove drawers when you came in and... oh, Mrs. Everly, there are some new green gloves that exactly match this beautiful green piping on your suit!" Having just put them away, I was able to have the correct drawer on the counter within seconds. "Let's see, you'd be what... size nine?"

Mrs. Everly was properly impressed. She took the gloves, which were quite soft and lovely, and fingered them. "They do match," she admitted, then could not resist removing her own, black kid glove, and slipping a green one on. "Oh, so soft!"

"It's French suede," I confided, leaning closer. "I just this minute put them into stock. No one else has even seen them!"

She fingered the price tag and raised her eyebrows.

"I'll just put them back," I said serenely, taking up the second glove and reaching for the box. "They're so unique I knew you'd enjoy seeing them."

Mrs. Everly held on to the glove she had worn. "I might take them," she speculated. "After all, they are a perfect match."

I smiled at her warmly. "And make a lovely outfit!" Then I noticed her black bonnet, which was adorned with a spray of black, iridescent feathers.

"Do you know, there is a white silk rose with velvet leaves

just this same color of green; so much more spring-like on a bonnet! One may hope for spring; it's only a few months away! Do look, it's just down here."

By now, of course, all the clerks in Findings were staring. I was grossly overstepping my bounds. I looked questioningly at Miss Bailey, but she merely nodded, so I sold Mrs. Everly the rose.

In the next few minutes, I interested her in a unique ebony purse frame (like Mother, she made many needlepoint purses) and one of the dear little pots of French scent.

"Alta, I must leave at once! I'm late for Mrs. Poncemore, and if you tempt me anymore, I shall have a dreadful lecture from Mr. Everly!"

"I cannot imagine Mr. Everly ever saying boo to you," I teased her, writing up the sale while picturing that balding, sedentary septuagenarian. "And, if he does, just tell him to speak to my father," I added demurely, sending the cylinder away with a satisfying *whup*, all charged to her account, of course.

"Well, Alta, I will be back to see you soon, no doubt," said Mrs. Everly.

"I shall be prepared," I promised, and we laughed together like two conspirators. Her receipt came back, and I sent her off with a smile.

I turned to find all the clerks gaping at me. Several looked pleased to assume I was now in trouble. Miss Bailey eyed me speculatively.

"Alta, you surprise me," she said after a moment, and I felt the departmental indrawn breath of anticipation. What did they think... that Miss Bailey could fire the owner's daughter? Perhaps I would be demoted into the depths of the shipping department.

Miss Bailey tapped her pencil thoughtfully against her cheek.

"Alta, from now on, when everyone else is busy, I will expect you to step in and give us a hand, as you so helpfully did just now. You performed acceptably." She raised one eyebrow, ironically. "However, why did you not show your customer the new Venetian lace, or perhaps the fox tippets? Next time, think higher, Alta. We must all think higher!" She chuckled and turned away.

The department let out its breath, seemingly satisfied, and turned back to their occupations. Did they think I had been rebuked? I was glowing with her praise.

After that, I enjoyed being at the store even more and often took customers. To be sure, not everyone bought so generously as Mrs. Everly, but soon several ladies were coming in regularly asking for me, and willing to wait until I was free. This did not make me more popular with the other clerks, but it pleased me!

Miss Bailey was also pleased. "Alta, you seem to have a gift for selling. I shall make sure to put you up to some of my more hard-to-please customers! Then we shall see how well you do!" she teased me. "I already have several in mind."

"Oh, please, ma'am, not Mrs. Noddingham-Smythe!"

"The very one."

"I shall fail miserably!" I moaned.

"That's a maybe." Miss Bailey walked serenely away down the counter to help a new customer.

Mrs. Noddingham-Smythe did come in, and she was indeed difficult, but I made the sale. After all, she had come in expressly for some pink ribbon. However, she would look at nothing else, and after she was gone, I acknowledged my defeat, and the others seemed pleased to find me only human. Miss Bailey was amused.

I did have one more small success, at least to my mind: Carlton & Hodges was a public store, of course, and not all the customers were *high society* by far. Most of them were quite ordinary people who found our prices high but dreamed over the luxuries we offered. I sympathized with them and felt, unlike some of the clerks, that they had a perfect right to look. I would show them an item or two, chat a bit, and then, discovering I was needed elsewhere, gently send them off about their business.

"I don't see how you can waste your time like that!" exclaimed Sofie. "They'll never buy a thing, and they'd look all day if you let them!"

I said nothing, but secretly, I wondered. Perhaps they had no money today, but who knew what tomorrow would bring? And, if it brought something prosperous, perhaps they would remember Carlton & Hodges with pleasure, and give us their trade.

One class of customer I did not welcome so kindly. Some of what Mother called "shop girls" came in; they tended to be boisterous and pawed through displays on the counter with gloveless hands that really were not quite clean.

I thought about this for some time, and then one day I brought in a small china basin filled with damp, rose-scented linen squares, along with a matching number of dry ones, which I stashed under my marking counter.

About mid-morning, two young girls of the type did come in, demanding to rummage through the silk flowers.

"Of course," I smiled at them, quickly producing my basin, and leaning confidentially toward them. "The fabrics of the flowers are so delicate and lovely! We all make it a practice to wash our hands before we so much as touch them!"

Taking a towel myself, I offered a cloth to each of the girls; they perforce accepted, somewhat bemused, and we stood there a moment, all diligently wiping. When I took back their towelettes, they were not quite white anymore! We dried our hands, and only after that did I open the case.

We proceeded to enjoy ourselves very much with the flowers, and I even showed them some delicate, lace-trimmed handkerchiefs that I was especially fond of before I "noticed" that Miss Bailey was needing me.

"I expect some new stock has come in," I confided. "We shall have to stop now so that I can go back to work. It's been fun, hasn't it?"

They agreed. It had been. But they were not at all inclined to stop.

"What's the problem? You're helping *us*, ain't you?" said the one.

"I wanted to see some gloves," complained the other.

"I'm sorry, I have no more time," I apologized. "But what are you doing with the rest of your morning? Will you lunch out?" I asked, putting away the handkerchiefs. "Have you tried The Happy Hen, just two blocks down toward the Park? It's a very nice tea house. Or there is Louie's. It's very good, too." They were immediately distracted and went away, happily debating dining possibilities.

No one in Findings said a word, but Miss Bailey inclined her head to me, and in the days that followed, several of the girls adopted my towelette technique. Of course, they used my supply—they did not bring any of their own!

Altogether, I was very happy at the store, and my mornings passed quickly, full of interesting events.

At home, Mother was so consumed with Agnes and the wedding plans that she did not pay much attention to me. No one accused me of lurking or looming, although there may still have been a little sighing going on.

I was happy to be allowed to spend my afternoons quietly reading or walking in the park as spring approached and the weather improved. Then, without my quite realizing how, spring was almost over, and it was time for *the wedding*.

Chapter Eight

I sat, listlessly brushing my hair at my dressing table. Warm May sunshine poured in through my bow window, and I was enjoying the otherwise unnoticed auburn sparkles it set off in my dark brown hair. This was no time to dawdle, but, frankly, I was not in much hurry to see my sister united to the man of my dreams, however tarnished he had become.

Mariah had rushed in earlier to lace up my stays, but I was not expecting to see her again to help me put up my hair in the proscribed bridesmaid sweep, ready for the wreath of carnations we were all to wear. Mariah, Mother, and Doris were all busy with the bride in her room, dubbed in our family as the "Miss Carlton Suite," traditionally given to the eldest daughter in residence and, therefore, eventually to be mine.

But not yet. After the wedding and the honeymoon summer abroad, Aggie would be bringing her husband back home to live in her quarters until the promised house facing Central Park could be found and fitted up for them.

While they waited, they would be quite comfortable here. The rooms were at the south end of the second floor and contained a very nice bedroom, a dressing room, a small bathroom, a cozy sitting room with a fireplace, and a view from the front of the house onto leafy trees and the gaslit street. Plenty of room for two.

I honestly didn't mind waiting. I was perfectly happy in my own dearly familiar room. I especially loved my window seat, lavishly upholstered in dark red velvet, scattered with several of my needlepoint masterpieces. I had done one pillow cover of a gray cat on a black background, which I thought had turned out quite well, plus another of a ship in full sail which now always reminded me of Mrs. Warren.

Mother and Father had a larger suite at the other end of the floor, and in between were several guest rooms as well as my own. Above, on the third floor, were more bedrooms and some of the servants' quarters, reached by the back stairs, with others in the basement near the kitchen.

It was a large and comfortable house, surrounded by great trees, well-kept lawns, and a rose garden—Mother's great hobby and pride. Here we lived in comfort, due to Father's genius at storekeeping, and there was plenty of room for all of us.

There were swarms of servants to take care of our every need: groundskeepers and the coach and driver. I'm afraid I had come to take it all for granted—I had never lived any other way.

Today, the house was full to the eaves with out-of-town relatives and their various *entourages*. The upstairs floors were clamorous with servants, rushing back and forth, coping with newly polished boots, garments to be pressed, last-minute repairs, and frantic requests for forgotten necessities.

Downstairs was worse. Noisy workmen were putting up fifty little tables with chairs in the drawing room, on the back veranda, and on the grass in front of it. Servants were unfolding chairs and setting each table with the linen and utensils necessary for the wedding breakfast. The florist got in everyone's way, creating arrangements, large and small, and putting up ladders to nail great garlands of fresh flowers and greenery in every possible doorway and arch. The house was a bower.

Wonderful aromas and surprising noise came from the kitchen, where Mrs. Croft and four extra helpers prepared the feast, apparently at the top of their voices.

The wedding was to be held at eleven o'clock at our church, St. James Presbyterian, a ten-minute carriage ride across Central Park. It would be attended only by family, close friends, and such of the servants as could be spared from their tasks.

After the brief ceremony, all would return to the house for the festive breakfast. Here we would be joined by many more guests, friends, and business connections. There would be a receiving line and a photograph. The breakfast would be served from long tables on the veranda, as the dining room table was filled with wedding gifts on display.

Once breakfast was cleared away, three wedding cakes would be cut and served on the veranda: the enormous, decorated, flat-sheet wedding cake, the tiered bride's cake (white), and the flat groom's cake (dark—in our case, a spice cake). There would be champagne and many toasts.

In the late afternoon, the bride would change clothes and the new couple would depart to spend their first night at the Plaza Hotel. Tomorrow morning, all who were able would gather at the steamship terminal to cheer them on their way to London, the first stage of their wedding journey and three months of honeymoon bliss.

Agnes could have been quite properly married more simply —in a morning gown or her traveling suit, as many girls chose to do, especially when leaving immediately on their wedding journey. Agnes's suit was elegant grey linen, with the smaller puffed sleeve and modified bustle we were beginning to see, and was trimmed in black silk. The drapery of the skirt was especially becoming. It would have been my choice for the ceremony, especially considering the darling gray hat she was to wear with it.

But Agnes was comparing herself with Adelle, and Adelle had wanted the white wedding gown, with a full complement of ushers and bridesmaids.

Aggie's wedding dress was a confection of ivory silk, lace, and seed pearls with a short train. It had a high, beaded neck, great puffed sleeves down to the elbow, then tight to a beaded cuff at the wrist. The dress was slender, with a draped apron-front pulled to the back in a mock bustle held by a large bow. There was to be a wreath of white carnations with a short veil down to her shoulders. She would wear gloves and carry a great bouquet of white carnations with satin ribbons draping to dainty, white satin slippers.

As to the carnations, Aggie was quite specific: "It's our love flower! The very first flowers Charles ever gave me," she had proclaimed, leaning adoringly on his arm, and trying to look happy about it. Charles looked like a cat with cream. Sometimes you have to opt for the romantic symbol.

Therefore, in the name of love, the bridesmaids and I (the maid of honor)—since Adelle, in her condition, could in no way take a part—were to be arrayed in various shades of carnation pink. Fortunately, mine was the deepest shade, quite a pretty silk morning gown with the same high neck, a modified sleeve, and lovely apron-front draping up to just a hint of bustle in the back. I would probably be able to wear it many times again if I could stop associating it with this occasion.

On my dressing table lay a velvet box from Tiffany's, containing the pearl earrings Agnes had given each of us. Three small, but genuine, pearls dangled down a gold chain, not too long, not too short, very delicate, and just right. I liked them. Mother had excellent taste.

I sighed, and, hearing myself, had to laugh at my lapse of

reform—I was hopeless. I began to remove the hair gathered in my brush.

It was impossible not to be aware that once this was to have been *my* wedding day. Wryly, I reflected that Charles's plans had hardly changed at all; he had only changed the bride.

Yesterday afternoon had been exhausting. It was spent with Agnes and the bridesmaids, all of us laboring away to make the favors for the wedding guests. These were small fancies of ivory silk, lace, ribbon, carnations, and silver leaves, to be fastened onto lapels or shoulders with an ornamental pin.

It was the custom for the bride to make those favors for the groom and ushers with her own hands, and to give Aggie her due, she did that. But afterward, she could not seem to stay seated, and was always putting down her work and rushing away to confer with someone, leaving the other five of us (three friends of Aggie's and Cousin Donna from Philadelphia) to finish up the remaining two hundred! It is no small favor to agree to be a bridesmaid.

Today would be worse. Besides disbursing the favors, it would be our duty to cut up the wedding sheet-cake, a dark fruitcake, into two hundred little packets, wrap them in silver gilt paper tied with pink ribbon, and then make sure every guest had one to take home!

Last night had been a formal dinner for the wedding party and all our relatives, which was a great success. It ended up being more like a banquet and had lasted long into the evening since everyone was feeling festive. This celebration dinner was why the house decorations had to be left for this morning, Saturday. The crews meant to transform the front rooms arrived early, shortly after six a.m., and disturbed everyone's sleep. Since then, the noise had never abated.

A shriek rang out from the room across the hall where the bridesmaids were dressing. Without much caring, I wondered what fresh calamity had befallen them. I would have to join them soon. The hair I could manage, but I would need someone to do up the buttons on the back of my dress.

I wondered what it would be like to live in a world where buttons were in the front. How I wished it were so. Women would have no problems dressing then! One could do it oneself.

Automatically, I began to stuff the wad of hair from my brush into the round ivory chignon box that always sat on my dressing table. It had a slot in the top and when it was filled, one painstakingly added the saved hair to a growing braid, which would be used to supplement hair arrangements later in life.

Mother had introduced us to this practice when I was thirteen, and although Aggie brushed off the task as too boring, just like embroidery, I came to find great pleasure in mastering a smooth, uniform plait and watching it grow over the years.

"You will be very glad to have this when your hair begins to thin!" Mother assured me. She, herself, had several long braids by now and would sometimes show them to me. You could scarcely see a change of color as the blonde turned subtly into gray, then silver. They were quite remarkable, and Mother used them frequently. My own, I supposed, would be piebald. Perhaps I should start a new plait each time my color changed and have many different ones.

Fresh shrieks from across the hall—what could be happening now? Rather than find out, I self-indulgently took out my carefully-stored braid and began the exacting process of adding on to it. It was calming and enjoyable, and I felt quite relaxed when it was done. What was all the rush about, anyway?

It only took me a moment to twist my hair up and secure it. Others might have more elaborate coiffures, but I was satisfied with this. It would look fine with the headband of carnations awaiting me across the hall, along with my bouquet.

I stepped into my gown and went across the hall to be buttoned up.

All was in pandemonium there. Cousin Donna had split a seam and had to remove her dress so that one of the maids could sew it up again. The fabric had torn, and although the maid was doing a fine job, it was clear the mended bodice would be even tighter now. The other girls were trying, ineffectually, to re-lace Donna's stays more tightly, while she protested that they were too tight already and she would never be able to endure more.

At that moment, Aunt Adah appeared in the doorway to quench the commotion.

"What a fuss! Stand aside, girls," she scolded and, taking over the task, gave a series of mighty tugs on the laces, which caused Donna to yelp.

Aunt Adah calmly tied her off, ignoring Donna's moans. "Stop your caterwauling, girl! This is better for you, anyway. Puts all your parts into the right position. You're fine. Just stand tall and breathe shallow. Look what a tiny waist you have. Your gown will fit now." And it did.

Aunt Adah asked for the button hook and proceeded to do up Donna's fastenings in half the time it would have taken us, and then she hooked me up as well. We put on our carnation headbands, took up our bouquets, each matching the individual color of our gown, and we all trooped off to see the bride.

We found Agnes swooning over a note which had just been delivered from Charles, professing eternal devotion to his own *personal carnation* and his impatience to see her coming down the aisle to him.

"It's all so romantic!" Donna breathlessly remarked.

"I think she really prefers gardenias and orchids," I muttered, but only got a startled look in return; Donna paid no attention to me, but then I think she needed all her wits just to keep breathing.

Agnes tucked the note into her stays next to her heart and was helped into her lovely dress. With the tighter skirts coming into style, one wore only a single petticoat. Agnes looked slender and somehow taller. I would have, too, in her place.

The veil was fixed with silver combs, and the wreath placed over it all. She looked a dream bride—ethereal.

We heard a great commotion outside, the carriages arriving to ferry everyone back and forth to the church.

The bridesmaids were rushed off in the first one to give the groom and ushers their favors and be ready to hand out others as guests arrived. When that first carriage returned, all three began taking people to the church and coming back for more. The last carriage took Father, Mother, me, and the bride.

Mother was seated while we waited in the foyer. Charles and his best man (Larry from college) stood at the altar with the minister.

The bridesmaids were each taken down the aisle by an usher, with me going last—alone. The organist was playing something churchy that I did not recognize but sounded just right.

Chords struck dramatically and Father came, bringing the bride. It was certainly an emotional moment, especially when Father gave the bride's hand to the groom. Both were in tears of joy; no one could doubt this marriage was a love match.

The ceremony was brief. In no time, Agnes was taking off her glove to receive her ring, and they were pronounced "Man and Wife." They came swiftly back up the aisle, trying hard not to look right or left as it was supposed to be bad luck, while noisy friends tried even harder to tempt them to peek at some outrageousness.

Such a ridiculous custom! I would have hated it. Charles

and Agnes, however, knew just how to handle it. Of course, they looked, and then everyone enjoyed teasing them about it and predicting the many types of bad luck which were bound to ensue.

Then they were outside the church and Charles was gallantly lifting Aggie into the special, all-white wedding carriage, drawn by four white horses, and they were driven home while the church bells pealed with joy. Very touching, but the noise was deafening.

Other carriages now drew up, and so began the task of getting everyone back to the house, where champagne was being drunk and preparations were being made for the taking of a huge group lithograph. More guests began to arrive with a great hullabaloo, and all was festive.

I had to stand in the reception line, of course, although Adelle was spared that task, sitting modestly in the drawing room throughout. Then the buffet was served and we took our plates to whichever of the little tables we fancied, inside or out.

Mrs. Croft and her helpers gave us a breakfast fit for royalty: a handsome strata, layered with eggs, cheese, and sausage, warm cinnamon rolls, great bowls of the exotic fruit salad called "ambrosia," great slices of ham, delicate waffles dripping with maple syrup, platters of sausages and bacon, and succulent chunks of chicken a la king, in tart-sized pie crusts so delicate they broke with a touch of the fork.

It was a breakfast beyond my imagination. I couldn't believe my ears when I heard Uncle Basil complain to Aunt Dorothy, "Where are the potatoes?"

"There are no potatoes, Basil," she responded. "Isn't that just like Horace and Antoinette?"

I wanted to rush up and say something scathing to them, but I was too full to move.

When the cakes were cut on the veranda, I could still hardly walk, but dutifully did take up my station with the bridesmaids to begin wrapping and dispersing the favors. This was not an easy task, and quite unpleasant, as we were expected as proper young ladies to keep our gloves on; they quickly became soiled.

It was the tradition to bake into that cake a great number of tiny trinkets, which were supposed to tell your fortune: silver horseshoes for luck, new pennies for fortune, and so on. A tiny satchel meant a trip, a bell meant you would marry soon, and a button meant you would never marry.

Naturally, each bridesmaid made sure there was no button in her own packet, nor those of her particular friends, to the further peril of her gloves. I wondered why I was the only one who had thought to bring an extra pair to change into when our task was done; it seemed obvious to me.

Waiters brought huge trays of champagne. There were more toasts and we all stood around eating cake.

Father made a pleasant speech, welcoming Charles to the family. Charles's father made another, praising Agnes. Glasses were refilled. Everyone was merry.

Around three o'clock, Mother signaled, and Agnes went away upstairs to change into her going-away clothes, the bridesmaids trailing after her to help. Mother frowned at me, so I went up as well.

I'm not proud of it, but I coveted Agnes's grey suit, and especially the little matching grey hat, trimmed in black feathers and veil. She looked wonderful, sophisticated, and married. I would have, too.

Servants brought down her luggage, surely excessive, and loaded it into a carriage. Why did someone who was looking forward to shopping in all the major fashion centers of Europe need so many valises? There were three hat boxes as well, yet I knew she would be buying at least half a dozen more in Paris!

Larry, doing his duty as best man, rode off in the carriage to deliver the luggage to the awaiting suite at the Plaza Hotel, from whence it would be conveyed tomorrow morning to the steam liner at the docks.

Eventually, Mother came upstairs and pronounced Agnes ready to go. Agnes emotionally pulled a carnation from her bouquet for each of us attendants. Traditionally, we were to dry it and always remember this day. Personally, I had had enough of carnations already to last a lifetime.

After much kissing and hugging, we all came down again. Agnes kissed Father and then Mother. Charles was trying to shake hands with everyone. The white wedding carriage drew up once more, and the couple ran out to it amid showers of rice and silk slippers—for luck.

It was meant to be extra good luck if any of the slippers managed to fall into the carriage. Some of the fellows had strong throwing arms, and Agnes and Charles were trotted briskly away, calling goodbyes and waving, with at least three guarantees of the very best fortune.

Festivity went away with them, and our guests began departing as quickly as their carriages could be brought up. Soon enough, all that remained was an appalling mess and our house guests.

So many months of planning, so much expense, the labor of so many people—all over in a few hours! Still, Mother and Father seemed extremely pleased and were enjoying compliments from the family. I suppose it was the *Wedding of the Year* in our circle.

The next morning, we all caravanned down to the port to board the great liner and visit Charles and Agnes in their stateroom suite—and leave them champagne, flowers from the wedding, and a basket of fruit.

Charles was, as always, jovial and enthusiastic. I looked hard to see any change in Agnes on this second day of her marriage, but she was a mask of vivacity—talking on and on about the wedding. If she seemed a little overly animated, that was probably my imagination.

The great bell rang and it was time for all visitors to debark, leaving the privileged passengers to line the decks and throw down rolls of streamers. On the dock, people tried to catch hold of one, and for some minutes the great ship seemed tethered by ribbons while the band played a sprightly march, and everyone cried farewells and tried to spot their loved ones in the crowds lining the railings.

At last, the ship began to move out, blasting its horn. The streamers stretched tighter and tighter and finally broke, setting the mammoth free to roam the ocean. We watched as long as we could see. Then, we all went home.

Within a few days, all our guests were gone, and Mother, Father, and I began new lives.

Chapter Nine

We now entered a period of perfect—and totally unexpected—tranquility. When Agnes had first left home last year, I was still involved with my friends, bringing crowds of young people into the house, and always begging permission to use the carriage or to host a little tea or dance.

Now, I went off every morning with Father to the store. In the afternoons, I sometimes went calling with Mother. About once a week, I began visiting Margaret. Otherwise, I practiced the piano (Chopin études) and read.

We enjoyed quiet evening meals, where Father and I vied to amuse Mother with tales of the store, and Mother brought us up to date on the latest gossip.

After dinner, Mother and I stitched together companionably for an hour or two, chatting of nothing very important, but we were perfectly content.

Father would retire to the library where I suppose he read the papers or worked on projects brought home from the store, but, having the most social nature in our family, he could not help coming in to see us every now and then to rant about local politics, or complain about the latest hapless doings of President Arthur, or the economic decline and how it might affect the store. Each time he left us again, Mother would share an indulgent smile with me.

At an early hour, we would all retire upstairs. There, happy in my room, I would read for hours before wanting to sleep.

About once a week, there would be a few people in to dine with us, often family, followed by several hours of socializing.

Once a month, Mother held a formal dinner party—with invitations, formal courses, and either cards or musical entertainment afterward. Often, we were invited out ourselves.

I was surprised to find myself enjoying these occasions. Our friends and relatives were interesting people. It was not so hard to converse with them when you were genuinely interested.

To keep my promise to my parents, I did go out with a group of friends from time to time, even to an evening of cards or to see a play. It was good to see my friends again—it had only been my sister and her beau I had wanted to avoid.

Add to this several visits with Margaret every week, and it made for a life I could sink into very comfortably, and I was quite content.

Early in July, Adelle produced young Hudson number two without complications, and we went to meet him as soon as we were allowed.

We found the new mother in her massive bed, all rosy with pleasure. And when Nurse brought the infant to us and placed him in Adelle's arms, it was obvious she was besotted.

"This is Adam Owen," she announced, covering him with kisses. "Isn't he beautiful?"

She unrolled him from the swaddling blanket so we could see him in his full glory and began kissing little arms and legs with many fond coos.

I thought him a squirming, damp, red bundle, rather like a gowned and diapered lobster, but I praised him along with the others. When he finally opened his eyes, they were a startling blue, and even I could see there was a forceful little person present.

John Jr. observed all this with a frown and, I thought, some malicious speculation, to which Adelle seemed oblivious. I hoped Nurse would be on her guard; she seemed quite efficient.

"The heir and a spare!" John Senior exulted handing out cigars to everyone, including me. I would give it to Father later.

Agnes was an indifferent letter writer, but we did receive a few brief missives describing a whirlwind of activities, first in London and then in Paris. It sounded as if they were having a wonderful time. It was easy to put them out of mind.

One evening, when Aunt Adah and Edgar had dined with us, and we ladies were enjoying our coffee in the drawing room, my aunt turned to me with an agenda.

"Alta, this is a quiet life for you, now that the lovebirds have flown."

"To my liking," I assured her.

"You are still going into the store?"

"Yes, but only in the mornings. I wish I could stay all day, but Father says I am too young."

Mother put in, "No one intends you to make a career of the store, Alta!"

"No," I agreed, "but it's quite good fun."

Aunt Adah regarded me, thoughtfully. "You like being with the public, I take it," she commented. "No doubt it is in the blood, Antoinette. You can't fight it."

"Not my blood," Mother demurred.

Aunt Adah turned back to me. "Do you ever do any sewing other than that needlepoint, Alta?"

Why did everyone criticize my tapestry? It was a mystery to me.

Mother answered for me, "Of course she does. Her seams

are perfect; such tiny, regular stitches. And she cuts out patterns with no trouble at all. I can never make heads or tails of them."

"That was ever true," retorted Aunt Adah. "Alta, you know I have been volunteering at that charity downtown—the one on the lower east side that Stanton Colt started, the *Neighborhood Guild*?"

"I have heard of it, but not that you were involved. I thought it was one of those new 'Settlement Houses,' and that all the staff lived in."

"I'm not staff, obviously," Aunt Adah sniffed. "But I can help with my money and the odd hour, here and there."

She leaned forward, a woman with a mission. "There is such urgent need among the emigrating poor! Such a privilege to work with families living in the worst of urban slums—poverty and illness everywhere, ignorance, mothers trying to support whole families with just the work of their two bare hands! We try to enrich their lives, if only a little. We teach them English— so many speak none, and more coming all the time. We help them find jobs and better places to live; and with their legal problems, they are so grateful for any help!"

"I'm sure they are," Mother stitched serenely on.

"And the children!" Aunt Adah continued. "We have a nursery for the youngest, so that their mothers can work. In the afternoons there are classes for the older boys and girls. Alta, some of them can't even read! I know the very thing for you! Could you not come in several afternoons a week, after you are done at the store? That is, if your mother could spare you?"

"I can get along perfectly well on my own, Adah," Mother replied placidly.

"You could have a sewing class, Alta! For perhaps seven or eight of the older girls? They have not even the most basic of skills; you wouldn't believe it! And they will be expected to go out to work at thirteen or fourteen. How much better they would fare with a skill like sewing!" She sat back and looked at me expectantly.

I pondered. Last year this suggestion would have had no appeal; this year, much was different.

Aunt looked at me and went on very casually, "You could come to us directly from the store. We would give you lunch. The girls would be, say, ten through twelve in age—if you could handle that?"

"Of course I could," I said, perhaps unwisely, and Aunt scooped me up.

"Wonderful," she congratulated herself, which is how I became a sewing mistress.

I added just one thing: "Aunt, I think I know someone else who would be interested in your Neighborhood Guild. "

Margaret was, indeed, and nothing could have worked out better. Mother, who was concerned about my going into such a disreputable section of the city, however charitable the work, was mollified by my having a companion. And, of course, it was just what Margaret had been wanting.

We went down to the lower east side together for our first afternoon. Our cabbie was disapproving when he let us out. It was certainly not like the part of Manhattan where we lived! Here were narrow, dirty streets full of trash and sidewalk stalls, with wagon vendors putting the many pedestrians in danger. Yet, despite the squalor, there was an air of vitality, of things about to happen. The people did not seem to walk about sunken in despair; I sensed purpose and hope.

The Neighborhood Guild was grim on the outside, but when we walked in we could appreciate that attempts had been made to make it all more cheerful.

Aunt Adah was there to meet us and took us to the dining room—painted the most appalling yellow—where we were given a small lunch. Then we went to the babies, where

Margaret settled in, presumably as an observer, but almost immediately she became involved with several demanding little boys.

My aunt took me off to meet my class. Handing over authority to me on the spot, she hurried away.

I surveyed my domain. It was daunting, but I had not expected much. The room was too large for our purposes. It was painted an uncomfortable green. Three windows did not let in much light, even though they had no curtains. There were some chairs, so I set them in a circle where we would get the best of the bad light.

Seven little girls of assorted ages regarded me with solemn eyes. One darling with a mop of red curls and many freckles attached herself to me at once. She sat as close as she could pull her chair and grasped my skirt with a grubby little hand.

"Oh, Miss, you are so pretty!" she whispered.

"What is your name, dear?" I asked gently.

"Maggie," she breathed, so quietly I could barely hear her.

"Maggie, and everyone, the first thing we must do when preparing to sew is wash our hands. Will you please show me where we can do that?"

They did, giggling, and we washed. The soap was full of lye, the towel a horror, but we returned to our room with cleaner hands. I began a mental shopping list: rose soap, linen towels, and hand lotion. I had been in this situation before!

After much thought about a possible curriculum, I had decided to begin with simple dishtowels as our first project. I brought with me all the supplies, courtesy of Carlton & Hodges, a contribution Father was happy to make, although he laughed.

"Alta, I hope your projects don't get too ambitious! Next, you'll be wanting to carpet the whole settlement house!"

"Not to fear, Father," I assured him. "There is no carpet

made that would go with those green and yellow walls! You can't imagine!"

"Now, Alta, you're not to use your own money for things like this," he scolded me, more seriously. "Of course, I will support your charities, just as I do your mother's. It's only that your sisters never had any. I'm beginning to see that you are quite a different person."

Nevertheless, I resolved to go to the bank soon and take out a little stake, from funds accumulated over years of generous family gifts. Somehow, it seemed important that the small amount involved should come personally from me. It was my commitment. I had never really made one before.

To start my class, I had each girl choose a thimble from my collection to fit the middle finger of her left hand. Best to make this a habit from the very beginning, as blood-stained fingers spoiled many a project. I had thought this would take only a moment, but I learned my first lesson immediately.

One girl simply could not make up her mind. Two sisters had a brief but vicious battle over a flowered china thimble, the elder winning and the younger retiring into a sulk. Another girl refused to wear a thimble at all, saying it was uncomfortable and made her hand feel like a mitten!

After spending far too much time on this, I taught my young ladies how to thread a needle and make a knot and finally had them stitching away, folding and basting their first hems.

It was hard going at first, especially for redheaded Maggie and the youngest, who both couldn't possibly be older than six, but they came along. There was a sweet Italian girl named Gina, the two sisters Nancy and Mary, another Mary (who would not wear the thimble), a girl named Cecelia but called Cici, and a tall, thin, blonde girl of twelve who impressed me very much, Ellen O'Conner.

I encouraged them to persevere at their toilsome task,

promising as a reward that when the towels were hemmed all the way around, I would teach them to embroider a pretty, straight-stitch flower in one corner. They were charmed.

It seemed we had barely begun serious hemming when my aunt re-appeared to admonish me that class was over. We began to gather up our supplies when I belatedly realized there was no way to tell the girls' projects one from another!

This required a delay while pencil and paper were found; then it took forever for each girl to laboriously write out her name and pin it onto her towel. At least they were all able to do it! I was pleased to notice Ellen quietly helping several of the younger girls.

They were devastated to realize they were meant to give up the thimbles until the next class!

I could see I had a great deal to learn myself.

"Aunt, you will be sorry you ever asked me to do this," I apologized when they were all gone.

"Nonsense. You'll soon have it all sorted out. Although I must say it was a good deal noisier than I thought a sewing class would be. I suppose I had a vision of a sedate circle of pretty girls patiently stitching while you read to them from *Aesop's Fables*!"

"My expectation as well," I confessed.

"Well, Alta, shall we say Tuesdays and Thursdays, then?"

It was settled. A cab was called for us and Margaret and I started home. She was brimming over with enthusiasm.

"Alta, it was wonderful! There really are several babies, not just toddlers and tear-a-rounds. I learned how to change diapers! I love the babies; they are so dear with their big eyes staring at you! But best of all are the ones just learning to creep or walk. They are amazing! And the three- and four-year-olds, just beginning to perceive the world and needing to be intro-duced to everything! Alta, do you know, they have hardly any

TOYS! Not even alphabet blocks! Only a few spools, and old pots and pans and such. No little trains or horses, or dollies, even! Alta, no picture books!"

"Margaret, we shall have to go shopping!" I laughed, hugging her and telling her about my group of problems. We agreed to shop together on the coming Saturday.

"I intend to go with you regularly," Margaret further assured me. "They say I may. I don't know when I have spent such a worthwhile afternoon."

We were both exhausted.

I admit I was still tired the next morning but got up as usual and went to work with Father. If I showed how tired I still was, they might say it was too much for me to take on. Surely, I would develop stamina.

On Saturday, I took the trolley and met Margaret in front of our mutual bank, presided over by our mutual friend, Mr. Warren, where we each made withdrawals to fund our exciting new projects. Then we had a lovely lunch at an upstairs tearoom.

While I was still determined to use my own money, despite Father's offer, I was in no way averse to using the family discount at Carlton & Hodges for my own supplies, and would gladly have extended that to Margaret, but our store had no toy department. So, Margaret and I set out to find one.

There, I am afraid, we ran amok. I had not known it would be so much fun! Margaret found her alphabet blocks, a wooden train set, and an actual barn with all sorts of wooden animals, not just horses.

There were cuddly, simple rag dollies, and I spent a long time examining them and their clothes, mulling over future sewing projects. Making doll clothes would be an excellent way to introduce dressmaking. Margaret acquired an entire shopping bag full of brightly colored rubber balls of varying sizes.

Then, we spent far too much time picking out picture books. It was exhilarating!

I reflected briefly on the tedium of the wedding preparations last spring. What a chore that shopping had been, not at all like this. I had not before realized what a shopper I was!

It was all far too much to carry, of course, so Margaret arranged to have it all delivered to her home. She would take it into the Neighborhood Guild piece-meal over the next few weeks.

We found another tearoom and collapsed together over sarsaparillas, as the weather was extremely hot and muggy. We beamed fondly at each other.

"Alta, I am enjoying myself so much," Margaret beamed. I agreed. A worthwhile day well spent.

Chapter Ten

On Monday morning I did my shopping at the store with my discount, and in the afternoon picked up Margaret, still beaming, bearing the great bag of rubber balls.

In my class, after we had all washed our hands with the rose-scented soap, I passed around small, inexpensive manicure sets, and spent a necessary half hour showing them how to clean, file, shape, and buff their fingernails.

"When a lady sews, it is important that she takes good care of her hands," I instructed them. "Your hands are on display when you sew, and if they are rough and calloused, or if your fingernails are ragged, you will snag and spoil your fabric."

I was pleased to notice Ellen respond to this lesson. The oldest of my girls, she was tall, thin, and very pale. Obviously well-brought-up, she had lovely posture and always sat modestly and with composure, and, although frail, did her work earnestly, while the younger girls seemed always on the verge of boisterous fidgeting.

We were, by now, done with basting, and were actually hemming, but it was all proceeding at a much slower pace than I had planned. Despite the thimble, Maggie still frequently pricked her other fingers and bled onto the towel. Cici sighed constantly, giving me insight into my mother's objections. Nancy was soon bored and complained she couldn't see why we could not learn the embroidery first.

All the girls except Ellen had to pull out crooked, uneven stitches time and again and begin anew, at which they protested mightily. Only Ellen's stitches were consistent. I praised her and showed her towel around the class as an example; she glowed at my compliments and Mary-Number-Two hissed, "Teacher's pet!" Somehow, we got through it.

In the carriage going home, Margaret confessed to me with chagrin, "I'm afraid the balls were not the best choice. They caused so much noise and confusion we had to put them away, and then all the children cried." Margaret looked very sad, herself.

"Never mind," I consoled, "it will be better when they learn to play with them properly." Then I told her about "teacher's pet" and she consoled me.

A letter came from Rome. It was too hot. There was too much walking. There were too many pigeons and cats, no doubt crawling with vermin. Charles was eating too much pasta and getting fat. Perhaps she would like everything more when they went on to the seaside resort. So much for the grandeur that was Rome!

In August, for my nineteenth birthday, Father took us all—Adelle and John included—on a grand outing. John Jr. was left at home with Nanny (hopefully vigilant) and the baby. What he thought of *that* I never learned, as Adelle was so happy to have an outing that the subject never came up.

We took the ferry on a brief but exciting voyage to see the wonder of New York, the Statue of Liberty. We had viewed its erection from Battery Park, but we had never actually gone out to it before. It was becoming a popular attraction.

The gift of France, *Lady Liberty* was enormous and magnificent. I thought she looked like Margaret. We women could not possibly walk up the myriad stairs to the viewing platform on top, although many others chose to do so. Instead, we waited a very long time for our turn on the small elevator. We were only allowed to remain on the viewing platform for the time it took the elevator to descend and bring up a new group, but the view was amazing and we were well satisfied.

Father then took us to a waterfront restaurant for an oyster dinner and we all felt it had been the great treat of the summer.

One Sunday afternoon, Margaret came over to take a quiet tea with me, laughing over a clipping from the post which she could hardly wait to show me.

It was an article on the new *Harvey Houses* opening at railroad stations in the southwestern territories. Lacking a sufficient local pool of employees, they were imploring eastern young women to come West and become "Harvey Girls."

It was all very proper, we were informed. These lucky young ladies were supervised and chaperoned at every moment, lived in dormitories, and wore modest uniforms. Apparently, they married local gentlemen and retired at such a rate the company could barely keep pace replacing them.

There was a blurry lithograph of a Harvey Girl.

Margaret and I had an immodest fit of the giggles.

"Well, Margaret, shall you go West and become a Harvey Girl?" I teased. "You would look wonderful in that apron. So commodious."

Margaret drew herself up grandly. "I shall look very proper, and I shall meet a handsome traveling salesman, who will no doubt abandon me as soon as we are married!"

"No, no!" I objected. "You are too smart for that! You will meet a cowboy, who will be forever true... but rustic. Or a dashing soot-covered coal-stoker from a train. You will live in a shack by the train tracks and see him briefly every time the train comes through."

"We shall soon have eight children, and I will be very happy!" Margaret pronounced.

We collapsed in laughter, causing Harrison to peek circumspectly around the door to make sure all was well.

Margaret composed herself. "Seriously, a year ago I would have dreamed over that offer, and longed to go, although my parents would never have allowed it. Now, I just want to go to the Guild. I pray every night that neither Mama nor Papa ever deigns to go down there and see the dreadful conditions! That would be the end!"

I knew that Margaret had fallen quite in love with one of the babies, little Henry, who was just learning to sit up without a pillow as a prop, and that she was seriously considering quitting her hospital job in favor of going into the Guild every day, just to be with him.

As for my class, the dish towels were finally done. The girls had loved embroidery, enjoying placing the small hoop to hold taut that part of the towel with the design. Their stitches, with colorful, silk thread, were much more fun, and thus slightly more precise than drab old hemming. When the last one was done, I bore the towels away for laundering.

I brought them back for the next class, beautifully ironed and folded (not by me, I fear, but by Minnie), and the girls were so awed they could scarcely touch them. But when they came to understand I now meant us all to troop down to the kitchen and present these treasures to Cook for use in the house, there erupted a storm of weeping and wailing that could not be quelled for a full ten minutes. It caused several staff members to look in on us and was very embarrassing.

Ellen was a great help to me in the end, solemnly reminding the other girls that the Guild could never afford to give such expensive presents, and that, of course, the fabric and thimbles and all the sewing things were donations to the Guild, and we should all be very grateful. I was very grateful to Ellen. Fragile as she was, a persuasive force seemed to shine out of her dark eyes, unusual with her light hair. She was formidable for one only twelve years old.

We made the trek to the kitchen to make our donation, and Mary Donovan, the cook—who had been warned—made quite a dramatic production of gratitude, which did somewhat lessen the grief of parting with their handwork, at least for most of the girls. Mary-Number-Two sulked to the end.

My little sewing circle took a great deal more of my time and energy than I had expected, but it also rewarded me beyond what Aunt Adah may have expected. It might not seem much to others, but I had never dreamed I could teach. We were doing much more here than merely plying a needle and thread.

The class was deeply satisfying but did not decrease my pleasure at being at the store. I was, by now, such a fixture that the other clerks were more accepting, and I began to glean little scraps of gossip from them that were more than entertaining.

I garnered that many deemed our head of department, Mr. Demming, *past it,* and thought he should be urged to retire, and that old Mr. Hodges was not far behind.

Father confirmed this last, privately: "Fred is not well," he admitted. "He has no energy and coughs all the time, no doubt from those cigars of his. He dithers over the simplest decisions!"

Father calmly lit his pipe. "He should have some time off. Rest—perhaps take Mable on a cruise. But he insists on coming in. Confidentially, we have to find ways to work around him."

It was very pleasing that Father gave me his confidence. He trusted me not to repeat our conversations.

On the other matter, Miss Bailey remarked to me in passing one day. We could not help watching Mr. Demming dress down a perfectly innocent stock boy when it was one of the clerks who had misplaced a new shipment.

Miss Bailey shook her head. "Jonas would never have done that before. He used to notice and understand everything." She lowered her voice, "I believe his hearing is going."

Mr. Demming dismissed the crestfallen stock boy and walked away, clutching at his chest with a pained expression. The ashen-faced clerk had stood nearby for it all but confessed nothing.

"Do you think Mr. Demming will retire anytime soon?" I asked.

"Oh, heavens no!" Miss Bailey laughed. "Not for years, I hope. Things are just fine in this department. Who would want them to change?"

I wondered if that was how she really felt, or if she were speaking to the "owner's daughter."

I thought that she, herself, would make an excellent departmental head, but said nothing.

Of course, I repeated none of this to Father, nor did I repeat the other gossip I acquired. I was determined to be discreet. He should be told if I heard something deeply detrimental to the store, but the rest was none of our business.

We were now well into September, still enjoying the last fine days before fall began. There was a crispness in the air and it did seem the dusk was coming on a little sooner.

One evening, Father came into see Mother and me—again ranting about Mr. Hodges.

"I really think Fred would oppose any innovation I suggest, just because it is my idea!" he complained.

"No doubt, Dear," Mother agreed, serenely stitching on.

"What is it now, Father?" I asked to further the conversation.

"I have had a really good idea," he declared, striding energetically about the drawing room. "Several factories are beginning to produce already made-up clothing for women. They call it 'ready-to-wear.' Skip a seamstress, just take one off the rack and wear it home. Some of it is not bad quality. Not bad, at all!"

"I have heard of that," I agreed. "There is a little shop downtown by the bank selling it exclusively."

"I think we should try a line of them in the store; just a small, very carefully chosen collection, as a special feature. If it does well, as I believe it would, it could become a section!"

Father's enthusiasm was catching. I thought it a grand idea, myself.

"And Mr. Hodges?"

"Fred opposes and is not willing to discuss it at all. He says it would destroy our image as a quality store."

Father paced some more. "He is quite wrong, you know. We will lose that image much faster by failing to stay in the forefront of innovation!"

"Now, now, Horace," Mother protested. "You are not in the board room."

"Father, I could not agree with you more!" I exclaimed. It was exciting to hear my father verbalizing his ideas. I was inspired by his vision and found I had ideas of my own.

"Beyond that, Father, we lack a number of departments other stores are opening. We should have, for example, a *toy* section. We are losing out on a great opportunity there. And perhaps... books?"

Father looked at me with surprise. "Alta, you go further even than I," he praised. "But Fred will have none of it!"

Father paced and I sewed, and we speculated on how Mr. Hodges could be got around, and then Father began suggesting ideas for expansion—perhaps a second store in Brooklyn? It was a very stimulating evening.

When we retired, I was not at all ready to sleep, so I curled up in my window seat with my current book.

It was Gibbon's *Decline and Fall of the Roman Empire*, recommended by Margaret—heavy going, but undeniably interesting. After a dutiful half hour, I put it down and took up Mark Twain's *Life on the Mississippi*, which I found much more entertaining. I read far too late for a businesswoman with work to go to in the morning.

Chapter Eleven

SEPTEMBER 1887

In early September, Charles and Agnes came home from their honeymoon bickering. She looked pale and tired. He looked petulant.

She ordered him about like a servant, and he could not even carry valises and hatboxes upstairs to the Miss Carlton Suite in a manner that pleased her.

They brought with them an astonishing amount of new luggage because of all the shopping. In addition, packages began to arrive—shipped home from abroad. There were gifts for us all: perfume from Paris, strings of Venetian glass beads, and an amazing hat for Mother, trimmed with peacock feathers.

I did not go into their quarters, but I wondered how there could be any room left for them to turn around.

Agnes modeled every new gown for us and lingered over showing us every purchase, reliving her days of glory. She was nervously animated and far too touchy. Every little thing annoyed her. She chattered incessantly in a high, shrill voice, and spoke slightingly of Charles at every opportunity.

Dinners became unpleasant. Agnes dominated the conversation, retelling stories of their trip. She openly criticized

Charles. If he took a second glass of wine, she accused him of drinking too much; if he accepted second helpings, she said he was eating too much and getting fat (he was, rather); if he were talking, she didn't hesitate to interrupt him and change the subject.

Charles did not react to any of this, just continued what he was doing. He was polite to her, loving even—as if she never said a bitter word. It was a bit eerie.

The drawing room was too cold, he must go upstairs to get her shawl, but then he had brought the wrong one, or he took too long doing it. Never a *thank you*.

She could not sit still for five minutes but must be up and pacing about. She would pick up a book, then after only a few pages throw it down and resume pacing. Yet, she did not want to retire for the night. It was very disrupting.

I cautiously remarked to Mother, "Aggie seems a bit... agitated."

"Many women take a while adjusting to the demands of marriage," Mother replied, placidly. "She will settle down in time."

I was glad to hear that.

Fortunately, they went out with their friends most evenings, and I was mostly gone during the day.

Agnes was contemptuous when I told her about the Guild.

"Good heavens, Alta, what is it with you? First, it's all work, work, work, and now it's *good works*!"

I held my tongue. No one could say I had not learned to hold my tongue.

Father was full of ideas these days, and in his own way, almost as restless as Agnes. He had begun talking to Charles about one day coming to work at the store as a lawyer in the business office. Charles was not at all averse. He confessed he was already disappointed to find the law firm mostly used its interns for filing and research for the various partners' cases. It would be years before he could hope for cases of his own, or anything leading to his presence in a courtroom. The store, on the other hand, was full of people and something exciting was always happening.

Having a *family* lawyer was one idea to which old Mr. Hodges did not object, as he was all for family participation in Carlton & Hodges—even me, I suppose. He was bringing in his own son, who was to start as an assistant manager after the new year.

Father was happy for young Fred to join the staff, but he was incensed that Fred would begin so high up in management.

"He should come in at the ground floor and work his way up!" Father objected.

Perhaps it was because of this that Father immediately began to develop a plan for Charles.

Deering, Mason, & Deering did a great deal of work for Carlton & Hodges, as it happened, and Father had no trouble convincing them that a dual internship, shared between the two firms, was beneficial to both.

In early November, a highly gratified Charles appeared in the breakfast room, ready to go to the store with us. He was to begin with an hour in the business office and then spend the rest of his mornings in Shipping and Receiving. His afternoons would be back in the research library. He was to spend a few months in every department at Carlton & Hodges, before settling in the business office.

Charles was to learn the mysteries that so intrigued me. Once again, it did not seem fair. I supposed Father was accepting Charles as a man of the family, if not the son he never had.

I supposed a woman could not possibly work in Shipping and Receiving.

The most I could hope for was that Father would, in time, allow me onto the staff in Findings full-time. In my mind, he surely would by the time I turned twenty-one.

Agnes was not so pleased as Charles.

"You shouldn't have to start in Shipping, like a common employee!" she complained. "You should be upstairs running everything, like Father."

Learning the store from the ground up was not a concept Aggie understood, nor the fact that it would take Charles years to learn what he needed to know, about both merchandising and the law, to become the adviser the store would need— should it begin the expansion Father had in mind.

"I intend to corrupt Fred Jr.," Father said with a devilish grin. "Get him on the side of progress."

I had no doubt that would happen.

That fall we had a beautiful Indian summer. Agnes continued going out in the open carriage, looking at houses alone while Charles was at work. The warmth of the lazy sun and glory of riding through bursts of falling red and gold leaves seemed to make Agnes feel better, and for a few weeks, she was more like herself.

Then they received devastating news from Charles's father. There had been a fire in the shipyard—several ships had sunk to great financial loss. The timing could not have been worse. An alarming financial slump was requiring drastic economies. He was very sorry, but there would be no wedding gift of a house after all.

Agnes was greatly disappointed, but the truth was, they were well situated where they were. Mother and Father were delighted to have them living with us. If I was not so pleased, I kept it to myself.

The weather turned cold and windy. There was talk of the first snow. One morning, as I waited in front of Carlton &

Hodges for my cab, a strong gust blew a sheet of newsprint against my skirts. I reached down to disengage it and was looking about for a trash receptacle when I noticed a small headline in a lower corner: *Go West, Young Woman!* How intriguing! The paper was not soiled, so I folded it into my reticule to read later, thinking it was probably more about Harvey Girls.

I did not remember this incident until that evening in my room. Retrieving the page, which was from the *New York Times*, I smoothed it out and read:

GO WEST YOUNG WOMAN

Are your prospects dim? Is your life confining and not prospering as you had hoped? If you have a spirit of adventure, we can offer you a possibility you will never have considered! Amazing job opportunities for women are opening up in our **Spectacular West***! Through our agency, if you have experience as a teacher, nurse, librarian, clerk, stenographer, cook, housekeeper, or seamstress, etc. we can assure you of an excellent position! You need only to pay your own passage West. We will arrange, for a modest fee, everything else. Our agency has excellent references and many testimonials from already satisfied clients. Are you* **A New Woman of the West***? Take your future into your own hands, and at the same time make a meaningful contribution to the expansion of* **Our Glorious Nation***! Write to* **Odyssey West, New York City Main Post Office, Box 20** *for more information and our references.*

I was very amused by this article and folded it away neatly. I could hardly wait to show it to Margaret.

She thought this offer was even better than the one for the Harvey Girls, and we laughed over it and fantasized for a while. More soberly, we hugged each other and told ourselves how lucky we were that our own lives were so full and our prospects so bright.

Neither of us were *A New Woman of the West!* We had used up all our *Spirit of Adventure* on the Guild.

At the Guild, my current sewing project was "A Gift to the Guild," clearly named beforehand, of window curtains for our grimy, bare windows. Used for a variety of meetings and activities, I intended to make the oddly green room more pleasant for the people who had to spend time in it. It was the simplest project possible; we could do it in two class periods, I was sure.

Each window was to have two panels, hemmed wide at the top for inserting a curtain rod and narrow the bottom, with a ruffled valance at the top. This meant a simple panel with only two hems for each girl. Ellen and I would do the valances since she sewed faster and better than any of the others. I found the fabric in the store remnant bin: eight yards of cheery red-and-white stripes at a reduced price. Father contributed the more expensive double-valance curtain rods.

I had estimated incorrectly. It took us three sessions to finish them, but we did get through it, mostly because, by now, I had learned how to get things done.

My bribe awaited the girls in a basket on my shelf: dainty, thin cotton, cut to size, to be hemmed and trimmed with thin Irish lace. There was a needle and embroidery thread to stitch a small flower and leaf in one corner, each rolled in a bundle ready to begin. They would be my presents to the girls. Perhaps the girls, in turn, would like to give them to their mothers.

The little angels were fairly sure they would prefer to keep the projects for themselves but succumbed to the bribery and sewed. Although I fear their stitches were as big as their hurry to be done.

On the great day, Mrs. Margolis came in to help us hang the curtains, bringing a young man and a short ladder to deal with the rods. The staff stood to watch and clapped as the curtains went up. They did look very nice.

"Well, my dear," Mrs. Margolis commented, "it certainly looks like Christmas in here!"

I was taken aback, not having had seasonal color schemes in mind. I remembered seeing the special window display in Macy's and hearing someone say that red and green were the new Christmas colors. I myself always thought of midnight blue with stars. Mrs. Margolis took pity on my chagrin.

"Never mind, we all congratulate you. Who would ever have thought you would complete such a project! And you girls are to be complimented! Everyone will enjoy these curtains, all year 'round."

The girls were made much of by all the staff and were quite full of themselves. We had punch and cookies. It really was quite an occasion. I was as bad as my students and felt I was a great success.

The next week—our first meeting in December—I passed the hankies out and we all sat in a circle and began. The girls were enchanted with pretty things, and for the first time my class looked as I had first pictured it: a ring of sweet girls, foreheads pinched in concentration, with the cleanest of rose-scented hands, stitching delicate lace. I was tempted to read to them, to complete the fantasy, but thought I had better leave well enough alone. They might forget to sew!

"Ellen, do you have a cold?" I asked. She sat beside me, coughing more than usual and had a red blotch on each cheek.

"Yes, ma'am," she confessed. "We all do at my house. It's this time of the year. It's so cold in our flat. Anyway, I always am getting a cold." She sighed resignedly and hemmed on.

I took advantage of the unusual calm to show Ellen how to do her flower and leaf in solid stitch since she was so much more advanced than the others. She gave me the sweetest smile. I was so fond of her that it was hard not to show her special favor.

Later that same week, the Sherwoods came to dine along with Aunt Adah and Cousin Edgar. Over our half-glasses of sherry in the parlor, Margaret casually told me something momentous.

"Alta, I have begun receiving a caller."

I looked at her amazed, not sure I understood her meaning. She laughed at me.

"Is it so hard to imagine that a man would wish to call on me? Mr. Albert Gorman, a friend of my father's. Father has instructed me that I am to receive him with a view toward marriage."

"Good God!" I could not help responding, although a lady does not use such a phrase.

Margaret was all composure. "He is a widower with two small children. That is all to the good, of course, with my experience at the Guild. I should be quite able to manage them."

I was startled. "You mean to accept him?" I asked in disbelief.

"I may. I don't really know him, yet. He has only called once."

Should I congratulate her or commiserate? "What is he like?" I compromised.

"He is older, of course, thirty-five, I think. Not tall. Rather stout. He has a mutton chop beard."

"Oh, Margaret!" I chose to commiserate.

"Now, Alta, don't be like that. This is a great opportunity

for me. You know I have no other prospects. He seems a very nice man, and there are the children."

I contemplated my sherry in silence and then drank it off.

"Don't be so tragic," Margaret scolded me. "Father hopes I will agree, but he assures me it is to be my own decision. Nothing is going to happen soon, at any rate."

We went into dinner in a solemn mood.

Mrs. Croft cheered us up with a great cod, backed in spinach and garnished with lemon and ginger sauce, and a savory bread dressing. Dessert was my favorite—Floating Islands—which improved my mood greatly.

It did not, however, improve Aggie's. Incredibly, she behaved in front of company just as she did when our family was alone.

"Do not take a second glass of wine, Charles," she called to him the full length of the table. "Harrison, do not pour him a second glass! He is bad to drink so much."

Charles ignored her and signaled Harrison to go on pouring. Eyebrows were raised, and people looked at each other askance.

"I would not let my wife talk like that to me!" I heard Cousin Edgar mutter to my aunt.

"How fortunate that you do not have one," Aunt retorted with some asperity, by which I gathered he was no longer calling on Eugenia Moffit.

Agnes's shrill voice sounded again and again. It was not always to discipline Charles. She told a French joke, very badly, and then told us for the third time about Mother's peacock hat.

Through it all, Charles continued patient and solicitous and made no response when scolded. Mother refused to take any notice. Honestly, I was incensed! How quick the reprimands would have been were I the offender. But I'd learned my lesson and said nothing, although Margaret and I exchanged many meaningful glances.

The next day being Sunday, I went to Margaret's for one of our private teas in her comfortable suite, which looked out over Central Park. The weather was cold and gray, and all the leaves had fallen, but we had a cozy fire and were ready to discuss serious matters. The first topic, of course, was Agnes.

"How can she be so hateful to Charles!" I cried. "He is so patient and attentive, but she has never a good word for him!"

"He can't be very happy with her," Margaret agreed. "Do you have any idea of what the matter can be?"

"Well, I did hint to Mother, but all she said was that it sometimes took a while for a woman to 'adjust to the duties of marriage,' whatever that means."

We both laughed, but then Margaret looked at me rather speculatively. "What do you think she meant by that strange phrase?"

"I don't really know, but that was all she said."

We both sipped tea and looked out the window. Perhaps Margaret was thinking about Mr. Albert Gorman.

I looked at her. I was beginning to know her well. "Margaret, I think you know something you are not telling me."

She sighed. "Well, some time ago, when I... became a woman, my mother told me that 'husbands will have demands, which the woman will not enjoy, but babies will come of it as a compensation.' Of course, I wanted to know more, but by then she could barely speak to me from embarrassment and went away." Margaret now looked uncomfortable herself but went on: "Naturally, I continued to think about it, and several months later I sneaked down to our library and searched out a book that had been forbidden to me. *Grey's Anatomy*, do you know it?"

"I have heard of it."

"They needn't have hidden it, it could have been written in Greek for all I could understand, but I was motivated to persevere and found the right section." Margaret rose and from the bottom drawer of her dresser removed a giant tome, brought it to the tea table, and opened it to a double page of diagrams.

"Alta, you and I are both educated. We have been to all the art galleries and seen the pictures and statues of those magnificent Greek and Roman men... those undraped men. An educated mind must assume there is a reason that they are so different from women in their... anatomy."

Maggie, who never blushed, had grown quite red in the face, and I felt the heat rise in my cheeks as I looked at the page.

"I think these diagrams explain everything," she said bravely, with the air of one taking an evil-tasting medicine.

I studied the drawings for some time, and read over the accompanying paragraphs, quite scientific and difficult to understand. The drawings were much more revealing.

Finally, I put the book down, firmly closed it, and reached to pour more tea. "No," I said, rejecting the theory entirely. "I cannot believe any woman would ever allow that!"

Margaret shook her head in some agreement. "It does not seem likely."

"Although, that would explain why Aggie is so upset," I acknowledged.

"Perhaps she refused," Margaret suggested.

I considered this for a moment and then dismissed it. "No, I can't believe it. We must be misunderstanding something."

In complete agreement, we put away the hateful book and dropped the subject.

Easy to speak of the weather, which was inclining toward snow, harder to dismiss our thoughts. Margaret had to be thinking what I was thinking: that, should she accept Mr.

Gorman, she might be expected to perform something of that nature. Unthinkable!

Another pot of tea was required before we regained our composure.

Toward the end of November, a quiet rumor passed through my family and out into the world. Agnes was "in an interesting condition." In fact, she was quite far along and was expecting the great event around the end of March. This explained a great deal but, in my opinion, did not excuse bad behavior.

Charles was puffed up with pride, but Agnes did not seem compensated.

"Now Christmas is ruined, and the whole season! I won't be able to go anywhere. It's not fair," she complained. But that did not change anything, except that there was yet another great round of shopping for dresses and robes and pelisses of a different kind.

I wondered how much Father had spent on her clothing in just the last two years. First, there had been her debut, then the wardrobe for her year abroad, and then the elaborate wedding clothes and trousseau, followed by shopping in Europe, and now this. But I did not envy Aggie her wardrobe. I was surprised to find I no longer envied her for her husband, either.

In deference to Aggie's condition, Christmas was quiet and not the usual festival of guests and feasting. Mother and Father went out only a few times. Mostly, we tried to create little festivities at home. Agnes did not appreciate our efforts.

The best gift I received, by far, was at the Guild, from Ellen: her treasured, beautifully stitched hanky. In addition to the spray of blossoms, Ellen had entwined my initials.

It was an exquisite gift of love, and I shed a few tears as I hugged my thanks.

I was so fond of Ellen; I wanted to shower her with

presents, but she must not be treated differently from the others. The best gift I could give her was sewing skills.

My class being on vacation for the holidays, I spent my time preparing for our next sewing project: dollies, inspired by the ones at the toy store, but simple enough for my beginning seamstresses.

How hard could it be? I made a pattern of two flat pieces to be sewed together, turned inside out and stuffed, and sewed one up to see if my idea would work. I stuffed it with cotton batting from Mother's sewing basket. It was flat, but definitely a doll, so I embroidered a pert little face and topped it off with a curly mop of fluffy, brown mohair yarn leftover from an afghan. The doll was appealing in a way, and simple. I thought my girls could do it.

I made patterns for several simple outfits: a dress with pantaloons, a coat and bonnet, and a flannel nightgown. The girls would love it and it could lead to making garments for themselves.

During the cold weather, we more or less lived in front of the parlor fireplace, and my project was necessarily untidier than my usual needlepoint—but Mother was amused and kindly overlooked my clutter.

"This is very cunning," she approved, holding up a little coat. "I'm sure your students will love this project."

Aggie thought it all nonsense. "You get so excited over nothing, Alta! And make such a mess. It's very irritating."

Mother said nothing, but later, took me aside to remark, "Some young women find it hard to approach motherhood."

I could see that for myself!

Chapter Twelve

N ew Year's Eve was even more subdued than Christmas had been. We stayed at home and at midnight, drank a toast and listened to the bells ringing. I loved the sound of it: *1888,* and said it to myself over and over, hoping it would be a better year.

It snowed some more in early January, pretty at first, but a slushy mess afterward, and it was freezing. As always, sales were slow just after the holidays, and we were less busy at the store.

Father had wanted to try a special sale to bring in customers and clear out old stock, to make room for new items, but Mr. Hodges thought that was brazen commercialism and would not hear of it.

"Things cost what they cost," he growled, getting very red in the face. "People will never buy anything at regular price if they know they can just wait and it will go on sale. Ruin everything."

Father let it go.

Still, people did come in. I thought, perhaps, they were just looking for someplace warm to go while waiting for better weather. The store was warm, heated with radiators and steam; our heating bills must be enormous.

Father laughed at my theory and said, "That's as good a reason as any to come in, which is what we want."

Charles had been transferred to Haberdashery with the New Year and was learning—with some success, I heard—to become a salesclerk. I knew Father was very pleased with his progress.

One evening in the parlor, just to make after-dinner conversation, I asked him what he was learning about selling to customers. He lost his look of perpetual gloom and was beginning to reply to me with animation when Aggie jumped up and hissed at us.

"The store, the store, the store! Is that all any of you can talk about? Come, Charles, we shall retire." And she flounced away upstairs, leaving Charles to grimace at me apologetically and follow her with obvious reluctance.

We both shrugged it off as due to her *condition*.

A few mornings later at the store, I was gathering cartons for disposal when, hearing a great hullabaloo, I turned from my counter and saw Charles running up the main aisle, toward the door, shouting, "Stop that woman! She's a thief!" Catching up to a figure almost out the door, he grabbed her arm and detained her.

Mr. Holloway, head of security and floorwalkers, was instantly there as well. As they turned the woman around, I saw with horror it was Mrs. Warren! She was extremely upset, trying to jerk her arms free, and shrieking "Let go of me!"

Charles grabbed her reticule, reached in, and brought out a handful of silverware, brandishing it above his head. "Look here," he cried. "Thief!"

Mr. Holloway began to drag her back from the foyer.

I turned to Miss Bailey. "I know that woman," I said

urgently, and she nodded. I left my counter and hurried up to them.

"Mrs. Warren! Oh, dear Mrs. Warren, what is wrong?" I asked, elbowing out Mr. Holloway and embracing her.

"Alta, thank God, it's you. Tell these dreadful men to let me go!"

"I'm afraid we can't do that, Miss Carlton," protested Mr. Holloway. "She did take these items."

"And I'm sure there will be an explanation. But upstairs in Father's office, Mr. Holloway. Not here. Will you please escort us?" I gently took her arm and, murmuring reassurance, urged her toward the elevators, the fastest way to get out of the public view. We already had attracted a circle of gawkers. This was no time to walk in full public view up the grand staircase.

Followed by our "escorts," we soon reached Father's office. I steered Mrs. Warren toward a comfortable chair in the reception room and said to my father's secretary, "Mrs. Clayton, please tell my Father there is an emergency. And then, could you have them send up a tea tray very urgently?"

I returned to Mrs. Warren, settling her in her chair, patting her arm, and in general trying to calm her. Mrs. Clayton, a paragon of efficiency, quietly did as I asked. Charles waited, fidgeting. Mr. Holloway stood like a sentry before the door. Father came.

"She stole these!" Charles accused, brandishing the handful of silver, for Father's information.

"Oh, for goodness' sake, give me those!" I snapped, simply taking them away from Charles. I laid them out on the small table beside Mrs. Warren's chair: a dinner knife, two forks, and a spoon. We all regarded them.

"Hmmmm. English Tea Rose. The very best," Father remarked.

"Oh dear, oh dear," wailed Mrs. Warren.

Father pulled up a chair, sat down, and took both her hands.

"Genevieve, what has happened?" he asked gently.

"Oh, Horace, I don't know! I was just standing there, and they were so pretty, and I saw that no one was looking, and I just put them in my reticule and walked out. It was very exciting. But then someone started yelling and chasing after me... and it was Charles! Oh, Horace, it was dreadful! They wouldn't let me leave the store!"

"Genevieve, you understand I shall have to send for Packy."

"Oh, no! Please don't tell Packy. He'll be so disappointed in me! I promised I wouldn't do it anymore."

"You've done this before, Genevieve?"

"Never here. Oh, never here; you're our friend! But today, somehow, I just couldn't help it."

"Don't worry about it, Genevieve. It will be all right." He patted her hands. "Charles, thank you for your quick action. You can go back to your post now. I will talk to you later. Mr. Holloway, that will be all."

Mr. Holloway pursed his lips and inclined his head. He turned to go, but then turned back. "It is a theft."

Father stood, and I saw in him every bit of the authority and control I so admired. "There is a good deal of difference, Holloway, between *theft* and a confused, unhappy woman who probably needs the help of a *doctor*, not the *law*."

Mr. Holloway inclined his head again and left. Father went to send a messenger to Mr. Warren at his bank, just down the street. The tea arrived and seemed to put some heart back into Mrs. Warren. We drank tea, and I talked to her quietly about other things.

Mr. Warren arrived more quickly than we could have thought possible. Father kissed me, thanked me for my help, and sent me back to work.

That evening, Father took me into the library and told me how it all came out. According to Mr. Warren, this had been going on for some time. Nothing helped—not understanding and gentle reasoning on his side, nor earnest promises on hers. Scolding made no difference. Now, they would try one of those German doctors. Father was skeptical. She was also, now, to have a live-in "companion" who would make sure she never went out alone.

"Now, that might help," was Father's opinion.

I thought it harsh. What a terrible life it would be! But there were unthinkable consequences if she were not watched. To actually run afoul of the law! Not all store owners would have been as understanding as Father. Poor Mrs. Warren. If only she had stayed home with her tapestry!

Father thanked me for my intervention. "Your instinct was exactly right. We are lucky you were able to stop it so quickly. I am very disturbed by Holloway's method of dealing with such a problem. If he cannot agree to a more diplomatic procedure, we shall have to part company!" Father also spoke to Charles—gently, but at length, about handling all issues arising at the store with calmness and dignity.

That evening, as we gathered for dinner, Charles came to me and enthused, "Alta, you were wonderful! You knew just what to do. I learned more from you in just those few minutes than all these months in the store!" He gazed at me with such admiration that I blushed; however, for the first time, I thought the expression in his beautiful, brown eyes was like a... puppy-dog? Also, I couldn't help wondering, since he was stationed in Haberdashery, how he came to notice the theft?

Aggie saw him talking to me, and at once came over and dragged him away, looking daggers at me. This was beginning to be annoying! Mother seemed to be looking at me reprovingly as well!

At work, I was applauded, but at home, I was considered a troublemaker! It was very upsetting, but nobody seemed to care about my feelings. I stomped off to bed in as bad a mood as Aggie, and could hear Father behind me—possibly the only Carlton in a good mood this evening—inquiring of Mother, "What's the matter with Alta now?"

I was still upset about the situation at home—and worrying about what would happen to Mrs. Warren—when I next went to the Guild and found that Ellen was not in class. She had never once missed before. The girls clamored to be the ones to give me the news.

"Miss, she's been drug away to a *'torium*!" Cici informed me, with huge eyes.

"Yes, and they took her sister and brother, too!" confirmed Mary-Number-One.

"It was the *Public Health*, Miss. They came right to her house and took them all away," explained Mary-Number-Two.

Little Maggie wept. I set the class to work on their dollies, put Susan in charge, to the outrage of Mary-Number-One, and went off to find Mrs. Margolis.

"I'm so sorry, my dear, I had hoped to tell you myself. I know how fond you are of Ellen—we all are. She is an outstanding girl, but I'm afraid her future is not very bright. She has tuberculosis, and you know that the Health Department is very severe on that now that it is known to be so contagious because of those *bacilacus* things."

"Bacilli," I whispered, remembering articles from a few years ago about the cause and spread of this terrible disease some called *the modern plague*.

"Yes, and you know the treatment they are trying here on the East Coast: isolation and fresh air. Ellen has been taken to a new sanatorium in the Poconos. It's a hard-luck family; her father died of it only six months ago, her mother a year ago in childbirth."

I had not guessed it was so bad. "But who was taking care of the children?" I asked.

"Neighbors, I think, and a married sister looking in. It was a bad situation; they'll be better off in the sanatorium."

"Poor Ellen!" I cried, feeling guilty. I had not bothered to find out about her situation. "She will be so frightened! I must go visit her at once."

"No, Alta. You will not be allowed to see her, because of the contagion, you know. But you can write to her." Mrs. Margolis brightened at this thought.

I did, too. "That's what I'll do. And I can send her some sewing, to help her stay busy."

"That's a wonderful idea. Let me find a book to tuck into your package as well." Mrs. Margolis gave me the address and promised the book the next week.

I wrote at once, saying how sorry I was and promising a package to come. Mrs. Margolis gave me a copy of *Jack and Jill*, one of Louisa May Alcott's delightful children's novels, and I enjoyed myself at the store, putting together a well-stocked sewing basket. Now, sadly, I could give Ellen the kind of gifts I had wanted to before.

Ellen had loved the doll project, so I packed the one she had been working on, then designed and cut out four more little outfits, delaying my mailing for several days while I spent evenings painstakingly writing out sewing instructions for them. It all made quite a sizable package.

Ellen wrote back even before I had managed to send it off, and soon we were exchanging a brisk correspondence. I coached her sewing, and she shared lively stories of the goings-on in the sanatorium:

We girls sit outdoors in lounge chairs with all our clothes on and three blankets and hats and coats and mittens and watch the snow fall. We take turns reading to each other. They love "Jack and Jill" and say I am the best reader. It is such fun, and we are as cozy and warm as bears in their caves.

I only hoped it was all as congenial as she made it out to be.

I wished I could have more of Ellen, and less of Charles. He seemed to be in my vicinity far too often. At the store, he found excuses to leave Haberdashery and stop by my counter "just to chat." The other clerks thought him "so good-looking" and pretended to swoon when he left.

"I wish he would *chat* with me," teased Myra, not very nicely.

My heart still leaped when I saw him, but for some time now it had leaped with apprehension. Did he have no sense of decorum? I was very cool to him but could not bring myself to be publicly rude. It was a dilemma.

At home, Aggie grew quite enormously *interesting*. As we progressed into February, she often did not bother to dress at all, despite her new wardrobe, but crept about the house in gown and wrapper, only to go back to bed. There, she played endless games of patience on a bed table. The *patience* was not contagious. She even came to meals—which she never missed—in a wrapper.

Considering that she could not bear to see Charles having any conversation with me, one would have thought he would avoid me at home as much as possible. He showed no awareness of that at all, repeatedly opening topics with me. I tried to reply as curtly as possible. His puppy-dog eyes seemed always upon me, admiring and beseeching. How could he possibly think such attentions would be welcome to me? Had I really once found him charming?

In mid-February, Mother once more took me aside. "Alta, I cannot believe I have to have this conversation with you again, but how in the world do you explain your behavior?"

I couldn't imagine what she was talking about.

"Why are you continuing to try to attract Charles's attention all the time? Aggie has complained of it, and I see it for myself."

"But, Mother, to the contrary, I try hard to rebuff him," I protested.

Mother raised an eyebrow. "Is that what you call it?"

"I don't want to be out-and-out rude," I was getting angry.

"That would be better than being come-hither! I see you looking at him very often. And he obviously retains some warm feeling for you. You both act as if Agnes were blind."

As often, Mother left me speechless. There was no arguing with her. When I could control my temper I asked, "What would you have me do, Mother?"

She regarded me seriously. "Perhaps, be what you call *rude*."

My rudeness rolled off Charles like oil.

Time moved inexorably on; it was March, and Aggie's confinement was now expected in early April. That seemed far away.

Toward the end of the month, it grew bitterly cold. Rolling dark clouds covered the sky. One morning, as we left for the store, it began to snow heavily—great puffy flakes that stuck together even as they fell and did not melt.

Within just a few hours, the snowfall had thickened to an alarming degree and streets were already becoming impassable. Deciding to close the store, Father sent everyone home while they could still safely travel. Going last, to make sure all was properly locked up and Mr. Holloway's security team well on guard—we barely managed to get home ourselves.

By noon, the storm was a blizzard. You could not see your hand before your face. It was no longer pretty, but frightening.

We set up camp in the drawing room, putting up screens to block the drafts, and eating from card tables before the fire. We wrapped up in afghans and fur throws from the carriage. The servants did the same in the kitchen. It was rather fun at first, like an outing.

The blizzard kept on relentlessly: the wind howling, drifts building up to an alarming degree. It would not have been possible even to reach the sidewalk, supposing one could open the blocked front door. By evening, all of New York City lay buried under feet and feet of snow. And still, it fell!

Everything was at a standstill. The streets were impassable. There was no communication of any kind. It was worth one's life to try to flounder through the deep drifts. No one could remember any storm remotely as bad as this one.

Agnes went into labor.

It was instantly clear there would be no doctor. I had never seen Mother lose her composure before—she went pale and shaky, and literally wrung her hands before her. This filled me with fear.

Minnie, the little parlor maid, came to our rescue. She slipped away and returned with Mrs. Croft, wiping her hands on her apron, all rosy smiles and anticipation.

"Having a baby, are we? Now, don't you worry, Mum. We'll be fine without the doctor. Don't I have plenty of experience? Five sisters I helped, and all the neighborhood besides. Don't you worry about anything!"

They went away upstairs "to make the little mother more comfortable," and soon Minnie and Doris were running back and forth with basins of hot water, towels, and pots of tea. A footman was allowed into Aggie's suite to keep the fire going. Mother went in and out. Charles was allowed nowhere near.

Father, Charles, and I communed before the fire. I read, Charles paced, and Father smoked his pipe. At dinner time, Minnie brought us chicken sandwiches and soup. Around midnight, we could hear Aggie beginning to cry out. It was quite nerve-racking; there was no possibility of sleep. Still, it snowed, and the wind howled.

Father and Charles deserted me in favor of the icy billiard room, fortified by their greatcoats and a bottle of brandy, firmly shutting the door. They left me alone in front of the fire to hear what was happening upstairs, the cowards! Mother would not allow me to come up, although I offered. I thought it might be valuable knowledge to acquire, like Mrs. Croft. You never knew.

With dawn, the cries became screams, and the blizzard was worse than ever.

With a surprising air of command, little Minnie took over the kitchen and began delivering a stream of delicious, if simple, meals from our well-stocked pantry and root cellar. We were assured all was well upstairs, but it sounded awful.

At last, in the early evening, the storm began to abate. At midnight, Charles Oscar Buford Jr. was born. His mother was said to be "just fine," although I doubt that was her personal opinion. Charles seemed both pleased and alarmed all at once. I thought his was a realistic reaction.

It took some time for the city to sort itself out and recover —the storm had been a disaster. For days, it was impossible to go anywhere, until the roads and sidewalks could be somewhat cleared, for it remained icy, as nothing was melting. There had been many deaths in the city, due to cold and exposure. No one had ever seen snowfall so deep; the blizzard itself had lasted unabated an unprecedented thirty-six hours!

At home, Mrs. Croft returned to her kitchen, but Minnie had new status in everyone's eyes. Charles had settled on pride and was smoking cigars. Charles Jr. was large and red and mostly screaming at the top of his lungs. Agnes would have nothing to do with either one.

Finally, it was possible to get out and find a woman to nurse Charles Jr., since Aggie was said to be "unable" to do it. Jenny, produced by Mrs. Croft, was to live with us, with her own infant in the room next to mine. A little later, on the recommendation of Mother's friend, Muriel Evans, we found Nurse, who took care of Agnes and baby and also lived in. Later, there would be Nanny.

Agnes declared she would never go through this again and would not even let Charles sit on the bed. Everyone thought this was humorous, but I thought she meant it. The truth was, she flinched from Charles's slightest touch, as anyone could see, and he was temporarily sleeping in one of the guest rooms until his wife should be "recovered."

He lost his initial elation and began to go about with a helpless, hang-dog expression that should have evoked compassion, but instead made you just want to shake him and say, "Get a hold of yourself, man!" He looked at me with the eyes of a basset hound.

In the room next to me, both babies cried incessantly. I couldn't sleep. It was unbearable. I had to do something. There had to be a change!

I went to Father privately in his library and asked him outright if he would consider taking me into the store full-time. I did not want to give up my class at the Guild, but if there were a full-time salary, I explained, I could perhaps move into an apartment and become independent—if I could find a roommate to share the cost.

No help from Margaret as a prospective roommate. Her parents would never have allowed it. Besides, she was now being officially courted by Albert Gorman and had less time for me.

But there might be a girl or two from the store. Granted, it was a bold idea, but not unheard of in these modern times.

Father's reaction was astonishing. I think I really had believed he would consider it. First, he got very red in the face, then he sputtered. At last, he erupted into furious words. "Your mother said no good would come from letting you go into the store! As always, she was right. Not to be thought of, Alta. Put it out of your head. You will live at home until you are married."

I tried to protest, but he would hear no reason. "Not a word, Alta Belle! I am now strongly of a mind to put an end to your career in Findings at once! It cannot be good for you if it puts such foolishness into your head."

Feeling a bolt of fear, I completely caved in and tried to take it back. I could not lose my wonderful days at the store! After I gave him fervent assurances that it had just been an idle thought, and other promises I was not sure I could keep, he let it drop. He promised not to tell Mother about my foolish idea, but now I feared he might at any time put an end to my delightful romp through Carlton & Hodges—for my own good, of course.

One night, toward the middle of April, I was tucked up on my window seat, happily weeping over Dumas's *The Count of Monte Cristo*, when suddenly, without ceremony, my door was flung open, and there was Charles, lounging against the door frame with a glass of brandy in his hand. I gasped.

"There you are," beamed Charles, toasting me. "The beauteous Alta, with her book. What a charming sight." Then he walked straight toward me with his arms extended. "Give us a kiss, Alta! It's way overdue!"

This was beyond any kind of manners! I jumped up and, battering him with my book, drove him back toward the door, imploring him as quietly as I could to leave. He thought it funny.

"Alta, quit your teasing!" he cried, trying to embrace me and dousing me with brandy. "You know you want this as much as I do."

"You are mistaken! Get out!" I managed to push him back into the hall.

Now he looked reproachful. "Alta, what's the matter? You've been flirting with me for months!"

"No, Charles, I have not. I have been trying to make you leave me alone." I shut the door in his face but immediately opened it again. "Charles, if you ever try this again, I will tell Father!" I hissed. He went pale. "Now, get out of here before someone sees or hears you!"

He went and did not bother me again. He was so cold and distant that Mother gave me a further lecture on "keeping harmony in our family."

Never again could I feel safe in my room. We had never used locks in this house. Now, each night I pulled a chair before the door; but it did not make me feel secure.

It seemed to me that I could not possibly tell my parents why I felt unsafe in my own home. Mother had sided with Agnes before; she would say it was my fault for encouraging Charles. Father was so pleased with Charles's progress in the store and was counting on him for the future.

And Agnes! How could she remain married to a man who made advances to her sister?

If I spoke, I would destroy my family.

I spent a great deal of time in introspection. My prospects were dim, and my future seemed limited.

In May, I wrote to Odyssey West.

Chapter Thirteen

AUGUST 1888

My inquiry was answered with flattering speed. They sent me references and urged me to make an appointment for an interview. Determined to be both sensible and cautious, I wrote to all the references and made no move until I had heard back from them.

One woman, whose daughter had gone West last year, agreed to meet me for coffee, and face-to-face, she delivered a glowing endorsement. The daughter, who had gone to a Montana ranch as a cook, was about to be married, it appeared, to the rancher. The agency had delivered everything it had promised and implied. The family was pleased and the girl was thrilled. I was happy for her, but supposed she would continue to be the cook, but without salary now!

The second reference merely wrote me, but it was enough. Their daughter was now two years happy as a schoolteacher in Arizona. Everything had been as promised, the trip was arduous, but the job had been worth it. They certainly recommended Odyssey West.

The others responded in kind. I don't suppose you would

put any on the list who had not been pleased, but still, I felt reassured.

Thinking about the interview to come, I did not feel like a very promising candidate for a real job. I had no special training, little practical experience, and, considering my lack of any serious training, it struck me that I did not have much to offer. I could see that I needed recommendations of my own. There were only two people who could say anything about my abilities: Mrs. Margolis at the Guild and Miss Bailey in Findings.

There was no problem in approaching Mrs. Margolis. I very briefly explained to her that I had decided to relocate and had found an agency that would help me find a job. She was happy to write me a letter but expressed surprise that a young woman of my social status would consider giving up such a comfortable life for one decidedly less advantaged. I murmured a few things about "meaningful work" and "contribution to society" and hinted at my family problems—she then assured me of her complete understanding.

"My dear, other young women have come here with the same problem. Times are changing, for goodness sakes! It is no longer surprising that a woman might wish to be independent."

She asked me several questions about the agency and was satisfied once I assured her I had investigated carefully.

She sat down, then and there, and wrote me a very nice letter. She did not fail to mention that I had recently been helping with a reading class.

As I was leaving, she embraced me and had one more thing to say: "As an independent woman, you must always live decorously, and be very careful to preserve your reputation."

Good advice, I am sure.

For the second letter, I took my heart in my hands, and asked Miss Bailey to lunch, to discuss "a serious situation."

She accepted, and in due course, we were seated at a

window table in Louie's Fine Italian Food. We ordered. I decided on spaghetti in a meat sauce, and she upon the ravioli. Wine was suggested, but neither of us would have dreamed of ordering it, so we declined. There were already glasses of carbonated water on the table—that was quite adequate. The food arrived promptly, steaming fragrantly; and at our first tastes, we could not help making little groans of pleasure.

"How in the world would you make something so delicious?" I wondered. "It must be the spices. What could they be? Our cook makes nothing like this."

"Find a book of Italian recipes," Miss Bailey advised me, sensibly.

I explained what I had really asked her out to discuss, and minimally described the situation, barely mentioning "problems at home" and growing much more eloquent about the dream of independence I had begun to foster.

Her eyes grew larger and larger, and she nodded, repeatedly. She knew my family well, but in a different way, through the lens of the store. She had not missed Charles's frequent visits to our section. She would certainly have heard the inevitable gossip.

When I had run out of things to imply, she nodded emphatically. "Alta, I must say, you are a very sensible and brave young lady. I am impressed by your determination to deal with a problem I fear is not that unusual. Certainly, I will write you a testimonial. And, let me say, you underrate yourself. You are a well-trained and excellent clerk. I should know, I did the training!"

That very afternoon she wrote me a glowing letter. Thus, armed with two recommendations and sure of Miss Bailey's discretion, I wrote for an appointment at Odyssey West.

I mentioned I had Friday afternoons free; they wrote back suggesting the following week. Telling Mother I was going shopping, I arrived for my appointment promptly, heart in my throat but trying to appear composed. Several years of disciplining myself at home had taught me much about that.

Besides my letters, I brought my graduation certificates: Miss Morrison's Private School, and—because my family was very forward-thinking—Brindle Academy for Young Women, with two years of fine arts, geography, simple mathematics, and literature. And as a sample of my sewing: a needlepoint bookmark and a doll in coat and bonnet.

Odyssey, in the person of a Mr. Ulysses Brown and a Miss Simpson, dismissed the sewing, barely glanced at the certificates, read the letters quickly, nodded at each other, and welcomed me to Odyssey West. It was surprising but gratifying.

"Miss Carlton, you are obviously a superior candidate for us, in every way," Mr. Brown assured me. "Do not worry so much about specific training. You are educated, clearly intelligent, and have experience teaching. Let us see what we can do for you."

They bowed me out, effusively promising to be in touch very soon. And they were. Within two weeks, I was offered six positions to consider and another appointment. After some discussion, I took their advice and we agreed on a request from a place called Black Butte in the New Mexico Territory, for a teacher in a one-room school, all grades, with perhaps a dozen students (although they regretted to inform us there were often fewer, due to bad weather, impassable roads, or the need to help out on home ranches). In addition to a salary, which Mr. Brown assured me I could live on quite well, they promised to provide full curricula for all the grades, which they would send to Odyssey to be forwarded to me so that I might arrive fully prepared. Finally, they promised to find me a place to live.

I was hesitant, but Mr. Brown and Miss Simpson were quite sure I could handle this overwhelming job. They assured me that with my background, I would very quickly "get the hang of it" and pointed out that the promised curriculum would be very specific about what I was meant to teach, so there would be no problem. They seemed so certain of my success that I finally decided not to worry about it anymore and put myself freely into their more experienced hands.

I wrote them, accepting the offer, and received a letter back naming a date in early September when I should be in Black Butte to meet with the school board. Mr. Brown advised me to leave by the second week in August to allow plenty of time.

My journey would be by both train and stagecoach. I would be twenty years old, a schoolteacher, and independent! My excitement grew as tall as the statue in the harbor. I, too, would be a *Lady of Liberty*, and now, *A New Western Woman*. Who would have thought, just one month ago?

Now that all was certain, the family could be told. They could not change it. I had written an acceptance.

Having had a long time to consider how I should break this news to my family, which would fall on them like a bolt of lightning, I had settled on a plan I hoped might prevent a full-on eruption. Mother had always looked up to her older sister, Adah, and I thought Father did, too. Her wry wit and tart remarks certainly endeared her to me. Armed with my new and growing confidence, I requested a private tea with my aunt, and abandoning all restraint, put her fully in the picture, as I had done for no other.

She *tut-tutted* and *tsk-tsked*, and when I delicately referenced Charles, she nodded sharply several times, her mouth a very tight line. My aunt did not miss much, however serenely Mother presided over all. When I mentioned that Mother seemed to think I had been at fault, she grew quite incensed.

"That's Antoinette for you! She never wants to rock the

boat. I'd like to give her a piece of my mind! Horace coddles her too much."

Feeling somewhat reassured, I told her about Odyssey West. She was quite shocked when I revealed my plans and what I had done to make them a reality. She paced the room awhile, which was quite a worry, but came back to me chuckling and sat down, taking both my hands.

"Alta, you do beat all when you take a mind to it! Horace and Antoinette will have a fit. But I do fully see your situation here is impossible, and I think you have made a very brave and intelligent plan. What a surprise! You are at an age when young people should try to make their dreams come true, or this old world would never get any place at all. Very boring."

I had hoped for her support, but she surprised me! Then, she dashed my hopes.

"But surely you don't really mean to take such a drastic measure?" she went on. "I should think when your father hears what you are thinking about, he will quickly reconsider his refusal to take you into the store. You can leave your mother to me. And I would be willing to talk to Charles, myself, and put the fear of the Lord into him."

I stared at her, quite dismayed. "But Aunt! I intend to go West. I have accepted a position. And, besides, that would be blackmail!"

My aunt looked at me as if to see if I were serious, and then lifted one eyebrow—an admirable talent.

"Alta, dear, I think of it more as the 'social oil that makes the world go around.' I believe you will find it would work. No need to leave your home."

I was shocked to the core. "Aunt, this is not a trick to get my own way with my parents. I have accepted the challenge to go West and help to build our Nation. I love my family, but I truly believe I will never be allowed to be independent as long as I live here in New York City."

It was a full half hour before she finally came to believe I might really mean what I was saying. I held firm. I had got the taste of going West in my mouth, and West I would go. There truly was nothing left for me here. Finally, she gave in.

"Well, Alta, what can I say?"

"Will you help me tell them? Without the part about Charles?" It was asking a lot.

She eyed me speculatively, then resurrected her usual wry attitude. "I wouldn't miss this for all the tea in China!" she assured me. "You are my favorite niece, Alta. You have created more dissension in this family than anyone since Great-Aunt Asphitilda ran off with the Hungarian Hussar!"

"Oh?" I responded with interest. "I never heard about her."

"Never you mind," huffed Aunt, and we then spent another half hour discussing the problem at hand, planning our little conspiracy for the following Wednesday when she and Edgar had already been asked to dine.

Wednesday night, I was so anxious I could scarcely eat a bite of Mrs. Croft's lobster Thermidor, nor the truly spectacular crown of lamb that followed. Alas, my midsection was in such turmoil, even the aroma of the food made me feel ill. Such are the wages of... surely, not sin, in my case—perhaps deviation.

As always, we ladies withdrew to the drawing room and enjoyed our choice of coffee or tea. As soon as the men joined us and were settled, I sat up tall, and in a few rehearsed sentences worded as carefully as possible, told my family what I intended. Mother, pouring a second cup of tea, nearly dropped the pot. Father went maroon, which I was getting used to, and sputtered so much I feared he was choking. Aggie's whole face creased in confusion, and she appeared to think I was "getting something over on her." Charles went white. Cousin Edgar was chuckling so much he had to get up and walk over to the French doors. Aunt placidly watched everyone's reactions.

"Good for you, Alta!" Edgar guffawed. "You have flung your bonnet right over the Brooklyn Bridge and jumped in after it!"

"Don't encourage her, Edgar!" Father fumed. The new bridge, a modern miracle of engineering, might very well represent to all of us a great leap of faith, but no daughter of his was to make another!

"Alta, you must be insane. It is an outrageous idea, completely unsuitable to our position, and dangerous besides! I will not allow it!" What had happened to the doting father I had grown up counting on to be indulgent?

I looked him full in the face and did not back down. "Father, it is done. I have accepted the position. I leave on August 12th on the Acheson, Topeka, and Santa Fe. The ticket is booked."

Father sputtered some more, not used to being opposed.

Aunt Adah regarded him with a raised eyebrow: "Horace, get off your high horse and come sit down with the rest of us."

Now, Father found words: "But she has been raised for something so much better than this!"

"She is a debutante!" Mother was so appalled; she could barely speak.

"For goodness sakes, Antoinette, let's not pretend we are society, here!" Aunt said wryly. "Our mother was a lady's maid and Father put himself through law school by working on the docks at night. And, for that matter, Horace's father was a saddle maker, and his mother took in wash. They all worked like slaves so that we could be educated and have better lives. Which we do, thank you very much. But the idea of a woman wanting to work should not be so amazing. You have to admit, it's 'in the blood,' Horace!"

Father sputtered some more. Aunt fixed him with a beady eye.

"Horace, you refused to take her officially into the store. She wants to work. What would you have her do?"

This lecture did not end the discussion, although it did calm things down. They continued for some time about "appropriateness," but eventually were willing to listen to the particulars of my plan, which I now was at last able to explain in detail.

Agnes put in her opinion: "I think Alta should be commended for wanting to be independent," she said, giving me a sweet smile and lowering luxuriously long and thick eyelashes, "especially if she does not plan to marry."

"Thank you, sister dear," I said, lowering my own, equally lavish lashes. "That does so help."

"Besides," Aggie went on, all animation, "we are so crowded in the house, now. It would mean we could remodel her room and the one next to it into a very nice suite for Nanny when she comes!"

Everyone frowned at her. Father *harrumphed*; Mother straightened her pearls.

"Thank you, Agnes," Aunt said. "Very practical, as always."

Aggie preened a little, quite pleased with herself. No one was pleased with me.

They did not endorse my plan that evening. The discussion went on for days. At one point, Father said he would change his mind about taking me into Carlton & Hodges, just as Aunt had predicted he would, but it was too late.

"I could not possibly take a job obtained by blackmail," I refused, loftily. "And that is what it would be."

In the end, they did reluctantly accept my going. I had accepted a position. It was *a fait accompli*.

The news of my imminent departure inevitably got out. It

caused a great deal of consternation at first but came to be accepted in an amazingly short time. At the Guild, they gave me a little tea with cookies and many warm wishes. My sewing class was in tears but liked the cookies. Mrs. Margolis told them a new teacher had already been found since they were doing so well. This piece of news stunned the girls, as they had assumed my departure meant an end to boring seams and hems—we placated them with more cookies.

At Carlton & Hodges, there was another tea in the clerk's lounge. Miss Bailey presented me with a departmental gift of a cunning small traveler's sewing kit. The clerks were all astonished that a Carlton would leave a veritable dynasty for such a speculative venture, but I doubted they would miss me much.

Miss Bailey gave me a private gift at the end of the brief event, as everyone else hurried back to the department. She handed me a prettily wrapped package, which proved to be an Italian cookbook. She was one person who wholly approved my venture and looked for great things in my future. I promised to study it so diligently that, when she came to visit me in the West, I would serve her a meal almost as good as Louie's. She said she would look forward to it, but I could tell she thought she would never see me again. I would miss her continuous support very much.

"Will you write?" she asked.

Touched, I promised that I would.

Telling Margaret had been unexpectedly difficult. For whatever reason, because I had been so caught up in my scheme of secrecy, or because of her defection in the direction of Mr. Gorman, I had not taken her into my confidence, and now, seeing her reproachful expression, I realized that not telling her had been a breach of our friendship. Trying to explain that I had not shared my plans with anyone simply compounded the offense.

Margaret, a true friend, instantly and graciously accepted this explanation and politely asked for details, but I felt a distance grow between us. I had made a mistake. She would have kept my confidence, as I well knew. I had been quite full of myself and not once thought of her feelings; perhaps I had also been a little afraid she, the practical one, would disapprove.

Margaret gave her full support now, which I did not deserve, and said that she should have done something similar herself but was not brave enough. Now, her life was turning in new directions.

"Will you have news for us soon?" I asked delicately.

"Not at all," she replied, demurely. "I did not see much of Mr. Gorman this summer. He always sends his children to the shore during the hot weather, to his mother's house on Long Island, and usually drives up to spend the weekends with them. I see him only on Wednesday evenings."

I could not tell how she felt about that and did not know what to say.

She laughed at me. "We are not in any hurry, Alta. At least, I am not. We shall see in the fall."

Margaret gave me another book as her farewell: a small, delightfully compact copy of Melville's *Moby Dick*, bound in morocco leather with a sailing ship engraved on the cover. It was one of her recommendations, which I had tried several times to read and failed. She urged me to try again, as she felt it was essential to an educated reader, especially a teacher-to-be.

I promised to read it on the train. We said goodbye with a tearful embrace, promising to write, but there was restraint.

My family's goodbye was more painful than I had expected. Father and Mother's drawn faces surprisingly stayed in my mind and even haunted a dream or two. Aggie's complacent smile and Charles's wounded eyes were easier to dismiss. Fortunately, Aunt Adah and Edgar came to the train station to see me off as well. Their matter-of-fact presence saw us through. Edgar gave me a two-pound box of chocolates, as he called it a "*bon-bon voyage.*" Edgar's jokes were terrible, even the bi-lingual ones, but he was always delightful company.

At last, the long, silver train came into Grand Central Station, and I settled into a compartment where two businessmen were buried in the *New York Times*, with my modest hand luggage. My one trunk was stowed in the baggage car.

Now, I could put all the struggle and unpleasantness behind me and think only of my exciting future. Or better yet, just enjoy the present journey and the new things I would see. How lucky I was! How amazing that it had all come true. I was actually going West!

Being August, it was sweltering hot on the train. All the chocolates had melted by the time we reached Chicago.

PART TWO

A New Woman of the West

Chapter One

D espite the summer heat, the train was more comfortable than I had been led to expect. It was somewhat disconcerting to share the compartment with strangers, but they were polite and mostly ignored me. It was noisy with the constant *clickity-clack* of the wheels on the rails. One was constantly jostled, and it was worth your life to walk down the center aisle, with the car swaying back and forth. If you opened the window to get a breath of air, you also got a liberal helping of coal soot and dust.

The businessmen left me at a brief commuter stop in Connecticut and I had the compartment to myself until the next day in Chicago. There, I was joined by a pleasant couple: Mr. and Mrs. Donlevy. They were on their way to Topeka to visit a married daughter. A grain salesman on his regular route, Mr. Eckles, took our fourth seat, but we did not see much of him. Mr. Donlevy thought the young gentleman no doubt preferred the livelier atmosphere of the smoking car, where card games were in progress.

Mr. Donlevy explored the train and brought news back to us. He had heard there were several professional gamblers aboard. We *tut-tutted* and hoped Mr. Eckles would not lose too much money. He did not share with us tales of his luck, or lack of it, during his rare appearances, but we agreed he looked more and more glum as time progressed.

I was well pleased with the Donlevys. In their company, I felt much more comfortable in the dining car, and we even spent some time in the parlor car having tea. Some things are awkward to do alone.

Mrs. Donlevy, Martha, had an unending store of conversation, and shared their history with me, including the story of her daughter's courtship. Then, she went on to the unfortunate marriage of her sister's son, her nephew, who had rescued a young girl whose reticule had been stolen on a Chicago street, brought her home to his mother, as she had no family, and eventually married her, more or less because it was the decent thing to do—only to be confronted by an angry brothel owner who said the girl owed him one hundred dollars for her keep, and could not leave his employ until it was paid. Needless to say, it was not a happy marriage after that, and she left him a month later. Still, they were legally married and his life was ruined. Such a sad case.

After hearing a carefully edited version of my own story, the Donlevys thought me quite the pioneer. Martha said she had thought her daughter brave just to move to Topeka!

One day out of Chicago, there was a great rainstorm with thunder and lightning, very frightening. We felt very exposed in the train out on the bare prairie and feared a lightning strike. The porter looked in and assured us we were quite safe, insulated on the tracks, so we allowed ourselves to enjoy the brief, but violent, display of nature's fireworks, and afterward felt the bond of survivors—fast friends forever.

Martha and I visited with many other people, which was

quite enjoyable, but I enjoyed most of all our meals in the dining car, which were surprisingly good considering the tiny space in which it was prepared. We were served plain food, well prepared: chops, steaks, and stews with fresh vegetables and salads brought on board at brief refueling stops. All was enhanced by a real table-cloth with linen napkins, china of good quality, and even a fresh carnation in a small bud vase. I viewed the carnation with a some-what jaundiced eye but was otherwise surprised and pleased with the unexpected elegance. What pleasure to dine leisurely while the scenery flowed by our window. We lingered for as long as we were allowed, over slices of Baltimore cake and cups of coffee, chatting on many subjects and speculating about the other passengers.

At about ten at night, it was time to retire to our bunks in the sleeping car. I went down the aisle to the tiny dressing room with my night bag, and changed into a nightgown and duster, feeling grateful that my traveling stays laced in front, as did the jacket of my neat, dove-gray gabardine traveling suit. Although it did not approach the style of Aggie's coveted wedding outfit, gabardine was much more practical for the train; linen wrinkled so badly.

My sleeping berth was an upper. It was perilous climbing the ladder to enter, but once there with the heavy curtain pulled closed, it was cozy and safe. I hugged myself, amazed to be abed in such a strange place. I liked the movement of the train, it rocked me to sleep.

The train traveled on for several more days and nights, rushing across the great American plains at an amazing thirty miles an hour, we were told. We saw cattle grazing on free-range and many rabbits with very long ears, called *jackrabbits*, that darted away from the train. Our passing startled aloft great clouds of birds that swooped and soared away from us. The train tracks were lined with sunflowers and a shrub with huge white flowers called *morning primrose*. We traveled under an immense blue sky.

Only a day out of Topeka, the train rolled to a stop so gently, it was a while before we realized we were no longer moving. This was alarming and we all speculated as to what could be wrong. Martha was sure it was train robbers and entertained us in the parlor with tales of several bands of desperate bandits known to operate on these barren plains.

The porter came to inform us that no such adventure was to befall. It was just trouble with the boiler. This was being patched up enough to get us to a side rail three miles ahead, but there we would have to wait for parts to be brought up to us from Chicago.

"Why can't we wait in Topeka?" Mr. Donlevy wanted to know, but apparently, that was too far for the patch to hold.

So, wait we did. I didn't mind at all—it became rather like a party. There was plenty to eat and drink. We were allowed to get off the train and walk about on the prairie. We played cards and drank tea, and the waiters arranged a concert in the parlor. They gave us all glasses of sherry and we were entertained by one of the cooks, who was an excellent classical guitarist. Two sisters sang beautiful duets.

I was almost disappointed when the train finally started up again. I had an important deadline, but there was plenty of time. Others had been inconvenienced much more than I had.

We were barely underway when there was more excitement: a small herd of buffalo ran briefly alongside us. Martha and I were horrified to hear gunshots ring out and saw several of the majestic animals fall. Mr. Donlevy came to report that there was much excitement in the smoking car, where gentlemen had lowered the windows and were betting to see how many they could shoot down. We were aghast, but apparently, everyone else thought it great sport! Mr. Donlevy hurried back to the action.

The Donlevys got off in Topeka, Kansas, and two burly miners took their place in the compartment. I waved out the window as my friends were driven off in a wagon by their daughter and her husband. I missed them intensely, but at dinner that night met a very nice couple, the Tortolas, going all the way to Santa Fe, and after that, I dined and chatted with them.

There were now dry plains and mountains in the distance. A day later, our speed slowed to a crawl through some foothills, but at last, we pulled into Santa Fe, after a journey I was beginning to think was long enough.

A wagon took me and others, with our luggage, to our hotel, *La Fonda on the Plaza*. My room was quite intriguing, decorated in Western motif, as was the whole hotel. I imagined it was like staying at a Spanish rancho—all dark wood and leather, with game heads mounted on the walls. There were arches and open spaces, a patio with a fountain, and all the floors were of dark red tile.

It was a relief to be on solid ground again. For some time, I felt the swaying of the train as if I were still aboard!

Checking in with the Butterfield Stagecoach office, I was told there would be a three-day wait for my stagecoach, due to a stretch of washed-out road after a cloudburst. I was a little worried to hear this, but I was tired from the journey, and now there would be time to bathe and wash my hair, to have my laundry done, and my traveling suit cleaned and pressed.

There was also a little time to explore the bustling town. I enjoyed walking around the plaza, looking into the shops, and examining the curious Indian wares being sold on the street. Besides my first Indians, I saw Mexican people and even some

Orientals—and heard strange languages being spoken. The New Mexico Territories were decidedly a foreign country.

It was six days before we were able to leave, and I tried not to worry. I spent my time writing long letters home telling of the wonders of the train trip, and the time passed pleasantly.

Finally, I was informed that the coach would leave the next morning. I packed and decided that I would treat myself to dinner at the Harvey House since it was my last night. I walked down to where it was located next to the train depot and went in, feeling uncomfortable as an unescorted woman, but I needn't have worried. I was welcomed and given a table to myself to one side. The room was crowded and noisy, with many long tables full of boisterous men and women eating enormous steaks and drinking beer.

The men were nearly all dressed in Western-style: large felt hats, heavy shirts, and work pants, with elaborately embossed leather boots, complete with spurs, which made a jangle of metallic noise when they walked.

They did not seem to be carrying arms; perhaps that was not allowed in a metropolis such as Santa Fe.

I was surprised to notice, however, that many of the men wore what could only be called jewelry: bracelets and rings, and great silver belt buckles set with big blue stones.

The women wore simple cotton dresses, since the weather was hot, with shawls and, to my New York eyes, outmoded bonnets rather than a stylish little hat such as mine. I couldn't help noticing several ladies giving me very sharp looks over the tops of their menus. They might be Western, but they were still interested in style!

The Harvey Girls lived up to the promise. They were all attractive and modestly gowned in black, with white pinafore aprons, their hair tidy in buns. They were exceptionally efficient waitresses—taking orders with dispatch and bustling about with huge trays held high, loaded with steaming dishes. I wished Margaret were here to share this meal with me.

The food was excellent. There was much more to choose from than the gigantic steaks, which I did not feel at all up to. I was able to order a chicken salad—which came fresh and crisp, and with hot white rolls and plenty of butter.

My Harvey Girl, Elly—according to her name badge—was not at all averse to spending a few minutes explaining things to me. The big felt hats were, she said, called *Stetsons*, after one famous maker in Philadelphia. The jewelry was made by local Indians and highly prized; it was pure silver, and the blue stone was turquoise—although other gemstones, such as onyx and petrified coral, were also used. This silver-smith craft had been taught to the Navajo, Zuni, and other tribes when they had been moved onto the reservations, and many had proved to be artisans, devoted to making beautiful jewelry using Indian symbols and designs. After all, these people had been making fine pottery and weavings for centuries. Silverwork came naturally to them.

I thanked Elly for the information and complimented her knowledge.

"All of us girls are collecting it," Elly explained, showing me several bracelets and rings that she wore, and I had to admit they were lovely.

Elly inquired, as she poured more lemonade, whether I would be staying on in Santa Fe. When I briefly explained I was leaving on the Butterfield Stage for Black Butte the next morning, she looked me over with a critical eye.

"Miss, forgive me for speaking out, but I've been in one of those stages, and you're heading for trouble if you travel in them cloths."

I was extremely surprised.

"You're the best dressed thing has come in here for months,

and everyone is enjoying looking at you," she went on, "but, excuse me, if you travel in them stays, you'll ruin yourself."

I blushed, deeply.

Elly went on, determined to put me on the right track. "The roads are real bad, and the stage will be crowded. You'll be jounced around something awful. Modesty is one thing but being jabbed black and blue is another. Take my advice; you won't be sorry."

She started to walk away, then turned back to add, "Besides, you're real slender. Nobody will even notice!" Then, she absolutely winked at me as she walked away.

I was still blushing as I doubled her tip and left the restaurant. Her advice was unconventional but rang with truth. It was bad enough riding on the train; my stiff corset had made it difficult to bend and sway as needed to keep my balance. Ahead of me was a trip of at least four days—on dirt roads, with overnight stops at rustic inns, and without servants. I determined to pack my stays away in my great trunk for the duration. Time enough to put them back on in Black Butte, before meeting the judgmental eyes of the school board!

As travel-wise as she was, Ely was wrong about one thing, I thought. Anyone who bumped into me in the coach would know I was not wearing stays.

Walking back to La Fonda, it was impossible not to want to linger in the gaslit plaza, and after much looking and wavering, I did, in one of the little shops, buy for myself a small turquoise and silver ring, to wear on my right hand. It might not be a sapphire, but I would not have to give it back.

The clerk, a small bespectacled man with a fuzzy white beard, turned my choice over to show me: stamped into the inside band, the tiny *mark* of the maker.

He explained, "This mark is proof it is genuine, hand-made Indian jewelry."

The ring was a bit dear, but I had the money. Father had not sent me off into the furthest wilderness of our country without a substantial deposit into my banking account, now waiting to be transferred to Black Butte. As Mother pointed out, it was not sensible to carry with me all my heavy winter clothing. It would have taken too many giant trunks.

"It will be better to buy what you need when you get there," she pointed out.

Father had agreed. Personally, I thought he had a bargain in me when compared with his continued investment in Aggie! Since her confinement, she now needed everything new again, in a slightly larger size. What were a few winter cloaks and gowns in comparison!

Grateful for my family's generosity, even in disapproval, which allowed me to indulge myself, I treasured my new ring. It was, in a way, a promise to myself of an independent future; the perfect symbol of a *Western Woman*, with enough spirit of adventure to leave off her stays to ride in a coach.

Chapter Two

At dawn on my sixth day in New Mexico Territory, I joined a surprisingly large group in front of the Butterfield Stagecoach office, preparing to board a huge black and gold "coach and six." Our coach awaited us—quite a large, black conveyance, with a string of around six matched horses.

The driver, a great, burly man in a sheepskin vest and battered felt hat, sat in state, three reins in each hand, ready to leave. Beside him sat a smaller, similarly garbed man. I smiled to myself, already possessing a great store of Western lore from my reading. This would be the *shotgun*, and indeed, a rifle was tucked in beside his seat.

My great trunk and my valise, with a parasol strapped to the side, were being hoisted to the roof, along with other luggage, some going on the back, or *boot,* as it was called. The agent was noisily directing all this. Then, consulting his watch, he urged us to board.

I could not believe it—seven of us climbed in and began trying to arrange ourselves! In addition, two young men, cowboys from their appearance, were clambering up to the roof! When the dust settled, there were four of us seated on my side of the coach, backs to the driver, and three others across.

"We're lucky, today," commented the man beside me, who had the window. "Usually, they cram in nine or ten." I could not believe it. It was impossible that the seven of us could be even minimally comfortable as it was!

Across was a small man dressed all in black at the window. In the middle, a large woman in a large hat and a gown so commodious, I could only think it completely inappropriate for such a journey. She appeared to have a full, stiff bustle and could not sit completely back. She was accompanied by an over-weight man, no doubt her husband. The three filled up their side of the coach as fully as we four across the aisle!

On my left side sat another couple—fortunately, both quite thin. And of course, the man on my other side, at the right window, dressed all in gray. We fit, but it was impossible not to jostle against each other. So unseemly!

"Where in the world would more fit?" I whispered to the man next to me.

"Oh, they would have to sit forward," he explained. When he saw that I did not understand, he pointed upward. "Sit on the edge of the seat and hold onto one of those straps," he expanded.

"How very uncomfortable," I commented.

"Don't worry, none of us will be comfortable," he laughed. "The only thing important in coach travel is how many paying customers you can stuff inside—or, on top, depending!"

I understood and was determined to make the best of it. The coach lurched forward and swayed back and forth as we drove the main street of Santa Fe, bouncing up and down over rocks that felt like boulders, and falling into potholes like canyons. People cheered us from the wooden sidewalks, and little boys and dogs ran after us.

Then we were out of town and commenced to drive at speed through the country such as I had never seen before.

The sky was vast, without a cloud, and an intense blue I had never seen before. Great red cliffs and buttes came and went, red as the dirt of the road. Everything was either red or blue, except for punctuation marks of stunted green pine trees, or occasional white rocks. At places, there were great white patches on the red earth. The quality of the light was amazing, everything so crisp and clear, and almost colorized—if that is a word—as if tints had been deliberately added. I remembered reading how great painters spoke of the *quality of light* in certain locations in Italy and thought I now knew what they meant.

The coach seemed to fly along despite the road, which was worse than in town. "Should they not slow down?" I inquired of my new acquaintance.

"Honey, we're only going about four miles an hour. We'll be lucky if we can keep up this pace," he replied, and tipping his hat over his eyes, appeared to go to sleep. How could he sleep? Appalled at the liberty of his address, I determined not to speak to him again. A brief trial of sitting forward and holding a strap, to see if that were any better, quickly proved it was not.

The morning wore on interminably. We began to be acquainted. The small man all in black was the Reverend Tomm, returning from a sabbatical in the East to his parish in Bagnold—a small town beyond Black Butte. The overweight couple, Eulalia and Morris Bysbee, were connected with a copper mine in Arizona, also headed for Bagnold to visit their son's nearby ranch.

The couple to my left was Bilethia and Jake Moser, going to Texas for reasons they did not divulge. They had a very long trip ahead of them! I shuddered to think of it.

The gentleman on my right continued to sleep on, so we

did not learn his name. Mrs. Bysbee pursed her lips in his direction, and said to me behind her hand, "I expect he's a gambler."

Around ten o'clock, we arrived at a hill so steep the driver stopped the coach and asked us all to step out and walk up the hill to lighten the load, while the poor horses labored mightily to haul the ponderous vehicle to the top. I didn't mind at all. It was a relief to get out and stretch and move about.

Mrs. Moser remarked to me that we should lag behind, and when the coach was at a suitable distance, we could relieve ourselves behind a boulder she spied. We did so; I felt quite the pioneer! It was the most unconventional thing I had ever done so far—much worse than leaving off my corset! I amused myself while toiling up the rest of the hill trying to devise how I might write Margaret about this in words less offensive than the deed.

Mrs. Bysbee complained every step of the way. Mr. Bysbee seemed to think it was his fault since he apologized to her at every other step. I thought she would be much more comfortable without such heavy stays, especially in this heat! But perhaps she felt it obligatory, given her size.

At noon, we stopped briefly at a grove of alders by a small stream, and had an *alfresco* luncheon of water, bread, and cheese, making the acquaintance of our driver as he portioned these out. He was Mr. Robert Stimpy, his *shotgun* was simply "Buck," and both had been driving this route for years.

"Ain't nothing to it, these days," Mr. Stimpy assured us, "Now that the Injuns is put down. I could tell you some stories! How-some-ever, the company don't like us to talk about them days."

We were quite willing to leave it at that. I certainly did not wish to hear more. Imagine, trying, at four miles an hour, to outrun Indians on their powerful ponies!

The cowboys kept to themselves, and we happily did not

have to make conversation with them. What in the world would you say to a cowboy?

As we got back in the coach after this welcome break, Mr. Stimpy suggested we change sides in our seating, so we did. It seemed only fair; half the day traveling backward and the second half facing forward.

It was nearly dark before we reached our stop for the night. Dewar's, a small structure, but with extensive stables, rose up out of the dusk with welcome lantern light and the promise of hot food. We had made thirty miles in a little more than ten hours, considered excellent for this first stretch of our journey. We were not expected to do nearly so well tomorrow. It was only twenty miles to the next station, Martinez Wells, but we would be going through hill country, and the route was much rougher.

Inside the posthouse was a warm and welcome fire; despite the heat of the day, it was now growing cold. We were served stew and plenty of hot coffee and then shown to our accommodations: one room for the women, another for the men. We slept on bunks, which were not overly clean, and we all opted to sleep in our clothes. After the day we had endured, the only alternative was sitting up all night, which had no appeal for any of us.

Mrs. Bysbee complained about the stew (not enough meat), the coffee (too strong), and the bunk. She didn't specify what was wrong with that, but privately, I thought it was probably too small for her to have any comfort. By now, Mrs. Moser and I were practically best friends and on a first-name basis. I slept through the night like a child, and I think Bilethia did as well.

In the morning, we were awakened at break of day for a bracing breakfast of bacon, pancakes with molasses, and boiling hot coffee. As we exited to go to the coach, one of the cowboys held the door for us. He lifted his hat to me.

"Hope you had a comfortable night, miss," he said.

"It was fine, thank you." I nodded at him, surprised to find such good manners in such a rough context.

We had a new team of six horses this morning, less well-matched, but looking fresh and sturdy.

We boarded the stage, taking the places we had chosen yesterday. Seating was apparently set in stone. With my row once again traveling backward, we set off at a great pace, but within the hour slowed to a plod while going uphill. Going downhill was frightening—with Mr. Stimpy cursing at the horses and hauling on the reins. Twice we had to get out and walk.

Around noon, we were traveling through a kind of natural canyon with great buttes on either side, going slightly uphill once more. The gentlemen had been discussing economic conditions until I thought I would scream with boredom. At first, it had been interesting, especially when they spoke of a terrible blizzard of the past winter which had killed up to 90 percent of the stock in some cases. This appeared to have happened just before our blizzard in New York. But they went on endlessly about so-and-so losing his homestead, and who else probably would, and what that would mean to businessmen in the little towns—until all was gloom and doom, and I could scarcely bear it.

As a low accompaniment to this, Mrs. Bysbee was telling Bilethia and me about the confinement of her dear friend Mrs. Allen-Brown, at which everything possible had gone wrong in the grisliest manner. Unbelievably, both mother and child seemed to have survived.

These two daunting conversations met and crossed in the tight confines of the coach, and being in the middle, I could not avoid hearing both and was beginning to get a headache.

Suddenly there was a flurry of yells from outside. The coach lurched and began to go faster, throwing us about. There came a rattle and pounding on the roof, like hail, then big thuds. There was now yelling and cursing inside as well as out, and a roaring sound—when suddenly, there came a great impact on the right, and the coach was flung violently against the opposite embankment!

I was screaming now—flung out of my seat and jammed against the door! I could feel the knob of the latch grinding against my side.

Unbelievably, the coach was still skidding forward as if on two wheels, and then rebounded and tipped over completely onto its left side. Screaming and flailing, we were all dumped to the right.

All was noise and confusion. I found myself, as it were, on top of a pile of people, with no way to relieve them of my weight. Then, voices came from outside, and efforts were being made to open the door behind me. It came open with a screech and strong arms were lifting me out onto the wheel—passing me down to someone below. What a relief to stand on solid ground! But the road was gone; all around us was a devastated landscape of rocks and dirt.

"Are you all right, Miss?" Asked the man who had lifted me out. *The cowboy,* I thought, who had held the door that morning.

"I'm fine, it's them! You've got to get them out!"

He looked me over with cool blue-green eyes to confirm my claim, then turned back into the doorway of the coach and climbed higher up on the wheel to get better access. He produced Bilethia, who seemed reluctant to leave.

"Jake," she kept saying. "Get Jake, he won't talk to me!"

"We'll get him out, ma'am. You come now. Careful, you seem to have hurt your arm." Gently, he levered her out the door and passed her down to the other cowboy on the ground as if she weighed nothing. I helped as much as I could.

Next came Mrs. Bysbee—quite a different proposition. It required the combined efforts of her husband and the Man in Gray from inside as well; she was nearly dropped to the ground, wailing and protesting all the way. She was covered in blood and something else, all over her face and arms and down the front of her dress.

At first, I thought she had been horribly injured, but she kept flailing at her hair and garments and wailing, "Get it off! Get it off!" I began to realize that the blood and matter must have come from someone else.

Mr. Bysbee and the Man in Gray passed up Mr. Moser next —limp and comatose. I helped to receive him as they passed him down, and we laid him in the dust of the road while Bilethia knelt and took his head on her lap, caressing his face and exclaimed over him in distress, trying to get him to respond to her.

The Man in Gray came out next, and it was clear at once that he was injured. He moved very stiffly and seemed to be having trouble breathing.

"It's my ribs," he explained. "I seem to have broken a number of ribs."

Mr. Bysbee then got himself out, apparently uninjured, although scratched and battered and bleeding here and there. He jumped to the ground and immediately went to the aid of his wife.

I stood expectantly by the door. "Reverend Tomm," I urged. "We must get him out."

My cowboy jumped down from the wheel and gently steered me away from the coach, urging me to sit beside Mrs. Bysbee. "We better just leave him there, Miss. He... didn't make it."

"Dead?" I couldn't believe it. But it explained Mrs. Bysbee's condition. He had been sitting on the side where the terrible impact had come.

Now the cowboys left us and ran to help Mr. Stimpy, who was overwhelmed with the horses. Two lay dead in the traces, with giant boulders near them. The rest, panicked by the noise and the smell of blood and death, reared and kicked and trumpeted their distress. It was clear they would do themselves more harm if not put under control at once.

Even as we turned to look, one horse went down, having broken its leg in the traces, and began to scream in a horribly human way. It was a terrible sound—to chill the soul.

Mr. Stimpy, nearly pulled off his feet trying to hold two of the rearing monsters, cried out, "Whit, Whit! Do you have your gun?"

Then, the cowboy who had done so much to help me was running up to the downed animal and pulling a pistol from the holster at his side. He calmly stepped up to the poor, flailing, screaming animal, placed the muzzle against its skull between the ears, and pulled the trigger. There was a bang, and then, for a moment, blessed silence.

But only for a moment. The remaining three horses panicked anew and began once more their deadly rearing and kicking at the traces. The cowboys both began to help Mr. Stimpy, struggling to untangle reins, in great danger of being kicked themselves. They were trying to draw them away from the coach toward a clump of stunted but sturdy trees, just ahead up the road.

Three horses left, three men to control them. Six passengers huddled in the dirt beside the overturned coach, one dead inside. There was one person missing.

I walked around the back of the coach and began to

examine the bourn on the other side of the road. I found him in a clump of dried grass, amid assorted boulders.

"Oh, Mr. Buck!" I mourned and knelt beside him. He lay there on his back like one of my rag dollies, arms and legs straight out. One of his legs was obviously broken, in a most grievous and life-threatening way. I could see bone sticking out and the leg was bleeding profusely. His face was covered in blood and he was unconscious—at the least. I couldn't tell if he was breathing or not.

I reached for an out-flung wrist and felt for a pulse. Yes, there was one! I was no medical person, but there was a rhythmic throbbing. Although badly injured, he was still alive.

I stood, and without giving it a thought turned toward the horses and called loudly, "Whit! Whit! I need you!"

He heard me and turned. I saw surprise, but he instantly handed the reins of the horse he had gentled to the other man and came to me with gratifying speed. He looked shocked at what I had found.

"Ah, Buck, what'd you do to yourself?"

"He's alive," I insisted. "There's a pulse, I felt it."

Intense eyes turned on me quizzically.

"I'm not trained medically, of course not, but I felt it! See for yourself!"

He did, and then examined the wound. He unbuckled his belt and used it to make a kind of tourniquet above the break in the leg, and the bleeding mercifully slowed to a slight seep.

"Have to loosen that every now and then to let some blood through, but at least he won't bleed out," Whit remarked. "The face, we can't do much. Probably broke his nose."

He sat back on his heels and regarded me once more. "What were you doing out here? Who's taking care of the others?"

"Mr. Bysbee is. I counted and there was one of us missing. I came looking."

The intelligent eyes now looked green. What color were they, anyway? He shot a look at me, such as I had never experienced in my life. For a moment, his eyes simply blazed at me, and I was transfixed.

"Well, that was danged smart of you!" he said with approval and... was it possible... admiration? "You sure keep a cool head in an emergency, ma'am. All the rest of us plum forgot about Buck, here. I thought he jumped off with Larry and me, but I guess he didn't get the chance."

Whit thought for a moment, then stood. His demeanor changed completely as he took charge.

"Buck's out cold. Let's leave him here for now. First thing is to get those dang horses settled. Come here." He led me back around the end of the coach, where he unbuckled and manhandled down a keg that was strapped to the boot.

"Here's water," he explained, producing a huge knife, and prying off the lid. "Cup's hanging around here somewhere. Give everybody a drink. And wash that stuff off Mrs. Bysbee, it's giving her fits. But don't waste the water... we're gonna be here a while and that's all we got."

He moved decisively toward the horses, calling ahead, "Larry, take the lead horse and ride for the Wells. Tell them to bring a wagon and Doc. Or Maria if Doc's gone. She's as good as a doctor, herself."

He then joined Mr. Stimpy, helping wrestle with the two remaining horses. It was wonderful to watch the play of muscles in his lean body as he pulled and stretched against the power of the great animals. Like a carving...

I controlled myself, with dismay. There was a job for me to do! Belatedly, I turned my attention to our little band of survivors. Looking into the boot, there was no trouble finding the cup, dangling on a leather thong, more trouble untying the knot that secured it, but eventually it came loose.

I could take charge, too, I assured myself. "Mr. Bysbee, I'll take care of Eulalia now. Please see that everyone gets a drink of water. We all need it."

Mr. Bysbee came to his task with alacrity.

After only a moment of reflection, I raised my skirt and tore a strip off the bottom of my petticoat. Dripping the cup in the barrel, I poured a little water over it, gave the cup to Mr. Bysbee, and, returning to his wife, began cleaning her face and hands while she continued to weep. The washing did seem to calm her. I got what I could off her dress, but it was hopelessly stained.

The drink of water helped everyone. I carefully made sure the lid was restored and that the keg sat solidly and would not be accidentally overturned.

The horses secured, Whit returned with Mr. Stimpy and surveyed us, satisfied. "Bysbee, come with us. Stimpy, can you get us a plank off of somewhere?" It took all three of them, but they did rip one off the boot, and in a while returned with Buck, as if on a stretcher, and set him down in the road beside Mr. Moser, who was still unconscious but occasionally emitting a low moan.

"I got a tarp up front," Mr. Stimpy offered. "Rig us a bit of shade. It's dang hot. Bysbee, give me a hand."

I knelt by Buck. He showed no signs of regaining consciousness. Whit came up with four sticks, stout but not very long.

"He's going to be in a lot of pain when he comes to. I think we should straighten and bind off that leg before. Save him some real bad minutes."

"What can I do to help?"

"If we can bind these sticks to the leg, we can at least hold it straight until Doc comes. That's probably about all we can do."

I stood. "Right, binding." There was nothing else for it, so I raised my skirt again and pulled down what remained of my petticoat. It was made of fine broadcloth, and I easily tore off the waistband, ripping the rest into as many strips as I could. Whit straightened the leg, which I could not have borne to touch. The horrible wound, with the bone sticking out, was filled with dirt. I brought a cup of the precious water and we cleaned it as best we could, then placed the sticks and wrapped it all, stopping short of the tourniquet.

"Not too tight," Whit warned. "It will swell something awful."

While he tied knots, securing our makeshift cast, I retrieved the piece of cloth I had used to cleanse Mrs. Bysbee, used a tiny bit of water to dampen it again, and tried to wipe the blood off Buck's mauled face. As I did so, I couldn't help thinking about Ellen's doctors and *bacilli*, but what could I do? It was unthinkable to leave Buck as he was.

Whit regarded me with approval: "Miss, you've been a real help. Lucky for me you're not some *Lizzy in a Tizzy*." He nodded toward Mrs. Bysbee.

I blushed at the compliment. "Please, you can't go on calling me 'Miss,' after all this! My name is Alta."

He looked at me straight on, and once again, his eyes did that strange thing and absolutely blazed for a moment. I had to take a very deep breath.

"Thank you, Alta," was all he said, and moved away.

After the tarp was up, secured by ropes from the recumbent coach to various taller rock piles, we moved everyone under its relative shade and sat there in the dirt, amid the rubble of our disaster. Luggage, fallen from the roof, was strung out on the road behind us and everywhere were boulders of many sizes, mixed with piles of dirt and gravel.

Now, Mr. Stimpy resumed command of the ship and explained our situation.

"Well, folks, we've had a bit of bad luck," he began. Quite

an understatement! "Actually, we was somewhat lucky at that. It was a really big landslide, but we only got the tail end of it. We was almost out of it... how-some-ever, here we are. There's no going back to Dewar's; road'll be blocked up for weeks. Larry's rid ahead to Martinez Wells. They'll come get us in a wagon. That's better anyway, they got a Doctor there, and Albion and Maria run a real nice inn. They'll take good care of us, best care we could get south of Santa Fe."

He looked expectantly around, hoping we would be cheered, before the bad news.

"Thing is, the Wells is still about fifteen miles away, over some real bad road. Larry will do good to get there by dark. They'll start back for us at daylight, but truth is, they won't be able to get to us much before dark again, assuming they bring a wagon. And 'course, we can't start back for the Wells until the next morning. So, what we're looking at is, two nights of camping out here. Mebbe three, if they can't start out right away."

We all looked glum.

"We do got some supplies," he went on, in a more cheerful vein. "We got coffee and cornmeal and beans. We won't starve. This is our only water, though. There's one more barrel, but we got to keep that for the horses. The rest all got busted. So we got to be real choosy how we use it. Strictly for fixing our food and for drinking. No washin'."

Mrs. Bysbee moaned.

"Now," Mr. Stimpy went on briskly, "it's gonna get real cold here tonight, and I got no blankets. Lord knows where all the luggage has got to, but those who are able-bodied should go now and drag all they can back up here. Them as has shawls or coats should get 'em out, you'll be needing 'em. 'Course we'll be able to have a fire. That'll help a lot."

Mr. Stimpy went back to the horses, still nervous and jittering about, although securely tied in their bushy thicket.

Able-bodied. Well, that was Whit, Mr. Bysbee, and me. We looked at each other and then set out to see what we could do.

Chapter Three

We left Bilethia, who was clearly in pain, in charge of Eulalia—now complaining that her "insides" hurt—Mr. Moser, and Buck, both still unconscious.

As we three started back down the way our coach had come, I did not fail to hear Eulalia hissing to Bilethia, "Did you see what she did? Absolutely raised her skirts and pulled off her petticoat! I saw it! I saw her legs! Shameless!"

I couldn't help but laugh, but also blushed. Whit chuckled and winked at me. "Lizzy in a Tizzy," he repeated.

If Mr. Bysbee heard us, he didn't show it.

The luggage was strewn quite a way back, down the road. Several trunks had burst open, the contents scattered everywhere. Fortunately, mine was still intact. I was grateful my stays were not draped decoratively over some sagebrush! We found my valise as well but never did see the parasol. My smart little hat, so admired in the Harvey House, was still somewhere in the coach—no doubt trampled underfoot. I would not be retrieving it.

Picking up everything we could find; we made several trips dragging it all back to what was becoming our campsite and set about seeing what we could do to make ourselves more comfortable.

Mrs. Bysbee (no more Eulalia to me!) traded her previous distress for a new one. Hers was one of the burst trunks, and—although she did not get up—she practically ordered us to bring all the loose things we had gathered to her, and sorted through them for her own belongings, continually exclaiming in dismay.

"It's filthy! It's torn! It's ruined!" was her constant refrain. She refused to use her own cloak as something to sit on but readily accepted when the Man in Gray offered his, also from a burst trunk, and made herself quite comfortable. I thought he should have kept it for himself. Eulalia spent the whole rest of the afternoon going through her things: shaking them out, folding them, and repacking the damaged trunk. Her constant little cries of "It's ruined!" were much easier to live with than the previous weeping and moaning.

I dug into my trunk and found a light shawl to make a kind of sling for Bilethia, who had sat through it all, grim-faced and silent. Her arm was clearly broken, but in the lower part, and seemed to pain her less with the support.

"It would be my right arm! I'm useless with my left," was her only complaint. Mr. Moser was beginning to move a little and trying to sit up. She begged a bit of cloth from me, and a little water, so I tore my rag in half and gave one to her. She sat comforting her husband and wiping his perspiring brow.

"I would rip my own petticoat, but it's buckram, and too thick to tear," she apologized softly to me.

I leaned down and kissed her cheek. "Don't worry," I reassured her, "Eulalia doesn't bother me. And you're a dear. Just take care of your husband."

"I won't take any water for myself next time we drink," she promised, speaking of the water I had used to wet her cloth.

"For goodness sakes, let's be sensible about this!" I scolded.

"Taking care of our injured is a priority, too! You'll drink with the rest of us." She gave me a small but grateful smile.

Mr. Moser began to babble a little, and I saw her put her hand to his mouth to stop his words a time or two, but nothing he said made any sense to me, and I paid no attention.

I went through my trunk again and shook my head. I wasn't giving up my cashmere shawl to make another sling, but the Man in Gray clearly needed one. Smiling a little to myself, thinking how shocked Mrs. Bysbee would be, I sacrificed my second-best chemise. There was enough fabric to hold the arm and the straps conveniently would fit over his head. If we needed more bandages for Buck, well, I would have to give up my last petticoat. If we needed more than that, I was down to pantaloons.

I was easily able to construct a sling for the Man in Gray. He found it to help some, but his arm was not the greatest cause of his pain. He tried to thank me, but it clearly cost him an effort to speak. He leaned back against the embankment panting, but now his face was almost as gray as his suit.

During the past half hour, Mr. Bysbee, who had been perfectly well all this time, had become quite pale and begun to shake, as if, in this heat, he was cold. Whit prevailed upon him to lie down by his wife and insisted that she stop defending her cloak and use it to cover her husband. Protesting that he couldn't possibly be cold, she gave in to Whit with ill grace, and now had something new to complain about.

"Alta, we've done about all we can do for now," Whit said, taking my arm and leading me out onto the open prairie beyond the embankment. "Let's gather up some firewood for tonight."

And so, we wandered out onto a patch of open land, not having to go far to find sticks, bits of branches, and thick bunches of dry bushes. I wondered aloud if there would be "buffalo chips" for burning, which I had read about in pioneer stories. Whit laughed and said more likely "cow patties," but if there were any, we did not find them.

"Whit, who is that man in gray?" I asked. "We never have heard his name."

"Him? That's Dale Danvers, from Albuquerque."

"Mrs. Bysbee says he's a gambler."

"She would!" Whit laughed full-out. I liked a man with an honest laugh. "Well, in a way, he is. He's an assayer for the mines. Silver, copper, coal, whatever. He finds out what it's worth. We don't get much gold out here." He then turned to me very seriously. "Alta, I'm worried about him. In my opinion, he's the worst injured of all of them."

I was shocked. "Surely Buck..."

"Buck is bad. He'll maybe lose that leg. But Danvers, he's in a bad way. He's got a broken collar bone as well as the arm—but it's the ribs. A while ago, he started coughing up blood. Alta, I'm afraid he's punctured at least one of his lungs."

"Oh, Whit!" I moaned.

"The worst of it is, even when help does come, we've still got a full day's travel to get to the Wells, in a wagon, over real bad road. It'll keep tearing at his lungs; I don't know if he can survive it. It'll be real hard on Buck, too. On all of us. But it may kill Danvers."

On this solemn note, we carried our wood back to camp, and went out for more, until we had what Whit judged was enough to last the night.

In the late afternoon, Mr. Stimpy built a modest fire and produced a cast iron pot, then boiled up a large amount of cornmeal mush, which we ate after dark in the light of the campfire, on chipped enamel plates with assorted bent forks or spoons. Never had anything tasted so good. He cleaned the kettle with sandy grit, filled it part way up with water, and made boiled coffee, magically producing "cups" to go around, most of them old tin cans. The hot drink put some heart back in most of us.

We sat around the fire, warming our hands on our coffee cans, for it was now indeed growing cold. The hot coffee especially seemed to help Mr. Bysbee, who stopped shaking and was embarrassed by his episode.

Mr. Moser had been able to eat a little and now sat up, but his words were confused and his eyes strange in his head. Bilethia was worried about him and kept patting his arm.

Buck was groaning now, and conscious from time to time, asking what had happened. Whit took very gentle care of him and got him to drink some water, but he fell unconscious again before we could offer him mush.

Mrs. Bysbee continued to complain that her "insides" hurt. I whispered to Whit that perhaps we should remove her stays to relieve her, but he vehemently rejected that.

"Whatever's wrong with her insides, those stays are what is holding her together. By no means let her take them off, at least until Doc comes. He'll know better than we do."

I couldn't help but agree. This was a surprising entry in the *Stays: Good or Bad?* debate going on in my head. Suppose I had been sitting where Eulalia had been and found myself almost at the bottom of that deadly pile in the coach, instead of mercifully on top of the heap... with no stays. It didn't bear thinking about. One way or the other, I had been incredibly lucky.

Mr. Stimpy now filled up the big pot with beans and water, to cover and soak overnight. "We'll feast on beans tomorrow!" he promised.

I couldn't help noting with alarm how much our water barrel was going down. A whole night, and one more day... and what if help did not come at once?

"Is there really no water around here anywhere?" I asked Whit.

"No, nothing but alkali until you get to the Wells."

Fortified by the hot meal and heartened by the fire, everyone began to prepare for sleep, gathering what clothes they could for coverings. It was clear we were minimally better off than we had been.

Whit took me away from the fire, leaving Mrs. Bysbee's disapproval behind us, and we sat on the borne across the road —our backs to the tall butte—and watched the moon come up over the expanse of prairie before us. I had never seen so many stars or such a sky. It was overwhelming. At first, we just sat and took it in. After a while, we began to chat—easily. How wonderful it was to be out West where things were simpler and rules were more reasonable, and we could talk as if we were old friends. I felt safe with him, and he was so admirable. Mother might disapprove of our growing friendship, but Mother had not been through what we had just survived.

I was curious about this unusual man, seeming so *rough and ready* on the outside, but able to slip into—and then tactfully out of—command, as necessary. He was much better spoken than Mr. Stimpy but deferred to the older man with becoming respect.

I thought of him shooting the poor horse, going close despite the murderous flailing hooves. Bilethia had said to me of that incident, "He's a right good shot. A horse has got a very little brain. If you don't get just the spot, you've wasted your bullet. Most folks don't know that."

Whit responded to my questions without reserve. He was indeed not *just* a cowboy. His father owned a sheep ranch near Black Butte. He had a sister and two brothers. His mother had died shortly after the birth of the girl, Mildred.

"Paul, now, he went off to Denver and got be a lawyer. By rights, he should have been the rancher, but Pa says, if the law is what he wants, he can do a world of good for us and all the other sheepmen. So, by default, that makes me a sheepman, too —what with the cattlemen trying to run some of us out. Pa's in charge, of course, but I'm sort of his foreman. My little brother Phillip is never going to work the ranch. All he wants to do is breed horses."

He made himself more comfortable, leaning back on one elbow on the grass.

"When we get back, Phillip's going to want me to go up in the mountains with him after wild mustangs. He wants to breed appaloosas, Indian ponies. It is kind of exciting."

I could see that. It was an exciting idea.

"Were you in Santa Fe on sheep business?" I asked.

"Nope, Denver. I've been on the road for a month! Larry, he's our head wrangler, and I went up to talk to our insurance company about all the stock we lost in the blizzard last winter."

I, too, had been through a blizzard last winter. I told him a little about my life in New York and what that terrible storm had meant to us. He was amazed.

"I would have thought you had the best of everything there," he marveled. "How strange, that one bad storm could travel on and make you as much danger and trouble as we got here out West."

"It's interesting that your ranch is near Black Butte," I remarked. "That's where I'm going, too." I blushed and lowered my eyelashes, not that he could see them. "I'm the new school-teacher."

"Really?" he seemed surprised. "I thought they would have given that job to my Aunt Izzie. She used to be the school-teacher until she married John Quimby. But she's only been widowed a little while. Guess six months was too soon."

"Six months," I reflected, counting back.

"Yes," he responded. "It was that dang blizzard. They had a little place just out of town, a few heads of stock, mostly pigs.

John went out; you have to feed the stock. You couldn't even see the shoes on your feet if you looked down. They had rigged a rope from the house to the barn so he could find his way back and forth, but it broke. We figured he never did get to the barn. Found him out in the back pasture after it was all over, and the snow melted down some."

"How horrible! That's the worst story I ever heard!" My eyes were welling with tears. "Had they been married long?"

"About two years."

My tears spilled over. It was just too much, on top of all the dreadful things that had happened over the last few hours, and concerns over the immediate future. Sobs were not far behind.

He put his arms around me and pulled me close. He was so firm, so warm, so safe. Keeping one arm around me, he tipped my head up and wiped away tears with one thumb.

"You have a tender heart," he said. And then... he kissed me.

It was nothing like when Charles had kissed me. His lips were dry, warm, and soft. So soft. My lips molded to his, I could hardly press close enough and could not help kissing him back ardently. And when he began to pull away, I clung to his mouth and did not want the kiss to end.

After a long and lovely interval, he set me back from where I lay—practically in his lap and sitting cross-legged— and laughed at me tenderly.

"Well, now I've done it! I've gone and kissed the school-marm!" He beamed at me.

His eyes told me how much he had liked the kiss. I was so stunned I could hardly talk at first, but my heart seemed to soar with joy. I looked at him sitting there, smiling at me in the moonlight, and he delighted me.

"I shall have to give you an F in deportment," I warned him. My God, I was flirting with him! I couldn't believe the playfulness I heard in my voice. A lady does not flirt. True, and a lady does not kiss like that, either.

He pretended to be crestfallen. "Surely not, teacher! I bet that kiss was worth at least an A—from the way you kissed me back."

He was right, but I was certainly not going to tell him that! A lady would never... well, I might as well give that up. Clearly, however well I had been brought up, in however many deport- ment classes they had put me, I was no lady. I lowered my eyes, hoping he could still see my eyelashes in the moonlight.

He turned somber. "I reckon I shouldn't have done that, Alta, but I'm not sorry one bit."

This jolted me like a rock on top of the coach. He spoke as if it meant something to him, more than just a playful romp under a starry sky, a brief vacation from calamity and death. It certainly meant everything to me. I began to fill up with happi- ness, and I matched his solemn demeanor, although I knew a woman was not supposed to be so honest—so forward. "Nei- ther am I," I whispered. Once more his eyes blazed at me, like sealing a vow; it was the third time. The moon was full in his face, and I could see it, even in the dark. I was not at all sure I would survive a fourth time.

He took my hand but sat so still I was almost alarmed. "Alta..." he began, but then shook his head and simply pulled me to my feet. I would rather he had kissed me again.

"We'd better get back to the others. Time to get some sleep." And he led me back to the fire. I did not feel compro- mised in the least. I felt elation.

We found the others well settled down—except for Mr. Danvers, who remained sitting upright against the embank- ment, breathing shallowly. Buck was moaning and thrashing around.

Whit knelt by him, urging him to lie still. Buck didn't seem to understand what had happened, despite being told. Each time he slipped back into unconsciousness, he seemed to forget. He was perspiring heavily. I got my cloth, wet it with a little more of the ebbing water, and came back to them.

"Let me do this," I said to Whit, and began gently wiping Buck's forehead and talking quietly to him, about nothing much, but he did seem to respond to a feminine voice and lay still.

"Why don't you try to get some rest," I urged Whit.

He nodded. "I'll sleep an hour or two and come and relieve you." He went back to the fire, lay down in the dirt, and appeared to go to sleep at once.

I talked quietly to Buck, on and on, since that seemed to be what comforted him. I told him about the moon coming up, the thousands of stars, and all the beauty I found here. Then, I talked lightly about life in New York, and how different it was. Finally, really at the bottom of the barrel, I told him about the train, and the stories I could remember of the lives of the people I had met there.

Whenever I thought he had fallen asleep, and stopped talking, he would rouse and try to sit up, and begin to groan, so I would resume my endless narrative. His fever was worse than ever. I got him water and made him drink. I thought he was very badly off.

My voice was nearly gone by the time Whit came to relieve me, and I was very glad to see him.

"Go get some sleep, Alta," he sent me off with a warm smile.

But first I took some water to Mr. Danvers and asked quietly if he needed anything else.

It took an effort, but he said, "Listened to your stories... it helped. Thanks, *Scheherazade.*"

I laughed at his reference. "Hardly that good, Mr. Danvers. Not quite literature!"

"Circumstances... make it better." He gestured that he could not talk anymore, so I bade him goodnight and went to roll up in my cloak and lie down. I thought it would be hard to sleep. He had put that old *Arabian Nights* story in my head, only if the stories stopped, it was not me who would die. I wanted to weep but must have fallen asleep at once, because the next thing I knew it was dawn, and Mr. Stimpy was building up the fire and brewing the most wonderful smelling coffee, in a number of the cans this time, since the big pot held our beans.

While we all drank our coffee, he put the beans on the coals, intending to cook them all day long over a low fire.

Breakfast was hard crackers and, for each, a tiny piece of cheese. We took stock of our situation. Bilethia was gray and grim, but she said nothing of herself, giving all her attention to her husband. His eyes were still odd, but he talked less and made sense when he did.

Mrs. Bysbee was probably in genuine pain by now, whimpering as tears ran down her cheeks, but I don't think she would have removed her stays even if I had suggested it. She would not even change her dress to a cleaner one from her trunk and looked at me as if I were a hussy for expressing the mere idea.

"That would be entirely improper!" she informed me huffily. "There is no privacy here." So that was that.

Whit took me aside. "You wouldn't have any laudanum in that bag of tricks of yours, would you? Or Lydia Pinkham's, same thing."

I was shocked. "No, I would not! I'm not a user of laudanum," I retorted, perhaps a little primly, because he laughed.

"Medical use only, Alta," he assured me. "Not accusing you of anything."

"Sorry," I apologized. "But the answer's still no. How awful! We have nothing to ease any of this pain!"

Mr. Bysbee was completely fit again and did his best to support and distract his wife, sitting beside her and fanning her with her own ostrich feather fan, now dusty and tattered.

Perhaps Mr. Danvers had been able to sleep upright, but it was hard to tell. He seemed much the same. Buck was worse. He was more awake and aware of his pain, which must have been extreme. He tried stoically to contain his groans but that effort, combined with his fever which continued to rage, caused him to drip with sweat. At the mid-morning drink, I gave him my share as well as his own. I thought no one noticed, but a little later, Whit took me aside.

"Alta, don't stint yourself. It does us all no good if you go down!"

I knew he was right; it was only what I had told Bilethia, but the water was very low.

Mr. Stimpy tended the horses and the beans. We gathered more wood. Somehow the day passed.

At dusk, we ate the beans, which were delicious. At full dark, we heard the wagon coming to save us.

Chapter Four

There was water.

There were warm blankets and oats for the horses.

There was no doctor.

Instead, there was Maria, and even that English heroine Florence Nightingale could not have had more capable hands. Mercifully, she had laudanum for Mrs. Bysbee and Bilethia. For Buck and Mr. Danvers, something better: whiskey.

Maria spent a little time with each of us—the injured first. She was quite concerned about Buck. I noticed her douse some of the whiskey over his wound before she re-bandaged the leg, discarding our sticks and using several wooden splints she had brought with her. I asked about the whiskey.

"Alcohol in it might kill off some of those nasty little critters," she responded. Ah, *bacilli* again.

Maria left Buck's nose to heal as it would, merely cleaning his face and beard. His forehead and brows were very clean, but I hadn't done such a good job on the rest.

"You wasn't much to look at, before. Guess it won't make no difference," she said, and Buck did not seem to disagree with her. Mr. Danvers she handled delicately and said little about his condition, but I saw her exchange looks with Whit.

She thought Mr. Moser would be all right in a little time, but we would have to wait and see. She approved of Bilethia's temporary sling but taped her broken arm, saying it already had a nice start healing and we didn't want it to go crooked. The doctor would decide about Mrs. Bysbee when we got to Martinez Wells. The rest of us she pronounced hale—albeit with assorted scrapes and bruises.

She dispensed tea and distributed blankets, helping everyone to create as good a bed as possible. I felt a stab of envy at her ability to make everyone feel reassured. How wonderful to have her kind of knowledge and know what to do in dire emergencies. Perhaps I should consider a medical career, myself.

The briefest consideration brought me back to my right mind. Maria was admirable. I had not been able to even touch Buck's wound. It was Whit who had handled all that. I did have skills of my own. I should concentrate on them; I was very good at sitting with patients and wiping fevered brows. Credit where credit is due!

Our second night of camping out was better than the first. We were warmer and somewhat medicated. It was a relief not to feel responsible anymore for our injured. Still, I awoke over and over—I thought the night would never end.

In the morning we had breakfast, loaded up the wagon, and started on our way. Very soon, I wished with all my heart that we were motionless as before. The wagon was old and creaky. It must have found every rock and pit in the road. The bumps and jostling were twice as bad as when we had been in the coach. Buck tried manfully to be silent, but even with more whiskey, he could not keep from crying out when the wagon lurched severely. Mr. Danvers groaned once and then fell unconscious.

Mrs. Bysbee, cushioned with laudanum, still moaned and wept in her husband's arms. Bilethia did not speak of her arm at all and only concerned herself with Mr. Moser—who was almost rational today.

Our situation was not improved by the fact that our wagon was crowded by a bundle rolled in our old tarp. He had died there, but the Reverend Tomm was not to be abandoned in the wilderness.

Whit and Mr. Stimpy rode the two coach horses beside or ahead of the wagon—to avoid the dust—using saddles brought from the Wells. Larry rode a new, fresh horse. I would have also preferred to ride, or even walk, given the option, certain I could have kept up with the slow pace of the wagon, but Maria asked for my help with Mr. Danvers. I wished I could believe my slight efforts were doing any good, but I tried with my own body to cushion him from some of the worst jolts. He was awake from time to time but had great difficulty breathing.

At noon, we had a most welcome halt for a brief lunch, but Mr. Danvers neither got out of the wagon nor ate.

"Just... let me... rest here," he begged. He did take some water.

The afternoon was worse, much worse. There was no shade, and the sun was like a furnace. I wished for my lost parasol. At least I could have kept the sun off Danvers. The road seemed to get progressively rougher. We were moving through magnificent terrain with an extraordinary play of shadows on the red rock cliffs and canyons, and the intense blue sky billowing occasionally with puffy clouds, but under the circumstances, no one was looking at the scenery. The poor horses tired, and we seemed to go slower and slower.

In the late afternoon, Mr. Danvers died. I was holding him at the time.

Well after dark, we finally reached Martinez Wells. The doctor was there, at last, back from a difficult birth out in the canyonlands. He took over our remaining patients with Maria now assisting him.

The Inn was basically a dirt shack, which I later heard referred to as *adobe*, but after the past two nights, it was a haven of comfort. A young woman named Conchita showed me to a room and promised me a bath, which duly appeared in the form of a large, tin sit-tub with two young girls forming a bucket brigade for hot water. It was the extreme of luxury after our ordeal, and such a solace that I did not get out until the water was stone cold.

Then, I lay on my bed and cried for Mr. Danvers.

Later, Whit knocked on my door to give me a tea tray and ask if I wanted anything to eat. I did not.

"Just go to bed then, Alta, and get a good night's sleep. In the morning, we'll all catch up with each other," he said, but as I took the tray he stole a quick kiss. "That's twice!" He teased and vanished down the hall.

That effectively banished all my tears, but now my heart was beating far too hard for sleep. I lay long awake, savoring the extravagance of sheets and pillows and remembering every moment spent with Whit.

The next day, Mr. Stimpy gathered us in the parlor before breakfast and clarified our situation. I was glad to see Bilethia with us, her arm well wrapped and in a real sling. She looked much better and had some of her color back. Mr. Moser was rational but wobbly. Mr. Bysbee seemed fine, as usual, but was alone. Larry was there with Whit, who gave me a sweet smile.

"First off, you'll be wantin' to know about Buck," Mr. Stimpy began. "As you can guess, he's real bad. Doc says that leg has got to come off, but Buck won't hear of it. They're arguing about that right now. I expect Doc will win.

"Mr. Moser, here, has a right bad concussion, but Doc thinks he'll be okay. Mrs. Moser's arm was already set, and she'll be fine, too. Mrs. Bysbee, I'm sorry to say, is not so good. Turns out she has a bunch of busted ribs, herself. However, them stays of hers kept the ribs in place so they didn't punch a hole in her lungs. That's what got Danvers, Doc thinks. He has Mrs. Bysbee all trussed up now, but she's got to be real quiet for two to three weeks, no traveling. If she can do that, them ribs should heal fine, and she'll be good as new. That means they'll be staying on here until they can travel again. Mebbe there'll even be coaches coming through from Dewar's by then."

So that was the final word in the *Great Stays Debate*. Sometimes, they could save your life. *Life* versus *comfort* should end the matter, but, after my days of freedom, I did not feel like putting mine on again.

Mr. Stimpy went on, "The rest of you, we'll get you out of here in a wagon. It'll be some slower than the coach woulda been, but you'll get there. They got the telegraph in Black Butte, and we can let Butterfield know what all's happened out here. You can get in touch with your folks. Butterfield's will fix you up one way or another, but obviously the stages won't be running regular for a while.

"This afternoon there'll be a funeral for Mr. Danvers and Reverend Tomm. Those of you going on, we'll leave first thing tomorrow morning. Well, that's pretty much it."

Our various farewells were very moving. Interestingly, it was the doctor who read the funeral service. The following morning, Mrs. Bysbee shed more tears; no doubt feeling abandoned, and actually patted my arm. Mr. Bysbee gave me a firm handshake, looked me in the eye, and said it had been a pleasure to know me. I believe he was sincere and returned the sentiment.

Then, like a recurring nightmare, the Mosers, Larry, Whit, and I were back in another wagon—Mr. Stimpy driving, with a man named Sam from the Wells acting as our new shotgun, all of us bouncing and jouncing without mercy.

Five miles outside Hockney, the next stop, a wheel broke. The men were able to temporarily fix it, but we had to spend another night "campin' rough." We got to Hockney by mid-morning the following day, but it took until well after dark for the smithy to restore the wheel to permanent usage. We spent the night at the Hockney Inn—the rest of the town consisting entirely of the smithy, the stables, and three houses.

During all this time, Whit and I spent every possible moment together, talking about everything under the sun, but mostly wanting to find out all about each other. We tried to talk quietly, but I'm sure we were an annoyance to the others.

I told him what it was like to live in New York City and about my family. In fact, I told him more than I would have thought to tell such a new friend.

He told me about his family and the ranch, what it was like to live in the West, and how they had come to be sheepmen, rather than running cattle, which had apparently been by the merest chance—his father having won a flock of sheep in a card game!

Whit explained that cattlemen and sheepmen disliked each other intensely because of the different way their stock used the range, especially once sheepmen began to use barbed wire fencing; the one thing that did seem able to keep free-range cattle out and the sheep in.

Sometimes, these fences prevented the cattle from access to the vast public lands the cattlemen relied on to supplement grazing. It took as much as ten acres to feed one single cow with a calf; no ranch could support that without depending on some outside grazing. There had been bitter animosity, and even violence, over this issue. Whit's ranch was fortunately not located in an area where his lands competed with anyone's free-range, but even so, they could not help occasionally being involved through friends and other sheepmen.

It was alarming to think of Whit being in such a situation, but I was fully aware that he always wore the pistol in its holster at his right side.

A lady should always tell the truth. Actually, it was a bit thrilling to glimpse the gun on his hip. He never took it off, except at night when we rolled up inside our blankets around the fire. Even then, he kept it close at hand.

I was no stranger to firearms. Father, a sometimes sportsman, occasionally went on hunting trips "up north" with various business associates, from which he returned with little to show in the way of game, but often with a new contract or supplier.

He thought it important that we three girls should know something about the sport, just as we had been taught to ride horses, so, over Mother's protests, he once took us to a firing range to shoot rifles. Adelle had obediently done as told, but flinched terribly when the gun went off and was so shaky, she was a danger to everyone else on the range. After that, Aggie refused entirely.

Never one to miss an opportunity, I tried very hard to stand steady and not to flinch, and on my fourth shot actually managed to nick the edge of the target, although I never got near the center. Father was pleased with me, but we were not taken a second time. Because of that lesson, the thought of guns did not horrify me.

Poor Father, he would have so much enjoyed a son who could share such masculine pastimes. Was it possible that Charles could fill that role? It was hard to imagine, but I was willing to wager that Father would soon be trying to mold him into such a companion—for business reasons, of course.

Whit said he liked sheep well enough, but they were not

intelligent animals, having been known to perish of thirst in a pen with a gate wide open, lacking a *bellwether* to lead them out. Not that cattle were much smarter, just more independent.

Whit said water caused even more trouble on the range: either the having it or the lack of it.

"We're all right," he told me comfortably. "We have an artesian well." He explained that was water spurting straight up from deep in the earth, which would never run dry and was completely pure. "Wait until you taste it!" he bragged. "Some artesian water tastes awful, but ours is sweet. You'll never have tasted water so good!"

I expressed a great desire to taste it.

Whit said the ranch shared its water with several homesteads on the ranch's boundary lines. Those people would have no water otherwise, and, after all, the ranch had more than it could use just running away and soaking back into the soil. However, some water-holders saw no reason why they should share, and even sold water at very high prices.

What a strange world I was entering! I hung on Whit's every word and could not hear enough of all that he was telling me.

From Hockney, we set off early on the last stage of our journey. One last full day of travel, one last night of camping out, and, barring further calamity, we should reach Black Butte around mid-afternoon of the second day.

That evening, Whit took me away from the campfire one last time. We climbed a little hill and sat on a huge flat rock to watch the sunset. As always, it was like cosmic theater: as the sun sunk low, colors blazed in red, gold, and all the shades in between, intensifying as it touched the horizon and began to disappear. Suddenly, between a breath and a gasp, the sun was gone. One last blaze of fire, and then all the colors began to mute, fading into the palest mauve, ocher, and deepening blue, and then into a black as soft as a fur robe. The stars came out. This sight never failed to move me deeply. I was a girl on a rock in a desert, yet somehow profoundly part of it all.

I know Whit felt the same. He took my hand, but we did not talk until some minutes had passed.

Then, he began to tell me quietly about Black Butte and the people I would soon be meeting.

"They'll love you, Alta. You'll be a great addition to the town. We can use a little refinement." He then grew serious and took my other hand as well.

"Alta, you've been splendid through all this bad time, not at all like some fancy *Miss from New York City*. I never once heard you complain. You took care of everybody. I just wanted you to know how much I respect and admire you."

Then, somewhat abruptly, he took me back to the fire and we rolled up in blankets with the others for our last night of "sleepin' rough."

The next morning, he seemed to respect and admire me from something of a distance.

I was a little puzzled, but as arrival at Black Butte became a certainty, my thoughts were diverted by worry about my immediate future. I was going to be in a schoolroom. Thank goodness my trunk was intact. It still contained the curriculum for my classes—the curriculum I had not studied! I felt the approach of panic. I had put it off, telling myself there would be plenty of time to prepare. Now, there was no time. I didn't know the present date, but a little calculation produced the fact that we were at least six or seven days late. When was school supposed to start? I could not remember; it had not seemed important; they would tell me what I needed to know when I arrived. Now, such thinking seemed idiotic!

We stopped for lunch and went on again through the

foothills. After several hours, the wagon laboriously mounted a low hill, and there was the metropolis of Black Butte laid out below us. My new home.

Chapter Five

B lack Butte looked like a *real city* after Martinez Wells and Hockney.

The black butte itself stood out starkly against the surrounding red rock hills and cliffs. Whit informed us it was the site of the Black Diamond Coal Mine: a seemingly inexhaustible source of bituminous coal, which everyone around here burned for heat and cooking. The town had gradually grown up at the crossroads, where the trams full of coal came down from the mine to intersect the road. At first, there was just a livery stable and a grocer, then a farrier and a hotel for all the mine people coming and going. That was when it became an official stage stop on the Butterfield line, and after that, growth was rapid. The coming of the grange hall and the telegraph line—housed in the Butterfield office—and finally, the opening of the post office, made it official; the settlement was declared a town, with a sign to mark the boundary line, announcing "Black Butte, pop. 5,012." Now, I guess, 5,013—counting me!

We drove slowly down the hill into town. I examined each feature with great curiosity. First, we passed the cemetery, then small houses set close together with fences but no lawns and very few plantings or trees. There were no sidewalks, only dirt paths. It was nothing like what I was used to back East.

Black smoke poured out of chimneys, and it was obvious that everyone burned coal, for the burning left behind porous, lava-like lumps called "clinkers," and every yard had its pile.

We passed the post office, a doctor's office, and several small shops, and suddenly, we were in the heart of the business district—passing a hotel, an enormous saloon, and a livery stable with a central open area on our right, pulling up in front of the Butterfield Stage Office. Our arrival brought towns-people running from every direction, who crowded around to listen as Mr. Stimpy dramatically informed the agent of all that had befallen us. This caused a great stir. He had to tell it over and over again. Many people rushed back and forth. Some of them, I thought, looked at me strangely as Whit helped me out of the wagon, but no wonder!

A sheriff's deputy escorted the Mosers and me to the hotel, along what was probably the only boardwalk in town. The deputy made sure there were rooms for us and promised our luggage would soon follow.

I had hardly been in my room long enough to wash my face and hands—in the pretty pink and white ewer and basin—and tidy my hair, when a soft knock on the door produced a maid who told me I was wanted in the parlor. I went down, feeling dusty and tired.

Whit stood there with two strange men. Whit seemed ill at ease and was turning his battered hat around in his hands look-ing, I thought with an interior giggle, a little sheepish.

"Miss Carlton," he said with strange formality, "this is Mr. Beemer and Mr. Weems, of the school board."

"Howdy, Miss," they said, almost in unison, removing their hats as well and turning them around and around in their hands, just like Whit. It was clear that everyone here but me was ill at ease. That made me instantly nervous.

"Gentlemen, I am very glad to meet you. I must apologize for being late to our appointment." I offered my hand. We all shook energetically.

"Well, about that..." Mr. Beemer began hesitantly.

"You see, you didn't come." Mr. Weems looked disapproving.

"We thought you changed your mind," Mr. Beemer stated.

"Wouldn't have been the first time!" Mr. Weems nodded in agreement.

"We didn't know about the accident, you see." Mr. Beemer now sounded as if he were apologizing. "Of course, we knew the stage didn't come, but Butterfield's didn't know why."

"They'll be sending a telegram to Butterfield's main office right now," Mr. Weems informed us, cheerfully.

"School started Monday." Mr. Beemer was not cheerful. "And you weren't here. And Mrs. Quimby kindly stepped in and said she'd do it."

"How good of her," I responded, at a loss. Quimby? That name did sound a little familiar.

"We would have asked her in the first place," Mr. Beemer hurried on, "but we thought it was probably too soon, her being such a recent widow and all. But she said no, she needed work to take her mind off of it."

"Makes sense. Her being the teacher before she got married, you see." Mr. Weems was pleased with the appropriateness of it all.

I looked at Whit. He nodded.

"My Aunt Izzie," he confessed.

"So," Mr. Beemer took a deep breath. "We all signed the contract, and she opened the school."

"But we had an agreement!" I protested.

"An agreement, Miss Carlton, not a contract."

"But it wasn't my fault I wasn't here on time! It was the accident!"

"Of course, it wasn't your fault, ma'am, but, neither is it ours. School had to start, and you weren't here. Mrs. Quimby was. And now it's done and done."

I stood transfixed. A contract had been signed. My agreement had only been an expectation. I had been too late for my new life.

"Ma'am, we do not abandon you. Don't think that for a moment." Mr. Beemer was now all compassion and concern.

"Certainly not, after you coming so far!" Mr. Weems seemed to sincerely wish to help.

"You'll be comfortable here at the hotel," Mr. Beemer hurried on. "We'll send off some telegrams of our own, see if we can't find you another school."

They looked at me expectantly. Every thought had been shocked out of my head, but it was clearly my turn to say something.

"Yes, of course. Thank you. You are very kind."

"Until later, then." The two gentlemen bowed, put their hats back on, and left the hotel.

Whit still stood there—definitely sheepish. "Will you be all right, Alta?" he asked. "I feel kinda guilty."

I looked at him, surprised.

"My aunt," he explained.

"Oh, Whit, it's not your fault!" I was surprised I could laugh, but it made me feel better.

"You're taking it real good," he approved. "Something will work out. These're good people. It just may take a while."

Then, he shrugged and turned toward the door. "I got to go out to the ranch. Larry and me, they'll be wondering what happened to us. I'll be around, though." He nodded, put on his hat, and started for the door.

He couldn't be leaving me, not just like that, after all we had been through!

"Whit, wait!" I cried out and ran a few steps after him.

He turned, looking very startled. That pretty much took the starch out of me.

"I..." I faltered. "I don't know your name!" I made a helpless gesture.

He laughed. "It's Charlie. Charles Demont Whitaker, at your service, ma'am." He made a little bow himself, tipped his hat at me, and was gone.

Charles? It wasn't possible! What I had taken for his name was a nickname. Of all the names in the wide world, he bore the one I would least have wanted him to have!

Well, I supposed the world must be full of men named Charles. I wondered inanely how to make Charles a plural word... *Charleses?*

Scolding myself, I tried to govern my thoughts: *What did that matter? What mattered was whether this Charles was about to abandon me, as my first Charles had done. Were any Charleses trustworthy?*

I went to bed troubled, anxious, worried about the future, and so worn out—both emotionally and physically—that I lay down, expecting I would never be able to sleep, and settled in for a long night of tossing and turning. I recall thinking how comfortable the bed was, with its feather comforter and mattress, after so many nights of sleeping on the ground. I must have fallen asleep before I could begin to agonize. I slept the whole night through—possibly without moving.

The next morning, I awoke to the soft cooing of doves under the eaves, drowsing awhile in the sunlight pouring in on me through my window, surprised to feel tranquil and calm. My situation hadn't changed, but it seemed my attitude had. Nothing like a good night's rest! I couldn't seem to summon up much concern. Perhaps, after all, a true *Woman of the West* was emerging, who would face whatever might come and turn it to the best advantage.

My new attitude was surprising, but I assured myself it was based on fact. People were taking care of me. They would find me a new job. Meanwhile, I need not worry about money for a while. Thank goodness I had followed Aunt Adah's sound advice and worn the "traveler's pocket" she had given me. Most of my money stayed on my person night and day while I traveled, in the secret pocket I wore hidden under my garments around my waist. I wondered how to tell my Aunt how sage her advice had been, without giving her hysterics. I might never be able to thank her properly. My lost reticule had contained only a few dollars in change. My main supply of cash remained perfectly safe, and I saw no reason to end a practice that had proven so effective. My money would stay where it was until the time came to open a bank account.

I had no desperate worries and could afford to enjoy myself while I waited for something to happen. I had a whole new town to explore. Surely it would have a good store and a library. That was all I really needed to fill my time. I would be quite happy and occupied.

As to Wh—Charlie, I would miss him while he was gone, and hoped he would return soon. I had only to remember the flash of those blue-green eyes and the two soft kisses to know he cared for me. Based on his competence during the accident and its aftermath, I had no reason to doubt his integrity. A finer man I had never met, nor one so attractive. I had no reason for alarm, and every reason to enjoy myself for what should prove to be a brief vacation.

Truth be told, I also felt a tiny measure of relief. I would not, in the next few days, have to face a schoolroom full of children of assorted ages, trying to match them up to my unread curriculum.

I had never, myself, been entirely confident of the "schoolmarm" role assigned to me, which everyone else seemed to take for granted. Teaching sewing was one thing, the "three Rs" quite another. However, I didn't have to worry about it today. I made a firm decision to wait calmly to see what would happen. I had a little money; I was all right for now. If I was fated for another teaching position, time enough to worry, then.

There was a quiet knock at my door, and the maid opened it and peeked in. Seeing me awake, she shouldered the door wider and entered, burdened with a teapot and cup on a tin tray and also a jug of warm water to replenish my ewer. Wishing me a good morning, she put the tray in front of me on the bed and, opening my window, threw out last night's cold water from the ewer. She shut the window and withdrew, leaving me quite speechless. If I had needed a reminder that I was no longer in New York City, this was a big one! Imagine just dumping water out the window!

I drank my tea, enjoying a little fantasy of indignant shrieks, followed by the angry intrusion of policemen, and a maid hauled off to jail.

I washed and dressed in a fresh, although wrinkled, cotton gown—the last in my trunk—chosen to bring because it buttoned in front. Ready to face the world, I reflected ruefully that at least I did not have to sit down to study the massive curriculum that lay on top of my belongings in the trunk. That should probably go to Whit... no, Charles's Aunt, now.

The maid reappeared and told me I was again wanted in the parlor. Whit stood there, as I had hoped; I flushed with joy to see him.

"Good morning... Mr. Whitaker," I said, teasing him. At

this late date, not much use trying to act like a lady. I felt a fool, but happy.

"Gosh, Alta, you can still call me *Whit*." He grinned.

"No, no, that's not appropriate. It's very embarrassing that I misunderstood," I apologized, more and more flustered.

"Charles, then?"

"I could not possibly call you that!"

"How about Charlie. A few people call me Charlie."

"All right. Charlie." Minimally all right.

"Alta, pack up your stuff. We're going to move you over to Mrs. Hoaglund's Boarding House. Aunt Izzie says you can't stay on here at the hotel, it isn't fitting for a single woman. Anyhow, that was where the school board was meaning to put you up, before. Mrs. Hoaglund's agreeable, and you can stay there until they find you a position. You'll like her. She's a nice lady."

I did like her, as well as the second-floor room she gave me in the back of her three-story frame house. It was on the street behind the hotel, barely a block away. My room, although small and drab, was clean, and the window looked out over some sheds, into the paddock of the livery stables. The horses grazed peacefully amid clumps of tall cottonwood trees, and it was a pretty country scene.

The room was furnished with a bed, a dresser, a small table with two wooden chairs, and one comfortable stuffed armchair, with a lamp on an end table beside it. A large rag rug covered part of the floor. In one corner, sitting on a tin square, was a small coal-burning stove with a scuttle of coal beside it.

For further needs, there was provided a plain ewer and bowl on a corner table and a chamber pot. If one wanted an actual bath, there was a tub room at the end of the second-floor hall, baths to be scheduled ahead, so the maids could carry up hot water. Further accommodations extended to the privy out back, down a boardwalk path somewhat screened by a vigorous honeysuckle vine, a rare and welcome planting.

Mrs. Hoaglund offered breakfast and dinner six days a week. On Sunday: breakfast, and a cold collation set out in the late afternoon. She extended kitchen privileges to me, which she said she offered all of her feminine guests; I was welcome at any time I might wish to make a cup of tea and take it up to my room, assuming there was already a fire in the kitchen stove.

The rent was acceptable. We shook hands. I might not have a job, but I did have my first home. I felt almost independent.

Charlie then took me back to the main street and around the little square, which was quite bare, to a café—O'Toole's Stew House. It was run, he explained, by the widow O'Toole, and always featured three different kinds of stew: beef, lamb (Irish), and a Mexican stew made of beans, beef, onions, and hot chili peppers. He introduced me to Sally, who was hostess, waitress, and cashier all in one; Mrs. O'Toole commanded the kitchen.

"You're the teacher who didn't show up!" Sally greeted me enthusiastically. "Everyone's talking about you. What a horrible trip you had, all the way from New York City, and then blood and guts everywhere!"

I tried to make as light of that, as was decent, given the seriousness of it all, and at last, she allowed us to order.

Despite the name of the place, we did not have to eat stew for breakfast. Sally served us perfectly cooked bacon and eggs, with truly delicious hot biscuits. We both ate heartily, starved after our days of rough living, and soon were chatting comfortably again, all awkwardness gone.

Charlie told me of his family's amazement at his story of our misadventure. He told me his aunt was most distressed about the confusion at the school and would never in the world have taken my job on purpose. She wanted to meet me to apologize in person. Very nice, but I noted to myself she did not offer to step down in my favor.

Then he told me he was going out with his brother, Phillip, after wild mustangs, as had been planned, and would be gone for at least a week or so. After all our hardships and forced camping out, he was going to do more—for pleasure!

After the meal, we went by the hotel and visited for a little with Bilethia and Jake Moser. Her arm was still in a sling but mending well, and he was suffering no aftereffects of his head injury. Butterfield's was sending them on tomorrow morning in a carriage to Albuquerque, where they could pick up a regular coach and continue their journey. It was a restrained goodbye. We had been through an ordeal together but were perfectly aware we would probably never see each other again. Perhaps it was just as well. They seemed to be surprised at my continued friendliness with Charlie, and for my part, I was reminded how little we knew about them, by how cautiously they talked to us, and especially by what they planned in Texas. They were secretive people, but for a while, we had shared the strong bond of survivors.

Whit then escorted me back to Mrs. Hoaglund's, made his little bow, and departed "on business." I did not see him again before he departed on his expedition.

I set myself not to resent his leaving. I have never had any trouble occupying myself. I concerned myself with settling in and finding a place for things that might be needed in the next few days. There was not much sense in completely unpacking the trunk; if a new position were found, they surely would expect me to come at once. What if I had to leave before Wh— Charlie came back from the mountains! That was a truly alarming thought! With great strength of character, I refused even to think about it, and, instead, took an inventory of what possessions I had left.

In truth, I now owned little enough. Minus a chemise, my hat, reticule, and parasol, and all but one petticoat, there was not much left. My traveling suit had been ruined beyond repair. Spattered with blood and dirt, one arm ripped half off, jagged rents in the skirt, torn at the hem—there was no recovering it. I had left it in the dust bin at Martinez Wells, along with my filthy cloak.

My entire wardrobe now consisted of the light dress I was wearing, along with my kid boots, sadly scuffed, and my last remaining petticoat. I had the dark-black serge skirt I used to wear to Carlton & Hodges, which I had worn with a blue gingham blouse to travel from Martinez Wells. Both were badly soiled, but with only a few tears and lost buttons, completely reparable. I had my precious cashmere shawl, a few unmentionables, my stays—which I wished I had lost—and my nightgown and wrap.

At the very bottom of the trunk, wrapped in tissue, was my rose silk bridesmaid dress. Mother had insisted I bring it along since I absolutely had refused to bring the gray silk with mignonettes.

"There may very well be some important occasion where you will be expected to attend as the teacher, and you will need something like this before your dressmaker will have had time to replace your wardrobe," Mother had insisted, with unfailing logic.

I had given in. It took little enough space and my defiance was all used up. From what I have seen, the Western Territories are harsh on clothing, and there will be little call for a fancy dress.

I still had the sewing kit, *Moby Dick* (unread), a tapestry sewing bag containing my needlepoint pillow covers, traveling compactly without stuffing, a sample dolly with wardrobe and patterns, and basic supplies, such as scissors, needles, and embroidery thread. I had my morocco grooming kit.

By some miracle, tucked into a pocket in the kit was a small velvet bag. On the train, I had carried it in my reticule. For no particular reason, when re-packing my trunk in Santa Fe, I had tucked it in with my hairbrush and tooth powder. My reticule no doubt remained at the bottom of the wrecked and bloody coach, along with my hat. Even had the small, velvet bag still been in it, I doubt I would have tried to retrieve it.

My jewelry! Fate must have wanted me to have it. Inside the bag, by the merest chance, was my suite of pearls from the debut, including the silver combs, the drop pearl earbobs from the wedding, and a single strand of garnets with matching ear bobs from my sixteenth birthday. My dowry, one might say.

These things comprised my entire belongings. Not very much with which to start a new life!

Chapter Six

The general store was easy to find; it was across the square from the Stew House: Burke's Mercantile. I opened the door in great anticipation and went in, savoring my first deep breath of familiar air... the scent of wares laid out, waiting to be sold. This store had a strong overlay of leather, saddle soap, and oil, but I saw at once that I was correct. It was a general store.

To the right side, as one entered, was a large section of various leather items, which accounted for the aroma, but also shelves of hardware, containing nails and tools, and of housewares, containing pots, pans, and dishes. The middle space was open, leading to the far wall, which contained a pot-bellied stove, with a bucket of coal beside it, and several comfortable chairs that could be pulled up in front. Even today there was a small fire, perhaps to maintain the large coffee pot occupying the top. There was a counter with a cash register, and against the far wall, a grandfather clock. To the left was a section with many shelves and counters of canned and packaged foods, and a counter of remedies such as cod liver oil, Epsom salts, and bottles of Lydia Pinkham's. All was dimly lit with only a few kerosene lamps, relying mostly on whatever light came in from the front windows.

Peering into the dusk, I drew a second happy breath. At the far left end of the store was a small area that appeared to have yardage and findings.

A jovial gentleman came from the stove to serve me.

"Morning, ma'am! You're the teacher who came after school already started, aincha?"

"I suppose I am," I laughed and offered my hand. "I'm Alta Carlton."

"Pleased to meet you. John Burke." He shook firmly back. "How can I help you, today?"

I explained my immediate sewing needs, and he cheerfully led me off into the maze to the left and measured off a foot of needlework netting. He could show me only a small selection of colors, but he did have basic yellow, blue, and brown, if not all the shadings I might have liked.

As my final purchase, I asked for writing paper, ink, and envelopes, guiltily thinking of all the letters I needed to write, and how little I wanted to write them at present. Mr. Burke took some time looking, but finally produced a small box of stationery and a little pot of black ink. Unthinkable to have packed that in my trunk! What if it had spilled!

"Guess you'll have plenty of time to write letters, what with the stagecoach accident, and then not having a job!" he laughed, good-heartedly, and continued to chuckle while wrapping up my purchases in brown paper, tying them up in string.

"Mr. Burke, could you tell me how to get to the library?" I asked.

"Yes ma'am, just go across the street to the livery stable there, rent you a gig and a horse, and drive on into Albuquerque. Hear tell they got one there." This set him off chuckling once more.

"But what do people do for books?" I asked, truly surprised.

"Cultivate Mrs. Brewster. Old Mr. Wooten Brewster, he's got a heck of a lot of books." This set off another round of chuckles. He seemed extremely good-natured. "Or get a high school kid to borrow you some. They got a library there."

I thanked him for his help and prepared to leave.

"You'll probably meet Mrs. Brewster at Church," he told me. "She'll probably lend you something."

I thanked him once more, politely said I would probably meet her, and left the store. I walked the short block home. Mrs. Hoaglund had a few books on a shelf in her parlor. I found a Bible, an abridged dictionary, and the complete works of Shakespeare in two volumes. I wasn't that desperate. I would have another go at *Moby Dick*.

The late afternoon was spent happily starting my needlepoint pillow, with my chair pulled up to the window, watching the horses outside, and for the first time seeing the shadows and colors of the surrounding red buttes change color as the sun lowered in the sky. The room was quickly becoming like a home to me.

I thought about the problem of my correspondence. I must let my family know I had finally arrived, but I did not plan to tell them about the disaster—it was too much like what they had predicted. It would be even worse that I had forfeited my job. They would no doubt order me to come home straight away! I had no intention of going home. What I would do was in doubt, but that was now the responsibility of the school board, was it not? Let them find a niche for me. I determined to send a telegram to my parents telling them only that I had "safely arrived," and promising a letter to follow when I would not be so busy. Perhaps in a few days, I would have something reassuring to tell them.

When dinnertime arrived, I washed my face, repaired my

hair, and presented myself at Mrs. Hoaglund's boarding house table.

Currently, there were five other residents: four gentlemen and a maiden lady. Mrs. Hoaglund assigned me the chair at her left, at the head of the table, and introduced me as "the teacher who came too late." It was plain they all knew who I was. They were friendly enough but reserved.

The lady was Miss Myra Blodgett, the postal mistress. Two of the men ran the local grange—some kind of granary, I deduced. Mr. Donald Passmore would doubtless be encountered at the bank, where he was the teller. The final gentleman, Mr. Eugene Ignacio, was the telegraph operator. We were quite a select company, except for me. I was a transient.

Mr. Ignacio informed us that his entire output the last few days concerned the stagecoach accident and its repercussions. This latter included me, apparently, and he regaled us with names of the many places the school board had sent inquiries.

I was somewhat surprised at the interest everyone seemed to take in what was, essentially, my private business.

Miss Blodgett assured me a number of letters had also gone out on my behalf. In her opinion, it would all be a wasted effort, since the schools would certainly have started by now, and would be fully staffed already. She hoped I wasn't counting on an immediate situation.

We were served an agreeable dinner of sliced ham and gravy on potatoes, with corn and beets, and apple pie for dessert. We then adjourned to the parlor where Mrs. Hoaglund served coffee, after which Mr. Ignacio entertained us with several musical offerings on his accordion—an instrument completely new to me.

I retired to my room after an unexpectedly social evening, which equaled, in its own way, any of my mother's dinner parties! I wondered if it would be a nightly occurrence.

The next morning, I took breakfast downstairs and, waiting until well after Mr. Ignacio had left for work, followed along to the telegraph office. My brief message merely stated that I had arrived safely, but late, due to a stagecoach delay, and that a letter would follow. I did not promise that it would follow *soon*, but really that was carping. I was not proud of myself, but why alarm people so far away who could not, in any event, do anything to help.

Returning to the boarding house, I sat down to my stitchery. At one, I took advantage of my tea privilege and lunched in my room on tea and biscuits.

Wanting a change, I took out my new stationery and ink, and my old pen, and wrote a long letter to Ellen—the only one of my correspondents I could truly think of as a confidant at this time, young as she was, as she had no contact with any of the others! I would have written to Margaret, but she would be seeing my parents regularly, and given our current estrangement, I would hardly win back her regard by asking her to keep distressing secrets from my family! Although I thought she would keep them if I asked, she was a very forthright person and would despise me for it.

I wrote to Ellen in a vein to amuse her and her ward mates in their cold outdoor fresh air regime, while relieving myself of all I desperately wanted to discuss.

No need to cushion Ellen from the hard facts of life, for she lived with death, much more than I ever would, and the bloody ravages of disease and painful medical procedures.

Not quite thirteen, she was mature beyond her years, the ravages of the *White Death*—as I have heard it called—having stolen her childhood and her family, her younger brother and sister separated from her in other sanatoriums. When her brother died, she had written movingly of missing him, but dwelled on her sister, Daisy, who seemed to be getting better.

Ellen told what had to be told but was always optimistic. I took her for my ideal of letter writing.

So, I wrote honestly but briefly of the accident, deaths, and injuries, and quickly went on to other things—descriptions of Maria's inspirational nursing, and the bravery of a certain "cowboy" who did so much to help us all. I made a comedy of all the rest, waxing indignant about the discomforts of wagon travel and complaining bitterly of sleeping rolled up in a blanket by the fire, which kept spitting embers at you and burned holes in your cover. I accused her of living in the lap of luxury with her lounge on the open-air veranda while I endured such hardship. I quite outdid myself with an account of Mr. Beemer and Mr. Weems, although, in truth, I was absolutely counting on both those gentlemen to get me out of my predicament.

I was sure Ellen would enjoy the letter and thought wistfully of writing a similar one to Margaret, later, when I could be honest with her.

Still thinking of Margaret, I took up *Moby Dick*. I loved the book itself, its small size, the charming line drawings, the gilt-edged pages, the smell of the ink. I dutifully began to read but put it down with alacrity when the dinner bell rang before the end of the first chapter.

Tonight's meal was a pot roast of pork with root vegetables, sugared sliced tomatoes, hot rolls, and a dessert of vanilla pudding. We did not have a concert that night. We had conversation with our coffee in the parlor. This was a most genteel boarding house.

The next morning, I took my letter with me down to breakfast, thinking I could just give it to Miss Blodgett. I am sure she saw the letter, but she did not comment on it. I laid it beside my plate and fidgeted with it during the meal, while she regarded me with an increasingly jaundiced eye. I confess this lady completely daunted me—she seemed so disapproving. I did not want to offend the *postal gods*, nor to ask her to break some *federal law*, so, at the end of breakfast, I confined myself to asking when the post office opened. She grew quite red in the face, answering frostily, "Nine o'clock, of course." As if that put me in my place. No doubt it did, and the whole world knew what I had to ask. In despair, because I could do nothing right, I merely nodded and thanked her. I'm sure my face was bright red, too.

I fled to my room and waited until she had been gone for a full hour before I made bold to walk up the hill on Main Street, to the building I had seen as we drove into town, to mail my offending letter. Handing it through the window into Mrs. Blodgett's hands to be franked was almost as bad as breakfast had been!

Then, relieved, I returned to Burke's Mercantile, and on a happier note, found Mrs. Burke on duty, as well as her friendly husband, who remembered me and introduced me to his wife.

"Myrtle, come here! This is the teacher came a week late! I want you to meet her."

"I was only a little late," I protested, quite tired of this fact always being appended to my name.

"Heavens to Betsy, John, who cares!" she exclaimed compassionately, giving me a warm handshake. "Miss Carlton, is it? Just call me Myrtle."

"I will, if you will call me Alta," I agreed, liking this plump, friendly woman.

The Mercantile was not very busy, and they both seemed inclined to visit.

It seemed she usually helped in the store during the day, slipping away when business was light to do a little housework in their home just behind the store. They had owned the store for some twenty years and were a great font of information about Black Butte.

Mrs. Burke was very kind to me and, when I hinted about my wardrobe problems, she instantly became my adviser. She made a pot of tea and sat me down by the stove to seriously discuss remedies.

Apparently, we were in the *back-of-beyond*. It was not going to be as easy for me to get a new wardrobe as Mother and I had assumed. Although the store carried heavy work clothes, overalls, jackets, and even long johns for men, no women's wear was available anywhere in town.

There were two resident dressmakers. One of them took no new customers, period—unless someone died. I needed to introduce myself at once to the other, Mrs. Sara Farrogot, in the hope she might accept me as a client.

"But what if we are just in the middle of it all and I get a job somewhere far off?" I worried.

"Perhaps Timbuctoo!" Myrtle joked, and we laughed merrily as if it were funny. It wasn't really, it was a predicament. But Myrtle did not see it as a problem.

"She can finish it and ship it to you, wherever you go. You have to have cloths, one way or the other."

Mrs. Burke was right, and she gave me great advice about what a southwestern schoolteacher should be wearing, from long underwear, heavy coats, scarves, and mittens, to woolen stockings and skirts with warm flannel petticoats. She strongly urged a good, solid pair of leather boots, and said the ones I was wearing (my treasured kids) were little better than slippers and wouldn't last a month. It seemed winter here was not going to be much like winter at home. Here, there would be slush, mud, no sidewalks, no central heating, and drafty wooden houses with a privy out back. I should prepare to be cold in a whole new way.

But that could come later. For immediate needs, she generously lent me her dog-eared, much used, ten-year-old copy of

Godey's Ladies Book—to take with me to Sara Farrogot in search of my most urgent need: a new suit and cloak. With luck, I would soon be traveling again, although I did not much want to think about that.

I duly went off to Mrs. Farrogot, armed with the *Book* and a scrap of dark blue serge from Burke stock. That lady received me genteelly but made a great fuss over not knowing me. I explained briefly why I needed new traveling clothes, and that Myrtle Burke had sent me.

Mrs. Farrogot lifted her lorgnette, which hung around her neck, and surveyed me skeptically, raising her left eyebrow. At last, she placed me, disapprovingly: "You must be the school-teacher who didn't come!"

Beginning to dislike her, I admitted it, curbing my tongue, as her services were needed. I explained that, in view of expected travel onward, I needed a suit, cloak, and hat quite soon, as mine had been ruined in the accident.

She drew back as if offended. "Oh, well! I don't do hats, don't-chou-know," she said, raising the eyebrow again. Fascinating.

"Just the suit and cloak, then?" I suggested, trying to keep a pleasant expression.

"I'm very busy right now. I don't see how I could fit you in." She spoke with finality.

I mentioned that, of course, there would be a commission for a rush job. She screwed up her mouth, as if in doubt of my ability to pay. I did realize that I did not look very respectable in my light dress and shoes, with no bonnet or parasol and only one petticoat. Well, she might wonder.

I was tempted to walk out and leave her, but then I would get no clothes. As a sewing project, it was beyond my ability, at least the tailored suit jacket with its lining and trim. I might manage the skirt and cloak, but it would be an ordeal. I'd had enough ordeals lately. Besides, she made me angry, and I was determined to get the better of her.

I drew myself up in true debutante manner and began to speak of New York, Carlton & Hodges, and my dressmakers there, and said that she had been recommended to me as capable of the standards I was used to, although *local* (that was not nice of me, but it just slipped out). Both of her eyebrows went up.

I showed her Myrtle's *Godey's Book*, which proved to be more recent than her own copy (scoring another point), and said I wanted something quite up to date, which could be achieved by only a slight alteration of the design I had chosen. She invited me, at last, to take a cup of tea, leaving me briefly to make it herself. Then, she accepted the book, perusing the illustration with her lorgnette. I explained the change I had in mind.

She drank her tea with her little finger in the air—an affectation I particularly disliked.

We had one nasty little spat. I was determined that the skirt should have no actual bustle, just a suggestion of one. She was horrified. I had traveled in a coach with a lady in a bustle and was not about to inflict that on anyone else, including myself!

Mrs. Farrogot could not be identified with such an unstylish garment; the eyebrow rose again.

I sighed, gathered myself together, and pleasantly reminded her that bustles were definitely going *out* in New York City, as I was sure she knew. I think she did not know this. I casually mentioned places like the Plaza Hotel and St. John's Presbyterian Church and remarked that my own sister's wedding dress had barely a suggestion of a bustle. This was true, but I did not mention that it had been, after all, a morning gown.

Mrs. Farrogot's expression changed from offended, to skeptical, to resigned. Finally, we were agreed.

She took my measurements, exclaiming over my *genteel*

figure, and said that she would, herself, purchase the required yardage of my sample serge at Burke's, adding the cost to my bill (with further commission, no doubt). The trimming, lining, and other findings would be more difficult, but Mrs. Farrogot assured me she would sell me what was needed from her private stock, and that we would "make do, don't-chou-know." The cloak would not be a problem, as she had a supply of heavy brown worsted yarn. She would return Myrtle's book as soon as possible.

I returned to Myrtle at once and she took me off to the back storage room, where she had made herself a more private little corner to serve tea to her friends—she served me not tea but a glass of sherry, to restore me after my ordeal. She wanted to hear the full account, gave everything a comic twist, and we were quite merry. I was beginning to like her very much.

Two farmwives came in and she left me to welcome them. They said they were only looking and she told them to give a holler if they needed help, then returned to pour me a second sherry.

I soon had Myrtle in fits of laughter, putting on the New York airs with which I had subdued my interrogator. I said I had lost all my self-esteem, to find I had to interview to secure the services of a seamstress in Black Butte!

Myrtle thought I was "a card" and said she had never laughed so much in years. She promised that I should have one of her own hats, for goodness sakes, whichever looked better with the suit. I changed my mind about the tea; Myrtle's was better than Mrs. Farrogot's, and she served cookies, which we both needed because we were a little tipsy.

We had a lovely hour together, giggling like two schoolgirls. No little fingers were extended, but we did spend quite some time trying, unsuccessfully, to raise our left eyebrows. We were both hopeless at it.

I stayed much longer than I should have and hoped I had not intruded on her business hours, but Myrtle said she was glad to have found someone she could talk to and urged me to come again tomorrow. I returned to the boarding house feeling I had made a friend.

I did return the next day, and daily after that. Life fell seamlessly into a pleasant world where everyone was devoted to restoring my wardrobe. I endured tedious fittings with the genteel Mrs. Farrogot, followed by hilarious teas with Myrtle—growing more and more fond of that warm-hearted lady. I loved being in the old-fashioned store, watching customers come and go and the hospitable John Burke entertaining friends with coffee by the pot-bellied stove.

Because of the need for haste, I was assigned straight seams and hems on various undergarments. Even Myrtle helped, taking on a pair of pantaloons.

When I was not at the store, I sat by my window, stitching away at a flannel petticoat and watching the cottonwood trees begin to turn color. Myrtle pointed out that it was growing cold. She and I sat closer to the stove in her backroom retreat. She warned me that, although the days continued crystal clear with the glorious sun pouring over the red dirt road and the red hills, it would soon begin to freeze at night as autumn came on.

When my fingers needed a rest, I reached for *Moby Dick*, but it never held my attention and soon I would fling it away in exasperation. I desperately needed reading material, but Black Butte had very little, and I had yet to meet the elusive Mrs. Brewster.

Once again, Myrtle came to my rescue. One morning she greeted me with great excitement.

"See what I found," she cried, showing me an old trunk she had discovered in the back of the storeroom. It was full of dusty books. I fell on my knees in rapture, rooting around and pulling out one old friend after another. Here was reading material for at least a year! I borrowed several for a start, and in no time was running through Eastern hardwood forests with *Natty Bumpo*, while *Jane Eyre* waited impatiently for me on the table and the *Bennet Sisters* went for a long walk.

The time passed pleasantly, and I remained strangely insulated from concern. I should have been overcome with guilt about the letters I had not written. My nights should have been sleepless with concern over my situation, but I was strangely serene, waiting contentedly in Black Butte—not so much for a job, I suppose, but for Charlie to come home.

Somehow, it became October and nothing had happened. Charlie did not come home. Mrs. Hoaglund took me to church on Sundays and I began to meet some of the townspeople. I made my daily rounds. I sewed, I read, and dined well at Mrs. Hoaglund's table.

I daydreamed, staring out my window, picturing Charlie camping in the mountains with his brother, making friends with wild horses and cooking beans over a small fire.

I tried to imagine the Whitaker Ranch, shaded with spreading canopies of cottonwood trees and filled with galloping steeds, who looked much like the Butterfield horses grazing outside my window, and sheep like flocks of the fluffy white clouds grazing in the sky.

The leaves on the cottonwoods had all turned gold against that indescribably blue sky. Coronado had searched the Southwest for gold but had not found it. How could he have missed it when it was right here outside my window?

Several times, Mr. Beemer called on me—not to report any progress, no surprise, but to promise me that both he and Mr. Weems were dedicated to my welfare and that "something would turn up." I probably should have contacted Mr. Brown at Odyssey West but did not. I suspect I feared he was such a man of action that he would have responded with a new position in, say, Montana by return telegram, and here I was, with my foolish heart, unwilling to leave Black Butte. I needed to be here when Charlie came home.

My new *Sunday Best* chemise was done. I wrapped it up in a square of cloth and went to show Myrtle how well the embroidered roses had turned out.

In the midst of pouring my tea, Myrtle suddenly rose, made a strange, alarming sound, and fell forward, smashing the tea table and landing on the floor amid shattered cups and saucers, scalding tea, and little cakes.

I cried out for help and John Burke came running to the back room, followed by two of his friends. He rushed to Myrtle's side, lifting her head, and supporting her back. She was conscious but irrational, muttering inaudibly and having trouble moving.

John picked her up without apparent effort, then carried her out the back door and across the little courtyard toward their house, calling instructions as he went. Fred, the clerk, was to watch the store, while Biggers, the handyman, was to run for the doctor. I followed along behind to give a woman's support, opening and shutting doors. We climbed stairs to their back door, then climbed more to reach the second floor. John put her down on their bed.

Finding a bottle of lavender water on Myrtle's dressing table and wetting the hankie I carried always in my pocket, I sat, doing the thing I did best: cooling her temples with scent and murmuring reassurances. It was the handkerchief Ellen had made me, my great treasure. I thought of friends and illness and separation and tried not to cry.

John told me there had been a stroke last year, a small one with no apparent aftereffects. He feared this was another. When Doctor Grigg arrived, he confirmed that diagnosis but warned that this time she would not get off so easily. He was quickly proven correct.

Myrtle's left side was affected; she had difficulty moving her left arm and leg, and the left side of her face was drawn downward, making her eye droop, and giving her a strange "up-down" smile. For she did try to smile, but we were not reassured. Her speech was terribly garbled.

Of course—I stepped in to help at the store.

Chapter Seven

W e made Myrtle as comfortable as possible and Dr. Griggs arranged for a live-in nurse.

Betty was one of several young, local women he was training in that capacity. She came to us that very evening from a nearby farm, carrying her valise, and took charge of house and patient with warm and Maria-like competence.

Doctor Griggs was also training several young men, one or another of whom usually accompanied him wherever he went, learning medical procedures. Naturally, they would have to have some years of formal training in Denver or back East before they could assume the title, but he was giving them a start. Doc hoped that one young man, currently training in Chicago, would join him in his practice in a few more years. He desperately needed the help and was overwhelmed with patients. There often were serious emergencies—accidents not just in town, but on the surrounding farms and ranches. He went wherever he was called, to difficult childbirths, illnesses such as Myrtle's, and even gunshot wounds.

John was distraught and wanted to be with Myrtle every

moment, but the store needed to be kept open. The needs of the town did not stop because the proprietor was having a personal emergency. Fred seemed the more competent of the two clerks, but he was horrified at the idea of being in charge of anything. John tried to run the store, yet at the first free moment would rush back to the house to be with Myrtle— leaving the cash register untended and chaos looming.

The solution was perfectly plain to me, but John found my offers to help in the store annoying and brushed them aside for the first few days. At last, in complete frustration, I brought him my letter of recommendation from Miss Bailey. He glanced at it. Then, he sat down and read it over. He looked at me and read it again. "I've heard of Carlton & Hodges."

"John," I said gently, "I know everyone here thinks of me as a schoolteacher, but what I really am is a trained dry goods clerk. Beyond that, I learned a lot about business in my father's store. I can help you here."

"But the cash register. The men customers..."

"I did all that at Carlton & Hodges. Let me help."

He finally did, of course, because he wanted to be with Myrtle. The first day, he looked over my shoulder every moment, but after I had helped a housewife find a new kettle, and another to the correct packets of rice and beans, and especially as I greeted an imposing rancher inquiring about belts— and courteously put him into Fred's competent hands—John began to relax.

He saw that I could write up a sale and make change. He saw I knew, in general, where items might be located. In between trips to check on Myrtle, he saw me tidy the counters. Finally, he allowed that I could do it and after that, spent most of each day with Myrtle—generally, I believe, getting in Betty's way.

Fred was a big help to me and entirely willing to let me be in charge. Biggers, it soon became clear, was mostly useful for moving heavy items, loading up wagons, running errands, and sucking on peppermint sticks. We all got along very well.

At the end of the first week, John quietly suggested that I should be paid a salary, just as Fred and Biggers were.

"Does that mean I am an employee here?" I asked, quite pleased.

"I don't know," he responded. "I suppose so, for now. Temporarily. Let's see how everything works out."

That seemed fair enough to me. And after that, he paid me in cash weekly, just as he did the other two. It was enough to pay my board and room with as much again left over, and I was satisfied. It was a good salary; one I could live on.

Nothing more was said about "temporarily", and I certainly wasn't going to bring it up.

We worked out a routine that suited all of us. I came in at eight in the morning; the trusted possessor of a key, I let myself in and built up the fire to warm the great cavern. Second priority was to fill the huge pot with water (at the pump located outside the back door) and put coffee on to boil. At eight-thirty, Fred got the store ready to open and Biggers emptied the ash and clinker bin under the stove and brought in more coal.

Then they tidied the storeroom by opening up any crates or boxes we thought might be needed during the day, while I opened the safe to get out change for the cash register and double-checked the rest of the store. At nine, I unlocked the doors, and Burke's was open for business as usual—never in twenty years disappointing its customers.

At noon, I lunched on cheese and crackers, and John came in to help while Fred and Biggers, who worked a ten-hour day, took an hour off for rest and a meal. John stayed in the store during Myrtle's afternoon nap but went back to her as soon as it was over. At six, Fred and Biggers went off for an hour-and-a-half meal break. Fred was married and went home, Biggers was *not*, and I assumed he spent his break in one of the four saloons since he always came back to work smelling of beer. John relieved me with just enough time to get to Mrs. Hoaglund's for dinner at six-thirty. She frowned on late arrivals.

John, with the help of Fred and Biggers, finished off the evening, which I understood was usually less business and more of a social event, as a group of long-accustomed regulars dropped in to chat and drink coffee in front of the stove (with extra chairs from the back), gossiping and telling yarns. They called it "discussing the news of the day." At nine, John would evict his cronies, and he, Fred, and Biggers would sweep the store, tidy things, bank the fire, and lock up for the night.

I was not at all concerned about my job not being permanent. The Burkes needed me, even if they did not yet know it, and I was sure I could make myself indispensable. From the first moment in Burke's, I had felt at home, and my head was full of ideas to increase business. Anyone could see the store was hopelessly old-fashioned. Of course, it was not my business to modernize Burke's or make suggestions. For now, it was enough to keep the store running. Still, I couldn't help reorganizing a shelf or two.

Evenings were my own, but I often returned to visit with Myrtle until the store closed and John came home. Her speech grew clearer, but she still lost words and was distressed while she tried to remember. Her left side was weak and she needed Betty's help to move around. Betty and I would ensconce her in a comfortable chair, surrounded by pillows and warm throws, and then I would amuse her with tales of customers. Fortunately, Myrtle was right-handed; we could sew together and often played card games, always finding something to laugh about. Betty said company was the best medicine Myrtle could have and thought the card games were especially good. Betty firmly insisted that we should encourage Myrtle to keep searching for her lost words instead of supplying them ourselves. Myrtle did improve, steadily.

Now I felt free to write the letters that had been put off for so long. To my parents, I wrote a minimal account of the accident and the loss of my teaching position, making light of the intervening weeks of uncertainty. That out of the way, it was easy to give a glowing account of Burke's Mercantile and how lucky I felt that my time at Carlton & Hodges had prepared me for it. I made it clear that, in my opinion, I would be much better at this work than I ever would have been in a classroom. Then, I changed the subject and dwelled more lengthily on my genteel boarding house and my complete satisfaction with Black Butte in general.

To Margaret, I penned a little more exciting, although still edited, account of my adventures. While not mentioning anyone in particular, I did make it clear that "one man of the party" had been quite admirable, and I'm afraid I did rhapsodize about campfires, sunsets, and skies full of Western stars.

I wrote to Miss Bailey to thank her for the training that had prepared me to seize my opportunity, and much enjoyed describing to her a Western version of Carlton & Hodges— bemoaning for her amusement its various shortcomings, but making it clear I was much happier here than I would have been in a schoolroom.

I never wrote of people screaming, blood on my skirt, running out of water, tearing up petticoats for bandages, or waking in the middle of the night weeping for Mr. Danvers, who had called me "honey." And I certainly never wrote of any particular sheepman—who was surprisingly still absent.

Feeling quite virtuous after each overdue letter was written, I promptly walked my correspondence to the post office and handed it over to a frowning Myra Blodgett. Surely, I need not take her frowns personally; why should she care how many letters I wrote? Was there some unwritten law governing each person's share of the US mail? If so, I had never heard of it. Yet, each time I arrived, Miss Blodgett made it clear she thought I was up to no good with all these letters.

Mrs. Farrogot belatedly finished my traveling suit and I began, perforce, to wear it to the store. Mr. Beemer came into Burke's and delicately mentioned that he had heard I was working here, and how long did I mean to continue?

I lowered my eyelashes and cautiously replied, "For the interim."

"I see," he said and went away.

It was colder now, and the beautiful, golden cottonwood leaves were falling in splendor on the ground. The sky turned a *different* indescribable shade of blue. The red cliffs and buttes outside of town could be seen in a dozen different hues as the day progressed: crimson at dawn, pinks and reds throughout the day, changing into mauve at dusk. And then, the stars came out.

Today, frost crunched on dry grass and the wooden walkway was slippery as I went to the store. It was time to start wearing my cloak; a shawl was no longer enough. I was glad for the banked heat of the stove as I quickly built up the fire and put the coffee on. Fred and Biggers came. At nine, I opened promptly.

There were no customers at first, so I leaned against the cash register, surveying *my domain* with satisfaction. This was quite different from being at Carlton & Hodges—missing all the elegance and the army of clerks, but in its own way better. It was flattering to be in charge and to feel confident that whatever might turn up today could be handled without much trouble. My new life was entirely to my liking. There was just one thing...

A customer was coming in. I moved out in greeting—somewhat blinded by the sunlight pouring through the door.

"Well, I swan! A person can't go anyplace without running into you!" said a familiar voice.

"Wh—Charlie!" I exclaimed. "Where have you been?"

"Roping horses. Where did you think I was?"

"You said a week!"

"I said 'more or less' a week. Guess it was more." He sobered and there blazed that spark from his eyes. There was more blue than I had remembered. "Did you think I wasn't coming back?"

"I... I didn't know," I admitted. As always, I felt a slight confusion when I was with him and was always a little lost for words, which no one who knew me would ever have believed.

"What are you doing here at Burke's? I thought you'd be long gone, onto some new schoolmarm job."

I was taken aback by this remark. It sounded almost as if he had wanted me to be gone. What a strange idea! "No," I said, trying for coolness. "No, they never came up with one. This is my new job."

"You, Alta? A dry goods clerk?"

"That's what I was in New York. Remember?" I may have flounced a little.

He looked at me levelly. "Bet Carlton & Hodges was a lot fancier than this."

At least he recalled the name! "Can I help you with something?" I asked as if he were a customer.

"Don't be mad at me, Alta. Time kind of gets away from you out in the mountains. And we got some real good horses."

"That makes it all right, then, I guess." Cool was effective. I tried for aloof. "Can you come and have lunch with me?"

"Of course I can't. I'm working."

"Dinner, then?"

It was not possible to go on pretending I wasn't glad to see him. I was more than glad. I let out the entire smile I had been trying to stifle.

"Dinner would be very nice," I admitted.

He smiled back, and I thought my heart would leap out of my mouth. So I closed it, lowered my eyelashes, and looked at him through them. He laughed aloud. I guess he knew a flirt when he saw one.

He did take me to dinner—picking me up at the store at six and walking me around the plaza to O'Toole's. I had lamb stew and he had chili. Mrs. Hoaglund was not pleased with me when he returned me to the boarding house.

"I expect my guests to be present for meals unless they have notified me in advance," she scolded, tartly. "It is very inconsiderate and wasteful, as it affects the amount of food I need to serve."

I apologized profusely, if not entirely genuinely, and promised not to do it again.

The next few weeks were a happy time. I never knew when Charlie would appear, but I saw him nearly every day, if only to step into the store and tease me out of my "businesslike manner," or insist for my opinion of Dr. Carter's Little Liver Pills, which he swore he thought might help his horse.

Once, he brought news of Buck from an itinerant pot-mender who had come through from Martinez Wells. The leg was off, and Buck was furious about that but getting better. Doc Von Hagen was whittling a wooden peg for him and expected Buck would be back riding stage by Christmas.

I went to church with Mrs. Hoaglund; Charlie was there in

the back row, holding a songbook—singing lustily. I fancied I could hear his voice above all others.

He took me for lunch afterward and then for a *spin* in his little, black surrey, with red fringe across the top, out of town into the canyonlands—full of fall beauty, with aspen turned to liquid gold and the invigorating crisp cold air.

One evening he called on me at the boarding house—after dinner while we were all in the parlor, accordion again—and took me for a dusk walk around the little town, telling me who lived where. We had coffee at O'Toole's and talked and talked.

When he brought me back, Mrs. Hoagland was still sitting up in the parlor. I was surprised since she usually retired to her own room after the parlor hour. Tonight, she joined us uninvited, and we all three sat and chatted. I kept wishing she would leave, but in the end, it was Charlie who did, bidding us both goodnight and heading back to the livery stable for his horse. Mrs. Hoaglund remarked that it would take him at least an hour to ride back to the Whitaker Ranch and that she was quite surprised he would stay in town so late in the evening. Did she think I needed a chaperone? How presumptuous! I was angry at her and disappointed. If she had not been there—he might have kissed me again.

The next week, the stagecoach began running again, the road having finally been cleared between Dewar's and Martinez Wells. It caused great excitement in town and currents of news began to flow once more. After the fact, we learned that Mr. and Mrs. Bysbee had been on the first stagecoach, staying overnight at the hotel and leaving early the next morning. Personally, I was just as glad not to see Eulalia again, but I rather liked Mr. Bysbee and it would have been nice to know their plans.

Charlie took me to the café for dinner twice that week, carefully prearranged with Mrs. Hoaglund, of course! Charlie always had the chili, but I was too cautious to try it. Sweat poured off his brow as he ate it, praising every spoonful, and he drank glass after glass of water, all the same, declaring it the best chili he had ever had.

The second night he insisted I try, if only a taste. Against my better judgment, I did—and regretted it at once! I could tell there were marvelous new flavors, but all I could feel was pain, from just one bite! I needed two glasses of water and had to wipe my brow with my dainty, lace-edged hanky.

I must have left that handkerchief at the café, although Sally couldn't find it the next day. It was a great loss, but I was so happy, I didn't mourn it long.

Mrs. Hoaglund accepted my dinner excuses but seemed to disapprove. I didn't care. Any time I could spend with Charlie was golden, and Mother was not here to criticize my manners!

Myrtle's health improved daily. Doctor Griggs prescribed a temporary housekeeper. Betty moved home and only came in to help with exercises to increase strength in her left side. Myrtle hated the exercises but loved the idea of a housekeeper.

John hired one of Betty's younger sisters to come as a live-in housekeeper and cook. Although only seventeen, Virginia Kinney proved both competent and a good cook. Myrtle began coming into the store in the late mornings, just to observe and enjoy. We made her comfortable, close to the main stove, and she visited with anyone who came in, her speech almost normal again.

To pass the time, I mentioned a few of my ideas for improvements and was surprised by the enthusiasm of her response. However, she warned me John was not open to change. A few years ago, she, herself, had talked him into a greater variety of stock of interest to women, but the things had not sold, and John had said that proved she was wrong.

Myrtle told me she thought John's resistance came from the

fact that he saw Burke's as primarily a *man's* store. She still held out hope for the future.

"Things are changing. He hired you! It's not just that we needed more help, you're good at selling and you're an elegant young woman. More ladies have started coming in. John knows it. He mentioned it to me and said he could see they liked you to wait on them."

A little embarrassed by this praise, I tried to raise my eyebrow at Myrtle. I practiced the eyebrow whenever I could, but it wasn't really happening. I must have looked grotesque. She laughed at me, sputtered a bit, having lost the word, and then said conclusively, "Don't-chou-know!" Our *un-business-like* giggles caused John to frown at us.

That was the closest any Burke came to telling me my job was to be considered permanent—but it was enough for me.

That evening, I wrote a short note to Mr. Beemer thanking him for his efforts on my behalf but giving him permission to stop looking for a teaching position, as I had decided to remain permanently at Burke's.

Joyously, I told Charlie of my decision when next I saw him. I declared myself a full-fledged citizen of Black Butte. He welcomed me to the ranks, saying we would celebrate by going someplace *very special.* He would not tell me where, saying it must be a surprise! Aroused by curiosity, he talked me into playing truant from church on Sunday in order to get an early start.

As appointed, he arrived in front of the boarding house at dawn in the little surrey. I crept out quietly, so as not to awaken anyone, and we were off as the glorious autumn sun came up, shushing each other with all the glee of escaping children.

We drove across the drylands and up into the hills on a side road, and then into a fairy-tale canyon paradise, where red rock walls grew closer and closer, encasing the water of a stream clear as Mother's Waterford glass. We put down a horsehair blanket on a great flat rock beside it and picnicked on bread and cheese and sweet, clear water. I could not resist; no matter how unladylike it was: I made him turn his back while I divested myself of shoes and stockings so that I could wade in the water. It was melted ice!

Lovely little pebbles were everywhere. I picked up a small round stone, as green as jade. Charlie said it was mountain jade. Another rock, a deep, reddish-brown, he found and gave to me, calling it jasper. Did he see that it was in the shape of a heart? A third was a clear shard I could see through. Quartz crystal, he said. Treasures—to keep forever.

We lazed the afternoon away, driving home slowly in the dusk. It was full dark before we got back, and I had missed Mrs. Hoaglund's dinner yet again, but it was only the cold meal set out on Sunday, and it didn't matter. We went to the O'Toole's where Sally made us feel at home.

When we could no longer make excuses to stay on drinking coffee, Charlie dropped me back at the boarding house and drove reluctantly off. I ran up the steps full of the happiness of the day, clutching a little bunch of wilted wildflowers I had picked—my precious rocks safe in my pocket—to find Mrs. Hoaglund frowning at the bottom of the stairs.

"Where have you been off to all day, may I ask, Miss Carlton?"

"Charlie took me to Coldwater Canyon," I almost stuttered, taken aback. "It was so beautiful..."

"Well, another time you might tell someone where you are going. I didn't know if I should be worried about you or not. I guess maybe I should be worried."

I placated her, promising to keep her informed in the future, and brushed it off. I ran upstairs to put my flowers in a glass of water and my precious gemstones in my jewelry bag.

People certainly caused themselves endless trouble by intruding into other people's business! She was, after all, only my land-lady. I was not accountable to her for every little thing I did.

I put her meddling out of my mind. She would not be allowed to spoil the ending of the best day of my life!

Chapter Eight

That beautiful day was the last of the good weather. Fall came on in a serious way. It grew much colder and was cloudy and gloomy. People began to talk about snow.

I also began to hear of a great event planned for the end of October. There was to be a Harvest Festival—a dance held in the basement of the church. Charlie said that everyone would be attending, and he would meet me there.

Mrs. Hoaglund said it would be the social event of the year. By the time Christmas came, we might either be snowed in or too cold to go anywhere!

The fete was to begin with a potluck, to which all the ladies would be bringing their best dishes, followed by music and dancing until quite late—perhaps even until after midnight! It sounded very exciting.

"But what can I bring?" I worried. "I would have to use your kitchen, but I can't really cook, anyway."

"Not a problem at all, dear. I'm sure nobody would be expecting you to cook. I'll be making a big meatloaf; more than enough to be the share of all of us here at the house. But it would make a good impression for you to bring something. You may have the last of my tomatoes getting ripe on the windowsill, here. You can slice them on a plate, sprinkle on a little salt and sugar, and people will like it very well."

I thanked her profusely—glad to be back, apparently, in her good graces. She had always been more than kind to me. I resolved to be a better boarder and not miss any more dinners.

The matter of what to wear to the gala was more serious. I consulted Myrtle. Of course, she and John were planning to go, although there would be no dancing for Myrtle—doctor's orders.

"It will be a joy just to watch everyone else," she enthused.

As to dress, she thought a skirt and white blouse would be fine, or perhaps the navy and green plaid wool with the white collar and cuff, but that was what I wore every week in the store, hardly festive. Vowing to discard the memories of when I had last worn it, I confessed that I did have another option and told her of my dark pink carnation silk. She insisted I bring it to the store and model it for her. I was afraid it would be too dressy, for I certainly did not want anyone to think I was being *New York*, but Myrtle had no such reservations.

"This is lovely, and very appropriate," she insisted. "It will be a treat for people to see it. Look at this cunning apron-draped front, and hardly any bustle at all!"

On that exciting Saturday night, for once, John shut the store early so that we could all attend the potluck. I walked the few blocks over to the Ecumenical Church with Mrs. Hoaglund, feeling very grand in my almost-bustle-less dress, in my new cloak, proudly carrying Mrs. Hoaglund's good blue platter, layered with beautiful sliced red tomatoes and covered with one of her best dish towels.

The church basement was crowded with a surprising number of people. The Harvest Ball was non-denominational, as was the church, so even the Catholics and non-believers came

—as Mrs. Hoaglund joked. It was an event looked forward to every fall.

The large basement social room was festive—decorated with autumn leaves, pumpkins, and corn shocks. At the near end of the hall, as we came in, a long table held a punch bowl with cups and other liquid refreshments in pitchers: buttermilk, cold tea, cider, and water. Mrs. Hoaglund whispered that if I watched, I would see men going in and out of the hall very frequently.

"There'll be plenty of whiskey out back," she laughed, "and everyone pretends not to notice, as if we all don't know what they're doing out there! Never you mind, I'll give you a glass of sherry when we go home!"

The middle of the hall was closely lined with rows of benches and long trestle tables covered in white cloths that looked suspiciously like sheets. At the far end, six long tables were weighted down with more food than can possibly have ever been assembled in one place before.

The first table started with salads of every kind: potato, macaroni, aspic, canned fruit, even one green salad—surprising this late in the year. This was followed by rolls, biscuits, and loaves of sliced bread, with mounds of butter and a least a dozen kinds of jams, jellies, and preserves. Then came platter after platter of meats: ham, fried chicken, roast turkey, and beef, and varieties of game: venison, pheasant, rabbit, and duck. There were meat pies and Mrs. Hoaglund's truly monumental meatloaf. Then came dishes of assorted vegetables: beets sliced in sour cream, green beans with onions and bacon, potatoes in cream sauce with peas, mashed potatoes, scalloped potatoes, and sweet potatoes. Around the edges were dishes of pickles, relishes, crab apples steeped in red sugar water, applesauce, and I'm sure much more that I missed.

All this bounty, and yet to come were the deserts: cakes, pies, puddings, cookies, and sweets beyond my familiarity.

I ate it all with my eyes and was so full there couldn't possibly be room for one bite of actual food!

Then, Charlie was there. He came to me with two glasses of punch and walked me along the food tables, hilariously describing the various dishes and speculating on who had made them. He warned me off several delicious-looking casseroles, saying of one, "That's Sada Martin's black beans and rice. Do not touch even one bean of that! I'm serious! Last year three people got deathly ill, and they had to call Doc. I'm surprised she had the nerve to bring it again!"

I was sure this was completely spurious and was laughing so hard, I was afraid I would spill my punch.

Then he took me to a woman pouring herself a glass of cider at the punch table, saying, "Alta, this is my Aunt Izzie!"

She was tall with erect posture, and perhaps five years older than me. Very dignified, she wore her blonde hair in a complex braid on top of her head and was what most people would call *a fine figure of a woman*. I thought she was the perfect picture of a schoolteacher.

"Isobel Quimby, Miss Carlton," she corrected Charlie, warmly taking my hand. "I'm so pleased to meet you at last! And so sorry for what happened about the school! I should have made my apology sooner, but..."

"Please, don't think of it," I interrupted her. "It turned out for the best. Burke's is the perfect place for me. That's my training, you see. I'm not at all sure I would have made a good teacher!"

"I'm so glad you are satisfied," she beamed. "I wouldn't like to feel you were thinking evil thoughts of me for stealing your job! And, of course, then I could never have gone into Burke's again!"

We laughed. That was a pretty picture, indeed! I began to like her.

"However, I do think you sell yourself short. You would probably have made a fine teacher in the end. Most of us are quite green when we start. I, myself, barely got through my first week, back when I was twenty. It was very bad until some of the older children imposed a kind of discipline over the boisterous ones—until I could learn to do it for myself."

Her whole demeanor was so commanding, that was hard to imagine. "I apologize to you. I had meant to bring you the curriculum the school board sent me, but I never did."

"It's of no matter at all," she assured me. "I still have my own from before." Then she stepped nearer and said confidentially, "Charles told me you were splendid during the stagecoach accident. He said you are one of the few sensible women he has ever met."

I blushed and tried to turn the compliment aside. "It was Charlie who was splendid," I protested. "He saved us, got us out of the coach. Mr. Stimpy had all he could handle with the horses!"

Charlie gave me a little hug around my shoulders. "Perhaps we saved each other," he said.

Then everyone began to line up for dinner, and Charlie hurried us both to take a place before it became too long. The wait could have seemed unending, but Charlie kept us laughing, and there was so much to talk about, in no time at all until we had arrived at the food.

There was more laughter—trying to fill our plates without appearing too much the glutton. We sat together to eat, and everything was delicious.

The enormous meal went on for nearly two hours. We all went back for seconds. I was glad I had not resumed the practice of wearing my stays and wondered if anyone really could tell.

Actually, tonight, I didn't care if they could. I would hardly have been able to eat anything at all if I had kept them on! My dress was a little tight as it was, without the compression of whalebone, and I had opened several buttons in the vicinity of the waist—covering the gap with my shawl.

Charlie complimented me, in a way, saying, "I like a woman who really eats. All these ladies who have one little chicken wing and say they're full; they're too delicate for me!"

I lifted my eyebrow at Isobel—I was getting better at it, at last. She raised her own, we laughed together. She and I both would pass Charlie's test. I judged she was wearing stays, but not pulled in very tightly at all. Both of us were women who ate!

When people could eat no more, the church ladies cleared the tables and a group of men took away the trestles and used the benches to line the walls.

A small platform was put up where the food had been, and our musicians for the night began to prepare.

"Look," I pointed out to Charlie, "it's Mr. Ignacio from the boarding house!" And, indeed, he was there with his accordion, along with a small man whose heavy beard was almost as big as his violin, and a third man whose instrument looked for all the world like a washboard. Charlie assured me that was exactly what it was.

They began to play, and Charlie excused us to his aunt and swept me away into a polka. After that, we danced a Virginia reel. There were so many people dancing, we made eight full sets!

After that, Charlie said, "I must not hog your time. Lots of people will want to dance with you, since you're new." He looked at me very seriously. "Don't say 'no' to anybody, Alta. It doesn't matter if you know them or not—not at a dance like this. I don't know how they do it in New York, but here it really makes a man feel like a loose wheel when he comes across the room in public to ask a woman to dance and then she says no. Also, people would think you're stuck up, which you are not in the least. Have a good time." Then, he gave me a little bow and went off to dance with Isobel.

I looked around for a place to sit, being quite out of breath despite no stays, and saw John and Myrtle nearby with an empty chair beside them. I hurried to claim it.

"You look like you're having a good time," John beamed at me.

"The best time ever!" I enthused, fanning myself with my hand. To Myrtle, I said, "You were right about the dress, it's perfect. I don't feel too dressed up. And I'm certainly not cold!"

Myrtle looked at me a little strangely, I thought, although it was sometimes hard to read her expressions, now. There was still stiffness in her facial muscles.

"I didn't realize you knew Charles Whitaker," she said. "But of course, you do, from the stagecoach."

"Yes," I agreed. "He introduced me to his aunt, Mrs. Quimby, the schoolteacher. I like her very much."

"Yes, very nice, indeed." Myrtle concurred. And then we talked of other things.

Several gentlemen did ask me to dance and, honoring Charlie's advice, I accepted all of them. First was Mr. Passmore, from the boarding house. He steered me around the floor, perspiring profusely, and as I thanked him for the dance afterward, I feared we would be teased tomorrow by the others at the dinner table. However, one after the other, the two grange men claimed my hand: Mr. Watson and Mr. Peeples. Mr. Peeples trod on my toes three times. After he brought me back to my seat, he bowed and retreated; Myrtle whispered to me that he was a married man, but several years ago his wife had gone to visit her family in Omaha and never returned—poor man.

"Perhaps it was because of his dancing," I commented, and we giggled. I thought Myrtle was going to say something else, but she didn't.

After that, I danced with the deputy sheriff, Mr. Rowley; then a tall, thin lawyer named Matthew Spencer; then a very small elderly man who identified himself only as "Artie," and Fred, from the store.

Myrtle made John take me out for a square dance. "At least I can enjoy watching you," she said, "if I can't do it, myself!"

This was a new dance to me, although I had heard of it. John was a good teacher, the steps were actually simple, and soon I was *do-se-do-ing* with the best of them. I enjoyed it all.

Near midnight, Charlie came for me again and took me off for a set of waltzes. Charlie was an excellent dancer—very smooth. This should not have surprised me. I had seen him ride, after all, blending with the horse as one being. Charlie would never step on my toes, but the waltz was especially suited to his style, and we made excellent partners. I wanted it to go on forever. It was, for me, the high point of a wonderful evening.

When the waltzes were, sadly, over, he took me to the punch bowl. We were both quite thirsty. He regarded me solemnly for a few moments, then finished off his punch and set the glass down.

"Alta, I have to go now," he said. "Izzie's ready to leave. Thank you for the dances. It was incredibly special."

"It was," I agreed.

He made me his little bow and abruptly left with Isobel.

I walked home with Mrs. Hoaglund, carrying the now-empty blue platter and telling myself I had nothing to complain of. It would have been lovely if he had walked me home, and he had clearly regretted that too, but he had family obligations.

Looking up at the bright stars, for it was clear tonight, I compared this rustic *ball* to the night of my debut. So much money had been spent on that other occasion, so much fuss: the flowers, the gowns and jewelry, the large band, the lessons, the choosing of escorts. All for an evening that had been a dutiful ordeal—in no way a highlight in my memory. I never even thought about it, except to occasionally wonder what Percy was doing.

This evening had cost no one anything more than the food and drink they had been glad to share with their friends. Yet they had all enjoyed every minute of it. As had I.

As promised, Mrs. Hoaglund did give me a glass of sherry, and she only teased me a little about "dancing with all the gentlemen of the house." I went off to bed with my head full of music, and in my dreams, I waltzed with Charlie.

The next few evenings were spent writing more letters home, even though the first batch was barely on its way. I wrote in great detail about the Harvest Ball and even allowed myself to hint at a special dancing partner. I wrote glowingly of my new life in this beautiful place, new friends, and surrey rides out into the countryside.

I even wrote to Odyssey West informing Mr. Brown of my current employment so that they could correct their records. I wanted to be sure they understood they had miscast me and that being a schoolteacher was not the height of everyone's ambition.

Charlie was not at church Sunday morning. I expected to see him Monday, but he did not even come into the store.

On Tuesday evening, Mrs. Hoaglund came to my door to tell me Charlie was waiting for me in the parlor. I was pleased, although I thought he might have come to see me sooner, and ran happily down the stairs. Mrs. Hoaglund followed, looking severe, but I paid her no attention.

"Well, I'll leave you to it," she said and closed the parlor doors. We could hear her walking away down the hall.

"Charlie, where have you been? I was longing to see you!" I gave him a hug.

He guided me to a chair. "Alta, sit down. I have to talk to you."

"So solemn!" I teased. My mood was light as air today.

"Alta, I had a visitor this afternoon, out at the ranch—it was John Burke."

That was surprising. John had been out of the store most of the afternoon, he often did that now, but why would he go all the way out to Whitaker's?

"Alta, he practically had a horsewhip with him, and if he had, he would'a been in the right. I haven't acted decent by you."

"Charlie, what are you talking about? Why would Mr. Burke talk to you about me?"

"Well, Alta, that's the point. He figures he's kind of like a parent for you here, him being your employer. His place to speak up."

"Charlie, you are driving me mad! Speak up about what?"

"Alta, ever since you came to town... heck, ever since I met you, I been acting like a man who is courting you. Like a man who had a right to court you."

He had my attention now.

"Alta, I don't have that right. I can't court you, much as I would like to. I'm a married man."

The air around me froze and shattered. I couldn't breathe.

"Alta, I am so sorry." He stood. His eyes blazed at me, and then he turned to go, putting on his hat as he reached for the sliding parlor door.

There was a familiarity about this scene that shook me to the core. This could not be happening a second time! I leaped to my feet and practically shouted at him.

"Charles Demont Whitaker, don't you dare go out that door. Get back here and sit down."

He looked shocked but obeyed. I sat across from him.

"You can't just say something like that and then walk out the door! You have to stay here, like an adult, grown-up man, and explain it to me, until I can understand what in the world you are talking about!"

Then, his whole affect changed, and there was no question about the sheepishness. His head drooped, he hunched his back, and then he turned and turned his hat in his hands as he told me a sad little story that was beyond belief—except that it had the ring of truth.

On his twentieth birthday—he was twenty-five now—Larry and some of the other hands out at the ranch thought it would be a great idea to celebrate by taking Charlie to a house of... that is, a place...well, to be frank, a brothel.

I knew of it. It was on the outskirts of town, called "Auntie's." I had waited on Madam, herself, several times in the store, with one or two of her "girls." They bemoaned our lack of finer fabrics for gowns. Our broadcloth was too coarse even for their unmentionables. They had to send away for their merest needs and then wait weeks and weeks for the orders to arrive by stagecoach or wagon. It was hardly worth their time to come into Burke's. I agreed but was unfailingly polite.

At any rate, at this place, Charlie was introduced to a charming, dark-haired young girl named Velvet, who told him, after several passionate hours, that she was sixteen, new in the business, and that he was, in fact, her first "client." Midst many tears, she shared her dread of a sordid future and confessed that she had fallen in love with him at first sight.

Being a decent young man, he had naturally found all this quite plausible, and within two weeks they eloped, boarding the Butterfield stage at the last moment, booked to Albuquerque, where they were married, for an "extra consideration," by a dubious, but consecrated, Catholic Priest.

Feeling quite the hero, Charlie brought his bride home to the ranch and introduced her to his family. It was not a success. Almost at once, it became clear that she had been mistaken about Charlie's station in life. The ranch was not at all what she had expected: it was not grand, they were not rich, and he was not even the eldest son. She had envisioned servants—not that she would be expected to take an active part in running the large ranch house, nor the care and feeding of the family and some twenty sheepmen, horse wranglers, and other ranch hands.

Her name was really Minnie Scruggs, and she was twenty-four, not sixteen.

Six months later, she "eloped" again—this time with the ranch foreman. Nothing had been heard of either one since that time, although there was speculation they may have been headed for San Francisco. Or Denver. No one knew.

That was the whole deplorable tale. It had not even the distinction of being original. I had heard a story very much like it on the train, just before we got to Topeka.

I sat beside him, holding his hand while we both shed tears.

"Did you not think of a divorce?" I asked, after a while.

"Yes, but we were married Catholic. They don't have divorce. I'm not Catholic, but she is. Besides, we didn't know where she was, you see. And Paw doesn't believe in divorce, anyway. I guess we just hoped the whole thing would blow over. And it did, sort of."

"Do... other people know about it?"

He snorted—not elegantly. "Come on, Alta! This is Black Butte! Everyone knows about it. Regular topic of conversation, especially lately, I expect."

"I see." And I did. It explained several looks and remarks I had not quite understood.

"So," I speculated, "the whole town knows I have been... cavorting with a married man?"

"That's about it," he admitted. "I've managed not only to trash my own reputation, now I've pretty much ruined yours."

He made another manful attempt to apologize. "Alta, I'm so sorry. I'm an idiot! I enjoyed being with you so much. I was coming to love you, and I wanted... well, I managed to fool myself for a while that the other didn't matter. But it does."

"Yes, it does."

We sat in mutual misery. After a while, I asked, "When you came back from the mustangs, you seemed surprised I was still here. Had you hoped I would be gone?"

"I didn't hope it, but it would have sort'a solved the problem," he admitted. "But you were still here, and I just couldn't resist."

He stood, and this time I was ready to let him go. "Alta, I'll say goodbye. I... won't be seeing you again. Except, just to say hello, you know... if we should meet."

"Yes," I whispered. "We must always meet as friends."

We shook hands. It was an insane thing to do. He opened the parlor doors, and quietly closed them behind him. I heard him cross the hall, heard the front door open and close.

He was gone. I loved him.

Chapter Nine

NOVEMBER 1888

With eyes now rudely opened, it was clear I had been living in a fool's paradise. Nothing about my new home was quite what it had seemed. All had been made so easy for me: a decent place to live, a job by which I could support myself... had the people who seemed to accept me so warmly been only waiting to see if I made some mistake? Everything had to be reconsidered. In the weeks that followed my devastating introduction to reality, I began to see Black Butte in a vastly different light.

I had assumed I was being courted... no, I *had* been courted by a man I was proud to be seen with, in full public view. I had thought everyone was smiling at our association. That had not been the case. His situation was known by all; therefore, they assumed I must know as well. It was now generally believed I had knowingly been the companion of a married man who had abandoned me when public disapproval reared its head. No matter what glowing recommendations I brought from back East, I was now to be considered *no better than she should be*: that damning phrase that urged the imagination to do its worst.

Mrs. Hoaglund came to me where I sat in the parlor, tears

streaming down my face, and had seemed quite surprised to find me so.

"My dear, whatever is the matter?" she exclaimed, sitting beside me.

I turned to her, at a loss, and then said miserably, "Charlie... Mr. Whitaker has just told me he is a married man."

"You didn't know that?" she asked in apparent surprise.

"No, how could I? He hadn't said anything about it, and no one else did. It seemed to me..." Filled with shame, I mumbled the rest. "I believed he was courting me."

"Oh, my dear! I thought of course you knew! But you know hardly anyone, who would have told you? I should have spoken at once when I realized you were seeing him. That day out in his buggy, and then at the Harvest Ball, it was so apparent..." She shook her head and took my hands, which were wet with my tears.

"I must apologize. As your landlady, I am in many ways your guardian here. And, rather than be helpful, I have been judgmental. I was about to ask you to leave my house, as such goings-on were harmful to my reputation!"

This shocked me almost as much as what Charlie had said! Assessing my conduct from her point of view, I supposed it had been very bad. I stared at her in dismay.

"There, there, don't look at me like that. Of course, I will not evict you, especially as the blame is to some degree my own. You poor child, you have had a shock!"

At that, I burst into a new flood of tears.

She comforted me, and when I was capable of listening again, confessed to me that, after the Harvest Ball, she had gone to John and Myrtle with her concerns, and found them in a similar state, having seen the intimacy of the waltzes. This explained why John had gone out to the Whitaker Ranch. As my employer, and more than that, he had gone to rebuke

Charlie for his behavior to me. He and Myrtle were truly my friends.

"You should know, Myrtle was of the strong opinion that you must be unaware of Mr. Whitaker's unfortunate marital situation, or you would not have allowed the connection."

To hear of Myrtle's loyalty had sent me off into more floods of tears, despite which Mrs. Hoaglund managed to get me upstairs and into my bed. I did not get out of it, except to use the chamber pot, for the rest of the week.

I refused to go downstairs for meals, so she sent up trays of tea and toast and gave out that I was ill. She sent a note to the Burkes, who responded urging me to take as much time as needed. Myrtle wanted to come to me, but Nurse Betty said no, as the walk and especially the stairs would be too exhausting. Myrtle had, herself, been in bed since the excitement of the Harvest Ball. I longed to see her and confide in her, for I couldn't bear the slightest idea of her thinking badly of me, but even that could not persuade me to leave my room.

Besides, I was a mess. My eyes were red and swollen from crying, my face was blotched, my hair a tangled bush. Whenever I stood up, I was so dizzy I nearly fell, and my legs were wobbly and could barely hold me up. I stood on the shore looking into the mirror regarding the *Wreck of the Alta Belle*. I wished I could go down with the anchor into the deep, dark water at the bottom of the ocean where I would think and feel no more. Sunday morning, Mrs. Hoaglund came briskly into my room with a tray holding tea, toast, and a bowl of oatmeal, which she put down on the bed. Then she went to my window and flung open the draperies, allowing piercing sunlight to blind me. I cried out in protest.

She came to my bedside, looking very stern. "Alta Belle, you will eat everything on that tray. Then you will take a bath; it is being drawn for you now. You will dress. I will come up to help with your stays and your hair, which you have allowed to get into an awfully bad condition. Then we will go to church."

"Oh, but..." I began to complain.

"Not one word out of you! There is nothing in the world wrong with you except disappointment and embarrassment. Your reputation, however, is badly damaged and it's time to get up and see if we can get it back into some kind of decent shape. Going to church is the place to start. Now, do as you are told. I'll be back in an hour, and you'd better be ready." She flounced out and left me staring after her agape. Alas, Mrs. Hoaglund has raised the mainsail and I had to go to church.

I eyed the food dubiously with no intention of eating it but did take just a taste of the oatmeal to show that I had tried. It was surprisingly delicious, with brown sugar, melted butter, and cream; before I knew it, I had eaten every bite. I ate the toast, too, and by then, I had finished the tea. No self-control at all.

Lupe tapped on my door and told me the bath was ready. I went. It would have been wonderful to soak in the hot water until it grew cool, but I clearly didn't have time. The slate hung beside the door showed that Miss Myra Blodgett was waiting for the next bath.

I scuttled back to my room, and when Mrs. Hoaglund returned, I was waiting for her in my shoes, stockings, petticoats, and chemise, with the hated stays ready to be laced up so that I might take the first step back onto the path of decency.

We walked to church. It was very cold. Mrs. Hoaglund said it looked as if it might snow, although it was early for that. Even if it did, as happened several times a year, it would stay on the ground only a week or two.

The church was hardly any warmer than the out-of-doors. Several people nodded to Mrs. Hoaglund, but I paid little attention—having seen Myrtle and John Burke in a pew close to the front. We joined them, and I was able to sit next to Myrtle. She held my hand throughout the service, which started at once. We had barely been on time. Miss Blodgett was late, probably because of me!

After the last hymn was sung, we all stood and attempted to restore circulation—nearly frozen to the core. Myrtle invited me home for the mid-day meal and to spend the afternoon, which Mrs. Hoaglund thought was an excellent idea.

The church emptied row by row, starting in the back, and as we awaited our turn to walk out, Mrs. Hoaglund chatted briefly with all those around us, making a point of including me. "You remember Alta Carlton," she would say, and add something inconsequential, such as, "Alta was not used to dry cold such as this in New York City!" or "Alta works at Burke's Mercantile, you know." These people were then forced to acknowledge me, which, to a soul, they did—if coldly and with as few words as possible. This was so different from the cordiality of even a week ago, I could hardly believe it. Could one waltz make such a difference? Apparently, it could, especially if you added in those unchaperoned buggy rides. I tried to hold my head up and stand tall, answering civilly in as few words as possible. "Yes, New York is quite different," and "Yes, the Burke's have been very good to me." Myrtle never let go of my hand and whispered encouragement in my ear.

At last, we were able to walk out, but as we paused to compliment Reverend Michael on his sermon, of which I remembered not one word, I was conscious of receiving many critical stares, followed by low comments to nearby friends—some followed by a hint of laughter. Myrtle firmly held my arm and I stiffened my spine, nodding to everyone we passed by—even Mrs. Goring, who basically tossed her head and turned to whisper to her cronies, Mrs. McKnight and Mrs. Dooley.

It was a great relief to at last reach the warmth, in every way, of the Burkes house. Mrs. Hoaglund walked with us, then left with an air of some relief, as if "passing the baton," with John's promise to walk me home in the late afternoon.

Virginia said dinner would be ready in an hour and settled us before the fire in the sitting room with a pot of tea and a small dish of sliced apples and cheese. John went off to the store, promising to return. At last, I was free to weep in Myrtle's arms and she to console me to our mutual content.

Myrtle said there was a great deal of gossip since the ball, but no one was likely to confront me to my face, Mrs. Goring aside, and I must ignore it. It was merely the current scandal and would pass soon enough when something new and more interesting came up. My only possible course of action was to behave as if nothing had happened, carry on, and under no circumstances give them anything new to gossip about! I promised her fervently that I would never err again. Little did I know how difficult that would prove to be!

Myrtle did give a little sweet solace to my aching heart by saying that she still saw Charles Whitaker as basically a decent man who had been dealt an awful hand—not entirely his own fault. But his past had not yet made him wise, and he was still prone to follow his heart and not given to thinking things through. While this was, perhaps, damning him with faint praise, it did make me feel a little better. It was what I thought myself. His feelings for me had been genuine, I would never question that, but he very much underestimated the power of public opinion and had not considered the consequences to me.

I returned to work on Monday and tried for a life it might be possible to bear. On Tuesday evening, I discovered this placid town was not even a place of law and order! After dinner (savory pot roast and vegetables), as we sat in the parlor enjoying our coffee, a burst of what could only be gunshots rang out, perhaps eight of them, followed at once by another round. Miss

Blodgett yelped and dropped her cup and saucer, which, of course, broke; I, myself, may have gasped a bit. Mr. Ignacio leaped up, bowed slightly to Mrs. Hoaglund, and said, "I shall investigate and report back, ma'am."

He rushed off in search of his greatcoat, followed at once by all the rest of the men, and they tramped out with a great deal of noise, banging the door repeatedly, heading in the direction of Main Street. I was astounded.

"But, Mrs. Hoaglund, surely it is dangerous! Why do they rush out like that? Does no one stay to protect us?"

Mrs. Hoaglund smiled, sourly. "Men! They don't think of danger, or of us. Just afraid they might miss out on some of the excitement!" Noticing my uneasiness, she hurried to reassure me. "We are unlikely to be in any danger here. The shots certainly came from one of the saloons. Here, have some more coffee." She refilled my cup. "The men will be back soon enough and will want to tell us all about it. Don't worry about that broken cup, Myra, let me ring for Lupe. We'll get you another." I marveled at her composure behind her coffee tray. Perhaps this was not an unusual event.

She was right, of course. Within the hour, they all came trouping back, flushed with high energy, demanding more coffee, and bursting with details. It seemed a group of hands from the nearby Drummond cattle ranch had provoked an argument with the Conolly boys, who ran sheep. There had been a rousing fistfight, which resulted in the Drummond bunch being thrown out of the saloon. When the Conollys went to leave, the Drummonds ambushed them at the door and the ensuing exchange of gunfire had been mortal. Two Conollys were dead, two wounded; one Drummond dead, three wounded. Both the sheriff and Doctor Grigg were having a busy night, to say nothing of the undertaker. There was a full hour of discussion about what was to happen next, not so much in the legal sense—no one seemed concerned about that—but whether it would erupt into a full *range war*, as had happened in other parts of the Territory. It was quite late when we finally all retired, and I'm sure I was not the only one who had trouble sleeping. I was full of dread for Charlie and his family and hoped they would not get involved in this unsavory business.

The next day the town was all abuzz, like a beehive that had been roughly shaken. More people came into the store than ever before in my time, but they came to talk in front of the stove and drink coffee, not to buy. The only positive that came of all this was that people were not gossiping exclusively about me anymore!

On Thursday evening, Mrs. Hoaglund insisted that I accompany her to the weekly sewing circle at the church. I did not want to go, as I knew these were the very ladies who would most want to exclude me, but she would brook no excuse. She explained that the ladies were presently preparing "fancies" for an upcoming bazaar—a Christmas fundraiser for the church.

"Surely there is some little thing a New York lady such as yourself could contribute?"

Well, there were the dollies, which had stood me in such good stead with my sewing class at the Guild. Thinking of possible future school sewing lessons, I had brought the remnants of that project West with me. Mrs. Hoaglund thought that would do very well, so I shrugged and brought my Betsy with her sample clothes to show. If I had to do this every Thursday, as it appeared, I supposed I could make one for this bazaar.

The doll received a warmer welcome than I did, for it was immediately clear that these ladies were not happy to see me. While they admired the doll, they grudgingly accepted me only because of Mrs. Hoaglund's patronage—especially Mrs. Goring and her friends.

There was one exception: I was pleased to find Isobel there.

She greeted me warmly, made a place for me beside her, and chatted with me all evening. What I had thought would be a grim ordeal turned into the possibility of making a new friend in a most unexpected place.

Isobel was knitting mufflers at such a speed that she completed one this very evening. The other ladies knitted caps, mittens, and socks, or else embroidered doilies and antimacassars. Mrs. Goring, despite her chill, was finishing a set of three quite charming tea towels, featuring an appliqué of a small sunbonnet girl with a watering can, sprinkling a few embroidered flowers. I praised her project and then worried I had been too effusive.

She unbent so far as to remark that my doll was sure to sell and that she hoped I could turn out a good number of them in the few weeks remaining until the mid-December event. Thus, I discovered I was expected to continue the good works at home in my spare time when I was accustomed to reading!

The evening was rounded off with a caramel layer cake made by Mrs. Dooley, which was so delicious that I had to regard her in a slightly more favorable light! Fortified with plenty of hot tea, I walked home with Mrs. Hoaglund in a pleasant glow. It galled me to say it, but it was her due.

"You were right," I admitted, and she laughed with pleasure.

"Well, Alta Belle, you did fine. But it's only a start, mind. It isn't going to all be as easy as that." She was so right!

The following Monday, John sent me to carry several small packages to be shipped to customers from the Butterfield shipping office, as Biggers was busy loading a large order onto the wagon of a local farmer. As I crossed the rutted dirt road to the boardwalk in front of the hotel, I saw Betty Kinney on her way to see Myrtle. I told her Myrtle was at the house and made her promise to wait for my return, so we could share a cup of tea in the store and have a visit, a promise she willingly gave.

I crossed the rutted street, stepped back up onto the boarded walkway, and was going past the livery stables when I heard low calls behind me:

"Hey, Alta! Wanna go for a buggy ride?"

"It's kinda cold, but I bet I could keep you warm!"

"Har, Har, Har!"

My face burning with embarrassment, I held my head up and walked on at the same pace past the Wagon Wheel Saloon— grateful that the shipping office was just beyond the Butterfield Depot.

The shipping agent, a tall, blond young man, was very helpful. "Packages from Burke's. Sure, he keeps an account, no problem." He quickly weighed them, made notations in a ledger, and wrote me a receipt.

"That's it," he said and smiled at me warmly. "You must be Alta Carlton, working at Burke's."

When I admitted I was, he introduced himself as Danny Devers.

"Hope to see you around," he said politely. I left in a pleasant glow, enjoying his admiring glance. No matter how broken your heart may be, it's always nice to know that someone finds you attractive.

I cut through the unplanted central plaza to avoid the livery stable, stumbling over the ruts, and arrived back at the store without further incident. I put the unpleasant event out of my mind. Biggers was still loading the wagon, its owner, farmer John Dougle, supervising his every movement.

Going into the store, I was happy to see Betty and Myrtle just coming in by the back way, looking for me; the timing was perfect for a visit and, as there were no customers in the store, I took off my hat and joined them in front of the stove where cronies with cigars usually sat.

Betty explained that she had been introducing several new

exercises Dr. Grigg thought would be of benefit to Myrtle, who was not being very cooperative.

Myrtle, indeed, was pouting a little and said she did not want to have to do any exercises, but, after we fussed at her for a while, she gave in and promised she would try.

I went to make us a pot of tea and was just pouring it out when there was a gunshot, right in front of the store—startling all of us. Managing to set the pot safely down without burning any of us, I thought I would never get used to the sound of gunfire like this! How was it that there had been none the whole first two months I had been in Black Butte, and now it seemed to be happening every other day?

Biggers raced excitedly into the store exclaiming, "Big rattlesnake in the road, right in front! Dougle got him in the head with one shot!"

I was petrified! I had just come from there, not fifteen minutes before, and hadn't noticed any snake.

Farmer Dougle followed Biggers inside, modestly sliding his pistol back into its holster, and a number of things happened all at once: John and Fred hurried up to slap Mr. Dougle on the back and otherwise congratulate him, Myrtle began to bounce up and down and babble about the rattlesnake tail belonging to Burke's because it had happened out front, and Betty turned white as my petticoat, jumped up, and appeared to be trying to hide behind the chair she had been sitting in.

It was generally agreed that it was far too cold for a snake to have normally been out in the open, and therefore was an eerie event—perhaps even an omen. The men went back outside to cut off the tail and dispose of the dead snake, and we ladies returned to our tea, although we got barely a word from Betty, and she left almost immediately by the back door, I noted.

I looked inquiringly at Myrtle. "Mr. Dougle was 'walking out' with Betty, before the... you know..." She lost the word but mounded her hands over her stomach. I nodded my under-standing.

I was about to ask more when the men returned, full of talk, and awarded the rattle to Myrtle, who, it appeared, had quite a collection kept on display in one of the glass-topped counters, which I had barely glanced at before, assuming it was "man's" stuff. This was an especially large specimen. Wonderful, I thought to myself. Now, I have to worry about rattlesnakes every time I go out to the privy. Another danger no one had bothered to mention to me!

John shook his head as he put the large rattle in pride of place. "Probably been living under the store for years. Probably the reason we haven't had a rat problem. Expect we'll have rats now."

For the first time, I began to wonder what other unexpected calamities might be looming in my future, which no one had thought to warn me about. I had found Black Butte picturesque and friendly. The reality was guns, shooting, rattlesnakes, rats, and married men who thought nothing of stealing one's heart. I began to regard the ladies of this town, even those I did not particularly like, with some admiration for living here at all—and with such fortitude!

Mentally, I began to write a letter to Odyssey West advising them to amend their description of the ideal *Woman of the West* to include the word "brave"; but then, perhaps no one would ever apply! "Not afraid of guns, snakes, and rats" would be even worse. I'm pretty sure, had I the least idea of it, I would have got off the train at Topeka!

Chapter Ten

J ohn was right about the rats, but, fortunately, I was not
expected to deal with them. That was Biggers' job, and he
rose to the challenge with energy and expertise that made
me reconsider him altogether. He baited traps with aplomb and
was insistent about where to place them for maximum effect.
Now, opening the store in the morning, there was usually at
least one pathetic corpse to be avoided until Biggers came in to
remove it with, I thought, uncalled-for gusto. Walking through
the store became hazardous, and more than once I stepped on
—and set off—one of his traps, which Biggers had to be called
to remove from my boot. He seemed to find this hilarious and
made many jokes about catching a lady rat, which I tried to
endure stoically.

Luckily, I never saw a live one. Much time was spent
steeling myself for such an event, but with no certainty of what
my instinctive reaction would be. I could only hope I would not
be one of those "eek, eek!" girls.

Several days later, Mrs. Dooley came in, cordial enough in
the store, and soon had me busy measuring out endless yards of
stiff, resistant ticking. She was preparing to make new

mattresses, which her three young house helpers would stitch up in their free time. She had found them sitting idle over their afternoon tea break once too often!

She broke off her domestic story with a sharp, disapproving intake of breath. "I do wish John Burke would not serve that type in this store! He should have more regard for his regular customers!"

I looked up and saw a strange group of three entering, being warmly greeted by John. They could only be Natives: two men and a woman wrapped in a trade blanket.

The men wore heavy jackets and pants, just like everyone else, but the hats were strange: soft black felt with a high domed crown—not at all like Stetsons. I could see their hair was worn in long braids. The woman, wrapped in a trade blanket, wore her hair in a strange rectangular bun at her nape, which was bound in the middle with heavy white twine.

I hurried to finish measuring Mrs. Dooley's ticking, folding it up into a manageable bundle while she stood rigidly with tight, disapproving lips, refusing to look at the central part of the store. I wondered how such a sour lady could make such a glorious caramel cake; perhaps it was really baked by one of her servants.

"Just charge this to my account," she instructed sharply. "I'll wait here."

"Yes, ma'am," I replied. The Dooley account was running a bit high already, but this was probably not the right time to mention that. I went over to the cash register to write up the sale and wrap the ticking in brown paper tied with twine to carry home.

"Alta, I want you to meet Ruth Yazzie and her husband, Tom Nez. And this, here, is Ruth's brother, Sam Two-Horses. They're Navajo, live up by Antler Springs, come in from time to time to bring me some silver work. Belt buckles, watch bands, and such."

"How do you do," I said. Mr. Nez solemnly offered his hand, so I shook it—followed by the other two. Ruth smiled at me shyly, keeping her head down, but I could see she was young and quite lovely, with smooth brown skin and enormous dark eyes.

"Alta, you take care of Ruth, here. Anything she wants. Tom and Sam and me got business," and he led the men off into the "Hinterland," as I thought of the *forbidden* men's section of the store.

"As if we don't have business of our own!" I retorted, but quietly. Ruth laughed shyly. I asked to be excused for a moment and took Mrs. Dooley her package. She left the store in something of a huff, but I returned to Ruth with anticipation. She led me to the foodstuffs, saying little, but efficiently indicating what she wanted: coffee, cornmeal, rice, and beans. Although she never looked me in the eye. Someone had told me that Natives considered being looked straight in the eye to be a personal intrusion—rude in the extreme, and highly disrespectful. Ruth spoke good English and easily conveyed to me what she wanted to buy. I thought she lingered briefly by the variety of teas I had gathered into a minor display, which John said was "cluttering up the counter." Ruth lifted a packet to smell but then put it down. She made no comment and moved on.

After I had written up her purchases, I hesitated a moment and then asked, "Do you like tea, Mrs. Yazzie?" She nodded. "It seems the men are still busy. Why don't I make up a pot and we can sit here by the stove and enjoy a cup while we wait."

Her face lit up with pleasure. I suggested we try the Darjeeling she had looked at from the display and it was soon accomplished. The fragrant tea was a nice change from the usual Black Pekoe.

Ruth let her blanket slide off as she sat down. I saw she wore a purple satin long-sleeved blouse over a deep blue, velvet tiered skirt. Interestingly, she wore a great deal of jewelry: long dangle earrings, a large and ornate necklace of turquoise set in silver, several rings, and at least four bracelets. I brought the tea and poured, and then wondered what in the world we could chat about.

However, she saved me the effort. Respectfully, not meeting my eyes, she indicated my right hand and said, "You wear a good ring."

I splayed my fingers to better display it, took it off, and passed it to her. "I love it. I got it in Santa Fe."

"Yes," she responded. "You buy at the shop called 'The Hogan,' yes?"

"Yes!" I exclaimed. "How did you know that?"

She turned it over and indicated the mark inside. "Joe Nez made this ring. My husband's brother made this ring."

I was amazed. "It will be even more special now."

She smiled with satisfaction. "Joe uses only the best stones and always sets this oval cut stone in a ring of these little silver beads."

She handed it back to me and picked up her teacup. "Why you do not get ear bobs, too?"

"They had run out of matching ones in the shop," I said. I had asked and been sorry to hear that.

"I can take order. It's his favorite design, and this stone is medium blue with almost no color veins. He can make ear bobs that match rather good. You want?"

Well, well! And I had thought her shy. "I do," I said, chuckling. "As long as they are not too dear."

"Two stones this time, not one," she pointed out. "But, for you, a discount." She named a price which, like the ring, was more than I would have thought, but certainly good value if they turned out to match the ring as she promised. It was a matter of trust.

"All right," I agreed after a moment. "Please ask your brother to make them. Do I pay you now? Or perhaps a deposit?"

"No," she responded. "Pay when you get them, if you like them. If not, no matter. And, please, add a pound of this tea to my charge. I do like, very much." She gave me a sparkling little sideways smile.

A businesswoman to match my own heart!

After the Navajo had left the store, I told John about Mrs. Dooley's reaction. He snorted and dismissed her, saying "The *Yazzies* pay their bill!"

I giggled, although the Dooley bill was not a laughing matter. I told John about ordering the earrings.

"I wondered if Ruth would try to sell you something. Sharp as a tack. Never misses a chance. Well, she'll give you your money's worth."

"John, why do you call them 'The Yazzies'?" All the men seem to be called Nez."

"They are Yazzies. But the family all goes through the women. Men carry the father's name, but it's the women who pass the name on."

"John, you have some men's jewelry in stock. Why don't you carry any for women?"

"Not enough call for it. You saw Mrs. Dooley's reaction to them just being in the store. Do you think she would ever wear Indian jewelry? Besides, don't want too many valuable entice-ments lying around in the store, attracting attention."

"You have the safe," I protested.

"Alta Belle, a safe don't do a speck of good if some robber is pointing a gun at your wife," he chided me, and I had to admit he was right.

I knew that every afternoon, John took the day's proceeds to the bank just before it closed, but we would still be a temptation because of the ten dollars in change we always kept to *start* the till, plus anything he took in during the evening hours, to say nothing of the stock itself.

"John, have you ever been robbed?" I gasped, having never given a thought to this side of keeping shop in the West.

"Yup. About six years ago, man came in, cleared out the till, and was gone outta town before I could even get to the sheriff. Never did catch him. But don't you worry. We're prepared, now. Also, when I go to the bank, I always carry my pistol."

So reassuring! More dangers to worry about!

It snowed that night—enough to cover the ground with several inches. I sat at my window watching it fall and wondering what Charlie's ranch looked like in the snow, whether he would have to go out and work in the cold and wet.

In the morning, the town was beautiful—all covered in white, pristine and peaceful, like a Christmas scene, but it began to melt at once, and by late afternoon everything was a muddy mess. Biggers was unloading a wagon full of coal into the bin out back, against expected further storms, so John once again asked me to take packages to the shipping office.

Flinching inwardly at the thought of having to walk past the livery stables once more, I took the packages—exclaiming over the weight of one of the boxes.

"Ammunition for a sheepman out at Table Mountain. Can you manage?"

I assured him that I could. He told me the second package was one of Sam Two-Horses' leather belts, a special order, and the third was a turquoise watchband, which he was sending out to another rancher on speculation since the rancher had asked him to try to find such an item.

I didn't let it go. I had to tell him of Miss Hutchins, who

had come in just before noon with the two Collins sisters, all three of whom had noticed and commented on my ring.

"Huh," was all he replied. When I said nothing more, he grunted and said, "Well, I'll think on it." I imagined this was what Myrtle was used to.

I put on my coat, hat, muffler, and mittens, and, trusting in my sturdy boots, had the parcels packed in a string tote. There was not the slightest possibility of cutting through the plaza; it was a sea of mud. It was bad enough crossing the street to get to the boardwalk in front of the hotel. Some planks had been laid across to walk on, which helped a little, but I expected they would soon vanish in the mud. I gingerly crossed the second street to the walk by the livery stable, noting that the route I would have to take home tonight already looked ankle-deep in mud—dreadful. I wondered if there was any chance of a freeze before six o'clock.

"Hey, Alta! Wanna go for a sleigh-ride?"

"Alta, didja hear what happened to Auntie's girls last week when they went on a buggy ride?"

"Come on in here, girlie, we gotta nice fire, warm you up!"

Humiliated, I tried to walk by as fast as I could, but suddenly a strong hand took my elbow, and I saw that I was rescued by Danny Devers, the shipping clerk, perhaps returning from lunch at the hotel.

"Get out of here, you hooligans," he yelled at the livery louts. "You don't know how to behave to a lady!"

"Where? Where's the lady?" one voice hooted, and they all laughed, but we were well past now, and soon he was unlocking the freight office and sweeping me inside. What a relief!

"Thank you so much, Mr. Devers! It's nothing, of course, but it's so embarrassing."

"John Burke should know better than to let you go out

alone like this," Danny criticized. "You shouldn't be subjected to that lot!"

"I am perfectly fine, thanks to you," I said, and he took my packages, making jokes about the weight of the heavy one and saying it was too bad I didn't have a gun to go with the ammunition, for then I could get rid of the livery lot for good! He did his best to be amusing and soon had me laughing. When all was done, he put his coat and hat back on, turned the sign on the door back to "closed," and offered me his arm.

"Why don't I walk you back to the Mercantile by way of the Stew House and buy you a cup of coffee to buck you up? Won't hurt none to shut this office up another half hour, and John Burke can surely spare you. It's a slow day everywhere!"

Why not? I thought. And we set off cheerfully the long way around the plaza—carefully crossing the muddy street to the boardwalk, which served the east side. This went past a saloon called Mickey McGee's, where men idled outside, but it was no problem with an escort, and we soon reached O'Toole's at the end of that block.

Sally greeted us as we entered the welcome heat of the Stew House, and I thought she was surprised to see me, but she gave us a table by the window and quickly served us the promised coffee. I slipped off my outer layer, stashed my reticule on my lap, and gratefully took a large warming sip—sighing with pleasure.

"I'm real glad to get to spend a little time at Harvest Ball, but you had so many admirers, I couldn't get through to dance with you! It's my good luck to meet you in the way of business, Alta!"

I was surprised that he would use my first name on so short an acquaintance, but smiled at him, nonetheless. Westerners were so much less formal, and I was happy to make a new friend.

"If it wasn't the middle of winter, I'd take you out on a nice picnic so we could really be alone. But the way it is, I got a better idea." He smiled back at me warmly and took my hand. I was alarmed at this astonishing liberty and tried to pull away, but he held on tight.

"I got some real nice rooms above the printing shop, you know... across the street from where I work, and halfway down the block toward the jail. Tonight, after it quiets down in your boarding house, why don't you slip out the back way and come around the side street? There's a back stair, you just come up and knock on my door. I'll have it nice and warm, and get some beer for us, and we can spend some real pleasant hours together..."

I practically gasped in horror and tried to stand up, but he held my wrist in an iron grip and forced me to retain my chair.

"Sir, let go of me!" I demanded loudly. Every instinct screamed at me not to make a scene, but then I would be his victim—a role I was determined to refuse. After all, I had no more reputation to lose! "You are quite mistaken if you think I would accept such an invitation!" I said loudly.

He practically hissed at me! "Be quiet! People are looking at us! Don't pretend to be so hoity-toity! You went with Whitaker quick enough! What, you think you're too good for me?"

I was sputtering with rage but unable to free myself. People were, indeed, looking at us. Help arrived in the form of Sally, with a large, steaming coffee pot.

"Can I give you folks a refill?" She smiled as if everything were fine and set the pot down on the table, right against Danny's forearm. He let go of me fast enough then—cursing with pain. I jumped to my feet.

"What the blazes do you think you're doing," he spat at Sally, adding a vulgar word.

"Just taking care of my customers, Danny," she smiled at him pleasantly and turned to me.

"Alta, I'm so sorry, I seem to have spilled coffee on your skirt! Come on back to the kitchen, and Miss Abbie will take care of that so it don't stain."

I grabbed up my reticule, and with that she took my arm and ushered me out—leaving Danny, red-faced, behind, nursing his arm and cursing.

In the kitchen, when the swinging door closed behind us, I almost fell into a proffered chair, thanking her profusely. "I can't believe what he suggested, and he wouldn't let go of me! It was awful, and he seemed so nice before. You absolutely rescued me!"

Sally patted my shoulder. "I couldn't believe it when you came in with him. I knew you couldn't know what he is, so I kept my eye on you. Abbie, give her some coffee; she never got to drink hers and she's shaking like a leaf. I'll go get her things and make sure Mr. Danny Snake Devers is gone." She swished back out into the café.

Mrs. O'Toole did bring me more coffee and made me put three spoons of sugar in it "for the shock." "You obviously didn't know, dear, that Danny Devers is our local honey trap. 'Dan-the-snake-oil-man.' He could sell a line to any girl. Any number of them have found out the way you did, and sadly, far too many fall for it, to their great regret. And he don't confine himself to our part of town, either. Several real pretty girls in Beantown have sweet little *bebes* now—with no father."

"Beantown? You mean the Mexican section?"

"Yes, dear. East Butte. And, you know Betty Kinney."

I raised both my eyebrows in shock, and she shrugged. "Well, now you know, and Sally got you out of it real slick. Guess the whole town will be talking about it!"

Oh, no, not again!

Sally returned with my outer garments and gave them to me. She watched while I put them on, her arm around Abbie's waist. They were clearly dear friends, not just employer and employee. Sally was tall and lanky, with a mop of curly blonde hair; Abbie was short and round with ivory skin you could almost see through, and with two shining wings of raven hair swept back into a low bun.

They regarded me with approval, and so they should: they had saved me from a "bounder," and I was suitably grateful.

"Well," Sally became all business again. "The snake has fled, but he could be lurking around somewhere outside. Think we should have Miguel walk you back to the Mercantile."

She summoned the gentleman who was tending to the pots of stew, and he came to us, wiping his hands on a towel.

"This is señor Miguel Gomez. Alta Carlton."

"*Buenos tardes,* señorita," he said, offering his hand. We shook very firmly.

"She has just had an unfortunate run-in with our busy Danny Devers, as I'm sure you are well aware, and I think it best she be escorted back to work at the Mercantile, just to be safe."

"It will be my pleasure," he said, taking off his apron. He donned a blanket—rather like the Navajo one Ruth had worn, but with a hole in the middle for his head—pulled on a warm hat, muffler, and gloves, and offered me his arm. Forthwith, we exited through the back door, me throwing back more thanks, crossed the street, and continued along the south boardwalk of the square. We passed another saloon, the Black Diamond, but with señor Gomez as my escort, no one made the slightest remark. He barely came up to my shoulder, a little barrel of a man, but possessed of great dignity. I held onto his arm, head held high, and never felt safer. Thus, we navigated across the muddy corner street and back to the west mercantile side of the plaza boardwalk.

At the door, I thanked him warmly.

"*De nada*, señorita," he said, smiling broadly and bowing. I made him a little curtsy.

"Too bad señor Dougle did not shoot Danny Snake in the head, instead of *el amigo de su casa,* Old Gotcha," he said. "*Pobre perdido.*" He pulled off his cap, bowed again, and left.

I went into the store, somewhat stunned by the way news traveled in this town and feeling concern for the future, which manifested immediately as I had to explain why I came back to the store late, the long way, and under escort. I did explain. Some of it.

"John, you are not sending Alta on any more errands!" Myrtle scolded. "You can just wait until Biggers..." she couldn't produce the word and finally shrugged it off. "You know what I mean! A young girl needs to be looked after in this town!"

John agreed and berated himself for thoughtlessness. I was happy enough not to be an errand girl anymore. Apparently, it was not safe to let me out-of-doors at all!

I had hardly regained my composure when the door banged open and Whit stormed in, striding directly to me in Dry Goods. I shot a concerned look to John and Myrtle who were both watching with rapt attention. I suppose Fred and Biggers were as well. There was nothing to do but turn to face Whit.

"You had coffee with Danny Devers? Alta, are you a fool?" he berated me. "I can't even go to the grange without hearing about some new trouble you've got yourself into!"

I was dumbfounded, but hardly speechless this time. "Nobody told me about Danny Devers. Just like they didn't tell me about you!" I hissed. "What business is it of yours, anyway?" I had never been so angry in my life.

"Everything you do is my business!" he yelled and stomped out, slamming the door behind him.

"My stars and garters!" commented Myrtle, looking riveted.

I stood with both hands pressed to my flaming cheeks. I tried to express some apology for the scene, but Myrtle just waved me away.

"Think nothing of it, Alta. Men are very strange critters some of the time. Still, it does liven things up a bit!"

They were kind enough to send me home early. Myrtle hugged me and whispered, "You need to have a good cry!" So, I did.

Seeing Whit again had been excruciating. Although my anger had risen to match his own, the aftermath was grief—tears for the one who I must not see anymore. There was no way we could even meet for explanations. For him to have come to the store at all was a shocking violation.

There was no future in dreams of what might have been. No going back to the past, although I wryly noted that I had completely reverted to thinking of him as *Whit* once more. *Charlie* was gone; he had not been honest with me. Whit was a daydream, born out of peril and tragedy, and I had to forget him, too.

Chapter Eleven

M y future lay in Black Butte, however unwisely I had committed myself. Somehow, I must find a way to live here. How much those first few careless weeks had cost me! So much, in fact, that the true friends I had made all agreed it was necessary to wage an actual campaign, if I were ever to be acknowledged in this town as a *decent woman*. And now, I had just barely evaded another trap—saved only by the unexpected help of Sally. I was hopeless! I saw nothing until it was all too late. Well, that would have to end!

Fired up with firm resolution, I dried my tears and sat down to write a list of rules for myself:

First, no more useless dreams about an unavailable man.

Second, although I still hoped to marry one day and have a family of my own, no more casually falling into mutual admiration, or going for coffee with "a business connection." In fact, no more anything without a chaperone, until the right man should appear. I would know he was the right man because a friend would have introduced him to me. Otherwise, no.

Third, I would channel my dangerous excess energy into the

store and drag John Burke into modern times, no matter how much he protested.

Fourth, I would improve my friendships with interesting women such as Izzie, Sally, and Betty, and cherish my friend Myrtle. Perhaps Betty would teach me how to help with Myrtle's exercises.

Last, as a symbol of my new life, in my spare time, I would throw myself into preparing for the bazaar, barely a month away, thus impressing the church ladies—the largest and most difficult obstacle I had to overcome.

Re-fueled with good intentions, I leaped to my feet, got out my sewing, and went to work on my dollies with virtuous energy.

I resolved to make ten dolls each in an appropriate outfit, not the two I had grudgingly agreed to produce. I made a list of all I would need and went to the store to ask Myrtle if I could have fabric from the remnant box, explaining my project.

"Heavens, yes!" she agreed. "But, Alta, these are so little, you won't need much. Take whatever you like from stock. John will agree, we always support the bazaar in every way we can." She giggled and lowered her voice. "John outright gives them all the bunting they need for decorating. He says it's our *thank you* to the town for their trade, but he doesn't like outsiders to know that in case they might think he was trying to get more folks to shop here!"

We laughed together about the foibles of this un-businesslike man, but fondly. I did check with him before I let myself loose with the scissors, but truly I needed very little.

Making a game of it—as I had done seemingly so long ago during the Christmas vacation when I prepared for my sewing class, pretending I was a factory girl—I cut out everything at once for ten dolls and all their clothes. Three would have a nightgown, pantalettes, and sleeping cap, with a soft flannel blanket, like babies. Three would have a pretty dress with a white pinafore, pantalettes, and a big bow in their hair. Three would have a party dress, pantalettes, and a coat and bonnet. The final doll would wear a plain dress with the coat and bonnet, and carry a small satchel made of cloth containing all the other clothes: the fancy dress, pinafore, nightgown, sleeping cap, and blanket.

Myrtle loved my project. She thought I should charge one dollar for the dolls in dress and pinafore, one dollar fifty cents for the baby doll with the blanket, and two dollars for the ones with the dress, coat, and hat. She firmly insisted that the doll with everything should be priced at five dollars!

I had to sit down. I would never have had the nerve to ask so much. But then, I had never been to a bazaar.

"After all," Myrtle added comfortably, "it's for the church."

I stayed up far too late each night sewing like a demon—no reading of books allowed, nor lingering chats after dinner. I made all ten dolls at once, then all the pantalettes, all the plain dresses, and so on. To entertain myself, I made up little dramas about the "poor factory girl" and what her life might be like. This was *burning the midnight oil* indeed, and very pleasing proof of my new intentions. I even brought pieces to the store to sew in intervals without customers when I should have been straightening counters.

Thursday nights became something to look forward to, as I could sew, chat with Izzie, and have refreshments, too.

As to my other resolves, Betty thought it an excellent idea that I should learn how to help Myrtle, and John gave me time off from work before her nap to meet Betty at the house and go through the simple exercise routines of leg and arm lifts and stretches. After we had tucked Myrtle in for what we laughingly called her "long winter's nap," Betty and I would go down to the Burke's kitchen where Virginia, taking the opportunity to run a few errands, would have left us the makings of a pot of tea, which we would enjoy along with a brief but pleasant visit before leaving to get on with our work. After several such comfortable chats, I made bold to increase our intimacy by referring to my disappointing relationship with Whit.

Betty owned to having heard of it and was all sympathy. She thought Mr. Whitaker was basically a good man, pleasant and charming, but he had not behaved well. I alluded to another, more recent and extremely unpleasant, encounter with a charming man. With embarrassment and many blushes, she said she had heard of that, too.

With a deep sigh, she looked at me directly and said she guessed I might have heard that she had not been so lucky as was I in avoiding that particular man. I owned that I had heard of it. With more blushes and sighs, she briefly told me the story of a simple farm girl, with a very decent but solemn and taciturn beau, who had been unable to resist the teasing and admiration of the laughing, good-looking man-about-town, who truly seemed to believe he would die if she didn't kiss him, just once. And then, he had wanted more.

"Ma and Pa wouldn't let me see him, so I took to sneaking out, and he was very persistent, and finally... I just let him do what he wanted to do. You know the result."

We both sighed some more and blushed.

"I confess I don't know exactly what it is all these men seem to want so much, but I think I have a pretty good idea," I said, at last. "I must say, what I don't understand is why women would willingly take part."

I was fearful I had gone too far, but Betty looked at me very directly, with a rueful smile, and surprised me by saying, "Having actually done it, I couldn't agree with you more! He seemed to want it so much, and I thought I loved him... and then he was... very forceful. But after, I could only think *is that all it is?* Oh, I liked the kissing and hugging a lot, but the rest was... just... well, a farmyard thing. But he was over the barn about it. Kept wanting to see me again and again, so it went on a couple of months. But I think I wasn't very good at it. Pretty soon, he began to say I didn't act as if I liked it very much, and I had to admit that was true. And, then he said I was like a stick, and that a 'real woman' would enjoy it, and I thought, well, he's been with those fancy women and I don't know what it is they do. So, I told him to teach me, if it was so important, and he got really angry and said that was no good, a 'real woman' didn't have to be taught. Then, he just dropped me, stopped coming to see me at all. I thought my heart was broke, but then I realized I was... well, going to have Jojo, and my folks found out and there was a huge ruckus, and Pa went in town to see him, and I was all happy because I thought Danny would marry me then, because of Jojo, you know."

By now I was holding her hand with one of mine and wiping up tears with the other, just as she was.

"Well, what came of that was Danny got all high and mighty and said it couldn't be his, since he had a paper from a doctor saying he couldn't father a child because he was something— sterile? From having had the mumps. Pa saw the paper and that's what it said, sure enough. Then Danny said he wasn't marrying any bad woman, and would never accept another man's child, and Pa came home and whipped me with his belt something awful. Ma made him stop, and after a whole lot more ruckus, it came about that they let me stay home. And after Jojo came, everybody loved him. I guess it was all worth it to have Jojo. I can tell you one thing, though: he is not going to grow up to be a man like his pa!"

We embraced and cried on each other's shoulders. I could not escape thinking how easily this could have been my fate, not with Danny the Snake, but with Whit.

At last, Betty drew back and looked at me solemnly. "It wasn't true, you know. I never been with any man, other than those times with Danny. I don't care what that piece of paper said."

"Betty, I believe you!" I assured her. "And I hear there might be a couple of girls in... the Mexican part of town who would agree with you. What a snake!"

She nodded. "There's some who say it's a wonder he hasn't been knifed. But he's gone now, didn't you know that?"

"Gone?" I was surprised.

Betty actually giggled. "Yes, since last week. Right after Sally burned his arm so good. He was right pathetic, wearing a sling and complaining about 'interfering waitresses.' I think Sally ought to get a medal! But that wasn't why he left. Your Mr. Whitaker had... a word with him. The very next day, Danny said Butterfield's had transferred him to Albuquerque, and he left town on the next stage!"

We both had a good laugh and a big hug, and parted as friends forever. She had given me a great deal to think about.

Myrtle was now spending her mid-mornings in the store, as well as late afternoons. Although not a member of the church sewing group, Myrtle was making pillows as a contribution to the bazaar. She was finishing a unique appliqué pillow cover, depicting a large cactus plant and a coiled rattlesnake. I couldn't help wondering who in the world would want to buy it!

I sat with her during lulls and we sewed together, chatting contentedly.

Our conversations mostly consisted of her bringing me up to date on what was happening in the town, although I began to suspect her of editing the news she gave me. How she could continue to know every little thing was beyond me, since her callers were all church ladies, protected, I assumed, from the steamier goings-on; but Myrtle was always a fountain of information. She was certainly the one to tidy up a loose end I had been carrying around.

"Myrtle," I asked, "You remember that day Sally rescued me from Danny Devers at the Stew House, and Mr. Gomez escorted me back to work?"

"I certainly do!" Myrtle nodded her head and *tut-tutted*.

"One of the things those awful boys at the livery stable were yelling at me was something about several of Auntie's girls taking a buggy ride. They seemed to think it was very funny. Have you heard anything about that?"

Myrtle went pink—she clearly had. She loved to tell a good story. "Ordinarily, it wouldn't be fit to tell you, but you do work here and you have waited on those girls yourself. Do you remember Marie and Victoria?"

"Tall, frenchified blonde, and a little, dark jumpy one?"

"That's them. Seems they were set on a nice walk and a little lunch at O'Toole's, and were just sauntering along East Main street when a bunch of men from Bagnold come up in a big, closed carriage and grabbed them up from off the street. Nobody tried to stop them, of course, and they drove right through town and off down the road, just whooping and hollering. About five hours later, here come Marie and Victoria, walking back barefoot, bedraggled, and carrying their high-heel shoes, mad as wet hens. They said the worst of it was those men never paid them, neither." Myrtle allowed herself a little smile because she had told this story well, but I did not think she found it funny, herself.

"I guess everyone thinks that's hilarious," I said.

She nodded. "But I don't. And I don't think very many other ladies do. Auntie's girls is one thing, but maybe next time it's decent women. That was greatly the reason why I told John you were not to be sent off on errands anymore without a male escort. I don't know what times are coming to. Seems the streets of Black Butte aren't safe for any woman nowadays."

We stitched quietly for a moment.

"I walk alone every day," I remarked. "When I come to work in the morning, and when I go home at night." It was only two blocks, but still!

"I know," said Myrtle, biting off a new length of snake-green embroidery thread. "Morning's probably safe enough, but that's why Biggers is walking you home at night from now on."

"Thank you," I said simply, and was once more deeply moved by the depth of her care for me.

Our quiet sewing session was suddenly interrupted by the noise of a wagon pulling up out front, loud men's voices, and then the heavy thud of many boots on the walk. John shouted, "Stations!" Myrtle astonished me by agilely sliding out of her chair behind the tea table and grabbing the rifle we kept under the cash register counter. I saw John opening the door of the grandfather clock, pulling out another rifle, and was at the same time aware that both Fred and Biggers had emerged, armed, from the men's section. Four rifles pointed at the front door!

"Alta, get behind me," Myrtle ordered, in a voice I had never heard her use before. I scurried to obey.

The door burst open and five huge, scruffy men clomped in, with great noise, stomping of boots, and jingling of spurs. The man in front—heavily bearded and wearing a leather great-coat lined in fur, with a battered Stetson and heavy leather gloves—held his hands away from his sides, palms out, in a universal sign of peace.

"Jumping Jehosiphats, John, this ain't no hold up! We come to give *YOU* money," he protested.

John lowered his rifle slightly. "Sorry, Boomer, thought you might be the Floyd Gang, heard they was around."

"Yeah, we seen Bobby Floyd last week, over to West Creek."

John lowered his gun, but I noticed the others did not. "Well, sorry, gentlemen. Can't be too careful."

"Nope. Don't pay out to take chances. How-some-ever, it's just us, in for our regular supplies." He turned toward Myrtle. "How you doing, ma'am? Heard you had a bit of ill health." He removed his Stetson.

"Much better, thank you, Boomer." Myrtle put her gun away under the counter. "How can we help you today?"

"The usual, plus we need some long johns and overalls, and..." he ruefully held out his hat, which appeared riddled with birdshot. "I need a new Stetson."

"John, don't just stand there, help these men!" Myrtle snapped, and everyone seemed to relax a little. Fred put away his gun under the nearest counter and led the way out back; Biggers lowered his rifle but kept it on him and stayed up front near the door. John ushered the men forward with a hospitable gesture. "The Yazzies were just in, got a couple of rings you might like to look at, Boomer."

"Jake, you and Donny take care of the food stuff. Rest of you, come with me," the big man ordered and strode off after Fred.

The smallest members of the group, relatively speaking, a gnarly, bundled-up older man and what I now saw was just a fresh-faced boy, doffed their hats and waited meekly in front of Myrtle.

"Alta, help these men to whatever they need. After you write it up, Biggers will load their wagon." Myrtle sat down and took up her appliqué as if nothing were even slightly unusual.

I gasped but did as I was told, and soon was glad of Biggers's help. He stashed his rifle in the umbrella stand and then stoically lugged out hundred-pound bags of flour, beans, and rice, and two enormous bushels of potatoes, his muscles bulging and his cheeks tinged pink with excitement. I followed the older man around while he said things like, "Five pounds of salt," and the young boy stared at me with calf's eyes. While I rang everything up at the cash register, Myrtle quietly educated me.

"This here is the Dudly Gang. They're not so bad, mostly cattle rustling, though they don't avoid trouble if it bites 'em. Come in regular every few months. Lot of places won't serve them, but folks know they trade here; other gangs mostly leave us alone. It works out well. So, give them 10 percent discount, Alta. Everybody's happy."

Presently, John and the men came back with a load of clothing. The big man sported a handsome new Stetson, adorned with a silver and turquoise leather hatband. I noticed he was wearing one of the new Yazzie rings as well. John called out all the items for me to ring up, nodded at the discount, and together, we packaged everything up, either in carry totes or brown paper bundles. Biggers ferried all this out to the wagon, then the group made polite goodbyes and clomped noisily out. John carefully did not ask where they were going, and they did not volunteer. Everyone acted as if this were completely normal. I did, too—but, really, I was flummoxed!

John held up the large wad of crumpled bills with which the Dudlys had paid for their supplies.

"Better get this over to the bank!" he said jovially, stuffing it all into a bank bag. He nodded at us and walked out. Biggers retrieved his rifle and followed, walking *shotgun*, I supposed.

I sat down again to sew with Myrtle, but it was a long time before I could breathe comfortably again, and I jumped at every little thump or scrape of a chair. Myrtle, however, sewed away serenely and was quite at ease.

"Calm down, Alta," she soothed me. "There's nothing

wrong. This is just part of *doing business*. Didn't you have anything like this in New York City?"

I had to admit we did not. I had heard, of course, of bank robberies, and jewelers held up in dark alleys, even kidnappings, but it all seemed so removed from the world of Carlton & Hodges, something that happened in the *bad* neighborhoods. Mrs. Warren's petty shoplifting was small potatoes compared to politely serving an acknowledged *gang*.

Finally, I had to ask, "Wouldn't Sheriff Higgins arrest them?"

"What for? They haven't done anything around here. Just come in to shop now and then. Sheriff's happy to keep it that way."

There was absolutely nothing more to it. I began to stitch a small blue flannel nightgown for my red-headed doll. I shook my head. "Well, I swan!" was all I could think of to say.

"That about sums it up," Myrtle agreed, and we quietly sewed on together.

When John came back, we held a small conference. John said he had stopped by the Sheriff's office just to mention the recent sighting of the Floyd Gang, something of interest to all lawmen. He then apologized for not informing me beforehand about "stations," and said he guessed it was time to make me part of their emergency defense team. I informed him proudly that my father had taught me to shoot—perhaps exaggerating slightly—and that I was not at all afraid of handling a gun. He was pleased.

Several mornings later, I was sent off in the wagon with Biggers to a quarry north of town, where he competently showed me how to load, fire, and then clean the old rifle assigned to me. After two such sessions, he pronounced me fit, although he could not say much about my accuracy in hitting the target. At that point, John handed me a small pistol with a pearl handle and said I had better learn how to use this, too.

"Girl who gets in as much trouble as you, better carry it around in that bag of yours. Everyone knows you work at the store. Better safe than sorry, I say."

This meant several more sessions at the quarry with Biggers, causing him to lower his opinion of my skills. Apparently, a pistol was quite different from a rifle. He now said I was a danger to everyone around me, and "couldn't hit the broad side of a barn if it stood still," but eventually pronounced me minimally competent, and from then on I went armed, like most of the men on the streets of the town. I felt, perhaps foolishly, safe.

For a time, I once again considered writing to Mr. Ulysses Brown to suggest he amend his recommended preparations for passage West to include a course in firearms, but in the end, I did not. Surely, mine was not a common experience. Besides, it might be bad for his business to dwell too much on dire events. So much better to reflect on positives—such as church bazaars.

Chapter Twelve

A t dinner a few days later, in the middle of a very nice roast chicken with bread stuffing, Miss Blodgett turned to me and said, "Aren't you ever going to come and pick up your mail, Miss Carlton?"

"What?" I replied, still not very quick on the draw.

"Letters," she said brusquely. "Think you got three of them by now."

"Goodness me!" was all I could think of to say, wondering how in the world I was supposed to know. Couldn't she have said something sooner or, for goodness sakes, brought them to me directly, since we lived in the same house? Apparently not, from the aggrieved set of her mouth. Probably against postal code.

I counted to nine under my breath, and when I could speak pleasantly, inclined my head to her. "I shall pick them up tomorrow on my lunch break. Thank you so much for telling me."

She ungraciously inclined her head as if to accept an apology, strongly giving the impression that nothing could compensate for her extra trouble.

I could hardly contain myself until noon. I did ask Biggers to walk me to the post office before he started his lunch break, even though I was carrying my pistol as always now; a rule is a rule, as Miss Blodgett would say.

The post office was located on Main Street, up the hill from the hotel, just past Dr. Grigg's office.

Miss Blodgett handed me four letters, not three, and I knew how the gold country prospectors must feel when they hit the "Mother Lode." *Eureka, I was rich!*

It was only by the strictest self-discipline that I did not rip all my letters open and devour them on the spot, but I tucked them away in my reticule, beside the gun, and somehow tended to business through the long afternoon. I then endured Mrs. Hoaglund's fried ham and gravy dinner, which deserved better from me. However, enough was enough! I begged to be excused from coffee and accordion in the parlor and escaped, at last, to my room.

Lighting my kerosene lamp, I trimmed the wick for better light and laid the four letters out on my table. All my correspondents had replied. Which to open first? There was really no question. I opened Mother's letter. It was very thick.

They were well. Charles Jr. was well and growing like a weed. He had become the treasure of the household, although his mother found him a bit of a trial. Aggie was going out every day now to make calls with Mother or to see her friends. She and Charles went out several evenings a week. When she was home, she spent most of her time in bed. The baby nurse had been dismissed, and a live-in nanny installed, although Charles Owen Jr. was younger than usual for that. However, it made his mother happy and that was what mattered. Mother spent many happy hours with the baby and found him very bright and forward for his age.

Charles Owen Sr. was doing well at the store, and Father

was quite pleased with him. He was currently ensconced in the Dry Goods Department—she was sure I would be interested to hear. I raised my left eyebrow at that (I was getting better at it). Mother went on to say that Father was currently excited about the new idea of electric lighting at the store, although everyone knew it would be years, if ever, before such a thing could happen.

Father was finding young Mr. Hodges very satisfying to work with. Old Mr. Hodges was in a sanatorium in Connecticut, near death, it was said—so sad. She, herself, was busy planning some extensions to the garden, come summer, featuring a play area for Charles Jr. with swings and a sandbox.

Adelle, John, and young Adam Oscar were all well, although John Jr. was not yet an enthusiastic big brother, having recently tumbled the baby out of his crib, despite the vigilance of Nanny.

Mother then went on for three pages to express a myriad of concerns about my situation: the long wait for my letter, the loss of the teaching position, the comedown of my being *just* a clerk at the Mercantile—they worried about me, etc. etc. I skimmed quickly over all that, no surprise that they were not pleased. There was nothing they could do about it!

However, there was a little postscript in Father's hand:

Alta, tell me more details about this store of yours; sounds interesting.

Next, I took up Margaret's letter. It, too, was thick, full of support and encouragement, just as one would have expected, yet there was a distance that would not have been there before. Margaret would not forgive me for not trusting her with my plans. I was not, myself, entirely sure why I had needed to keep it all such a secret. If I had to tell the truth, I suppose I had been fairly sure she would plead common sense and talk me out of my escape from New York. Perhaps I had feared I could not hold out against her disapproval on top of everyone else's. So, her letter was supportive but cool.

She went on to update the doings of our mutual friends: several engagements, including Hortense and Larry, a few little scandals, and one nice surprise—Percy Ward was to be married at Christmas to his second cousin, Julia. I remembered her unfavorably as ill-groomed, always finding fault, and constantly complaining. Despite that, I hoped the two of them would find happiness, and that sweet, gentle Percy would not grow up to be a henpecked husband.

Margaret then gave me all the news of the Guild, which had now been renamed *University House*. She devoted an entire page to a young man who was teaching a controversial course in pugilistics: *People say we should not be teaching such a violent sport, but Joseph says it gives the boys self-confidence to be able to defend themselves on the streets. I think it is splendid and go to watch whenever I can!* Of her suitor, Mr. Albert Gorman, she wrote not a word.

How interesting! I would never have thought that Margaret, of all people, would be so bloody-minded. It was impossible to imagine her watching young men bash each other about the head with any kind of enjoyment. Perhaps I would write her about the Dudly Gang! Even mention my guns... but, no. Once more, I couldn't take the chance that she might inadvertently say something to Mother about things she didn't really need to know!

Margaret closed with compliments on my *new cowboy friend* and said he sounded like *a most romantic hero.* That was overdoing it, but I had been enthusiastic when I wrote her. I put her letter down sadly, wishing I had not written about Whit at all, and that I had not piled up so many things to be secretive about.

The note from Miss Bailey was all about the store, the new

winter merchandise, the girls in Findings—but, more importantly, the information that Mr. Demming, the department head, had just had a heart attack and his doctor forbade him to work any longer. That explained what Charles was suddenly doing in Dry Goods! The search was on for a new head, and she was thinking of applying herself. Diffidently, she did not have great hopes of being chosen, but there were several other female heads at Carlton & Hodges and she would always regret it if she did not try.

Good for you, Miss Bailey! I thought, and planned to respond very enthusiastically what a good head she would make, and how mistaken the committee would be if they did not hire her. I also planned to write the same to Father, but the reality was that the choice would have long been made by the time my correspondence could arrive. Nonetheless, I could hope.

Now, I took up Ellen's letter—the best saved for last. Her first page was all an enthusiastic response to my *adventures*, of which I had written to her more openly than to any other:

I hope you don't mind, but I shared that exciting letter. I have five quite intimate friends now and have taught them all how to make dollies, and we sit around all day, outside on our cold porch in the health-giving fresh air, making clothes for them, while we take turns reading aloud. The dolls were supposed to be for the younger girls, but now we brazenly claim them for ourselves and sleep with them at night. I named mine Betty; forgive my copying your 'Betsy', but I think of them as sister-dolls, and love mine dearly. Right now, we are trying to make them our idea of Western Outfits!

The girls were all agog at your letter, and it was quite the best thing for us since we read "Jane Eyre." I must confess to you, we are all in love with your cowboy, and think he is much more dashing than Mr. Rochester, or even Mr. Darcy, and you must write us more about him. Does he ride a horse like a wild Indian? Can he rope a cow? Most importantly, have you decided what color his eyes are? We need to know.

Oh, Ellen! How could I tell her? I would write in her own cheerful style, and just say that he had turned out to be a sheepman and had ridden off in search of other adventures; but it was quite all right, as I was now being bowed to at church by a tall Western lawyer in a large, black Stetson, with whom I had danced at the Harvest Ball, and time would tell.

Ellen went on to describe life in the sanatorium, the wonderful food, which, although plain, was so much better than what she had been used to at home. She said she was getting quite fat, and the doctors were very pleased with her progress.

You are right to accuse us of sloth. All we do is eat, and lay in our lounges on the veranda, wrapped up to our chins in blankets with great, woolly hats on our heads, and sew and chatter. The boys in the next ward tease us mercilessly through the lattice. There is one called Bennie who is always calling something rude to me. He is quite cute, with perhaps a million freckles, and red hair going every which way. I try to ignore him, but he makes me laugh.

Of course, Evangeline is lost to us now, and we will miss her forever, but as the nurses teach us, we try to think of positive things and of a happy future. This is why your letters are so important. Please write again as soon as possible.

Love, always, Ellen.

I vowed to write her every week, and certainly had a bushel of stories to tell her that could be given an amusing turn to share with her friends. I thought they would love the tale of *Old Gotcha*, and that I could make something amusing out of the shopping trip of the Dudly Gang. And I would definitely tell her of my semi-successful lessons in firearms, and Biggers's remark about the barn.

Chapter Thirteen

I t was now the week of the bazaar, and, despite longing to respond to all my letters, I must give priority to finishing the last of my dolls. It was hard to believe I had managed to turn out ten of them in such a short time. I still had a little stash of beloved price tags from my Carlton & Hodges days, and, carefully writing *Betsy Doll,* I attached one to an arm of each. I had the four nightgowns to finish but should be able to give them to the *Fancy Work* ladies on Thursday.

I was quite curious as to how they would be received and if Myrtle's pricing suggestions would shock them. I was also very curious as to the pricing of Myrtle's rattlesnake pillow—if a purchaser could even be found!

The bazaar was to be held on Saturday, in the basement of the church—where I had so enjoyed the Harvest Ball—as was, I believe, every public social event. Black Butte had no other meeting hall. The bazaar would start at noon and go on until nine that night; the church ladies would spend all day Thursday and Friday setting up the booths, decorating, pricing, and putting out the wares. One corner was being set up as a tearoom to be run by Sally, which, besides tea and biscuits, would also serve a light meal of chili and cornbread. Miss Abbie and Maria Pilar, Miguel's granddaughter, were preparing huge vats of chili at the Stew House.

I would not be able to take part in all this preparation, being employed, although it sounded like great fun. I must mind my counters at the store. We expected heavy business, with people coming in from the surrounding countryside for the church event.

Myrtle had always helped with the bazaar before, but it was out of the question this year. She was determined to at least go to the bazaar itself, and I believe Dr. Grigg came to feel it would do her more harm to be denied than to let her go! He allowed her one hour in the early afternoon, but only if she went with a companion. There was no question who that would be! John laughed and said I could go, and that he and the *fellows* would do their best to keep the store going until we got back. Myrtle and I were thrilled to be able to go at all.

On Thursday afternoon, Myrtle was wrapped up warmly by the stove, chatting with Mrs. McKnight, and I was trying to serve two very nice Hispanic ladies who did not seem pleased with my calicos. They spoke little English and I even less Spanish, so we were not making much progress.

A fusillade of shots rang out from the direction of the bank to the west. John at once shouted "Stations!" I scooped up my rifle from under the dry goods counter—to the horror of my two customers.

"Go back by the stove," I urged them, pointing. "Go to Myrtle!" They understood that well enough and fled.

We stood five-square, ready to defend our fort from all invaders. I was proud to stand with them and felt certain I could pull the trigger, should it be required. I was not at all afraid.

More shots, shouting, and then came the sound of galloping horses.

"Biggers, go find out what's going on," John directed. "But be careful."

Nothing could have pleased Biggers more, and he dashed off. I much doubt he even heard the word "careful." He came running back, color high and wheezing with excitement.

"Bank robbers! They got Passmore and rid off with a whole lot of money. But Sheriff got one of them and nicked another, so he fell off his horse. We gotta search for him, he could be hiding anywhere!" This was the most words I had ever heard from Biggers all at one time.

"How strange," I reflected as I put the safety back on the rifle, then stowed it safely under the counter. "He seems to actually enjoy extreme crisis." I do try to be honest, so I had to admit, I was somewhat excited, myself!

Biggers and John at once went out to search the courtyard and sheds between the back of the store and the Burke house. Fred stayed with his rifle to help guard the store and I joined the ladies at the stove, where Myrtle had also put down her rifle and was busy making a pot of chamomile tea to calm us down.

I was quite surprised to hear Laura McKnight talking to my two customers in fluent Spanish. I took the opportunity of an interpreter and asked her to find out what had displeased them about the yardage.

"Oh, they want patterns and plains in bright colors. They say John Burke only ever brings in dark browns and greens, and why ever does he think that is what women want to wear? We feel the same, don't we Myrtle?"

"Oh, yes," Myrtle agreed, placidly. "But John is very set in his ways."

At that point, Jack Warden from the butcher's shop ran in the front door. "Passmore's going to be okay!" He informed us in a high, excited voice. "Just nicked in the shoulder. Docs with him now. Where's John?"

"Searching for that robber out back," Myrtle said, pointing, and he ran out the back door.

We heard a great deal of noise from the street, and of course, we all ran to look out the front, no matter how dangerous. *We're really no better than Biggers,* I thought to myself! There we saw Sheriff Higgins and his deputy dragging a man between them toward the sheriff's office, a great crowd of townsmen accompanying them.

"That'll be the robber, off to jail!" said Mrs. McKnight, with satisfaction. "Good that they caught him."

John and Biggers came back, through the front this time, to tell us that the excitement was all over.

It was the Floyd Gang, they told us. The dead man was Bill Picker, and the wounded man, now in jail, was Joe Floyd, Bobby's younger brother. The rest had got away with a lot of money, maybe five-hundred dollars, but it was insured. Donald Passmore had been heroic—although wounded in the chest, his shot was the one that had taken out Picker. The Sheriff had gotten Joe.

That night at the sewing circle, while I finished the last little nightgown, I listened as the ladies categorized the behavior of nearly every man in town, not always kindly. It was clear they felt men could not be counted on to keep businesses running or make practical decisions during exciting emergencies and were prone to getting themselves damaged for their trouble.

"It's lucky the Floyds didn't kill anybody," proclaimed Mrs. Dooley. "If they had, Joe Floyd would be having a *necktie party* right now!"

Isobel quietly explained this strange phrase to me and I could hardly believe it. This was 1888. Surely nothing like a mob lynching could still occur, even though we were not a state and, I suppose, might be "in the wilderness." Isobel shook her head. All too possible.

I had also brought her Myrtle's pillow, which, to my surprise, was much admired. Myrtle had added a dark gold fringe all the way around. I guess it was imposing, but all I could see was the snake! I wouldn't want that on my couch.

Refreshments this night—although very pretty iced cookies —did not come up to Mrs. Dooley's caramel cake. However, we ate them all, along with copious tea, and Mrs. Hoaglund and I walked safely home to the boarding house—without a single gunshot or disturbance of any kind.

Friday was an ordinary day, except that as before, after the shooting at the saloon, many people came into the store just to chat. I thought Myrtle was much too excited about it all; she shouldn't get so worked up, but she would not hear of going back over to the house with Virginia and missing any of it.

Friday night, Mrs. Hoaglund canceled coffee in the parlor and instead marched Miss Blodgett and me into the kitchen, where she stationed us at the table and put us to work cutting out, baking, and decorating a great many gingerbread men for the bazaar bake sale table. Carmelita had already made up our dough. Mrs. Blodgett rolled it out while I cut and put them on baking trays. We were to decorate them with white icing and candy red eyes and buttons. It was actually rather fun. Miss Blodgett became almost human in an apron with flour on her face, instructing me exactly where to cut and rejecting misfits in a bossy, post-mistress kind of way.

Meanwhile, Carmelita stirred a huge pot at the stove, making chocolate fudge, while Lucy kept the fire going, and Mrs. Hoaglund, at the counter, somehow miraculously was turning out six of her famous lemon meringue pies, each in its own tin pie pan, a donation, at her request, from Burke's Mercantile.

Altogether, it seemed to me, John had donated a great deal to the bazaar in one way or another.

How we all managed to finish our projects without getting in each other's way I could not imagine.

"We are a regular 'cooking bee,' don't you think?" I asked them, which they thought very funny. "Whatever happened to 'too many cooks spoil the broth,' I ask you?" I went on. Even Miss Blodgett laughed at that.

In the morning, Mrs. Hoaglund would commandeer the male boarders to carry everything to the church. Then, she would stay on to help all day.

Apparently, Miss Blodgett and I, who worked during the day, would never be considered as *real* church ladies, despite our best efforts. Whereas Mrs. Hoaglund, who also worked, but in a different way, free to come and go, was a pillar of the Sewing Circle. Could I be a *decent woman* even if I were not a *real* church lady? I hoped so, with all my heart, after all this effort!

On Saturday morning, I opened the store as usual and again, we had a surprising number of visitors. Farmers bringing in their families for the festivities lounged around our stove with John, and only occasionally bought a little something.

Myrtle and I cheated a little and walked over to the church at noon, reasoning that time to have lunch should not be considered part of the allotted hour. We were astonished at what the ladies had been able to do to the dull old basement: a Middle Eastern street bazaar with at least a dozen booths, tented in bunting of every color. Our stock must be exhausted at Burke's. I hoped John had already reordered bunting—Christmas was coming! I resolved to check the minute I was back in the store.

Mr. Ignacio played his accordion on a small stage in the middle. There was a crowd of at least twenty customers, with more coming in all the time.

Myrtle and I sat in the tearoom and were waited on by Maria Pilar, wearing a bright, Mexican skirt (I wondered where she found her fabric!) and with silk flowers in her hair. We enjoyed a bowl of the milder chili, which I still found "plenty spicy," as Myrtle put it. Then we strolled past the displays, heading for the fancy worktable. There, to my astonishment, I found my little dolls priced at three dollars each. In fact, the one with a hat and coat beside a frilly party dress was six!! I gasped.

"Well I swan!" exclaimed Myrtle in surprise.

"No one will ever buy her!"

"If no one does, then I will, myself," said a silky voice beside me, and I turned to see the lawyer, Matthew Spencer—the gentleman who had lately been bowing to me at church.

"How very gallant; but what in the world would you do with a doll?" I queried.

"How do you know I don't have a little niece?" he responded, taking my arm, and we bantered on in that manner quite pleasantly, somehow drifting away from Myrtle. He made amusing comments about various people we passed, especially all the attention being paid to our wounded hero: Mr. Passmore. The chest wound must be very slight, I thought, for he seemed in no way hindered by the giant sling, which supported his bandaged shoulder and arm, and was quite enjoying all the fuss.

"You know they'll be transferring Joe Floyd up to the jail in Santa Fe next week. That's where the trial will be held, and where the state penitentiary is as well." Mr. Spencer informed me. "The town won't settle down much until Floyd is gone. Everybody is wondering whether someone will get up a lynching or if Bobby will try to bust him out, so Sheriff Higgins can't wait to get rid of him."

I thought Mr. Spencer very good company, although he was not the one I would most have wished to be with. I reminded myself of my resolution to get on with my life and gave myself over to be mildly entertained by this urbane man. It was easy to be impressed with the way he bowed and handed me back over to Myrtle after we had traversed the room. Well done, without offending anyone and with perfect propriety. Mrs. Hoaglund saw it all and nodded her head at me approvingly. Myrtle teased me, but I laughed it off.

"Alta, look!" Myrtle cried suddenly. Doc Grigg strode by, carrying her rattlesnake pillow under his arm. The price tag on it boldly proclaimed ten dollars! Perhaps it would turn up on a chair in his office as a precautionary warning!

After that, Myrtle and I made one more round of the room. From the *White Elephant* booth of unwanted items, I found a lovely, framed watercolor of Coldwater Canyon, which I would enjoy on my wall; and a dear, little blue teapot for my very own. Myrtle bought a great many things; she had me gather them all to be watched at the coat check booth by the door until she could send Biggers over to get them. That service cost her twenty-five cents.

"It's for the church," she reminded me. "This is one place John doesn't mind what I spend."

At the Bake Sale booth, I bought cookies and Myrtle bought one of Mrs. Hoaglund's lemon meringue pies, which did look mouth-watering delicious.

"John will enjoy supper tonight!" she commented.

We spent the rest of our precious time in the Jumbles Tent, where, at last, I gratefully found another source of clothing than Mrs. Farrogot. There was clothing for men, women, children, and even a few items for babies. Most of it was "gently worn,"—such a nice phrase. I was happy to supplement my bare wardrobe with a second white blouse to wear to work, a print cotton dress, a pink wool shawl for evenings after work, and a fine pair of bedroom slippers.

More and more people kept coming.

"I think this bazaar is a success," Myrtle commented.

Just before we left, we took one last peek at the Fancy Work booth; only two of the Betsy Dolls remained. The expensive one was gone. I was ridiculously flattered.

Mrs. Goring cheerfully explained the rise in prices, "I thought it was high enough, like you, Myrtle. But Edna Michaels said we were way too low, and she's the one with the most experience of bazaars, being the Reverend's wife. She said they would sell, and she was right! These last two will be gone soon, I'm sure. Congratulations, Alta! You made us thirty-seven dollars for the church. You must make them again next year."

"Well, well!" Myrtle whispered in my ear as we left the building. "A compliment from Daisy Goring! You are on your way, Alta!"

It was gratifying. She must imply that I am accepted into the Sewing Circle if she talked about next year. But I had not thought I would have to become a doll factory to do it!

Chapter Fourteen

I t was now but two weeks before Christmas. The store was busy every day. On Tuesday, Lawyer Spencer came in and surprised everyone by coming directly to my counter.

"Miss Carlton," he greeted me, raising his hat, "I have just been to see Mrs. Hoaglund and have her permission to ask you if I may call on you at the boarding house tonight, after supper."

I was quite surprised—not that he would ask, but at the suddenness of it. However, one had to admire his sense of the correct conduct—the way these things should be done. After all, it was winter, with few opportunities for casual meetings. Perhaps being nodded to at church comprised a form of courtship in the West? I agreed, and that evening he duly appeared in time for coffee in the parlor, and we enjoyed a concert from Mr. Ignacio. After that, Mrs. Hoaglund shooed everyone else away: the two gentlemen from the grange, Mr. Peeples and Mr. Watson, as well as the invalid Mr. Passmore. They all teased us discreetly as they left.

"I will leave you two to your visit," Mrs. Hoaglund beamed at us. "I will just be in my sitting room across the hall, should you need anything." She left the sliding parlor doors open, as well as the door to her own quarters, and we sat together on the main settee quite properly chaperoned.

He stayed for an hour, and we did not lack for things to talk about, as he seemed interested in my background and my life in New York. As he was preparing to leave, he asked me if I would take dinner with him at the hotel on the coming Sunday evening. Full of my new resolves, I left him to seek Mrs. Hoaglund's opinion. The hotel being only a block from the boarding house made a difference, somehow, and she was favorably inclined. We would not be chaperoned, of course, but it was a public place—what could happen? And he had been so respectful and proper in his behavior. She gave her smiling approval; I accepted and saw him out with something new to look forward to. Apparently, I was courting again! I had never yet dined at the hotel and was curious, as it was the best Black Butte had to offer. Mrs. Hoaglund complimented me on my "conquest."

The hotel was considered *fancy*, although I preferred the Stew House, myself. There were linen tablecloths and candles, and we were served a pleasing steak and glasses of red wine. Quite "la-ti-dah," as Myrtle had promised.

As we came to the end of the festive meal, Matthew (as Mr. Spencer had asked me to call him) put down his napkin and reached for my hand, which was unexpectedly awkward, as I was still holding my steak knife. I was quite surprised by this familiarity.

"Alta, I was thinking we should forgo coffee and dessert here at the hotel and adjourn to my house. It's nearby, and I can give you a very nice glass of Madeira. We can get to know each other so much better that way!"

So much for all his good manners! I jerked my hand away.

"Mr. Spencer, I could not possibly go to your house! That

would be entirely improper. I'm surprised you would ask it!" I
hissed, not wanting to make a scene in such an elegant place.

"Oh, come, now, Alta," he persisted, trying to recapture my
hand, despite the fact I was keeping the steak knife pointed
toward him! "We get along very well, and I think we understand
each other. There is no need to waste time with these missish
protests. We should get straight to the matter at hand. We can
be very discreet, and you must be missing the company of a
man."

"Sir, you forget yourself! Whatever you think of me, you are
quite mistaken!" I dropped the knife and raised my voice, falling
back on previously successful tactics. Clutching my reticule and
shawl, I stood up, realizing at once that I had made a strategic
error—It had never occurred to me to carry my pistol to a
dinner engagement! Never again would I be without it. Saying
not another word, I stalked straight out of the hotel, causing
quite a stir, and knowing that everyone was looking at me.
What was it about the men in this town and restaurants! I could
not believe it was happening again!

I rapidly traversed the boardwalk and turned the corner into
the rutted street leading to the boarding house, but was only
halfway home when Mr. Spencer ran up behind me and
grabbed my arm, turning me forcibly around to face him. I had
never seen an angrier man.

"Did you think I would let you get away with that?" he
rasped harshly, twisting my wrist cruelly.

"Mr. Spencer, please let go! You are hurting me. You must
realize I am not interested in getting to know you in the manner
you suggest!" I tried and failed to pull away from him.

He practically spat at me. He was livid. "Who do you think
you are? A little tramp from New York! You weren't so particular with Whitaker, were you?"

I thought he would assault me right there in the street when suddenly the metallic sound of a gun safety clicking off froze both of us on the spot. I saw a tall man in a pale greatcoat, holding a large pistol trained directly between Mr. Spencer's eyes.

"The lady asked you to let her go, Matt," the stranger said. "If I were you, I would do it."

Mr. Spencer stepped back in a hurry and made a great effort to compose himself. "What, she's the exclusive property of you Whitakers?"

"Something like that," the stranger responded, the pistol never wavering.

"Well, you're welcome to her. She's a tease and a Nervous Nellie. She ain't worth it." And, making a remark about a female dog, he strode off, cursing.

The "Nervous Nellie" remark was quite accurate; I was shaking like an aspen leaf, my two hands clutching my useless reticule under my chin, with no idea of what to do. However, the first and third remarks had been quite uncalled for!

"Allow me to introduce myself," the stranger said, putting away his gun. "I'm Paul Whitaker. Sorry we had to meet this way."

"You're Whit's brother! That is, Charlie's. The lawyer!"

"Yes, regrettably, I share that profession with Spencer."

I sighed. "Not the right man to go out to dinner with, I guess."

"Alta... Miss Carlton, you shouldn't be going out to dinner with anyone without a chaperone. Or coffee, either, for that matter."

Did this man know everything about me? I petulantly replied, "Mrs. Hoaglund thought it was quite proper."

"Mrs. Hoaglund is deceived by appearances. Perhaps she thought he was a decent man."

There was not much to say to that! Paul offered his arm and

helped me over the ruts to the boarding house stairs. I thanked him profusely and sincerely. He politely offered himself as a chaperone, should I desire to socialize again. I said tartly that I believed I was done with socializing for the foreseeable future. He said that was quite wise, raised his hat, and was gone.

Mrs. Hoaglund was devastated when I described my fancy dinner at the hotel. She burst into tears, apologized, and blamed herself until I was consoling her, rather than the other way around.

"Mr. Whitaker is right, you know," she conceded in the end. "I was wrong to let you go anywhere alone, especially after dark. Another time, I will, myself, go with you." We gloomily regarded the future. "Or, better, I'll send Lupe!"

I laughed and hugged her warmly. "Don't worry, dear Mrs. Hoaglund. I don't want any more suitors. The men in this town have quite put me off!"

Beyond that, I was tired of having to be rescued. A Western woman should be able to protect herself. After all, I had the means. In my anger, a naughty little scheme suggested itself, first as an amusing fantasy, then as something I thought I could actually attempt. Perhaps, once people—and by that, I meant men—knew I carried a gun in my reticule and was fully prepared to defend my honor, they would behave more like gentlemen!

With that in mind, the next time there were packages to mail at Butterfield's, several days later, I asked John to let me take them, without an escort. He blustered and said Myrtle would "have his hide," but I persuaded him saying I had a little plan, which I was pretty sure Myrtle would approve of once she knew.

Doubtful, he saw me off, and I hoped to goodness he would not be sending Biggers off to trail along behind me. That would ruin everything!

Nearing the livery stable, I slowed my steps to a mere stroll, hoping my admirers were not otherwise occupied. I need not have worried. Right on cue, my tormentors appeared in the doorway and the catcalls began.

"Hey, Alta! Wanna go have a cuppa coffee?"

"Right, we could go to the hotel!"

"Maybe we can't afford her, guys. Maybe we should just go to Auntie's!"

I stopped walking and looked straight at them. By now I knew well who they were from the feminine grapevine. Smiling at them pleasantly, I spoke to them directly.

"Mr. Hooper, Mr. Burley. And Andy Goring! Good afternoon, gentlemen. Were you addressing me?"

This seemed to take them quite aback at first. Then, Andy Goring, whom I judged to be the ringleader, got up his courage and answered back, "Well, if the boot fits!"

"Mr. Goring, I shall have to ask you to address me more politely in the future," I said, and, opening my reticule, took out my pistol and pointed it straight at him. He took a great gulp of air and shrank back against the wooden wall of the livery stable. Biggers had told me never to take up a gun unless I expected to shoot it. I was eager to shoot it. Perhaps that showed. Certainly, they heard me click off the safety.

"Mr. Hooper," I continued, moving the pistol to address the second, and I thought the rudest, of the boys, "Is that an apple you are eating? Would you be so kind as to toss it up into the air?"

He hastened to comply, without at all understanding. I moved the pistol to the apple's trajectory and pulled the trigger in a flash. Of course, I came nowhere near hitting it but did have the satisfaction of hearing my bullet thud high up into the wall. All the young men cowered, and we had attracted considerable attention.

"Jeez, lady," protested Mr. Burley.

I shrugged, causing general alarm about where the pistol might now be pointed.

"Be careful, lady, it might go off again!"

"But, gentlemen, that is just my point," I said, smiling. They had walked right into it. The apple was a happy accident. "You see that I am not a particularly good shot. You also see that I always carry my pistol with me and that I will use it. I would like to point out that, although I know I did not hit the apple..." We all smiled at my feminine lack of proficiency... "I did come quite close to it, as I believe you will all agree." They nodded as one, however untrue. "That brings me to my final point. I am a lady, as I hope you will treat me in the future, and I would never, of course, shoot to kill. But I will shoot at a shoulder, or an arm, or perhaps a leg? And you can always count on me to hit somewhere near it."

The foolish smiles froze on their faces, and they shrank away, pulling themselves up, perhaps trying to look less of a target. Low bursts of laughter came from onlookers around us. I clicked off the safety and put the pistol away in my reticule, smiling at them. "So, gentlemen, how will you be addressing me in the future, when I find it necessary to walk past here?"

"Miss Carlton," they assured me.

"Good day, Gentlemen," I bowed slightly and continued on my way to Butterfield's.

"Good day, Miss Carlton."

"Nice to have seen you, Miss Carlton."

"Enjoy your walk, ma'am."

I am a wicked person. In this moment of triumph, I simply could not restrain myself from turning back for one final remark:

"Oh, and Mr. Goring, please give my regards to your mother."

Now, there was a roar of laughter from the onlookers. I supposed those three young men would hate me forever, but I did believe they would be polite from now on, and that this ridiculous incident might make the men of the town see me in a less vulnerable light.

Naturally, the story went through town like a stampede. I sincerely hoped this would be the last time I would be the cause of a sensation, but it would have been worth it—if the desired effect were achieved.

John and Myrtle laughed so hard when they heard my story that I feared for the health of them both.

"And to think that I was worried you wouldn't know how to use that pistol! Nobody ever did better!" John said, and I knew that was praise, indeed.

However, I'm afraid I was quite puffed up with my own self-importance after Paul Whitaker came into the store. He took my hand, bowed, and kissed it. "Alta Belle Carlton, you quite exceed expectations!" he declared and left. I shall never receive a better compliment!

Mrs. Hoaglund never mentioned it, but she did ask me to say grace before dinner, always a mark of favor. In weeks to come, I thought I detected the smallest little element of respect from the church ladies, but that may have been just my ever-optimistic imagination.

I thought I had done well, but apparently, I still needed one more reminder that a single woman must practice eternal vigilance. This gift I received on Christmas Eve.

Christmas in a boarding house cannot be expected to be like Christmas at home, and the last few days I had been finding myself nostalgically dreaming of past holidays and feeling a bit sorry for myself. Mrs. Hoaglund did her best, decorating the parlor and dining room with evergreen boughs, pinecones, and red ribbons. She gave us a Christmas feast with goose and all the

THE COURTING OF ALTA BELLE

trimmings, and we exchanged token gifts under a modest Christmas tree, having drawn names from a salad bowl the week before. I gave Miss Blodgett a very pretty lace-edged hankie, Mr. Passmore, our hero, gave me a nicely wrapped cake of fine-milled rose-scented English soap. We toasted each other in whiskey punch, and I retired to my room with glowing cheeks. It was, after all, a happy Christmas.

I had been cherishing a small packet just received from New York, planning to save it for Christmas morning. But I was feeling festive and decided to open it now. Inside was my real Christmas: a needlepoint purse from Mother with a lace-trimmed handkerchief inside, and a loving note from Father, with the news, as a postscript, of a large deposit into my banking account. From Aggie and Charles there was a card saying *Season's Greetings*, and from John and Adelle a small, but luxurious, packet of bath salts.

I was sitting enjoying my gifts and feeling happy when I thought I heard a sound at my door. At first, I dismissed it, thinking myself mistaken, but then it came again—a kind of scratch, with a low voice calling "Alta!"

Wondering what in the world it could be, I hurried over and opened the door to find Mr. Peeples, of the Grange, beaming at me with quite a red face, rocking back and forth on his heels, his hands in his pockets.

"Isn't this wonderful and convenient, Alta?" he said, and I saw I had been wrong; he was not beaming, he was leering. He was also quite drunk. "I can just slip down the stairs and tap on your door, and nobody will ever see me coming or going. We can spend as long as we like together without anybody ever knowing!" Yes, definitely a leer.

Fury rose in me until it was probably a good thing my reticule was behind me on the table. "Mr. Peeples, I am not available for any such goings-on," I said in a loud voice which, I was pleased to see, made him flinch. "If you ever knock on my door again, I will scream and tell Mrs. Hoaglund at once. Are we clear?"

He nodded, sputtering, and desperately gesturing for me to be quiet.

I started to shut the door, but then opened it again, saying in the same loud voice, "Just to remind you, I always keep my pistol very near!" Then, I did shut the door, loudly, and made sure the lock was engaged, enjoying the scuttling noises as Mr. Peeples fled back upstairs. I collapsed in my chair in a combination of laughter and tears. How had my life come to this!

Merry Christmas, Alta! I thought wryly to myself. How long would this go on? Would I have to actually shoot some man before this implacable town would believe I had a shred of virtue? Perhaps Mrs. Hoaglund was wrong, and no amount of propriety could reconstruct the first (bad) impression I had made. I descended into depression, but after a few days of introspection, concluded Mrs. Hoaglund's way was the only logical path. I resolved to continue to follow it, however many long and unpleasant turnings it might require.

I knew I was virtuous, even if the town did not believe it, and I would continue to insist on being treated as such.

I had come to realize that as much as I might ultimately desire to marry and have a family, after so many bad experiences I had to face the fact this might not happen for me. On a positive note—and I was determined to remain positive—I was better off than I had been at home. I was independent. I had a good job, which promised well for the future, and a few true friends who were genuinely interested in my welfare. I had achieved that much.

It was aggravating to have to encounter Mr. Peeples every day. His embarrassment and attempts to avoid me would have made anyone curious as to what might have passed between us.

However, no one seemed to take notice, and I hoped it would all soon go away.

By New Year's Eve, I was able to lift my glass of eggnog along with the rest in Mrs. Hoaglund's parlor while gunshots rang out from saloon row to toast 1889—whatever kind of a year it might turn out to be.

Chapter Fifteen
JANUARY 1889

At the first sewing circle of the new year, Isobel gave me quite a surprise. I was happy to see she had saved me a chair and sat down beside her. She was darning hose; I was making yet another flannel petticoat. After the rigors of preparing for the bazaar, there was no official church project for a while—we were all sewing on our own.

"Alta," Isobel said to me quietly, under the general chatter, "I've been wanting to talk to you. I have a proposition for you."

I smiled at her encouragingly, wondering what in the world. I liked her very much and was trying to get up my courage to call her Izzie, as Whit had done.

"I am in need of a housemate," she began, sedately. "You know my little house, on Ponderosa Street, five blocks south of the plaza. I bought it when I sold the farm and moved back into town. I am quite bored of living alone, and despite my being a respectable widow, I know it is considered not quite proper. Two mature women living together would be much more appropriate, but there has not been anyone before I cared to share with."

"Isobel, what a wonderful idea!" I responded, flushing with

pleasure at the compliment, loving the idea. But I looked toward Mrs. Hoaglund, full of doubt. She had done so much for me.

"You cannot go on living in one room in a boarding house," Isobel stated calmly. "You'll turn into Miss Blodgett!"

I could not help but laugh.

"I have already spoken to Mrs. Hoaglund, Alta, for I know the obligation you must feel toward her. She has been very good to you throughout all this... to-do. She thinks it would be a good opportunity for you. Besides, with all the surveyors coming through town because of the new road, and possible railroad spur going through to Gallup, she can easily rent your room out at once."

At my startled look, Isobel added, "She's a businesswoman, Alta, just like yourself. She can charge a railroad man on 'per diem' much more than she has been charging you!"

I wanted to accept but felt I must mention one more thing: "Will not my reputation rub off on you? You must not—"

She stopped me firmly. "Alta, my family feels responsible for your predicament. We feel the least we can do is offer you whatever protection the Whitaker name could offer. As my housemate, there would be a certain acceptance. Please let us make up for the wrong that has been done to you. It ought to help, at least a little."

"Isobel..." I had no other words.

She smiled at me warmly. "That's settled, then. Let us say no more about it. You'll come to dinner Sunday afternoon, and we'll see if it suits you."

It did suit me. The house was hardly *little*. It was a two-story clapboard, with a picket-fenced yard and an enclosed sun-porch entrance in front, facing a southern exposure. In the back, a spacious veranda faced north. Next to the kitchen door was a small enclosed outdoor washroom with a pump, a hand-operated washing machine, and a small stove to heat water.

Beyond, under a clump of cottonwood trees, there was a coal shed with the inevitable clinker pile beside it. That was the extent of her holdings, except for the necessary outhouse, behind the clump of trees.

Isobel's yard was dirt; no one had a lawn in Black Butte, nor plantings of any note. Due to the sparse rainfall, plantings had to be watered by hand, so most folks didn't bother. Isobel had more than most.

The back veranda supported an ivy-like vine, now bare but in the summer covered with green leaves and dark berries. Isobel said the leaves turned scarlet with the first frost—very pretty, I am sure.

By the front steps, she kept a great tub, which would be filled with yellow and orange nasturtiums—actual flowers, such a luxury!

Inside, the house had a parlor, a formal dining room, a bathtub room, and a spacious kitchen with another large dining table and chairs. It was what I have heard called a "country kitchen," with a sitting area around a fireplace. Upstairs were three bedrooms, with a fourth dormer room up a short flight of stairs in what had been an attic.

I was quite pleased with the room Isobel offered me. It faced east and so would get the morning light. It was much larger than my space at Mrs. Hoaglund's. There was a delightful window seat, which reminded me of my beloved room at home in every way except for the view. It was not Mother's rose garden, but vividly Western: the great, red cliffs north of town, the sky, yet another new shade of blue, and dark, leaf-less cottonwoods tossing skeletal limbs in never-ending intricate patterns. Great puffy white clouds marked the path of the wind. I must be careful, for one could while away an entire afternoon just sitting here watching the play of cloud and shadow across the land.

Isobel had made herself a charming home filled with lithographs of family, patchwork quilts, and hand-made rag rugs. I would have a five-block walk to work on dirt paths, not just one, but it was through a good neighborhood and not the rowdy main street of town with all the saloons and livery louts. I could not wait to live there. Not being such a green newcomer as I was last August, I suspected the house would be bitter cold and drafty through the rest of the winter months, and that the walk to the privy out back, not protected by a wall of vines as was Mrs. Hoaglund's, would be an agony. But Isobel's company more than made up for mere physical discomfort.

I would, however, miss Carmelita's cooking. Some considered her the best cook in town.

I wanted very much to live with Isobel for assorted reasons, some of which did not admit examination. I could not deny there was a tie to Whit. I was not sure that was good or bad, as I was doing my best to forget him.

Much as I wanted to just say yes, I did feel I needed to confess that as a housemate I had little to offer—I knew nothing of housekeeping or cooking.

"I can sew, and I can shop, but that's about it," I concluded ruefully.

Isobel laughed and said it was high time I learned those skills, and a good thing she was a teacher. She remarked my ignorance was in some ways a virtue, as she could teach me the *right* way from the start instead of having to overcome all the mischiefs which might have crept in.

We shook hands on a rent that was less than I had been paying and agreed to share food costs and to prepare and eat our meals together.

The next Sunday, John lent me Biggers and the wagon, and,

after a tearful goodbye to Hoaglund's, I joyously moved in. We were compatible housemates from the start, working together to establish an easy routine. In no time at all, I was calling her Izzie.

I loved the east bedroom and lost no time making it my own. It was past time to refill my needlepoint pillows. I felt I had a permanent residence now. I asked Myrtle's advice and she pointed me toward the cotton batting. John overheard our conversation and disagreed.

"You should use this kapok filler instead. It's much lighter, and best of all, it's easier to wash. Batting takes so long to dry. I got it from military surplus. They are using it for sleeping bags and, especially, for life jackets now, you know. It is much more buoyant than cotton batting. Keeps you afloat longer."

Myrtle and I had a good laugh about my urgent need to be kept afloat on the plains of New Mexico Territory. But when I saw it, it was so much lighter weight—and cheaper—that I did decide to use it despite its ugly appearance. It was a disagreeable yellow-brown, which John called khaki, but no one would see it, so I bought it. My pillows were good as new, and softer. They were perfect in my new window seat.

My framed watercolor of Coldwater Canyon looked marvelous on the wall. There was a wardrobe very adequate to hold my few clothes, with shelving for my hat—on permanent loan from Myrtle. There was even a rack for my two pairs of shoes. There was a large, braided rag rug on the floor, with prominent rows of yellow in it. The room had perfectly adequate white curtains, but at once I saw how glorious it could become if I were to make new ones, and a bed cover, too, of butter yellow! The whole room would light up with the dawn and even when it did not, would hold the memory of the sun and be cozy and cheerful.

I was measuring for yardage when I realized there was

nowhere I could get fabric like that. Certainly not at Burke's! Thoughtfully, I sat down and considered my prospects. It added a personal angle to my plans for the store, and a sense of urgency. I wanted to decorate my new room right now!

With reinforced determination to apply my energies toward the store, I lost no time in getting Myrtle and myself in a private corner and inquired more particularly into the items John had stocked at her request, but which had not sold. She ruefully told me that she had got some teapots in pretty colors, four eight-piece china table settings of middle quality, assorted veiling and trimmings for hats, along with an assortment of findings for dressmaking.

"I thought Mrs. Faraday would buy those, but she didn't like the colors they came in. She wanted black or navy, and the store in Albuquerque must have just sent us stuff they couldn't sell themselves. Let's see, there were also a dozen wind-up alarm clocks; I was really surprised no one bought them. And a bunch of fancy teas. It was all very disappointing."

But not surprising, I privately thought, having watched John's sales technique. If asked for a cooking pot, he reached back on the shelf and plunked one down on the counter; there was no offering of a choice. In fact, for the most part, there was no choice, just one of a kind. I had never heard him make any suggestion to a customer, except in the case of the Indian jewelry, which he seemed to regard as separate from the regular stock. He had a passion for it and himself wore a heavy bracelet, ring, and belt buckle.

I went around the store looking for Myrtle's treasures and understood more and more why they had not sold. The teapots were there, six very pretty ones: three of various colorful patterns, and three in attractive solids of blue, pink, and light green. However, they were on the back of an upper shelf, the standard brown pots stacked in front of them so you could not even see them.

The teas I finally located at the back of a drawer full of scrub brushes, in little packets, perhaps stale by now, although tea is quite long-lasting. The clocks I found after much trouble, shelved with the lanterns, which had also come to cover them from view. Unless you came in directly asking for a clock, you would never know we stocked them.

I knew where the findings and hat trims were in my own department and saw at once that I had fallen into John's manner of selling. In a new place and trying to fit into the store, I had not often tried to interest my customers in anything additional to their orders, and John frowned on "cluttering up the counters" with any kind of display.

When there were no customers, I took out my notebook and started a list of suggestions I wanted to make to John. It began with lighter, brighter fabrics—butter-yellow broadcloth —but grew at an alarming rate.

Such a gentle word, *suggestions*, but my list soon began to look more like *demands*. John, an experienced merchant who had done things one way all his life, would see my slightest request for change as criticism from an ungrateful newcomer who was too full of herself, knew nothing about the West, and besides that—was very young.

But my head was buzzing with ideas. I couldn't stay quiet when there were so many ways to increase sales! I knew now just how Father had felt when old Mr. Hodges would not listen to any of his ideas!

It seemed simple to me. For one thing, the stock was not organized logically. Wares seemed to have been put on the shelves wherever there was room when it arrived, and the result was chaos. There was no logical order and you had to memorize. Frying pans sat next to washboards, and if you wanted a plate, they were between the grinding mills and the mason jars, nowhere near the cups and saucers.

Among the packaged foods, one would have thought all the varieties of dried peas and beans would be found together; instead, they were scattered piece-meal throughout the section, as were the many varieties of soup mixes, noodles, and crackers.

Another practice that grated on me—nowhere were attractive items set out in easy view, even on shelves, things you might like and decide to buy if only you could see them. They seemed universally to be hidden away like the teapots. John expected people to ask for what they needed.

Equally irritating, the whole center of the store was wasted space in my view. Customers entered into an open area, reaching across the full width of the store to the back wall, from which John would come beaming in welcome, and lead them straight back to the stove with its welcoming chairs and cups of coffee. The cash register and a grandfather clock were also here, along with a storage room and the back exit. Nothing to entice one into sections to the right or left, only bare counters and shelves stuffed with jumble. The warm welcome was good, but prime counter space was lost.

Also, a clear message was sent: customers were not expected to wander about looking over merchandise for something they might like—they were to wait for assistance!

Naturally, I was most critical of the section I knew best, my own. Here was one, all-consuming complaint: it was not large enough! Although we were the sole source of dry goods in town, John stocked only the basics: one grade of cotton, flannel, or muslin; dressmaking fabrics, serge, and heavy woolens only in dark colors; bolts of ticking for mattresses and heavy duck for men's pants and overalls, but no drapery or upholstery fabrics.

We stocked no silks or satins, no moiré, brocade, or taffeta. Must ladies always wear wool? We had no delicate batiste, sprigged lawns, or dotted muslins for summer gowns. Our broadcloth was heavy enough for sheeting. We needed ging-hams and chintz and calicos, and all in colorful bright prints and plains! It was not just Auntie's girls who could find little to their liking.

In fact, I had been hard put to find attractive fabric for my Betsy Doll outfits. Myrtle had kindly given me free-range of her piecing bag, or I would never have managed.

I knew Myrtle was right—that John did not see Burke's Mercantile as a store for ladies.

How women here must long for color in their homes! There was plenty of color outside—one had only to look out any window—but the interiors I had seen so far were uniformly drab. I could picture myself suggesting sky-blue cushions for their settees, or bright curtains like the ones I wanted. Even red and white striped ones, such as those I had made at the Guild, impossible to supply.

No use daydreaming about New York! It was a dilemma. I could just picture myself, a mere chit of a girl, a stranger who had only worked for him for a few months, suggesting he could double his business by stocking for women! It was easy to imagine the jovial features of his face freezing one by one into icy dismissal, perhaps actual dismissal! To him, it would be presumption. Up to now, logical arguments had not swayed John, but what would?

It came to me that he would have to be shown. I determined that, somehow, I would sell Myrtle's *mistakes*—and in a way that would open John's eyes.

Paul Whitaker came into the store and, once again, came straight to my department. He greeted me most pleasantly, insisting that he was *Paul*, not *Mr.*, and asked for fifteen yards of plain muslin, for curtains the Whitaker housekeeper wanted to make. As I measured out this yardage, he discreetly inquired if there had been any more unpleasantness from a certain lawyer. I was happy to assure him that the gentleman in question no longer tipped his hat to me in church, although I always greeted him with a chilly nod of the head.

Paul laughed; he had expected nothing else. Looking around my section, he remarked that he was taking the train to Mexico City in a few days, regarding a land grant case, and wondered if I might have any exotic commissions for him, such as fabrics, pottery, or jewelry. I smiled, thinking of my curtains, but I could no more ask this elegant man to shop for me than I could accept his previous offer to be my chaperone! I said, only, that I knew my department needed brightening up and had ideas, but it would be slow going since John Burke was not open to them.

He looked at me with amusement and some speculation. "Well, that will be a good challenge for you, Alta. I will be waiting with anticipation for any surprising changes."

"Don't hold your breath," I advised him.

He *tsk-tsked* at me. "Alta, you are getting quite Western in your speech! You must be careful not to lose all your New York polish. It is quite attractive." He was one to talk! He was as far from a typical Black Butte man as one could get.

I laughed back. "I guess *Western ways* do tend to rub off. Izzie will rein me in if I get too country."

He said he was glad I was living with Izzie, now, and considered it most suitable. We parted with mutual good feelings. I was predisposed to think well of him, because he had saved me, of course, but also because he was a Whitaker... and because he was so interesting and easy to talk to. Perhaps he had got it from his studies and travels. He did have a wonderful air of worldly wisdom and languor which I much admired, although I thought it a bit of a pose, especially once having seen what he became when he drew a gun. That had been eerily thrilling—I was quite intrigued with Whit's older brother.

This conversation became another inspiration for me to begin my campaign against John if only to provide an amusing chat in the future should I meet Paul again.

The teapots seemed a good place to begin. Taking advantage of John being briefly gone from the store, I climbed up on a step stool and selected a beautiful teapot, patterned in the Chinese manner with oranges, blues, and reds on a white background. I found a tin tray and covered it with a scrap of linen. I found two white cups and saucers that were slightly thinner than our standard stock pottery. I found a silk daisy in my leftovers bin, taped it onto a pencil for a stem, and washed the label off an almost empty bottle of Milk of Magnesia for a vase; it was such a pretty cobalt blue color. I used two remnants of white broadcloth to make napkins and took it all into the Foodstuffs section.

At the end of the main counter there, which everyone would have to pass by, I set up a very credible little tea tray. I added a tea ball and several packets of Myrtle's fancy tea, tearing open the corners so that the individual aromas could be appreciated.

At the last minute, I added a small plate of cookies, brazenly ripping open a package of the small vanilla sugar babies we kept in stock. It was an odd item, but men often bought them. I was partial to them, myself, although I thought them a bit stale, as well they should be since they were made in Cincinnati! How strange, shipped so far to sell in a town where most women would produce them weekly from their own kitchens. Apparently, there were enough non-cooking spinsters, like me, and bachelor boarders in this town to make the sugary treats worth keeping in stock.

Shortly after I had completed my forbidden display, the

Collins sisters came into the store and came straight to Food-stuffs. They admired my little tea tray very much, and we had moved on to my helping them with small amounts of flour, rice, and cornmeal when John returned. He came at once to welcome the ladies. His hawk eyes missed nothing, of course, and he frowned mightily.

"Alta, what is this mess on the counter? I have asked you to keep the counters clear!" he began, but the elder Miss Collins interrupted him.

"It is a lovely little display, John. I had no idea you had anything so pretty in the store! Is that teapot for sale?"

Breathing a sigh of relief, I immediately responded in the affirmative, interrupting anything John might say, and named the price.

"I'll take it," Miss Collins said firmly. "And what is this most delicious-smelling tea? It's very unusual."

"That is jasmine tea, Miss Collins, from China. Myrtle and I often have some, as a nice change from pekoe. Would you like to sample it?"

The ladies were pleased to accept, and I quickly made up a pot, as Myrtle often did for her favorite customers, and soon we sat in front of the stove, daintily sipping China tea where there were usually men smoking cigars.

The ladies left, bearing away their supplies and their new teapot, not neglecting to add a quarter-pound of jasmine tea to their previous charges. I stood demurely at the cash register. John glowered at me.

"That pot and that stupid tea have sat here five years, and nobody wanted them."

"Nobody saw them! People find they want pretty things when they can see them."

"That's enticement!"

"I think of it as supplying a desire I know exists, as you did when you told Boomer Yates about the Yazzies' new jewelry."

"All right, Alta, you make your point. Don't rub it in." John stomped away, grumbling, into the Hinterland.

Within two weeks, I had sold all five remaining teapots and a great deal of tea. Myrtle was delighted, John ungracious.

I did not stop there but turned my attention next to the alarm clocks, which I found at the back of a bottom shelf, well out of sight. I moved them to the end of one of our glass-topped counters, removing the inappropriate nest of men's socks which in no way deserved such a showcase.

I set one clock on top of the glass counter on a little square of felt and set it to ring on the hour. John was more than annoyed, but, as Myrtle said, they "sold like hotcakes!" I had no idea what that phrase meant, as I had never known pancakes to sell especially well, but sell the clocks did. The hourly ring attracted attention to them and caused general hilarity in the store for everyone except John, who just *harrumphed*.

When all the clocks had sold, I turned my attention to the sets of dishes. Still not asking permission, but with Myrtle's help this time, we set out a display of one of her dinnerware services. The design was not much to my liking, but it was Myrtle's favorite: white china much thinner than John's usual *café grade*, hand-painted with overblown pink cabbage roses, each plate, saucer, and cup edged in gilt. John thought it much too fragile to be practical.

We used our previous tablecloth and napkin and set out one place setting with a few interesting serving dishes and a standard knife, fork, and spoon. The rest of the set of eight we stacked attractively on a shelf behind that counter—where they were highly visible.

To enhance our place setting, I found a white pottery cream and sugar and a set of pewter salt and pepper shakers.

I outdid myself this time with my centerpiece: I found a bit of dark red felt and rolled tiny strips into pretty good imitations of a rosebud and, adding a green felt "leaf," taped each onto a wooden skewer with green draft tape. I swiped a potato from Foodstuffs, stuck it in the bottom of a teacup belonging to the set, and had a nifty "frog" in which to stick my "roses."

"Alta, that is absolutely ritzy!" Myrtle enthused.

Even I had to admit it was. I almost didn't care if we sold the china or not—it was enough to give Myrtle this pleasure of seeing her "mistake" set out so elegantly.

However, it did sell within the day to Mrs. Laura Higgins, the sheriff's wife. In fact, she took the second, matching set as well, to make a service for sixteen. Biggers had to deliver all this to her home, making two trips afoot, being extra careful that nothing broke as it was too small a load to get out the horse and wagon.

Myrtle and I then set out the second design, two sets of a blue and white "willow" pattern, much more to my taste with its pleasing hint of the Orient. It sold within the week, this time to Mrs. Reverend Michaels, and, again, she took both sets!

"Thank you for saving me a trip to Albuquerque," she said to John.

He had a thoughtful expression on his face but said nothing.

"Myrtle," I asked privately, "how is it you did not sell these pretty things before? Didn't you show them to anyone?"

"Not really," she replied. "You know how strongly John feels about not 'tricking' people into buying things they don't need. And these things are certainly not necessities."

"Perhaps not to a man!" I replied tartly, wondering why John had ever gotten into this business. However, the answer was obvious. He saw himself as a men's ware supplier, much like the men at the granary supplied seed, not as a merchant. But a merchant was what this town needed!

I began to think I had grossly underestimated the amount of trade John was losing. I now believed that sales might double if we began to stock the kind of wares desired by women. Would John be willing to make such a very great change? I could not believe he would.

Chapter Sixteen

I t was with some trepidation that I set out to sell the remaining bits of "Myrtle's Mistake"—the hat trimmings. We would forget the findings; I fully agreed with Myrtle that, with their unpleasant colors (tan, grey, and beige), they were a dead loss and should be tossed. Hat trimmings were a different matter.

Wadding a large piece of our heavy brown wrapping paper into a sort of head shape, I swathed it in muslin and tucked it into an ewer requisitioned from Hardware to create a "head" model for a hat. Using the brightest fabric I could find—a brown printed calico, which had not been selling—I draped the ewer as if with a scarf. It was crude but utilitarian.

I constructed a kind of low-crowned boater hat out of the lightest cardboard I could find. Most of our boxes were far too bulky for me to cut. I covered the hat form in off-white muslin, using a paste made of flour and water. When it was dry, I let myself go—trimming it with a big, lavender silk ribbon hatband and bow. Cutting out of the purple felt a great number of small "violets," I spent the rest of the day ecstatically sewing them in artistic clusters onto the brim and band with yellow embroidery thread, creating a golden French knot center for each flower. I added a few small green felt leaves for contrast and finished by swathing it all in a lavender veil. It turned out rather showy, but it did look like a hat. I was quite pleased and proudly anchored it onto my display head with several large pearl hatpins. I set it out on one end of my main counter, surrounded it with a bit more veiling, and commenced making more fanciful felt flowers to scatter around the base as examples of what could be crafted as hat trim. I had no trouble thinking up flower shapes but was severely limited by the lack of colors, being confined to maroon, black, dark green, and brown—I had used up all the purple. I thought someone surely should congratulate me on my ingenuity, for I produced some very exotic (if slightly funereal) blooms.

The display served my purpose, which was to get ladies thinking about trimming their own hats since there was no milliner in town. Where they were to get new hat forms, I had no idea, but they certainly could spruce up their old ones.

John noticed the new display and scoffed but said nothing. My lady customers were most interested, deeming my "hat" stunning. One admirer said she would wear it—even though it was made of cardboard—if it were for sale! To a soul, however, they denied the ability to create such a vision, no matter how much I urged them to try. Perhaps I had overdone it with my sample! However, one fact was clear: this town needed a milliner!

It is remarkable but true that where there is a need, something will rise to fulfill it. Not necessarily what you had been thinking of, but perhaps something better.

On the third day, a woman came into the store, asking for veiling, whom I had never seen before. She was small and round, somewhat stooped, but very neat in her appearance, wearing a nice bonnet but heavily veiled.

She admired my hat. I complimented her own bonnet, and

she allowed that she had made it, herself. I remarked she was the first woman I had met in town who felt capable of such a feat. She laughed and said she could make a real hat just like my cardboard creation, using heavily starched buckram.

In response to my amazement, for I had thought the hat a mere fantasy, she said that much could also be done by way of shaping felt, but that the difficulty in hat-making was always where to find real hat forms of straw or other stiffened fabric.

My mind racing, I asked, "Are you a milliner? Do you ever make hats for sale?"

"Oh, no," she responded. "Most people are far too uncomfortable to be around me."

Lifting her veil, she permitted me a brief but full view of the deformity I had begun to suspect. She had a pronounced hare lip.

I returned her gaze steadfastly. "I should introduce myself. I'm Alta Carlton."

"Uma Deetz," she said, letting the veil fall. We shook hands.

"Mrs. Deetz—" I began.

"Miss," she interrupted, firmly.

"Miss Deetz, if Burke's were to acquire a stock of hat forms, would you consider making hats on commission through the store? The ladies could describe to me what they wanted, and you could make a hat on speculation. You would not have to meet."

Personally, I thought such aversion could be overcome soon enough if the hats were pleasing.

She was interested. I suggested that the store might ask for a 30 percent commission on each sale, with the remainder going to her. She, in turn, would buy her hat-making materials from Burke's, at a 15 percent discount. Everyone would benefit.

Miss Deetz said she would be happy to be able to augment her income. I guessed it might be meager. She gave me her address. She lived some blocks southeast of the plaza, an area of town I had not visited, up the hill toward the high school.

"Miss Carlton," she said, "I will make a real hat just like your model. If you like it, and if it sells, I will say we are in business!"

I cautioned her that I would have to get John Burke's permission, but I thought it such a good idea I was determined to try.

Was it possible I could get John to agree? For one thing, I was sure he would like to help Uma Deetz if nothing else about the plan interested him; but with a heart-pounding thrill, I thought my scheme might be the key which opened the door to the future of Burke's Mercantile.

Within four days, Miss Deetz produced the hat, and it was wonderful. I modeled it and swore I could not take it off.

"Please make me three more just like it!" I enthused, forgetting in the excitement of the moment that I did not yet have a hat shop! "I want one, Mrs. Owens will take one, and I'm sure the other two will sell quickly!"

Over a cup of tea—she chose Darjeeling—and very gently as if she in no way wanted to suggest she might know more about anything than myself, Uma Deetz schooled me in the art of selling millinery:

"A hat must be unique, you see. It is even more important, perhaps, than a woman's gown. Say that I do make up more like this; you keep one for yourself and sell one to your Mrs. Owens. The other two quickly sell, perhaps one to Rosita Gomez, and the last hat to Mary McGuire. *Señora* Gomez adores her hat and wears it to church at St. Bartholomew in Beantown. Mary McGuire does not go to church, except sometimes at Easter, but wears hers to visit relatives. However, you and Mrs. Owens both attend Rev. Michaels's Ecumenical Church; the moment she sees you wearing *her* hat, you will lose her as a customer forever and her friends as well. Worse, she will run all over town crying foul, and many other ladies will begin to regard you as a 'sharp dealer' who cannot be trusted." I listened intently as she continued: "God forbid Mrs. McGuire should suddenly decide to go to Easter services where she will run into señora Gomez. That will take care of the rest of Black Butte. Our hat business will decline and die before it is ever established. This is why every hat must be at least a little different from every other. If a lady asks us to copy a hat she admires, we must firmly decline. She must make do with *similar*. Can you agree to that?"

I could, and thanked her warmly for the good advice. I can sell, but in no way on a level to avoid the social pitfalls she had just described.

Miss Deetz was quite right. Selling hats in New York City, with its great population, was one thing. Here we were few, and it was quite another. Therefore, Burke's hats would be one of a kind. Black Butte was too small a town to survive a hat war!

I admired Uma Deetz as much as I liked her and thought she would be a valuable addition to the store. How I wanted, at that moment, to introduce her to Miss Bailey—my first teacher —and listen to them discussing sales; I should have to content myself with something *similar*, such as writing to Cora about her.

It was now imperative to storm "Fort John." I could picture as plain as day a small Millinery department, bringing many more women into the store. If only we had better stock, they would buy more than hats.

I took Myrtle fully into my confidence, and she, always eager for anything new, became my co-conspirator. However, the price I paid for her support was high. She also admired the violet hat, and perhaps I am a nicer person than I thought—or else much worse due to out-and-out bribery—for it was she who wore the hat to church the following Sunday. Perhaps she just outmaneuvered me.

Together, we carefully marshaled our arguments against John, stressing the growth of the town and how much times were changing. We iterated the most common requests we could not fill and finished with a generalized list of what we would like to add to our stock. Finally, we would crown our presentation with the idea for the hat salon, which would bring more women into the store. It convinced us, and hopefully, it would interest John.

All this in hand, we planned to bushwhack him the old-fashioned way—at Sunday dinner. Virginia, fully a party to the scheme, produced a feast of all his favorites: steak with baked potatoes, molded gelatin supreme salad with mayonnaise and canned carrots and peas, Parker House rolls, styled after those served in the famous Boston hotel restaurant, and chocolate meringue pie.

It is not possible that anyone in Black Butte dined better that Sunday afternoon. John looked surprised, but manfully ate his way through the entire meal, then sighed with appreciation, folded his napkin, and lounged back in his chair.

"Well, ladies, that's the best meal I ever got in February before. However, I expect there's something I must do to earn it. I'm ready. Bring on my bill."

Both Myrtle and I were surprised to have been so transparent, but he certainly did seem to be in a good mood, so I launched into my presentation as planned with Myrtle putting in her two cents every now and then. He sat through it all with benign acceptance, agreeing to every suggestion! He was aware that the town was changing and that what had served twenty years ago might not be enough now. He could see for himself that a modest Women's department would have customers. He was even willing to try my idea of commissioned hats, saying it was better than buying the hats outright, and, anyway, was what he was already doing with the Yazzies. He took our breath away by taking our reasoning even further:

"Here's something you didn't think of, Alta. If we don't expand soon, someone from outside is likely going to open up a bigger store that *does* cater to women. I always liked to think of Burke's as leading the way. I'm not partial to being second-best. And I'll own, it wouldn't hurt if profits went up. I just wondered how long it was going to take you ladies to push me into it!"

Infuriating!

It was all settled. It was actually happening! Myrtle and I, stunned, at once began the exhilarating process of putting together an order for stock appealing to women, being very careful to specify colors and quality this time, and beginning small, since this was all speculative. We could always reorder if something sold well.

We were engaged, as it were, in *sticking our toes into the Rio Grande, to see how wet it was*. We were pretty sure we knew, but there would be no more of "Myrtle's Mistakes." If some of the new things did not sell well, we would not be out much and could have our own white elephant sale. In fact, we liked that idea so much, we promised each other we would have one in any event, later, if we could sneak it past John! We knew the ladies of the town would love it. We meant to use up every drop of John's sudden new attitude!

We set ourselves to reconfigure the layout of what was now the Dry Goods section. We would need more shelving, new counters, and a partitioned "Hat Salon." It was great fun. Myrtle especially enjoyed it. She had wanted to do this for years.

What we did to create a Women's section, Fred did in a smaller way for Men's Wear, surprising us with several unexpected desires of his own: such as an upgrade from just work clothes to blazers, shirts, and slacks for social events.

John could not help *harrumphing*, but he was always a fair man and couldn't say no to Fred after having said yes to us! He did not join us in the planning, not even for discussions, just told us to do what we wanted and spent even more time around the stove drinking coffee with his cronies.

"Is that a problem?" I worried to Myrtle.

"No, everything is fine." She was sure.

We were ordering some housewares and linens, but meant to concentrate on our new department for now. If it were successful, we could redo Hardware and Foodstuffs later.

Actually, John did his part in the remodeling by writing to our supplier in Albuquerque, explaining our plan to enlarge, and hoping they could accept and fill an order much larger than anything before. He asked for a more generous discount and quick shipping.

Stewart's Trading Post replied quickly that they would be happy to fill the larger order and accommodate us, and, further, if John would supply a letter of credit from his bank, he was such an old and trusted customer that it would be their pleasure to increase our discount as well as to extend payment into monthly installments at the start, which John said would help us get over the hump of renovation. They would ship as quickly as possible, depending on the condition of the roads, with probably the first, immediate shipment being sent in no later than a month, followed by a possible second later on if they, themselves, have to order from back East. We looked forward to an exhilarating spring.

In the last week of March, we sent off our order in the mail via stagecoach. I, myself, delivered the large packet to the post office—without an escort. I had no trouble on the streets, of late.

In the mid-afternoon, we all gathered on the veranda of the store, despite the cold March wind, to watch the stage drive off bearing our massive order. My heart was in my throat. I fervently hoped the stagecoach would have no accident.

Visions of linen tablecloths and china tea services danced in my head, along with soft, light woolens, see-through lawn, and bright red calico—and definitely my butter-yellow curtains! All strewn with silk flowers of every color, like gardens in a park. My hopes for 1889 were rising to the sky. Just a few months before, I had thought it would be the worst year of my life.

Chapter Seventeen

I t was well we got our order off when we did, for a week later, the major snowstorm of the winter arrived—in an eerie echo of the year before. It snowed without ceasing for two days, and huge snow drifts covered everything. I was not even able to get into the store, but then, nobody else was, either. The snow stayed on the ground for several weeks and the roads were impassable. Everyone made light of it, saying it was only a typical storm and nothing near "the storm of the century." This was just snow.

Narrow paths were dug through the streets so that people could get to businesses. A holiday air prevailed, as normal activities were suspended. Outlying farmers could not come in. School was closed, no stagecoaches came through, and no supply wagons of any kind. Burke's had so few customers that John told everyone to just stay home. It was not worth braving the cold and the drifts.

Izzie took advantage of our house-bound days to give me an intense course in "how to manage a home," including both cooking and cleaning. At first, I demurred, informing her that back East we spent such days comfortably cocooned before the fire—reading, sewing, and drinking cocoa. She replied firmly that out West folks took advantage of their opportunities, and she set up the ironing board for my first lesson. I admired her determination and asked if she had ever met, while in the East at school, a Mr. Ulysses Brown. She said no, and very properly brushed that remark aside as what it was—a diversionary tactic — then handed me the iron.

She showed me how to heat the flat irons on the large kitchen stove, taking a hot one up to use by clicking it into the iron frame. She showed me how to sprinkle and iron my blouses and petticoats, somewhat appalled that I had gotten this far in life without knowing such a basic skill. I thought wistfully of Lupe at Mrs. Hoaglund's—but I learned. I did think it excessive to iron the sheets and pillowcases; Izzie did not.

"It's proper," she insisted.

Izzie taught me to make decent soups and stew during this time, but we both agreed my biscuits were barely edible.

On Sunday, Izzie insisted we must go to church. I went, although I privately thought we were in danger for our lives from the cold, and almost wished I was back at Mrs. Hoaglund's, just two blocks from the church. Izzie's house was eight blocks away, and I was really a bit surprised neither of us got frostbite.

After church, since we were already downtown, we decided we deserved lunch at the Stew House, especially since it was on the way home. We got a warm greeting from Sally and saw that O'Toole's was doing quite a business.

"Everyone's bored with staying home," Sally explained, making room for an extra table for us by shoving some boxes into the kitchen. "We're making a fortune!"

I was happy for her but wished Burke's was as well. We made sure to order biscuits, and I bit into mine with a mixture of pleasure and chagrin. My biscuits really tasted more like cardboard.

Izzie agreed. "We should ask Sally for advice," she suggested. "Go to the authority."

Sally was much too busy for that. Anyway, she pointed out it was Miss Abbie who made them and urged us to go into the kitchen when we were done eating and ask the biscuit queen herself. We did.

Miss Abbie was happy to take a little break to put her feet up and talk to us.

"They're working us to death here!" she half-complained, indicating señor Gomez straining to lift a new pot of stew onto the stove, and Maria Pilar peeling potatoes in a corner at such speed it made me fear for her pretty fingers! Abbie, herself, was covered in flour and had just filled the oven with four pans of new biscuits.

"I'm pretty sick of biscuits right now," she admitted, "but if you want to know the truth, it's not so much the recipe as it is the hands. You see, I can't tell you what the secret is, but I can tell you how to get it. Just keep on making biscuits. After about a hundred times, they will just get better. It's the hands."

I looked at her in despair, but Izzie and I agreed—Miss Abbie should know. She was famous locally for her tasty and very tall biscuits. She must have made thousands of them by now.

Izzie and I struggled home through the narrow path down our street, and that night I served for supper—along with pork chops and canned peaches—leaden biscuits, possibly batch number five. We had quite a long way to go. Izzie looked resigned but determined. She took the positive view that at least they were better toasted as leftovers and did make excellent crumbs to use on top of casseroles and brown Bettys. I was impressed anew with the force of her character.

In the week that followed, I made biscuits three more times —no improvement, but we found they were also more palatable floating in a bowl of soup (which I was very good at). Izzie did let me make oatmeal muffins instead one night, and if I do say so myself, they were delicious. At my suggestion, I made another batch topped with sugar and cinnamon for breakfast, and that became our favorite weekend morning meal.

I suggested that perhaps I had hands for *muffins*, but Izzie demurred, saying Miss Abbie had been quite specific, and it was biscuits. She said she had never heard of "hands for muffins"; but after reflection, admitted that, to be honest, she had heard the phrase used in association with making bread. I pointed out that muffins were a form of bread. Izzie then grew rather heated and said that there were no hands for muffins and it was ridiculous for me to claim it after only two batches! We let the subject go at that. But she did ask for my muffins very often.

That week, Izzie also introduced me to laundry, concentrating on linens. Although both of us were working women, we usually sent such heavy items out to Mrs. Reed and only did our personal wash ourselves. Izzie insisted that before you sent a task out for hire, you should know how to do it yourself to correctly value and supervise the service you are paying for. I'm sure she was correct—I was equally certain I would never commit to a life where I would have to be the one who washed the sheets—but I could have done without it. After a lifetime of never having to deal with the wash, my own underclothes, blouses, and petticoats were bad enough.

Izzie soon had me sweeping and dusting like a professional, and turning out palatable but simple meals, such as steak or chops with mashed potatoes, gravy, and canned vegetables.

Just as an excuse to get out of the house one day, and to check in at Burke's to see if I could come back to work yet, I struggled down to Mrs. Hoaglund's one afternoon and begged her for her famous meatloaf recipe. Many ladies would not have been so kind about their specialty; Mrs. Hoaglund told me how to make a meatloaf in general, but said she was holding back her own secret ingredients. I would have to use my imagination. Fair enough.

She did not, in general, share her recipes, especially the one for the Parker House rolls from the hotel in Boston. I had often enjoyed them at her table but *that* she did not share, nor ever explain how she had got hold of it.

John was not helpful in ending my exile and said to wait at least a few more days until the roads stopped running like rivers. He also scolded me for being out today when it was not necessary.

On the way home, I stopped in at the butcher's shop, but Mr. Warden had no minced beef for making meatloaf. His supplies were running low in general, and he made several remarks—ones that I did not care for, but believe were meant to be pleasantries—about a bad winter fifteen years ago when the town survived only by eating horse meat. He assured me we were not yet come to that pass and strongly urged me to try calf's liver, of which he had a good supply, fresh that day.

I did not ask him how he got it amid all this snow, as I did not want to know, but asked instead how such a thing was to be cooked since it had never been on the menu back home.

He recommended fried liver and onions, explained the simple cooking directions, and sent me off with enough for two.

It was a little off-putting, in the idea, but I knew many people ate it; in fact, I remembered seeing it on the menu at the Harvey House in Santa Fe.

I had meant to surprise Izzie with meatloaf; the liver was a bigger surprise. She said she liked it quite well and happily supervised as I sliced the onions and dredged the meat in flour, frying it all in lard so hot it popped at me out of the skillet. It was delicious. Heaven must smell like frying onions!

Izzie said this dish was her nephew Paul's favorite, and that we must immediately have a dinner party and invite him and his great friend, Jeremy. So, I made the meal again two nights later.

It was quite a pleasant evening, and I began to see that there were rewards for learning this cooking business. Paul was flatteringly appreciative, as was his friend. Izzie had not insisted on biscuits for this special meal, allowing me to make the oatmeal muffins. I served this up with baked potatoes and canned stewed tomatoes and was quite proud of myself.

Jeremy Wells was a delightful addition to our party. A small, roly-poly, bear-like sort of man with a well-trimmed black beard and twinkling blue eyes, he kept us laughing all evening with outrageous puns and droll stories of their recent train trip to Mexico City, usually at his own or Paul's expense. It seems he often traveled with Paul and was planning to go with him to San Francisco in the spring. They both spoke eloquently about the customs, scenery, and cuisine they would experience on that trip until I quite wished I were going with them. It was an unexpectedly pleasant evening in the doldrums of being snowed in, and Izzie and I vowed to invite them at least once a month. Only, Izzie was to cook the next time!

Amusing dinner party, nonetheless, on the following Monday, I insisted that I must go in to work at the store. I think Izzie thought I was making an escape. Izzie laughed while watching me slog off through the snow and slush, avoiding more lessons. She was a schoolmistress to the core, and I was helpless before her. It was a relief to be back at work.

When the snow did, finally, melt, I already knew what to expect and was not surprised when we were mired in a sea of mud for two more weeks. Although it was warmer now, I preferred the snow.

In late April the Yazzies came again, a sign that things were getting back to normal. Ruth delivered my earbobs—they were perfect, and I paid her happily.

With John's full approval, I asked if her brother would be willing to supply us with a modest assortment of lady's jewelry and whether she, herself a weaver, would supply a few small rugs. She agreed at once, saying they had a backlog of stock and would be happy to have an outlet so soon, and we shook hands on a second satisfactory commission arrangement.

Myrtle and I added plans for a special locking glass display counter, where we could lay out the jewelry while still keeping it secure and hang rugs behind the counter to add atmosphere.

The following Sunday, Izzie and I were chatting with Mrs. Hoaglund in the foyer of the church when we were ponderously accosted by Robert Dougle, the farmer. With daunting solemnity, he asked permission to call on me that afternoon at the boarding house, where he thought I was still living.

My instinct was to firmly decline, but, both eyebrows aloft, Mrs. Hoaglund drew me aside and pointed out that he was a most respectable member of the community and ran a successful farm. Izzie looked skeptical but shrugged.

I could not imagine such a man would want to court *me* and was somewhat curious. The thought did occur to me that he might have heard that Betty Kinney and I were friends, and perhaps he might want my advice. On that basis, I agreed to see him at two.

Izzie, the taskmistress, had me cooking our Sunday dinner. I had left a stuffed chicken roasting in the oven while we went to church. All I had to do upon our return was make the gravy. Izzie had made bread on Saturday, so I was spared the dreaded biscuits for one day. We had plenty of time to enjoy our little feast and clean up before our self-invited guest was due.

He arrived promptly and sat uncomfortably on the candy-striped settee in the parlor. It was so difficult to make ordinary conversation with him, I almost expected an hour of non-conversation, but he ended my suspense with breathtaking directness.

"Miss Carlton, as you may know, my wife died three years ago. I have two older children besides the infant, and a farm in desperate need of a woman's hand. I am here to ask if you will do me the honor of becoming my wife."

I honestly must say I had not expected this. After a stunned moment, I managed, "Mr. Dougle, we hardly know each other." What a stupid reply! A wagonload of *knowing* would not make him in the least attractive to me.

"My need is great," he replied, simply. "And I am told you are a hard worker." When I did not at once reply, he added, lowering his voice discreetly, "And you, perhaps, have not much chance at making a decent marriage."

My cheeks flaming, I rose and turned my back on him, staring out the front window until I could regain self-control. Would this town never quit? Perhaps born of pique, a most amusing idea came to me. Once more, I fear, I gave in to temptation with hardly a struggle. I was furious at Farmer Dougle. Assuming a semblance of composure, I resumed my chair beside the settee.

"Mr. Dougle," I began, as regally as possible, "I am extremely flattered by your offer. I know your reputation in this town. However, since you have already lowered yourself by asking me, I wonder why it should not occur to you that you might so much better ensure your future happiness by asking where there is already love and regard?"

He looked shocked.

"By that, I refer to Betty Kinney, as you must guess. I know she made a dreadful mistake, which has quite brought her down to my level, but there is a great deal to be said of the innocence which led her into that mistake, and she is very sorry now. I happen to know that she still esteems you, highly. She has all the accomplishments needed by a farmer's wife, and her nursing skill makes her even more qualified for motherhood.

"Since you have already stooped so low, why not take the one who loves you, rather than me? I am convinced I should make you miserable. I know very little of housework or cooking, have no experience caring for children, and, of course, I would not be willing to give up my work at the Mercantile. I regard it as my career."

He sat for some time, looking thoughtfully at his shoes. Then he stood up, made me a stiff bow, and retrieved his hat and coat. "Thank you for your candor, ma'am. I can see we would not suit," he said and left.

I had to stifle giggles with a hand over my mouth as, through the window, I watched him walk away. Then I sighed deeply. It was hard to accept but was as clear as the glass in the window: this was how the town still thought of me.

I went away to inform Izzie of the surprising conversation, and how outrageously I had behaved, and we shared equal measures of hysteria and rue.

"Wouldn't it be something if he accepted my advice?" I commented.

"He should," Izzie retorted. "It was good advice."

One thing you had to say about Black Butte: It was completely unpredictable and never ceased to surprise.

Chapter Eighteen

JUNE 1889

The stagecoach resumed its regular run, and John received a letter from Albuquerque announcing the shipping date of our wagonload of supplies, estimating its arrival in Black Butte at the beginning of May. It was to contain the main part of the order, with a small supplemental shipment to come about a month later, in early June.

The news of our intended expansion blew through town like a dust storm, and folks began coming in to see what was going on. We put them off with the promise of a "Grand Opening" when renovations were finished.

This brought down the wrath of John.

"This store can't 're-open!' Never been shut!" he growled. "Never going to be."

Myrtle and I made a strategical retreat, and after several days of debate, offered "Open House." John still grumbled but agreed.

"A war over words," I complained, quite put out with John for the wasted time.

"Be happy for what you got," Myrtle advised, serenely. Wiser, as always.

We turned our thoughts to what was more important and began to plan how to restructure the store in time to receive the first, largest shipment without ever closing the store, not even for a day.

Myrtle and I made a large floor plan on a swath of brown wrapping paper, working out exactly how to rearrange the store into better-defined departments. We planned where to put every shelf and counter for the best use of our space and how many new ones were needed. There had to be mountings for twenty new lamps. We moved the cash register up near the entrance and planned a new stove there. We would be twice as warm next winter and could even serve tea for women customers there.

We kept John's big stove and crony chairs where they were, along with the huge clock. It would always be the heart of the store, but it was no longer the focal point. We honored John's request to leave his Hinterland as it was. He and Fred would handle changes there, if any.

John saw and approved our plans in his usual way. He brought Chester Goode—of Goode Furniture, next door to the butcher and on the south plaza boardwalk—to the store.

"Show him your plans," he instructed us, and to Chester, said, "Do whatever they want. Just don't bother me about it."

I thought that was beyond gruff and was beginning to think John was playing a game with us, but Myrtle just smiled complacently and began explaining; Chester got very excited.

A few days later, a crew of four workmen arrived and began moving shelves and counters around according to our plan, even sawing and hammering to make new ones right in the middle of business hours! At first, the chaos was terrible, but it was amazing how quickly we adjusted to it, as did our customers. We did business over, around, and through it—and never minded the sawdust. Even more customers came in to see what the fuss was all about. I imagine we became an entertainment of sorts, as the new store took shape around us.

For Myrtle and me, the best of all was creating our tiny Hat Salon. The capable carpenters made a small lattice room in the front corner of Dry Goods. They made waist-high counters, with storage below, and a shelf all around at shoulder height, for display. They made a neat little vanity table set, mounted with a three-way mirror for trying on hats. It was a space that would be easy to make attractive with drapes and a rug.

Miss Deetz was quite pleased with it and set a goal of twenty hats finished in time for the Open House. Our only problem was how to display them.

Myrtle suggested a wire spindle with a circle on top. I preferred the idea of *papier-mâché*, made of newspaper with a flour and water paste, but that seemed too complex. We gave it up and decided we could all survive with just setting hats on the shelves, although it was not what we had envisioned.

One of Mr. Goode's workmen, a young Hispanic apprentice, overheard our dispute, and a few days later, approached me.

"Señorita Carlton, señor Goode permits me to show you this." He handed me a wooden form, surprisingly lightweight.

I turned it and saw it was an oval head shape made of pine, with the suggestion of a neck mounted on a small pedestal. It had been sanded, polished, and stained a light brown, as pleasing to touch as to look at.

"For the hats, señorita." A hat stand. It was perfect!

"I see it now," I said. "How elegant! Wherever did you find it?"

He laughed, and I saw how good-looking he was, although young for an apprentice. In his early teens, perhaps.

"I confess, señorita—I made it," he smiled broadly. "After I heard you and señora Burke speaking of your problem of display. Señor Goode liked it and said I should show you, and I could make more if you want."

"I do like it, very much. And I would like to order more if they are not too dear. This is as good as a piece of art! I'm sorry, I don't know your name."

"Joaquim Almaguerra, señorita." Again, the charming smile. "I am so glad you like it."

"How in the world did you make it so light?"

"It is not solid, señorita. I cut it in half, scooped it out, and glued it back together again. In the way the old artisans make the *Santos*, those large statues of the saints, to carry in parades on festival days."

Sakes alive! A genius artist in the guise of a furniture maker's apprentice. Not possibly more than fourteen or fifteen years old! Would the wonders of Black Butte never cease?

I showed it to Myrtle. She liked it, too. We ordered ten at one dollar each, although Myrtle thought that a bit dear.

"I don't care. If John thinks it's too much, I'll pay for them myself. He can take it out of my salary!" After seeing this, I couldn't bear to display my hats any other way!

"No need to get huffy, Alta!" Myrtle protested.

"Do as you like," was all John said.

Almost at once, we had to disturb him again. We had to bow to the obvious—we would need more clerks. It was not possible for three of us to watch over all the areas we had created, and Myrtle absolutely could not be allowed to wear herself out working the floor anymore. We decided to start with two, one for my section and one for Housewares and Foodstuff —under my supervision.

I had hardly begun to entertain this idea when, at Thursday Sewing Circle, Laura McKnight sat down firmly in the chair I was saving for Izzie, spread out a sheet she was hemming, and said, "So I hear you are hiring clerks at Burke's. What would you say to my twins?"

I was quite startled. How could she possibly know that?

Laura went on, "Do you know them?" They graduated from high school last spring and they are driving me mad at home. They need something to do. Loralee is the blonde one, Lydia is the quiet one."

I vaguely recalled them as customers, coming in with their mother and disagreeing with her choices. Well, you have to start somewhere.

"Send them in to see me," I agreed.

They came the next day and I was pleasantly surprised. They were attractive, well-dressed, and clearly very bright. Loralee was quite animated and charming; Lydia, the one with brown hair, was quieter, but impressively sensible and mature. They even spoke a little Spanish like their mother, having learned it from their housekeeper.

They said they would love to work in the store. What could be better?

I hired them on the spot and told them to come in on Monday wearing dark skirts and white blouses.

That was easy!

I found them quick to learn and thought they would do very well, although both tended to flirt with male customers—despite my efforts to instill professionalism. As an example: Dewey Hughes, the young reporter for the Beacon, took much too long interviewing them for the article he was writing for the weekly newspaper. They all three had better things to do. Flirting would never have been allowed at Carlton & Hodges.

Myrtle was in her glory, excited about the plans and contributing what was sensible to them. Of course, we did not allow her to do any moving of stock. Biggers helped me with that. But we had to keep an eye on Myrtle. It was against her nature to sit and watch while others were working so hard. It was so important she did not overdo it and tire herself.

John and I hoped we could keep her quietly seated at the Open House by appointing her cashier. Her station would be in front, at the cash register, where she could greet customers as they came in, take payments, and keep an eye on whatever was going on. To our great relief, she accepted this, saying she was glad there was a job she could do to be part of it all.

The goods arrived by wagon only two days later than estimated.

Shortly after that, the promised jewelry and rugs from Ruth Yazzie were delivered by more relatives: the Begay brothers. It seemed they had been part of the Appaloosa hunt and were great friends of the younger Whitaker brothers. They left us to go visit out at the ranch to see the horses.

This set me to missing Whit again. I had been so busy... I had spent less time thinking about him. I had been doing so well—this was a setback. I would have to start all over at the beginning. Taken so unaware, I spent a sleepless, tearful night before I could get my composure back.

I wished I could just see him from time to time. Just a glimpse at a distance. Would that be better? Or would it make things worse? I only knew I wanted desperately to see him. I wanted him to know what I was accomplishing at the Mercantile.

This was all so futile; I was disgusted with myself. Of all times to be moaning over lost love! I needed all my energy for the store.

The *great unpacking* needed the concentration of all of us. We had to get everything out, entered into the books, priced, and onto the shelves—while still waiting on customers. It was a daunting task; somehow, we did it.

Lydia and Loralee surprised us by being quite proficient. I

would never have guessed that organization and sensible time management were among their set of skills! It was a sight to see Lydia directing Biggers here and there with great piles of merchandise in his arms. We even "shanghaied" Virginia into helping as an extra pair of hands, and the McKnight sisters organized her, too!

Izzie offered her students as a day of "on-site business experience." I said no thanks, but I'm sure the McKnight's could have managed them as well. They must get it from their mother.

On Opening Day, Uma Deetz brought in the promised twenty hats. She had outdone herself, making them from buckram, felt, or duck for the forms. We displayed them all around the little room, with the ten most special on our beautiful wooden heads and the others attractively placed here and there, amid veiling and silk flowers. It was a gallery of hats! We were sure the ladies of Black Butte would adore this space as much as we did.

When John opened the doors, Mrs. Hoaglund was the first to enter. She said there had never been an event like this in Black Butte before. It was all a wonderful success.

I had only one disappointment once I got Whit off my mind: Paul Whitaker was not in town to see it. He and his friend Jeremy were still in San Francisco and we did not know when they would be back. I confess I had hoped to impress him.

However, it is probable that most other people in the area did come, at least briefly, to take a look. This included the Hispanic residents of East Butte and the outlying farms and ranches. It was an awe-inspiring number of people, far beyond any of my experiences in Black Butte—even the Harvest Ball— and many did want to buy. We dealt with the onslaught as best we could, but there never had been, and possibly never would be again, such a day's business!

We gave every child a balloon on a stick and offered everyone punch and sugar babies.

When John finally shooed out the last crony and closed the doors at nine, we all collapsed by the main stove and just grinned at each other. We had survived! It had been phenomenal, beyond expectations. We had sold out a lot of the new stock and would have to re-order at once.

Without a doubt, the Hat Salon had been the hit of the day. Only two hats remained unsold, and one of those was reserved for Gladys Reilly, who was only waiting for her egg money to come in to be able to pay for it.

We sent everyone home, and I went over to the house with Myrtle, John, and Virginia. We shared a celebratory glass of sherry. It was not so fine as Father's Amontillado, but the Burkes gave me a full glass. "Well, ladies, I suppose you are going to say, 'I told you so!'" John grumbled, but there was a twinkle in his eyes.

"Dearest John, never in the world would we say that." Myrtle smiled back demurely. "But we did!"

"Welcome to modern life!" John proclaimed, refilling our glasses. "Although, I, for one, am not sure I am going to like having to work this hard from now on!"

That was a sobering thought. It was true that we were much busier for a week or two, but then things settled down to a new level that we seemed able to handle with our competent new help. We reordered in larger amounts and soon were comfortable in our new routines, doing a great deal more business than before.

Chapter Nineteen

Lavinia Hoaglund invited Izzie and me to the Quilting Bee at church. Marjorie Adams was to be married in August, and her mother and aunts had spent the winter piecing an elaborate patchwork quilt for her, in the appropriate *double wedding ring* pattern. The church ladies customarily did the actual quilting for a fee, many hands making light of a task that would otherwise take many months.

A large frame was set up in the church's basement, then the quilt was fitted to it and basted on top of the cotton batting filler with a solid color backing. The Bee was called to quilt all this together with about a million tiny quilting stitches, finishing off with appropriate edging. The family had asked for the popular *Ocean Wave* quilting design, which would show handsomely on the reverse blue backing when all was done. Every possible decent seamstress, even vaguely associated with the Ecumenical Church, was asked to help on Saturday, if only for an hour or two, this being a great fundraiser for the church. They sat around the quilt and stitched all day, taking turns with as many sewers as could be squeezed in. There was a lovely potluck lunch, which was eaten in shifts—the quilting never stopped. Izzie went, but I could not attend because of work. I would go on Sunday afternoon after church to help finish up. I was eager to be known to help with the quilt as a compliment to the family because the fabrics and findings for the wedding gown and trousseau had all come from Burke's; although I believe her family had done the sewing, not Mrs. Farrogot.

Isobel and Lavinia were both there, along with others, and I sat in to learn the pretty wave-pattern stitching; it was a pleasure. I knew I was still only tolerated here, despite the success of my dolls at the bazaar, because of Lavinia's patronage. My friendship with Izzie and connection to Burke's helped; but I knew I could easily be asked to leave, as, it was whispered, young Mrs. Stewart had been for sloppy stitches and sticking her fingers so that she bled on the quilt! Thank goodness my stitches were still tiny and regular, and I made sure to wear my ivory thimble. Whose, I wondered, was the greater sin? Mine or poor Mrs. Stewart's?

I need not have feared; my stitching was praised, and I enjoyed myself very much. We did not manage to finish the quilt, but a few ladies came in and did edge binding during the week. I saw the finished item on display the following Sunday— it was beautiful.

A wagonload of re-orders from the trading post in Albuquerque arrived at the store on Monday, and we worked like beavers building a dam to re-stock the shelves. With increased mail coming and going from the store, I now made it a practice to go to the post office pretty much every afternoon after the stage came in. Wednesday afternoon I was rewarded with mail of my own—one of my regular letters from Ellen.

I saved it for the evening to share with Izzie, for I had told her all about my favorite student and she was kind enough to take an interest.

We read this letter with growing joy; it was the best possible news. Ellen was cured! There were no more bacilli in her blood. She was now installed in the *Well Ward* and the doctors predicted that she could leave the sanatorium by the end of summer if she still tested clear. She was to continue a regime of fresh air, exercise, and good food; she could hope that the disease would not recur. A relapse was to be avoided at all costs. A second cure, although not unknown, was not a certainty.

Through happy tears, I told Isobel even more about my Ellen, and I brought out all her old letters, carefully saved, to share. Izzie said she wrote exceptionally well, was clearly bright, and all the more extraordinary for having come from what could not escape being labeled an "immigrant slum."

The rest of Ellen's letter, however, had not been so promising. It was full of problems, although, as always, Ellen wrote in a positive manner:

> *They will be at some trouble to find out where to put me! Bridie cannot take me, as she already has Seamus and Eileen, as well as her own two, and they all live in just the one room. Shirleen would like to have me, but two of her children are already ill, and it would be the worst place for me to go as I might be re-infected. I shall probably be put into one of the dormitory houses, where they can keep me until I am sixteen. That would be best for me, and if I can then get a job, I would be ready for my independence.*

This cast us down. Wiping away tears, I told Isobel I had heard only bad of these dormitory houses, and how, one way or another, Ellen was going to be placed right back in the environment which had fostered her disease in the first place. It was not to be borne. She was only just fourteen now, the thought of her being on her own at sixteen was devastating. What kind of job could a sixteen-year-old girl hope to find?

Isobel surprised me, once again. I was going to have to get used to this Whitaker trait.

"Alta, from all you have told me, she is a unique and brave young girl, worthy of being rescued. Why don't we bring her out here to live with us?"

"Really?" I breathed.

"You know our climate is now being considered ideal for recovery from tuberculosis, being so dry and clean. I have heard of two new sanatoriums being built up by Santa Fe, with patients who come all the way from the East Coast."

"You don't mean that she should live in one of those?"

"Of course not, silly. We have two extra bedrooms! Is there anyone else you need to rescue?" She was good beyond belief, but shrugged off my thanks, pointing out that she was, after all, a schoolteacher, and would go quite far to get a hold of a truly outstanding student—such as Ellen promised to be.

After serious considerations and consulting Lawyer Paul, we came up with an audacious plan that thrilled us to the core. Izzie and I should go back East on the train and bring Ellen home ourselves! Two mature women traveling together would be quite proper, and I was longing to see my family. Izzie thought the train trip would be a brilliant overdue vacation, and the only impediment was whether Burke's could get along without me for the month such a trip would require.

The Burkes made everything easy. Although they had never rewarded themselves with one, they said I was young and deserved a vacation. There lived in town a retired widow who had once been a clerk at Burke's, Porphyria Forster, who, although well into her sixties, was still quite spry and said she would be delighted with a "vacation" back to work! Our road was cleared of all obstacles.

It did not seem possible to me that they would be able to manage at the store, and I dropped swiftly from euphoria to despair—perceiving this, Myrtle took me aside and poured some good sense back into me.

"Now, see here, Alta. Most of the ideas to re-organize the store were yours, and they're good ideas. The store works better now than it ever did, and you've trained up those two girls real well, even in this short time. Porphyria is an old pro and very smart. She'll catch on right fast. Land O'Goshen, girl! You got to have confidence in the good job you have done and let us function; if your system's as good as we think it is, we should be fine for the few weeks you'll be gone. That's the best job of all, you know, when you don't have to have your hand on the wheel every minute. And, besides, you need to see your folks!"

"Oh, Myrtle, you and John are too good to me!" I cried. "I shouldn't ask, it's such an indulgence—" I was prepared to go on in this vein for some time, but Myrtle had come to know me very well and knew how to distract me.

"You do realize, Alta, there is a condition," she said.

"A condition?" I faltered.

"Yes. You are not allowed to return unless you bring us a current *Godey's Ladies Book*." We laughed in each other's arms, and I promised.

I met Porphyria and took her through the store's new routine. Almost at once, I felt myself relaxing. Myrtle was not wrong; I wondered why in the world she hadn't been mentioned when we needed *all hands* in the run-up to the reopening! I guess they thought her too old for lifting and carrying, but just fine for waiting on customers!

Izzie and I were like two schoolgirls planning our excursion. I think I had assumed that my future life would be staid and uneventful.

Knowing I could never marry Whit, and after my truly dreadful experiences with the men of Black Butte, I honestly had given up any thought of a future marriage. I planned a life of work and would make a social life with my good women friends.

Izzie was my hero; she cherished the memory of her late husband and considered herself still married to him, even continuing to wear her wedding ring. I felt quite as she did: I would never marry. I had given my heart to Whit, and he still had it. It was unthinkable that I could live with any other man.

That was why I had given up any hope of children. I had never dreamed I would have something so exciting to look forward to as adding dear Ellen permanently to my life—it changed everything!

There followed a round of telegrams and then correspondence with Ellen's sanatorium, doctors, and Bridget, her eldest sister. After Mrs. Margolis, still at University Settlement House, spoke for me, there was universal approval.

Ellen was ecstatic. She was to be made my ward, and a date was set for me to take her away in early August. Izzie and I would take her back for the start of school the second week of September—how familiar that sounded!

We made reservations for the stagecoach to Albuquerque and the train to New York. I wired my parents. It was all a prospect too wonderful for words.

We needed traveling clothes. That made it necessary to take on the formidable Mrs. Farrogot once more. Izzie pointed out that our respectability as travelers would be greatly increased if we were *well-dressed!* We both needed to do something about that.

Mrs. Farrogot had made my replacement traveling suit last year, which I had been wearing to work until it got too hot for wool serge. Izzie had nothing even partially suitable to wear on the train.

So, we went together to storm the castle. I bore a modest gift, a small box of sugar cookies, my current success—no more sugar babies. Mrs. Farrogot received us frostily, which surprised me until she had made several remarks about Uma Deetz's hats, and I began to see that she bore some ill-will in that direction, which seemed to include me. This made absolutely no sense to me since she did not deal in millinery, but it was unmistakably real. Izzie and I practiced raising one eyebrow at each other and endeavored to get her off the subject.

At last, she allowed that, although totally booked up, she thought she could manage one traveling outfit apiece in the time remaining, and we got down to pleasurable details. Izzie, in her blonde fairness, would look marvelous in a buckskin-colored suede cloth; I should travel in blue-gray, heavy broad-cloth, which would wrinkle, but not so badly as linen, and had the great advantage of being washable.

We were each to have a suit: skirt and jacket, with two blouses and a matching lightweight cloak of the same fabric, lined with flannel. We should be very elegant, indeed, and most respectable.

After that, we practically sneaked to Uma Deetz's house to order our hats. We walked downhill a block, as if going back to town, and then cut over five blocks to Pine Street and up the hill again, just praying we did not meet one of Mrs. Farrogot's friends who would run straight to her to report on us!

Uma had suggested we come privately to her house, rather than rendezvous in public at the store. I must confess we three found it all hilarious, but we did agree that if we wanted our suits, Mrs. Farrogot must not know where we got our hats. Uma said she had no idea what the problem was, but there was a steely edge to her voice that made me think there might be more to the story.

At any rate, Uma made us tea and we sat down with drawing pads and pencils, happily perusing several books of basic hat design.

Uma's house was an eye-opener to me. I had never been in a living room more comfortable, nor more pleasing to the eye. There was nothing of value in any of the furnishings, and it easily could have been shabby and bare. But each pillow, each vase of dried flowers, and every picture on the wall had been chosen to blend and complete the elements of the room. Just sitting there was a lesson in good taste and interior design.

"Uma, you've had design training, haven't you?" I asked, approvingly.

"Well, only from the good sisters of Our Lady of Carmel at Santa Fe. Ma and Pa had no money for education. The good sisters took an interest in me, or I should have had no education at all. There was a group of wealthy Santa Fe parishioners whose contributions were the mainstay of the convent. At a bazaar one spring, we discovered I had a knack for decorating hats and that it pleased these ladies.

"The nuns sent me to a local milliner for training and thought I could make my living as a maker of hats, but they had not considered the personal contact aspect. People were very uncomfortable around me. It never did work out well."

I was deeply moved by this story and the fact that Uma trusted me enough to tell it. I wondered why she had come to Black Butte and what she could possibly be living on. It must be very little. I swore to myself that I would do everything in my power to improve her well-being.

At any rate, Uma was pleased to make us secret hats. For me, she designed a medium-blue pancake, tilted up on the left side and filled with blue and white silk flowers. It tied under the chin with a blue silk ribbon. I loved it so much that the day Uma finished it and gave it to me, I never took it off until bedtime, and seriously considered sleeping in it, except that would have ruined it. Of course, the next morning I had to put it away and not even think of wearing it until we were well out of town.

Izzie's hat was also nice, but then she was so much more suited for the formality of the little dark-brown-felt riding hat. It was a quite perfect miniature of English regalia and suited Izzie perfectly. I could never have carried it off. Uma was surprisingly knowledgeable about style for one who seemed to have lived a sheltered life. I thought her much more modern than Mrs. Farrogot.

It seemed to me that Uma Deetz was much more than just a milliner; she was also something of a student of human nature!

Toward the end of June, one night while Isobel was away at a school board meeting, I had just curled up in my favorite place to read, the comfortable divan near the kitchen, when there was a knock on the front door. Wondering who it could possibly be at this time of night, I lazily went to answer it.

I opened the door to Whit.

He immediately stepped in and took me in a strong embrace. Kicking the door shut, he proceeded to kiss me so passionately that I was without the ability to protest. He held me so tightly against him, that within moments I learned more about what is between men and women than I had previously surmised, and I began to understand for the first time why a woman might be willing to participate.

I truly did not wish him to stop, but at length, he held me a little away and gazed at me as if he could not see enough.

"Alta, I can't take this anymore, being away from you. And now I hear you are going back to New York!"

"Only for a visit," I protested, as if it mattered.

"You won't come back! Not once you see your family again and that New York way of life. I know it!"

"But I will come back! I am only going to get Ellen... you

remember the young girl I told you about? Izzie and I are bringing her back with us."

He seized me for another long, dizzying kiss. I struggled out of it—having regained a small portion of common sense.

"Whit, you must stop this. Izzie..."

"Izzie is at a board meeting. I made sure we could be alone. Alta, I cannot go on this way. Glimpsing you around town, hearing about you—it's making me crazy. You have to come away with me!"

"What?"

"Listen, Alta!" He pulled me down to sit on the striped settee in the parlor and held my hand. "I've been planning this forever, and I know it will work. My buggy is outside. We will just go away together, someplace like Wyoming or Montana where no one will know us, and we can live together as man and wife. We can have our happiness. You only have to go pack a few things and we can be gone in ten minutes!"

"Whit!" I protested, moving away from him. "That could never be!"

He instantly recaptured me in his arms. "Alta, I spoiled it for us the first time, don't you do it now! How can you not want this?"

"I do want it, with all my heart. But Whit, I can't just leave Black Butte! There are too many people relying on me! You must see that. Izzie and I have been working so hard to make a home here, and we are to have Ellen. She is my ward now; her whole future is at stake. And John Burke has done so much for me; now he pretty much needs me to run the store since Myrtle has been ill. Myrtle... It would kill her! And Mrs. Hoaglund would be so disappointed after all the work she put into restoring my reputation... and Izzie and I are leaving on the train in a month! We have paid for our tickets! My parents..."

He stopped trying to kiss me and looked at me, blankly at

first and then with rising anger. That shocked me and I drew away. I could see him fight for self-control.

"These things are more important to you than our happiness?"

"They are all counting on me, Whit. You must see that. And you... your father is counting on you, about the ranch. And you can't let down Phillip!"

He pulled back, looking bleak.

"But even more, think a moment, Whit—Charles. If we lived as you propose, it would be blissful. Oh, I can hardly bear to imagine the joy of the beginning. But then, after a while, there would be no way to avoid it becoming furtive... alienated from all friends and family... dishonest. To live together without marriage, always afraid we would be exposed. What if there should be children? How long before love became reproach and resentment? Whit, you must see all this!"

He regarded me for a full minute, and I had to endure watching grief once more cross his beloved face and fade into steely blankness. How I wished I could not read his emotions so well. At last, he spoke: "You're not coming, are you?"

I shook my head. "No, Whit. I can't."

He rose and made me his familiar little bow.

"Goodbye, Alta. Have a good life. I just wish it could have been with me."

He was gone. The door closed quietly. Dreams shattered all around me and my knees folded so that I had to grab onto the door frame to keep from falling to the ground. Steps crossed the porch, gravel crunched, the front gate clicked open and shut. A buggy started up and drove away. He was gone.

I was stone, and it was all my own doing. Heaven had been in my hands, and I had set it down. I had said no.

I spent a hideous night between weeping and picturing the route we might have followed to Montana. If I had gone with

371

him, where would we be now? At Blue Lake? Would we be approaching Gallup at dawn? By dawn, I could no longer imagine where we might have been and had to give up the slight comfort of that fantasy.

Only grief was left.

Chapter Twenty

The trip to New York was a great success! Izzie was a perfect traveling companion and we made a quite respectable pair: genteel and well-dressed by Mrs. Farrogot, wearing our fabulous hats. We met interesting people and were not unbearably uncomfortable.

I tried hard to present a cheerful face, and if Izzie found me less animated than usual, she was kind enough to say nothing. As far as I knew, she was unaware that Whit had called on me that ill-fated night of her board meeting. She must suspect something, or else she just believed I should be told, for the day we got on the train she said to me, "Alta, I want to tell you that Charles has left the ranch. He's gone away entirely, without saying anything to anyone. I just thought you should know."

How could he do that? When Paul and Phillip and everyone were counting on him so much!

"Thank you for telling me," was all I said. We never discussed it any further.

We did, however, have many other interesting conversations. Izzie inquired whether I had not been afraid to trust myself to a stagecoach again—after my first experience. I was honestly able to answer in the negative, pointing out it was very unlikely to happen again, and the train, itself, was no less dangerous. I had just been statistically unlucky the first time out. On this trip, there had been no untoward incidents, nor on the train, and we arrived safely and on time in New York City.

My family warmly greeted us at the station and bore us home. Their generous hospitality to Isobel pleased me very much; although her address and comportment were such that she would be welcome anywhere. They were not surprised to learn she had spent three years in Connecticut at Miss Haverstadt's Academy for Young Women before returning to Black Butte as a schoolteacher. There was no occasion to mention the detour to the hog farm, beloved as its master had been, nor that I was hopelessly in love with her nephew.

Aggie received us graciously enough, although she did remark reprovingly that I was "as brown as a gypsy," but perhaps it was no wonder, considering the rough life I now must live. We admired the little boy who had grown quite boisterous and undisciplined. Charles Sr., a little stouter with a little less hair, was very much the "Lord of the Manor"—although it was my father's house. He was obviously quite taken with Isobel and she raised her eyebrow to me more than once at his attentions.

It was a shock to discover that Aggie was in an *interesting condition* again. So soon! She was no more pleased than the first time, talking at great length about the inconvenience and discomfort of it all and swearing it would never happen again, if only she knew of any way to prevent it. I could see Izzie biting her lip to keep from saying there were several ways—besides one absolutely certain.

I spoke to Mother privately about this, thinking it would be a shame for Aggie to keep churning out infant after infant if she did not want them, but only succeeded in shocking and offending Mother. She asked if this was an example of "Western Indelicacy" and said such things were not to be spoken of, much less practiced. She was horrified that I should even know about them. Being indebted to Myrtle as well as Izzie, and even Betty, to say nothing of the Sewing Circle, I said no more. But I did not think she was right.

Charles took us on a grand tour of Carlton & Hodges, pausing at each innovation until we had praised it to his satisfaction before leading us on to the next. We were introduced to the new head of Dry Goods: a young man who had been brought in from outside; I was not too surprised.

It was delightful to be reunited with Miss Bailey and I was proud to introduce her to Isobel. They liked each other at once and we met her twice for lunch at the store in the new Rose Garden Tea Room, which Father had just opened. It was already immensely popular; we enjoyed tasty finger sandwiches and salads with, of course, copious pots of tea.

I took Isobel to meet Margaret as well, and she gave us tea in her private quarters, where she and I had shared so many intimacies. It seemed to me that the two regarded each other somewhat warily, but that was probably only my over-stimulated imagination. What was certain was that we both listened with great interest as she described the modern improvements at University House and the work she was doing there.

Then, after a sidewise glance at Isobel, Margaret entered into a confidence I was quite surprised she would give in front of a stranger.

"I must tell you that I am engaged to Joseph Pritchard, the teacher at University House I wrote you about, Alta. It is against the wishes of my parents. I tell you this as you are bound to hear it from someone during your visit, and I would rather you hear it from me. He is quite wonderful and very steady and hardworking. Our lifestyle will be plain, but I entrust myself to him entirely. The wedding will be on September 1st; my parents will not attend and say they will cut me off without a cent. I am sorry for their disappointment in me but also angry that they would have preferred another marriage—to one for whom I had neither affection nor respect. I hope they will come around to it in time."

"Margaret, I am so happy you have found love! If you can go to him with propriety, then, of course, you must. I hope you will be very happy." I also hoped she would not inquire into my own love life—especially in front of Izzie. Fortunately, she was too engrossed in her personal dilemma to be curious.

Isobel and I offered our hopes that her parents would be reconciled, and we left her contemplating her small, but treasured, diamond engagement ring.

It seemed I was passing everyone's inspection, even Isobel's, without showing the inner grief I carried everywhere. Perhaps a complete change of scene, such as a long trip, is a good way to learn how to live with sorrow and begin a new life.

Just before we were to take the train to Ellen's sanatorium to fetch her, Miss Bailey asked Isobel and me to dinner at her small apartment. What a good friend she still was. She served us an astonishing meal of Italian spaghetti in marinara sauce, and I had to confess to her that I had never, yet, sampled to the wonderful cookbook she had given me.

Izzie informed Miss Bailey that she oversaw repairing my womanly deficiencies and that now she knew of such a cookbook, she would make sure it became our autumn homemaking project, especially if everything were as good as this!

Miss Bailey advised us to buy Italian spices and pastas while we were still in New York, as she much doubted they would be readily available out West. We would need exotics, such as oregano and sweet basil, besides more ordinary herbs. We would need dried pasta of various kinds, or we would find ourselves making our own from scratch, a project she assured us would be too difficult right at first, although we might come to it with pleasure later.

While the dinner had been fun, it seemed to me that Miss Bailey was not as lively as I was used to seeing her. Perhaps one who hides a disappointment recognizes a sister more easily? Looking back over our various meetings, I became sure of it and took an opportunity of asking her delicately if she was finding it difficult to work under young Mr. Wheeler.

Waving me off in a self-deprecating manner, she admitted she had allowed herself to hope, but that she was sure Mr. Wheeler would prove quite competent once he was settled in, although he was a bit stuffy about following the rules to the letter.

"I really should not have expected anything else, but, still, it was a disappointment. It is just that now I know I will not advance any higher in the store. But never mind. I am quite lucky to have risen so high as the head of Findings."

Privately, I disagreed, but, honoring her for staunchly taking a positive attitude, took her for my model and said no more.

Father surprised and pleased me by taking time off work to escort Isobel and me to Hale House to retrieve Ellen.

"As she is to be a new member of our family. It behooves me to welcome her personally."

This was the dear Father I remembered and cherished. I felt grateful and close to him at this time.

We took the train, hiring a horse cab at the nearest stop to take us out into the country to the spacious, leafy grounds of Hale House.

We found Ellen in blooming health: grown rather tall and lanky now, still very blonde with her hair in one long braid, a sprinkling of freckles, and beside herself with excitement for the trip ahead. Her enthusiasm made her a delightful companion, and we all enjoyed the trip back to New York. Father treated us to dinner in the diner, and Ellen's enchantment with everything new made it special for us experienced travelers again.

We took advantage of the four days remaining in New York to outfit her with such clothing and possessions as a girl of fourteen would need, a project which Mother and Isobel wholeheartedly took on, becoming quite intimate over it. Aggie felt the need to remain at home in bed.

I was pleased to see an affinity form between Izzie and Mother, just as it had with Cora Bailey. I was proud to introduce Izzie anywhere, but when one's special people like each other it is a great pleasure; a gift, not a given. Only two people I loved seemed to be moving out of my orbit: Margaret and Whit. I would have to bear it.

The afternoon before we left New York, Father required my presence in the library, where he utterly surprised me. Up until now, only Whitakers had done that. Father outdid them all. He laid papers before me, expressing his personal interest in the future of Burke's Mercantile and my future there. If Father's figures were accurate—and I knew he was an astute businessman—he could supply us from Carlton & Hodges, giving us wares of much higher quality at a better discount and shipping cross-country by train at an only marginally higher cost than we were being charged from Albuquerque!

We could offer high-quality merchandise straight from New York in what most back-Easter's still considered the wilderness. It would be an excellent thing for Burke's Mercantile.

The miracles of modern times, which were bursting upon our nation, were beyond imagination—especially with the new rail lines already under construction.

"You would not stop ordering from your present suppliers, of course. That would be bad business. Continue with the staples. But we could send you, at a mutual profit, specialty items you cannot now procure. Such as English woolens, French laces, hat forms, fine fabrics and superior trimmings, Irish pearls, so many things."

My mind began to spin at once with a dozen ideas.

Father went on, "Also, I must confess a great scheme of mine: Burke's could ship me a stock of these Western leather workings you have described: boots and belts, vests and wallets, and such. I can order a supply of Stetson hats myself, from Philadelphia. Especially, if your Navajo contact could supply some of the Indian jewelry and rugs, we could have an exciting 'Western Roundup' at Carlton & Hodges to celebrate the Fourth of July next year. The tearoom could serve Western foods such as pancakes, chili, and steaks. It would create a great stir! The publicity would be wonderful! We might even set off a Western craze."

At one accord, we lost ourselves in several animated hours of speculation and planning, like two children on a delightful caper. We decided that during the fest, the tearoom would be called the Cactus Grill. It was such a pleasure to share this with my father, and he treated me so flatteringly as his equal that I knew I would love and honor him all my life. Any breach between us was ended.

I felt the greatest relief that I had not caused him dishonor and grief. I believe I began to heal at that time. It was a reward for choosing the straight and narrow—rather than the exciting but outlaw wild yonder offered by Whit. I would waste no further time wondering "what if?" I had made the right choice.

My parents felt the visit had been all too short but understood I had responsibilities to return to, as did Isobel since school was about to start. They saw us off with affection and warm wishes and promises to come West soon. They showered us with little gifts of books, magazines, and treats to enliven our travel days. Cousin Edgar, true to form, brought us a rather large box of chocolates, but when I described the story of my melted previous box, he did not object to opening it on the spot. We gorged on it and I offered it to everyone we met. It was just as hot as before, but this time, not a chocolate was left to melt by the time we reached Chicago.

Ellen proved a staunch traveler, but to our minds, she dwelled too much on memories of Hale House and her friends there. Izzie was of the opinion that Ellen would have a great adjustment to make, having twice had to leave everything familiar. First, she had left her tragic home for the Sanatorium, now she was probably forever leaving all she had ever known behind, including the remnants of her family.

Isobel was of the opinion it would help the girl to talk about her past, and so we listened to endless tales of institutional life—some stories amusing, others sad. When she spoke briefly of the death of the boy with red hair who had made her laugh, we all shed tears. I watched Isobel come to value Ellen's character and intelligence and begin to love her, perhaps not as much as I, but enough to do both credit.

Our journey home passed without incident—other than celebrating my twenty-first birthday on the train. We survived the less comfortable stagecoach segment, which was much shorter since we were able to stay on the train all the way to Albuquerque, and thence to Black Butte the back way via Bagnold. We were all three quite happy to finally arrive safely at our destination.

Ellen moved happily into the attic room after rejecting the third bedroom on the second floor. She said she loved the sloping roof and the view. Doctor Grigg took over Ellen's care and pronounced her perfectly healthy! Traveling did not seem to have undermined her recovery—there had been a small fear of that. I thought she would make a splendid adjustment to living in the West. As much as she had loved her family back East, most of them were gone now, sadly, leaving only a remnant of the family. My hope was that she would find a good, healthy life here. I was determined on it.

A week after our arrival, she was enrolled in Isobel's school, where, with her sweet nature, she immediately began making friends—despite it being known that she lived with the teacher!

Chapter Twenty-One

FALL 1889

From here and there, I quietly garnered little wisps of information about Whit. I overheard two customers complaining that he hadn't come to the grange lately and that an order had not been picked up. I heard that Paul and Jeremy had gone out of town somewhere, but that Whit was not with them. Porphyria asked the McKnights if they knew where he was. She said she missed him tipping his hat when he passed her on the street and "wasn't he good-looking?" They agreed, sliding their eyes toward me, but didn't know where he had gone. It was said there had been no letters.

I don't know why this should have increased my sense of loss, but it did. I felt ill whenever I thought about Whit. If only I knew where he was and could have the solace of imagining what he was doing.

I did not think I could count on Izzie to share if any news did come. I was pretty sure she would not tell me, for my own good, of course.

His father, Desmond Whitaker, was pointed out to me in town from time to time, looking grim. He had lost his future;

the son who was to have inherited the family ranch. I felt it was my fault. How he must dislike me!

If not for that, our homecoming with Ellen would have been a joy. At the store, I was welcomed with open arms, and every little change was shown to me over and over. Porphyria Foster had fit in perfectly and was to be kept on part-time.

The McKnight twins were still interested in young men. It seemed the high school music teacher was spending a good deal of time at Loralee's counter in Housewares, which was a strange place for him to be shopping, as he was unmarried. However, he bought something every time: a tea kettle, a fork, or some tea. Things I suppose a single man may need as much as any other. I had to admit that Loralee remained highly efficient, even while he was calling on her.

We made a special nook for Father's gift—the new *Godey's Ladies Book*—with a table, two chairs, and a lamp, set off by a small screen where a lady could sit and browse through it with a friend.

"It will soon be just as worn out as the old copy," Myrtle complained. But we were proud to display it and gratified by the number of women who came in to look at it. Never, however, Mrs. Farrogot. When I next came face-to-face with that lady at church, I invited her to come to study it. She turned her back on me and marched away as if I had insulted her, perhaps suggesting she *needed* to study it!

"Hah!" Myrtle snorted in my ear. "That woman! There's no living with her. She acts as if we 'got one over on her' on purpose."

What a shame, I thought. A collaboration would have benefited all of us.

Myrtle seemed well and seemed to be following instructions: half a day in the store, sitting at the cash register; otherwise, resting at home. I spent more time with her than I should have taken away from work—relaying tales of the journey to New York. Myrtle had an insatiable appetite for them, and I believe she would have loved to go on such a trip herself.

I put John in the picture of my father's ambitious plan, and to my satisfaction, he was pleased and receptive. After some inquiries of his own, he wholeheartedly accepted the offer in its entirety. He was most interested in the idea of shipping our leather goods East since he was always looking out for the good of the town, and this could not help being a profitable opportunity for the local leather workers. Father's *Western Roundup* was Eastern *fol-de-rol* to us, but Burke's would be glad to provide the wherewithal. People from the saddlery next door to us and the leather works across the street from Butterfield's came in and out of the store daily, becoming cronies sitting around the pot-bellied stove.

Ruth Yazzie, coming with her menfolk to deliver a regular consignment, was even more pleased than I had thought she would be. She could now employ several grandsons and nephews, otherwise idly beginning to get themselves into trouble on the reservation.

She gave me a beautiful smile and said, indicating the improved store, "Now, we enlarge, too!"

I thought her larger, personally, and she caught me looking and laughed outright at the joke. She nodded, cradling her belly. I congratulated her and hastened to make us some jasmine tea. She liked that as well as the Darjeeling.

Father had agreed to my suggestion that Miss Bailey should manage our account on the Carlton & Hodges side. This was slightly unusual, but a compliment to her, and it allowed us to be frequently in touch. She had many invaluable suggestions. We wrote back and forth weekly.

Myrtle would handle the orders on our end. It was the perfect kind of desk work as it would keep her sitting down. We fixed up a screen and desk where the old cash register used to be, a small kind of office. Dr. Grigg agreed to increase her hours in the store to include the afternoon, but only after her nap.

It was not "make do" work, but vastly important, and John and I were both gratified to see the pleasure Myrtle took in it. John got as deeply involved in the order as we could have wished, and we spent endless hours going over the catalogs they had sent.

We sent off our first exciting order to Carlton & Hughes: it included a large packet with descriptions of the Western regalia we could produce, carefully compiled by Fred. Fred had even brought in a photographer to take several lithographs of jewelry and leatherwork displays, to give them a better idea of what they might order. We were not ignorant of modern sales tactics, even out here *in the sticks.*

If they responded quickly, we thought we should be able to ship their Fourth of July order by the following May to arrive in New York mid-June—*Goodness sakes! That would be 1890, a new decade! Was it possible?*

We waited for their responding order practically holding our breath, so eager were we and all our vendors to leap into production.

Carlton & Hodges wired us in due course that their responding order was in the mail. They gave us an expected shipment date by the end of October for our order of New York goods. With luck, we should receive it before the really bad weather set in.

The orders were official. Our various vendors went to work with smiles on their faces. All we could do was cheer them on and await the arrival of the new merchandise.

As it happened, when the wagon pulled into our courtyard with the New York goods, Black Butte was enjoying an unusually sparkling October Indian summer. The new goods were a great addition to our stock and it was clear the collaboration was a great success, at least on our end.

Soon after, Ellen came home from school full of plans for the Harvest Ball. Izzie—always looking out for a chance to give her students hands-on experience in the community—had volunteered her school to do the decorating this year, an offer gladly accepted by the church ladies, who could thereby concentrate entirely on the booths.

Izzie's school taught the children of the town from first through eighth grade. That is to say, only the children of Black Butte; East Butte, as I preferred to refer to as "Beantown," had its own Catholic schools.

Many children did not go on to high school, although technically, they were required to by law. There was no one to enforce it; some parents simply put them to work on farms or ranches.

Those who did go on were sent into a five-room wooden structure with four teachers and a small office for the principal. The fifth room was used as a meeting room, library, music room, and anything else that required general gathering. There was an athletic field for football and baseball.

The truth was that our part of town had grown beyond Izzie's one-room grade school. She had twenty students this year, heavy on the sixth and seventh grades. Plans were already in place to open a second school next fall, for grades one through four. Izzie would continue with fifth through eighth.

I was glad Ellen could go to school with Izzie, and she was making friends quickly with the larger than usual class her own age.

Obviously, this decoration project was aimed at these older children, to give them a hands-on community service experience. Unlike the bazaar, the Harvest Ball decorations were not much different from year to year, but the young people were eager to take them on and wanted to make a few innovations. Careful to include the "babies," they set them to coloring and cutting out giant "autumn leaves," to be pasted up everywhere, an addition to the usual bunting-covered walls.

At first, Ellen was just on the committee to plan this grand event, but before we could blink, she was in charge of the whole thing and ordering people around as if born to it.

"We used to do things like this in the Sanatorium to keep busy. They always made me be in charge," she explained, philosophically.

It was she who came up with the idea of opening the event with a Harvest Parade, starting at Izzie's school, which every child in town was welcome to enter: decorating their play wagons and little carts with streamers and balloons, pulling younger brothers and sisters, or even their pets.

We saw no harm in the idea, but were quite surprised at how popular it became, almost at once. It seemed everyone was talking about it and planning how to enter their children.

Without even asking, Ellen took her new authority for granted and simply went to Alfred Long, the high school music coach—who also taught civics, history, and sports. He, like Izzie, seemed always looking for ways to take part in community activities, and promised the high school marching band would lead the parade, all five of them. It would be very festive.

Izzie and I just shook our heads. The girl was amazing. Not even one month in a new school, and everyone was already looking up to Ellen as a leader. Isobel blushed with pride.

Like the rest of the town, Myrtle seemed especially excited about this year's Harvest Ball. After the success of the store remodeling, she felt that she and John should contribute something special, more than just the usual bunting, as a thank you to the community for their support.

We had several conferences with Virginia without coming

up with the right idea. Anyone could give a whole ham or roasted turkey. The Drummond Ranch traditionally gave an entire roasted steer—and sent several cowboys to help eat it! O'Toole's would send a vat of chili. It was said that Jack Warden was planning a roast pig. What could we do to compete on a scale like that? We threw our hands up in despair.

At that point, Betty Kinney arrived for Myrtle's exercise session, gave me a big warm hug, and whispered into my ear that John Dougle had begun calling on her since last April and that he had asked her to marry him—very welcome news.

If she meant that to be a secret, she should not have told me because my reaction was congratulations and hugs. Of course, everyone had to hear, then. Virginia already knew; Betty was her older sister.

When the excitement wore down, we must have resumed our long faces because Betty inquired what was the matter. Over tea, we bemoaned our failure to think of a potluck "thank you," expecting her to commiserate. Instead, she laughed at us!

"Talk about making a mountain out of a molehill! Of course, you can't compete with things like a whole roast pig. But there is one obvious thing you do have that no one else can come close to." She beamed at us expectantly.

We looked at her at a loss.

She *tsk-tsked* at us. "A barrel of pickles, of course! Everyone loves your pickles. They'll be thrilled."

Why had we not thought of that? The barrel would look most impressive on the banquet table. We could station Biggers—who loved social events—to stand beside it with a long prong and fish pickles out as people filed by. While there might be dainty dishes of watermelon or little cucumber pickles, no one would have our back-East kosher dills! From the beginning, twenty years ago, John had always kept a barrel of them right beside the cracker barrel.

Betty was a genius; we gave her full due and congratulated her again for her coming wedding. She blushed becomingly, saying John Dougle insisted she must bring her creamed corn cakes to the potluck, which he considered the best he had ever eaten.

Betty told us John had asked that the wedding take place on the day of the Harvest Ball—so that it could be their wedding celebration. They were to stand before the Justice of the Peace, Red Wilcox, who was also the local mortician; and Betty and her son Jojo would move to the Dougle farm.

That was quite romantic, in a way. I couldn't believe the John Dougle I had encountered could have come up with such an idea.

Izzie was beside herself over this development. She whispered to me, "Alta, now you can add 'matchmaker' to all your new accomplishments!"

I was delighted to see Betty happy but couldn't help wondering how happy she could be—so fond of such a dour man. I bit my tongue to keep from asking if she were to be *allowed* to continue with her nursing once she was wed.

Betty had saved the day with the barrel of pickles, although I overheard Myrtle saying confidentially to Virginia, "I do think we better take a scalloped potato casserole and two of your cherry pies as well."

It was clear that a dish of sliced tomatoes would not do for me this year. Izzie and I conferred and decided on vegetable pot pie, for her, and Black walnut cake for me. Ellen volunteered to frost the cake as her contribution.

There was no denying the enthusiasm in Black Butte for the annual Harvest Festival and Ball. It seemed to burn more brightly in the heart of the town than any holiday—even Christmas! We all looked forward to it; it was as if a drift of accordion music swept over the town, increasing our anticipation.

On the morning of October 16th, I came into the store as usual. One look at John's face told me all I needed to know.

"No, John," I cried, running to take him in my arms.

"She's dead, Alta," John wept into my shoulder. "She died in the night. I never got to tell her goodbye."

Neither had I...

We wept together. The whole town wept. Myrtle had been our secret treasure; she was one of a kind.

John closed the store.

Her funeral was attended by many more people than the little church could hold. Those who could not get in waited patiently outside, despite the cold. It was an open casket ceremony; the church ladies had dressed Myrtle in her best bombazine dress and the violet hat. Reverend Michaels gave a beautiful eulogy, and the small choir sang the congregationalist hymn "Nearer, my God, to Thee," bringing us all to tears. A long cortege of buggies followed the coffin to the graveyard, atop the west hill out of town.

The cemetery was a desert compared to the green lawns back East, but now, with eyes more Western, I could see it was well cared for and had its own stark kind of beauty.

Several of the graves were adorned with mementos: a horseshoe, a dried evergreen wreath, and one heartbreakingly small monument bore a toy train engine. I thought Myrtle's communal teapot would have been most appropriate, but by now knew well enough that the town folk would think that disrespectful. It was all a great sorrow.

How Myrtle had been looking forward to the new merchandise, the Harvest Ball, and to the turn of the decade. She had already begun planning a New Year's Eve party. Now, I supposed we would at least make an appearance at the Ball, the merchandise would sell, but there would be no party.

John was inconsolable. He had no thought for the store, but wandered listlessly around his house. He spent hours in the graveyard or walked far out into the countryside, despite the weather.

I took over running the store. I was a Carlton. What else could I do?

PART THREE
The Courtship

Chapter One

June seemed to have confused itself with March. I walked to the Mercantile in a gusting wind that kept me fighting to keep my skirts down. Clouds scudded across the sky, but I knew it wouldn't rain. They would have all blown east by noon and we would enjoy the usual breezy, sunny afternoon.

At the Mercantile, I let myself in, battling one final gust. I greeted the night watchman, Walter Dobson, who was cleaning out the clinker box under the new pot-bellied stove in the front of the store. The new lamps and additional stove had proved too much for Biggers to tend, along with everything else he had to do. Besides, we needed more security with all the valuable new merchandise now in stock. Walter was the answer. He patrolled all night, saw to the rat traps, and swept up. Worth every penny.

With all the shipments coming in and going out, Biggers had needed an assistant, even after being relieved of stove and lamp duty. Jonah Benet, a boy just out of high school, was helping with all the unpacking for me to inspect and price so it could be taken out to the various departments. Then, there were deliveries to customers, trips to Butterfield Freight and the post office, caring for our old horse Chester and the wagon, hauling in shuttles of coal during the day; the list of Biggers' chores was endless.

I walked to my office—which had once been Myrtle's small, screened-off space—hung up my coat and bonnet, and sat at my desk to check my *to-do* list for the day. I greeted my employees as they came into work, coming past me to hang up their coats in the back.

First, as always, Fred—early like myself to make sure the Hinterland was ready for a day of business. He was my mainstay and support, a great font of knowledge about the workings of the store. He would have been the obvious person to run it after John abdicated, yet if any decision were to be made, he always stepped back, inclining his head respectfully to await my decision. In every other way, he was a superb employee, but he wanted to be told what to do.

"I wouldn't have your job for the world," he had told me a year ago. "I wouldn't want to be in charge. What if I make a mistake?"

"I make a dozen mistakes every day," I exaggerated, but he wouldn't hear it. Yet, he ran the Hinterland like a clock. Frankly, all John did was sit by the stove with his cronies smoking cigars or seclude himself in his office.

"Good morning, Miss Alta," Fred said, lifting his hat to me.

"Good morning, Fred. How is Little Fred today?"

The baby boy was teething and Fred and his wife, Gertie, had not been getting much sleep the past week.

Fred gave me a big smile of relief. "Better, much better! Two teeth came through last night, poor little fellow."

"I'm glad to hear that, Fred. My best to Gertie. Ask her to bring him in the store soon so we can all see him!"

"Thank you. I will." Fred bowed slightly and went off into the Hinterland.

Little Mary Gomez blew in as if she had been running. "Little" Mary was almost as old as I was, but so short and retiring, one couldn't help treating her like a child.

"Am I late Miss Alta?"

"No, no. Ten minutes to spare," I said, half laughing. The poor girl seemed to fear she might be fired for the least little thing, although her work had always been adequate. She was painfully shy, which didn't matter so much in Foodstuffs, where she had little more to do than write up and package purchases and help with Housewares if there was a backup of customers. A clerk didn't need to do much "selling" in Foodstuffs; customers always knew just what they wanted. She was some relation to my friend señor Miguel Gomez, the cook at O'Toole's. I thought it important that we had a Hispanic on the staff, but she would have been more useful if she were more forceful.

We had more Hispanic customers now than we used to, which was good for business. Our profit line was going to show it, despite the warnings of Porphyria and, indeed, some of our customers.

"Regular people won't shop here if it gets to be a Mexican store!" Porphyria had said with distaste.

It was true a few people did not come in so often as they had, but the store was booming! After all, where else could people go for what we offered, short of Albuquerque?

Porphyria served our new customers as instructed, but I often had to remind her to smile. Pursed lips and a nose in the air are not good for business. I tried to take those customers myself and asked Lydia McKnight to do the same whenever she could since she spoke some Spanish.

Ginny Brewster came in the front door next, cheeks rosy from the cold, with Porphyria right behind her. Ginny was our latest hire and worked wherever she was needed. It was bad business to make people wait too long.

"Good morning, Alta," Porphyria greeted me with the usual touch of condescension. She was, after all, my elder, and had worked in the Mercantile for years before I came, more or less running the Dry Goods section.

"Is Uma Deetz coming in today? We're running low on hats."

"I believe she is," I replied, hoping her attitude was softening. Porphyria had not been a fan of Uma Deetz, either.

"I sold the pancake with the pink roses to Edna Michaels yesterday afternoon." Porphyria sounded disapproving.

"Oh, yes?" I responded, wishing she'd hang up her coat and move on. At times, she rubbed me the wrong way and I had to work hard not to let it show.

She went on talking, her lips pursed rather sternly. "A bit showy for a minister's wife, I thought."

"Surely not," I frowned, putting down my pen. Sometimes, you must speak up: "It's so important for the minister's wife to make a good appearance, don't you think? Since she represents the church as much as Reverend Michaels does," I observed, firmly.

Porphyria needed to be reined in from time to time, but overall, I reminded myself, she was still my most valuable employee, next to Fred.

Lydia McKnight arrived last. Her sister, Loralee, had married the music teacher and moved with him to his new job in Las Cruces. Lydia stayed on, very capably handling Housewares and quick to notice where she might be needed to step in and help when the store was full.

"Good morning Miss Alta!" she called to me, and I had to smile. I liked her very much on a personal level and thought she had been the most capable of the two sisters. Lately, though, she seemed to have acquired a beau of her own: Dewey Hughes, the lone reporter for the Black Butte Beacon, came into the store much too often for the small amount of news we generated and always ended up at her counter. She was not much good for anything while he was in the store.

I frowned a little to see that instead of the regulation tailored white blouse, today she had topped her black skirt with a frilly pink shirtwaist. Very attractive, but not businesslike. I guessed it meant she was hoping for a visitor today. I decided to wait and see if that happened, then I could address my disapproval of the whole situation at one time; privately, of course.

At Carlton & Hodges, she would have been fined and sent home to change. We were hardly Carlton & Hodges here.

I wished mightily for a telegram from my father, telling me that our big April shipment of Western goods for his Fourth of July Roundup had arrived. It should any day now, but I would not rest easy until I knew it was safely received at Carlton & Hodges.

How hard we had all worked to gather and pack up the huge shipment. We had Navajo rugs and jewelry, Pueblo pottery, and Zuni baskets. Father was ordering his Stetsons directly from Philadelphia, of course. They would arrive in glamorous black leather hatboxes; our shipment would have the silver concho hatbands.

Black Butte craftsmen had worked late into the nights, creating leather vests and belts, the fringed leather jackets, the etched and painted high-heeled boots, and the wallets engraved with Western motifs. To complete the cowboy regalia, we included a good supply of checkered flannel shirts, heavy tight-legged work pants, wool socks, and cotton bandannas—and yes, even a dozen pairs of red long johns.

Finally, we sent along gear to help Father stage his scene: a selection of branding irons, a saddle, spurs, and lariats. All this paraphernalia meant a great deal of profit for Black Butte as well as for my friends, the Yazzies. Now, we all prayed for success for Father's promotional scheme. But first, it must arrive in New York City.

"Hair-brained idea," Old Mr. Hodges had called it, but young Mr. Hodges was proving much easier to work with and was intrigued.

"Why not let him try it? Not so much to lose if it doesn't go over," he argued, mildly.

"Fine, let Carlton hang himself. Maybe then he'll shut up with all these wild ideas!"

I hoped with all my heart it would not become a hanging. The order had been an unexpected boon for us, but my father's reputation rode on it.

Father had written that he was preparing a temporary department for his promotion in a corner of the main floor, with painted Western backdrops and fake cactus. He planned a staged "shoot out" in the store entrance, to open his event on the weekend before July 4th.

I thought of writing to him that his cactus did not grow here, but in Arizona, and that he could increase the drama of his "shoot out" by ending it with a hanging, but I wasn't sure he would appreciate the humor at this time.

At eight-thirty, Uma Deetz arrived carrying two big totes full of hats. Walter let her in, and she went straight to the Hat Salon and started putting them out. I joined her there.

"Uma, what do you have for us today?"

"Morning, Alta. Got a dozen. Who bought the pink roses?"

"Edna Michaels."

Uma straightened up for a moment, and despite the heavy black veil, which hid her features, I thought I could detect that she was pleased.

"Edna will look very pretty in that hat," I commented.

Uma nodded and took out a black straw with a black veil, scattered with white polka dots.

"Oh, I love that one!" I cried, seizing it and trying it on.

"Me, too," Uma agreed, and I swear she laughed when I took it away to have it charged to me at once.

The truth is, we who worked at the Mercantile were quite well-dressed. After all, we had the pick of the new merchandise before it ever went on display—at a 20 percent employee discount, a not-so-small perk of being in our business. Normally, I would reorder at once to replace what staff had bought; but I couldn't do that with Uma's hat. I had deprived some townswoman, but only felt a little guilty; not enough to put my delicious polka dots back in stock.

It was a marvel how Uma kept all her hats in her head and never made a duplication. There was always just a touch of distinction. There were two other black straws in this consignment: one trimmed with a bunch of silk daisies and the other with a white flower and veil. Mine was much the smartest.

I guess I was waiting for Uma to make a mistake and repeat herself, but so far as I could tell, that had not happened yet.

At the rate we were selling hats, the ladies of Black Butte must have been starving for them for years. They mostly had worn cotton bonnets they made themselves—this was so much better!

When I asked Uma to increase her production, she growled at me.

"Order some from Albuquerque. Can't keep up as it is!"

I hated to do that, but there was no one else. I had never understood Mrs. Farrogot's aversion to headwear. In fact, I had tried to include her in the new prosperity. Running into her at the post office over the holidays, I had approached her directly and told her Burke's was doing so much business these days I wondered if she would not change her mind.

"Uma Deetz' hats are a great success, but there's a limit to how many she can make. Could you not reconsider and make some yourself? I would be glad to carry them."

That was a mistake. She turned on me with such a fierce face that I stepped back in fright and bumped into Ms. Higgins, the Sheriff's wife, causing that lady to drop the package she was waiting to mail.

"I am not a milliner, I am a *modiste*!" Mrs. Farrogot informed me angrily. "You are very mistaken if you think I would ever demean myself to such a collaboration!"

This was such an overly forceful response that both Mrs. Higgins and I were mystified. Sure that I was offering her an excellent business opportunity, I forged rashly ahead.

"Well, if not hats, Mrs. Farrogot, have you considered opening a school for seamstresses? Black Butte is so very much in need of more dressmakers."

Mrs. Farrogot's expression of disdain turned into fury! Mrs. Higgins grasped my arm to protect me, or perhaps it was for her own safety.

"Miss Carlton, you are as misguided as you are rude!" she snarled. "I am no teacher, either. Why in the world would I give away the skills I have learned over these many years to a group of inept needleworkers unfit even to turn a hem? I would be poaching on my own business, as, indeed, are you, madam!"

She tossed her head and stormed out of the post office in such a huff she nearly knocked me over and left behind her mail, which now infuriated Mrs. Blodgett.

"I'm not a poacher!" I exclaimed to the air in general. "I never poach."

"Did you have some business?" Miss Blodgett hissed. "Or are you just here to interfere with mine?"

It was all quite upsetting!

"Never mind, Dearie," Mrs. Higgins consoled me. "Everyone knows Mrs. F is crazy."

That did not greatly help. I mailed my letter to Margaret and then waited for Mrs. Higgins to mail her package so that I could walk out with her.

"If you don't mind my asking, who makes your clothes?"

Mrs. Higgins laughed. "Not Mrs. *La-ti-dah*! She never took me on, not hoity-toity enough for her. My sister in Clovis makes my clothes, and she don't really have time for it. You were right, Miss Carlton, in saying we don't have enough dress-makers here." She went off shaking her head.

Since that day, Mrs. Farrogot had never again spoken to me at church, giving me only an icy nod. It was beyond belief. How could I possibly be injuring her business by selling hats, when she refused to make any herself?

There was a thick veil of misunderstanding here I could not seem to penetrate.

Which brought me back to Uma. I wished she would raise her veil so we could talk face-to-face, but I knew she would not. No one wants to have to see people shrinking away when they look at you, but the veil prevented intimacy. I had so many questions I would like to ask her. Our consignment agreement was working out very well for the store. Was it making a difference for her, too? Did she really have enough to live on? Her veil suggested it was none of my business.

At nine o'clock, John came in right on time, walked to the front door, and unlocked it. Uma left with Walter right behind her. We were officially open for business. John said not a word to anyone but went away to his office in the Hinterland. Business as usual.

Several Hispanic ladies came into the fabric section and I left the Hat Salon to help them. I recognized one as a frequent customer: a handsome woman wearing an attractive cloak and gown of dark red wool. It was our best grade of lightweight wool; she had bought it here.

"What a lovely outfit," I complimented her. "Did you make it yourself?"

She gave me a warm smile. "*Si, verdad*. I am Consuelo Martinez. We haven't been introduced, but you have been very helpful to me here, in the store, several times."

"Alta Carlton," I introduced myself, and we shook hands. "I do remember you, of course."

"This is señora Lopez and señora Costinado."

We all bowed to each other.

"*Con mucho gusto*," they said.

It seemed these ladies did not speak enough English to go on with the conversation. What an awkward situation.

"How can I help you?" I asked and was answered with a cascade of Spanish, of which I understood not one word.

Lydia McKnight, bless her heart, came up and asked if she might help.

"Oh, please," I responded with relief, remembering the McKnight family all spoke some Spanish from having a long-term Hispanic housekeeper. Lydia was promoting herself to my top employee on the spot.

"It's something about making dresses, but I don't know what," I said, letting her take over.

Lydia launched a stream of melodious Spanish, which seemed to relieve all three ladies. Animated conversation ensued.

"Señora Martinez did make her own dress and bought this lovely wool fabric for it here," Lydia reported. "Now, she is making dresses for these two ladies, but wanting a lighter weight fabric for summer, but heavy enough to wear through fall as well. I'm pretty sure."

"Ah," I nodded, my mind galloping ahead. "Tell her I have

some especially nice new worsteds that just came in and will ask Biggers to bring them to us. Then, tell her I love her cloak and dress and remember the fabric. How does she get her patterns?"

More exchange, with much assistance from graceful hand gestures.

Lydia said, "This is getting hard, I don't know sewing words, but I think she says she looks at ladies like you around town and goes home and makes her own patterns."

"Heavens to Betsy!" I exclaimed, always delighted to uncover hidden talent.

The señoras looked inquiringly at Lydia.

"*Muy bueno*," Lydia explained.

I knew that phrase, and it didn't really express my admiration.

"*Muy, bueno, bueno!*" I repeated, and everyone laughed at me encouragingly.

As we chatted about the intended gowns and what style and colors they were thinking of, my mind was stampeding over the edge of the real Black Butte on our horizon to the north. A very bold idea was occurring to me. It was exciting.

Why not? It wouldn't hurt to ask. I took the plunge.

"Lydia, ask her if she would be willing to make dresses like this for town ladies as a commission through this store if I made all the arrangements and sold her fabrics at a discount?"

With help from Lydia and an adjournment for a pot of tea, while Biggers brought the bolts of worsted, we managed to convey, in awkward Spanish, the basic workings of a commission agreement. Señora Martinez looked more and more receptive as she came to understand.

It seemed she would, indeed, be very interested. Beyond that, she knew several excellent seamstresses in her neighborhood who would also like to increase their incomes.

She warned me they would not wish to use those fancy

patterns that came out of my big book. No sham bustles, thick beading, piping, tight gores, or whalebone stiffening. Nor would they use the popular silks, satins, or heavy brocades that were so hard to keep clean. They preferred to make their own, simpler patterns and to use washable fabrics, or at least ones that could be restored with cleaning fluid. This would be a different kind of clothes, more comfortable and easier to maintain. Really, garments for a different kind of life.

That didn't mean there would only be housedresses and aprons, although even those did not have to be drab. There would be plenty of designs for smart, colorful suits and gowns for visiting and shopping as well, plus Sunday bests and even party dresses. All would be made of practical fabrics and trim. Clothes that buttoned in front so that one did not have to have help getting into or out of them.

I liked everything I was hearing. It was exactly what I had been wanting for myself! I felt sure there would be customers who would gladly pay for such garments once they heard of them.

This was obviously different from my other two consignment agreements. I proposed that all charges should go through the Mercantile. The señora and I would meet to figure out a fair wage for the seamstresses; a flat fee, based on a generous hourly fee. They would also have a percentage of the modest consignment fee, all to be paid as they preferred, weekly or monthly, by the Mercantile.

Customers would, of course, buy their fabric and findings from us. All meetings and fittings would be held at Burke's. Altogether, a favorable agreement for all.

By the time Biggers produced the promised worsted, we had reached an agreement to begin in a small way. I proposed myself and Izzie for immediate appointments, while I prepared announcements of the new service at the store. Izzie had been complaining she'd had nothing new since our trip back East, and I certainly needed a new skirt and blouse for work. Why not a new outfit for church to go with my polka dot hat? Why should I not treat myself? I deserved it.

I shuddered, thinking of Mrs. Farrogot's reaction on seeing the two of us at church in new smart outfits—which she had obviously not made. She was the one who had banished us!

She already thought I was a poacher. I might as well be hung for a goat as a sheep!

Then I had an awful thought.

"You don't have any objection, do you, señora Martinez, to Uma Deetz' hats?"

Lydia had to translate a bit. Once she understood, señora Martinez's reaction was obvious.

"She loves Miss Deetz' hats and has, herself, bought one. She says Sarah Farrogot was— how should I say? Frightened by a cat in a sack, or something like that. It's some Spanish idiom, I can't really translate, but I imagine you can guess the meaning."

I could indeed, and we shared a hearty laugh. There could be no further objection.

I felt no need at all to confer with John before making this unexpected arrangement. He would only say, "Do as you like." That's all he ever said. I was willing to bet my own salary that this venture would be a success. I was sure there would be customers. As to the financial arrangement, this was different from our other two consignments, but the señora and I came to a happy agreement.

All charges would go through the Mercantile. The seamstresses would work at fixed rates, which we would work out based on a generous hourly rate and an estimate of the required time. Fabrics and trim would be charged to the customer at the store's regular rates. There would be a reasonable service charge, which would be divided between the store and the seamstress.

All meetings for planning and fittings would take place at the Mercantile. It would be a favorable arrangement for all.

We formally shook hands on it and toasted ourselves in tea. I was now officially in the dressmaking business. Heavens above! Now Sarah Farrogot would indeed see me as a poacher, even if, technically, no one involved in my scheme would ever have been her client. I considered myself quite blameless.

My new partner left the store with her personal clients, all carrying packages of worsted and smiling as broadly as I was myself. What an exciting morning it had been!

I thanked Lydia profusely.

"You were a great help to me today, Lydia. You speak even better Spanish than your mother. I believe we are about to be very busy, thanks to señora Martinez and the customers she will bring in. Some of them will no doubt be Hispanic. I am giving you a raise of twenty-five cents an hour, starting today. You are now our official translator!"

Lydia was pleased, but she did remark, "You should learn to speak Spanish, yourself, Miss Alta. The ladies love you, but how much more effective if you could speak, yourself!"

I laughed and gave her a little hug. "I have too much to do already! Besides, why should I when I have you?"

I went back to my desk feeling I had done a good day's work already, although it was barely noon.

Of course, I did tell John at once of my new enterprise as soon as I could find him. He stared at me, but, as I had expected, he only shrugged.

"If that's what you want," he growled and went away across the courtyard to his house where his housekeeper would give him lunch.

I had my lunch at my desk: bread and cheese from home, with a cup of John's awful coffee and a package of sugar babies from Foodstuffs—too deeply immersed in planning how to announce and conduct my new business to go out to eat.

I planned a large poster on a stand to display prominently in Dry Goods for the announcement, searching for just the right words:

Apply at once for summer wear.
Plan ahead for fall with:
THE MERCANTILE MODISTES

I know I do sometimes take things a bit too far, but to choose this name for my seamstresses was baiting the she-bear—poking the coiled snake. What in the world possessed me?

I suppose the Devil made me do it.

Chapter Two

I had barely finished lunch when Ellen came running into the Mercantile with her best friend, Millie Whitaker. The two had become inseparable, which seemed especially appropriate, as they had been together in Izzie's school through eighth grade, and now at the small high school. Izzie and I highly approved of this friendship, although it did cost me a pang or two. Millie was Whit's younger sister. Izzie was Millie's aunt, as well as Whit's.

Millie often slept over with us, especially on the weekends, and on Sunday afternoons after church usually took Ellen out to the ranch with her once the weather had turned mild enough. Then, they ran free on the land—riding, exploring, playing with baby animals in the yards, or lazing on the veranda porch swing in a nest of pillows and afghans.

In the evenings, after dinner, Larry or one of the hands would drive Ellen back to town. Those afternoons were Ellen's idea of heaven. She was mad for the horses.

School was out. The two were celebrating the first day of summer vacation with a wild day *on the town*. Millie was to spend the week with us, and they planned to walk all over, exploring the town. Ellen was to spend next week out at the ranch.

Their day had begun with a visit to the livery stable, where they hung on the corral fence to visit with the horses—especially Paul's horse, Dandy. Paul stabled his horse and gig here, and the girls both cherished a hope that he would let them drive it out one day. Paul was not at all sure they were old enough, but there was always hope.

They had begged the last of our fall apples for Dandy. Wizened as they were, they were no good for Izzie's apple pies, but Dandy seemed to accept them good-naturedly. Perhaps he shared a horse's version of the belief that where gifts were concerned, the intention was the important thing.

I was surprised to see the girls had an escort today, the young Almaguerra boy—Chester Goode's apprentice who had made our hat display heads for Uma's Salon. Then I remembered Izzie telling me something about an agreement with Demont Whitaker.

After greeting me, the girls ran off into the Hinterland—ignoring convention—to find John, in the hope of peppermint sticks. Curiously, although John rarely conversed with anyone except his cronies these days, he had a soft spot for children, especially these two runabouts, and I knew he would not disappoint them.

Joaquim modestly hung back, not following the raiders. He was not a personal friend of John's.

"It's nice you have time to spend with the girls," I commented, in a friendly way I hoped would cover my nosiness. "You are not working for Chester Goode this summer?"

Joaquim smiled kindly at me and helped me out of my conversational difficulty. "Señorita Carlton, I now have two jobs. One with señor Goode when I can, one with señor

Whitaker, which is most important. To be a friend, yes, but more, to keep an eye on those two. They need watching!"

He indicated Foodstuffs, where John was now helping himself to the candy jar on behalf of the girls. Nothing could have better shown the differences between Ellen and Millie. Ellen stood tall and blonde with her hands behind her back, respectfully waiting—well-trained by her days at the Settlement House and the sanatorium. Millie, on the other hand, a tiny, vivid brunette, hung on John's arm, absolutely flirting with him. John was obviously enjoying it to the full. She had those big, soulful, blue-green Whitaker eyes; it would be hard to refuse her anything.

Joaquim felt his point was made.

"Ellen walks right into any situation without a doubt about being welcome and includes everybody, no matter how awful they are. Some people don't understand. And Millie, well... she flirts with anything male. That definitely gets misunderstood."

Joaquim shook his head with concern. "Millie's had boyfriends since she was ten. A couple of weeks is all it usually lasts, but they won't always go away when she's done with them. It's a problem."

I saw what he meant. The two girls were now distracting Lydia; they knew her from school. Millie was pestering Lydia to take them to the Hat Salon and let them try some on. Ellen didn't care a hoot about hats, but she would hang around, a friend to the end, while Millie tried on every hat in stock. I knew Lydia would succumb.

"Look at Ellen," Joaquim directed me, ruefully. "She tore her skirt on the corral fence at the livery stable. We stopped in at Mrs. Hoaglund's. She gave us a pin to do it up." He grinned, "Cookies, too. Snickerdoodles."

My goodness! Barely noon and the girls had already cut quite a swath through town!

The torn skirt was brand-new, of course. I had made it, myself. I mentally revised my plans for the *Modistes*. Ellen would have to be the first customer. Her wardrobe was deplorable; nowhere near what it should be. She was awfully hard on her clothes.

Acknowledging the truth of his remarks about Millie, I wondered at Demont Whitaker's choice of Joaquim to be *minder-protector*. He was far too mature to be around the girls so much, especially Millie. I remembered the reaction of the McKnight sisters when he first came into the store two years ago. Both the McKnight twins had outright flirted with him.

"You seem to know Millie pretty well," I remarked.

"*Si,* señorita," he agreed, pleasantly, once more giving me that knowing smile. "I am a *primo*. That is a kind of cousin to Millie. I am señora Rojas's nephew and have lived on the Whitaker Ranch since I was four. Millie and I grew up and went to school together. I always watched out for her, anyway. Now, I get paid." Therewith a hint of laughter in his dark eyes, fully aware, I feared, of my misgivings. He was much too handsome and smart for his own good!

I gave him two dollars to take the three of them to lunch at O'Toole's and sent them off before they could get into any more trouble here.

Just before closing time, an errand boy from the telegraph office brought me Father's message. For this important missive, he had not confined himself to the economical ten words, and had also splurged for rush delivery:

Shipment received in excellent condition STOP
Goods even better than expected STOP
Roll out the wagons, we're in business STOP
Check is in the mail STOP
Love, Dad STOP

Such a relief! But "Dad"? I could never address him so informally. However he thought of himself, to me he would always be "Father."

This summer promised to be a happy time for all of us. The craftsmen of Black Butte would be flush with the unexpected income of Father's order. At the ranch, no one would fall off their horse or be bitten by a rattlesnake or get lost in one of the enticing canyons. In town, no one would be run down by a wagon or wander into the middle of a saloon fight. No discarded young men or misguided older ones would bother Millie.

Chester Goode was prospering, despite losing time from his young apprentice. He had a full crew employed, making desks for the new high school—all full-grown men.

A good prospect for all.

The new high school was now the main topic of conversation around town. Although it was yet a year away, no one could talk of anything else. Some were against it, as well as any increase in school tax. Why should they pay to educate other people's children? Some saw how badly it was needed.

The main objection was that the Catholic high school was also closing, and the young people from East Butte would be included. Some were sure the sky was falling; others hoped it would help to unify a divided town.

My three visitors would still be in the tiny, old school this fall. They would be seniors in the new high school—the first class to graduate.

The new building was already under construction and would be imposing: a two-story brick edifice with ten employees, including a principal and a janitor. There would be eight teachers, ten classrooms, a principal's office, a library, a music room, a teachers' lounge, and an auditorium with a stage. There would be a large athletic field, with bleachers out back and a stable for those who came to school with horses and buggies.

It would be a wonderful improvement and, many hoped, a unifying influence on this divided town.

Around the middle of July, I received a letter from Father with a triumphant account of the success of his Fourth of July Roundup.

Apparently, New York City made quite a thing of July Fourth these days: fireworks over the Statue of Liberty and all that sort of thing. This year, the Western theme seemed to have caught the city's fancy, and a craze was starting for everything Western. Father said they had sold almost everything, even the saddle, and he included an even bigger reorder. Father wrote that if the craze lasts, he would keep on selling Western gear:

Tell your people to get to work now for an order twice as big next year. Everyone agrees we should make this a yearly event, at least for now.

Black Butte was flooded with speculative prosperity with this news. Leatherworkers laid on more staff. The Yazzies and their Zuni friends bought huge supplies of silver and turquoise.

I was flattered to be considered the cause of it all—back again to compete with the new school as the main topic of gossip!

The equal success of the *Modistes* was just as gratifying. Almost at once, we had as much business as we could handle, and before I knew it, I had five sewing with Consuelo Martinez and they were swamped with orders.

We had young señora Rosalie Alvarez (newlywed and quite beautiful), señora Emily Montez, Miss Maria Derecho (blessedly fluent in English), and the elderly señora Maria Gomez; yes, a relation. I feared this last lady was too old for the job, but, although her hearing was not good, her eyesight was great, and her sewing was exquisite.

All were booked up for the rest of the summer, and I was running around the Mercantile like a chicken with its head cut off trying to facilitate all this mayhem.

In August, Consuelo politely mentioned to me, with Lydia's help, about a new young widow she had met, Clara Gutiérrez, who was by no means an ordinary young lady. Consuelo organized a tea party for the *Modistes* and invited Clara to meet me. Biggers drove me to East Butte to attend, and Ellen came with me, for once on her own and bored.

This was the first Hispanic home I had ever been in, and I didn't know what to expect. It was a pleasant surprise—more colorful than I was used to, with a full embellishment of what John called "gewgaws," and that which ladies find essential to their decorating schemes: doilies, vases of dried flowers, what-nots filled with figurines, decorative pillows, and framed pictures on the walls. Added to this were various Catholic paraphernalia, which included a two-foot statue of the Virgin Mary with a small sort of shrine with votive candles and wax flowers, a framed painting of *The Sacred Heart of Jesus,* and a crucifix hanging by the door.

Altogether, more pleasant and comfortable than I had expected.

We had Miss Derecho to help with translations and were soon in animated conversation, fueled by delicious spicy tea and exotic sweetbreads I was told were called *pan dulce.*

I was seated by Miss Gutiérrez and was relieved to find her fluent in English. I liked her at once. Slender, tall, and dark, she dressed simply, but with style. I could see at once she would be an elegant addition to the staff of the Mercantile.

I told her outright that I needed a Spanish-speaking staff

member to coordinate the *Modistes* and oversee their meetings with clients.

She said that she had been widowed for six months and was eager to find employment.

"I should like to be independent of my mother-in-law and have my own place," she told me. "It would have been different if Carlos and I had had children, but we did not."

Delicately, I inquired, "Surely, you might wish to remarry? A future husband who might give you children?"

"Miss Carlton," she said wryly, "I am a graduate of the University of Mexico in Mexico City. I was a primary school teacher. My marriage was arranged by my family, and, while I am sorry that Carlos died, we were not a happy couple. Be honest, what do you think of my chances of finding a compatible partner in Black Butte?"

I had to laugh, remembering my own experiences. She was right—highly unlikely.

Clara continued, with great composure, "I am not interested to remarry, nor to teach. Business seems a good choice if I wish to support myself."

I hired her on the spot, on a "let's see how it works out" basis. If she proved unable to handle the complicated consignment job, she'd be a great addition to the staff. I knew not everyone would agree, but we needed a Hispanic on the staff who was not shy like Mary Gomez. Lydia couldn't be expected to do all the translating, and despite whatever anyone else thought, Beantown (that hated name) figured high in my plans to tap into an under-utilized source of income. Surely Hispanics had a right to shop at the Mercantile as much as anyone else.

I don't think John had meant his store to exclude. Frankly, the problem may not have come up for him, as his merchandise —leathers and Stetsons—did not appeal to Hispanic gentlemen who wanted *caballero* gear: silver-studded jackets and sombreros with dangling ball-fringe, and there were certainly none such among his cronies.

Clara agreed to start on Monday. I took a second serving of the enormous breads, a sugary pink one this time, very pleased with the whole affair.

Ellen had a good time, too. Consuelo had a daughter, Amanda, of the same age. They would be in the same class when they went to the new high school. Amanda took Ellen off to another room with several other girls who were also there, and we soon heard gales of laughter. No doubt they found Ellen's rudimentary Spanish hilarious, but I could not imagine a better or faster way for her to learn.

I was more and more pleased with the work my new *Modistes* were doing.

Frankly, I soon came to prefer the more practical gowns and suits they made, and our customers seemed to agree. Their creations tended to be less fussy with trims, more tailored, with front openings, and as often as possible, washable!

In fact, I realized that in general, I was much less concerned with high style now than I had been. Somehow, all that seemed far away on the East Coast, and here, in the New World, we were more concerned with practicality and freedom of movement.

A Western woman needed a shorter skirt, one not adorned with ruffles, lest, lifting the children into the wagon, she might put the heel of her sturdy boot through it and rip the whole hem off. There was no time for endless smocking or piping every seam, and our ironing was more a matter of a quick smooth down, rather than two hours of laying in tiny pleats. And, most of all, our gowns opened in the front. No time to find someone to do up eighteen buttons down the back of your dress, when company was already walking up the path to your front door!

Nowadays, Biggers often drove me to East Butte on business and ferried the señoras back and forth to the store for fittings and consultations. We were literally bursting at the seams. Even John saw the need, so we converted the storeroom into a fitting and sewing room. Then, onto the back of the building, where only the coal shed had been before, we built a commodious and much more efficient shipping and receiving room with a new coal storage bin in the back.

Our remodeled fitting department was a dream, and because of it, the dressmaking business increased yet again. On-the-spot alterations could now be made. We had a changing booth in one corner, and several large mirrors in another with a fitting platform. With our own stove, excellent lighting, and a tiny social area with chairs and little tables where friends could have tea and comment, we soon were doing a business, which quite rivaled Uma Deetz's successful Hat Salon. It could be said the two consignments went "hand-in-glove."

Clara Gutiérrez fit in, also "like a glove." She quickly learned the routines of the Mercantile and helped me figure out how to run the consignments. Of the staff, only Porphyria objected.

"You can't have Hispanics on the staff. There are people who won't shop here because of that," she predicted, her nose at a higher altitude than usual.

"They haven't seemed to mind Mary Gomez," I pointed out.

"Pooh! Marty Gomez is so shy they never notice her. Besides, she knows her place and never forces herself on anyone. This Clara person acts like a schoolteacher!"

"Yes," I agreed blandly, "she was a schoolteacher." I walked away without further comment.

Mrs. Fairweather Gordon, of the ice plant Gordons, did speak to me directly and told me she would not be shopping here in the future, or at least until "offensive people" were removed from the sales staff.

"I'm sorry to hear that," I told her. "I'm sure that will be very inconvenient for you."

But for every such client we lost, ten more Hispanic families came in, and they had good money to spend.

John made no comment on this big change, although I did hear Porphyria ranting to him one day. He just *harrumphed* and stalked off, never saying a word to me, even when I showed him the books that proved how much more money we were making.

I felt like a female Midas, "Queen Midas." Everything I touched turned to gold.

Except love...

Chapter Three

It was a beautiful Monday morning in early June—if a bit brisk. The sky was full of those little white puffs of clouds, marching east like a flock of sheep on the move to a high pasture. I went to work smiling, glad to be outdoors, enjoying the walk and my playful fantasy of shepherding in the sky.

I let myself into the Mercantile as on any other day. Fred arrived first, as always, and then the other clerks came one by one. Walter bid us goodbye, and John opened the front door on the stroke of nine. Business as usual.

A few customers came into Housewares and Lydia went to help them.

I decided to treat myself to a pleasant task before settling down to reorders: a shipment of small, beaded evening bags had come in from New York. I took the box out into Dry Goods and began to arrange a display at one end of the central counter. I chose the bag I liked best: black jet beads, because it reminded me of Mother and her needlepoint, arranging it with a pair of gloves, a corsage of silk flowers, and an evening scarf. I stepped back from the counter to admire the effect.

The bag was quite charming. It was hard to imagine where a

Black Butte woman would wear such a bag, but I was sure they would sell. A perfect example of what John called "enticement."

Guilty as charged, John! But wouldn't it be special if just displaying such a bag on her dresser top gave a woman joy? This was the part John had never understood.

I tried a silver bag instead but changed back. The black displayed better. I wondered if Mother still made purses or if she had gone on to some other project by now. She was sure to like these, especially the silver one I held. The bags came from Carlton & Hodges, so perhaps she had already bought one herself.

I was lost in a New York dream of home, stitching by the fire with Mother, when I became aware a customer was walking up behind me. I turned and received such a shock I dropped the little bag on the floor.

The man bent over and picked it up—making a show of dusting it off and examining it.

"Alta, what the heck is this?"

It was Whit.

My knees turned to water. Grabbing onto the counter, I managed to keep on my feet. It was the closest I had ever come to fainting in my life.

He handed me the bag, looking solemn as if scanning my face to see if anything had changed.

"Alta, we have to talk. Can we go to Izzie's?"

I couldn't have spoken to save my life. I just nodded and gave him my hand, still holding the beaded bag, and we started for the door. Ginny Brewster appeared in front of me glaring at Whit.

"Miss Alta," she asked worriedly, "Is everything all right?"

I looked at her and tried to focus.

"Ginny," I said, "I have to go home. You're in charge until Porphyria comes in at noon." I broke away from Whit to get rid of the annoying silver bag. It was getting in the way. I put it into Ginny's hands and patted her arm absently.

Ginny was white as a sheet.

"Watch the cash register," I said, as from far away. "Tell Fred."

"But, Miss Carlton, when will you be back?" wailed Ginny, who had never been more than last assistant.

I took Whit's arm and clung to him, looking back at her vaguely.

"When I can," was the best I could offer, and we went out the door and got into Whit's buggy.

He drove me home, holding my hand all the way. We said not a word, which was unusual for me, especially since I had about a million questions that needed answering at once. But I was still too shocked to speak. I didn't know why I had been given this chance to see him again, or who might be seeing us go by alone in his buggy—undoing the work of years! I just kept staring at his face. I wasn't going to miss a thing.

His seemed harder, more sharply cut. He had a scar on his left cheekbone and lines across his brow. He looked older. Well, we were both older.

He tied up the buggy on the picket fence, lifted me out, and we went inside the house without even thinking of neighbors who might be looking out their windows. The house was empty. Isobel and Ellen were both at school.

Whit kicked the door shut, seized me in his arms, and kissed me hard. It was not the way he had used to kiss me. I began to believe that nature did not design us as we are for nothing!

At that point, he held me slightly away from him and regarded me solemnly while we both tried to catch our breath.

"Alta, I came to tell you we can get married, now."

This made no sense and struck me dumb again, just as I had been about to burst out with questions. A tiny whiff of caution crept in around the edges of the trance into which I seemed to have fallen.

I took a deep breath.

"Whit, where have you been all this time? Not a word to anyone!"

He waved that off as unimportant. "Alaska, but that's not the point!"

As reality began to seep back with caution, my joy was turning mournful. I was thinking how I would miss him more than ever when he went away this time—after the kisses we had just exchanged.

"I haven't changed my mind," I said, sadly.

His eyes blazed at me in the old, familiar way—more green than blue today. He seemed to look into my soul and my knees began to buckle again.

He grabbed my arms and held me erect.

"Everything has changed, Alta. I am not really married to Minnie Scruggs after all. You and I could get married today!"

I just stared at him. "What...?"

"It wasn't ever legal," he beamed at me, and I saw a hint of the Whit I remembered. He chuckled at my confusion and hugged me again.

"I know, it's a lot to take in. Sit down, Alta. I'll tell you."

He pulled me down onto the candy-striped satin settee and captured both my hands. His hands, which had always been so soft and warm, were hard and calloused and crossed with scars.

Alaska. He must have been to the gold mines.

"Alta," he began, "it's all because of Paul and Jeremy Wells!"

That did not help me understand anything.

He laughed again and patted my hands.

"You made quite an impression on Paul, Alta. He says you're way too good for me and I should spend the rest of my life making it up to you. He's right, and that is my plan."

I was glad to have Paul's good opinion, but...

Whit began his story.

"Paul is a lawyer, as you know, and we always tease him he is way too heavy on right and wrong. But he felt strongly that because I had ruined your reputation, my family had a big obligation toward you, to right the wrongs I caused."

He paused, and a rueful look saddened his face.

"Alta, I never understood! I thought if I went away, everyone would forget I was taking you around. I never guessed they would think... well, as Paul pointed out, I'm a stupid idiot. His words." He sat back, looking apologetic, and then went on.

"So, Paul set out to see what he could do. It was right after he and Jeremy got back from Mexico City and found out I was gone, and things were kind of a mess out at the ranch, and Dad was pretty much in a black funk."

Whit resettled himself on the settee. The satin was slippery, and we both kept sliding off.

"So, they went back to the beginning, to Albuquerque, where we got married, you know, me and Velvet, Minnie Scruggs. That Wells is as good as a detective. The priest that married us was long gone, but Jeremy went right to the head of the Catholic Church and found out plenty about him, mainly that he did not have the right to perform the ceremony, being what they call 'defrocked.' It was never legally registered. He just took our money."

Whit stopped and chuckled. "Wells is persuasive in a different way than Paul. Doesn't need a gun! He got that Monsignor to write to the Bishop in Santa Fe, and soon Paul got an official document in the mail, declaring the marriage 'invalid.' Doesn't that sound fancy? But it means you and I are free to marry!"

At this point, we both found it necessary to stop talking and express our feelings more deeply without words. However, it was too difficult on the settee, and we both kept slipping off. Whit sighed and stopped kissing me. Still holding my hand, he went on.

"Alta, that would have been enough for you and me, but not for Paul. He didn't want any chance of Minnie coming back and making trouble. So, they went looking to find her. First, they went to San Francisco, but there was no trace."

"I remember them traveling," I broke in. "They were gone for a long time."

"*Yes*," Whit hurried on. "My Uncle Brendon lives there, Dad's brother. When I left Black Butte, I went to him, and he staked me to go up to Sutter's Mill prospecting for gold. So, that was where Paul wrote his letter to me, saying I was free. But I had moved on up to Alaska by then and only got the letter months later. It's a miracle I ever got it at all. It passed from hand to hand and was snowed in at the Chilkoot Pass for a while, but finally, it did get to me in Bear Flats.

"I left to come home as soon as I could get outfitted up for the trip. I had found a little gold and managed to stay alive to bring it back to San Francisco to pay Uncle Brandon back and get myself home. All this is all that's left!"

He pulled a little pouch out of his pocket and opened it to take out something wrapped in a bit of cloth... a cloth I recognized!

"That's my hankie! The one Ellen made for me. I thought I lost it at O'Toole's..."

Whit gave me that old, familiar, sheepish look. "Well, Alta, I'm afraid I stole it. I just wanted to have something of yours, like having you in my pocket. It smelled like you for a long time, but then... dag nab it! Why can't I stay on the subject? Look, Alta, this is all that's left of the gold."

He unwrapped the object and placed it in my palm: a small, very heavy, dull gold stone.

"That's gold?" I asked, amazed. It didn't look like much more than a dirty rock.

"Just enough to make our wedding rings, Alta!" He slipped easily to one knee beside the settee and clasped my hand tight, enfolding the nugget.

"Will you marry me, true and legal, Alta Belle Carlton? You're making me crazy! I loved you and missed you the whole time I was gone. All I ever wanted was for us to live on the ranch and raise a passel of kids. I swear, if you won't have me, I'll go back to Alaska and be one of those hairy old men who live out back in the woods!"

I wouldn't have thought anyone capable of laughter at a moment like this but laugh I did. "Whit, you don't have to threaten me! Of course, I'll marry you. I couldn't possibly marry anyone but you!"

It was a moment of profound happiness. He began to embrace me again, but we both slipped on the settee. He laughed, picked me up as easily as if I were a sack of flour, and carried me into the kitchen, where he deposited us both on the wide, soft divan in front of the fireplace, where embers from this morning were still glowing. That was much better. It was easy to lie pressed together there and kiss, and so we did for a while. Anyone peeking in the back-porch window would have thought the very worst of us!

With each kiss, our love grew more intense. Somehow, the pins fell out of my hair and it came down. Somehow, buttons on the front of my dress kept coming undone. His hands were warm, and the calluses were unexpectedly thrilling as they rasped across my soft flesh. Even more thrilling were the words he began to whisper in my ear, praising my skin and my soft lips. He pulled away. Cold air rushed in where all had been warm. I was devastated that he had stopped.

I protested, as I would have gone on forever, but he carefully separated us and sat up. We propped ourselves up in a pile of pillows, and he looked at me with great satisfaction.

He took back the nugget, which was still clenched in my hand, and wrapped it up, putting it safely away. I asked for my hankie back and he refused.

"Sorry, but no, Alta. I have to keep it. I pretty much regard this as my luck. I'm not superstitious, usually, but you're going to have to let me keep this."

I thought Ellen would find that as romantic as I did, so I let it go.

"Alta, I really got off the track this time. There's more to tell you."

"More!" I protested, not sure I could bear it.

"I got home just yesterday, and Paul told me the rest of it. He and Wells found her!" Whit nodded, smugly. His brother, the hero, could not have done less. "They went all the way to Denver, as the next best choice, and found her right away. She and the foreman she ran away with, Ernie Bagot, have a place there called Red Velvet, and I guess she's done right well. She remembered Paul and was willing to see him, and he told her the whole story. He said she had a big laugh about it, and then said she was sorry to have caused me so much trouble, because I was a 'nice boy.' Alta, listen to this! She said that even if the priest had been 'frocked' it wouldn't have been legal, because she married Scruggs when she was fifteen to get away from home, and she had plenty reason to know he was still alive because he is in the Colorado State Prison and will be for another ten years! She visits him there every month and says she will be his wife when he is free, as she loves him dearly. Guess Bagot will be out of luck there."

We both shook our heads that such things could be.

"So, that is two reasons why I am not a married man and never was. Paul is so brilliant! He got her to write this all down in what he calls an 'affidavit' and had her sign it in front of a notary public. So, now he's got two pieces of legal paper that prove I was never married. He's going to start showing them around all over town, to Sheriff Higgins, and in the saloons, and it will spread all over town, and in a couple of days everyone will know. So, I'd say we can announce our engagement next Sunday and be married as soon as I can get these rings made up, say end of May? I'll take you to Albuquerque for a few days for a honeymoon, and then we can settle in at the ranch."

He reached to enfold me once more, murmuring endearments; but he had said some things that filled me with alarm and my head began to clear. Trying to push him away, I practically had to climb out of his arms before I could get his attention.

"Stop!" I pleaded, "Please! There are some things we have to talk about!"

"What?" he protested, looking confused and trying to put his arms around me again.

"I listened to you, now you listen to me. I have a few things to say!"

Drawing myself up primly, I rearranged my clothing, which was in more disarray than I care to admit. I had to do up four buttons!

Whit looked stunned. "But you said you loved me!"

"And I do. But there are some things you need to know." It was hard to look serious while hunting for your hairpins!

"Alta, don't tell me there is someone else! You said you'd marry me!"

"I do want to, Whit. But you may not want to marry *me* now." I gave up on my hair and just rolled it into a topknot bun, sticking in all the pins I could find to hold it up.

Whit pulled back in alarm. "Is there someone else?"

"In a way, Whit. I have a ward, now. Ellen O'Conner, the

girl from my sewing class in New York? The one who made the hankie?"

He did not look as though he remembered my talking about her.

"She had consumption, but she is well now, and they let me bring her West to live with me. Izzie has been wonderful, taking her in to live with us! Did Paul tell you I live here with Izzie now? She insisted we must go get Ellen and bring her West. She went with me on the train. Whit—Izzie met my parents, and everybody loved her. But, if we get married, wherever we live, Ellen must live with us. I have promised her, until she is old enough to go out on her own. You may not want that, Whit."

He did not look enthusiastic. I felt my heart sink.

"One other thing, Whit. If we married, I would expect to go on working at the Mercantile. I'm not at all sure I want to live on some ranch."

He looked about as crestfallen as Farmer Dougle had been to hear the same news. I was cast down by his attitude. He simply didn't understand how much had changed while he had been gone. What I wanted now was not what I had wanted before.

I got up to make us a pot of coffee and, noticing it was nearly noon, some sandwiches from last night's roast; I began to tell him about my life since he had left.

He did not really want to hear and soon stopped talking to me. So, I stopped, too, and contemplated my life while I finished eating my sandwich.

Sadly, it seemed there would be no more conversation right now; we were at an impasse, and I needed to go back to work. Probably what we needed most was a referee.

When Whit had finished eating, I told him my immediate intentions.

"I have to go back to the store. You probably have things to do, too. Come back tonight for dinner. Izzie will be home, and you can meet Ellen."

He agreed morosely and I left him there, walking back to the store as he didn't offer me a lift in the buggy. I did leave a note for Izzie to forewarn her of our dinner guest. I don't know what Whit did.

The Mercantile was still agog from my walking out, but, as nothing bad had happened, I hoped they might forgive and forget. It was business as usual the rest of the afternoon.

By the time I got back to the house, Izzie and Ellen had been home from school for a while and had obviously heard Whit's story. He seemed in a somewhat better mood but inclined to be sarcastic.

"Did the Mercantile burn down while you were gone?" he asked when I came in the door.

"No," I returned mildly. "I have them too well-trained up for that."

He did seem to have begun talking again, if not to me, and while Izzie and I made dinner, he told us something more of his journey to Alaska and some of the things that had happened to him there.

He had crossed the Chilkoot Pass in winter and seen men around him die. He had found and lost gold, made and lost friends. He swore it was enough adventure to last him for the rest of his life, fingering the scar on his cheek.

It was plain to see that he was not the same young man who had walked away from Black Butte and all his problems. He was leaner, harder, and there was a watchfulness about him, as if he never allowed himself to completely relax. He was more solemn, almost grim. I missed the teasing, playful banter of the past, but this new version of Whit filled me with fluttering butterflies while taking my breath away. He was wildly exciting, and I was hard put not to show how he affected me.

431

We ate chops with mashed potatoes and gravy and Izzie opened a jar of canned green beans. Dessert was oatmeal cookies. Whit ate like a man who had missed a lot of meals. I wondered where he was staying.

We shooed Ellen off to bed and Izzie made as if to leave us, but both Whit and I asked her to stay.

"We need someone sensible here," he complained. "It's hard enough to understand what's going on without having to decide who's right or wrong. I feel like someone keeps punching me in the stomach!"

That made me cry, and Whit had to comfort me. Izzie spoke quite sharply to us both and said we would have to do a better job than that of keeping to the subject.

I then spent several hours, with help from Izzie, explaining to Whit again how much had changed while he was gone, what the store had become and why I felt obligations. I told him of Uma Deetz, who had put her whole trust in me and needed me to be the intermediary of her increased income. I explained about the Mercantile *Modistes*, whose incomes likewise depended on me, and the wonderful, growing partnership with the Yazzies, who, because of my consignment sales, had been able to bring the two wayward nephews and their families into the Yazzie compound near Antler Springs.

Whit perked up when I spoke about the Yazzies. He was amazed that I had met them and built a friendship with Ruth, saying he knew Joe and Sam from mustang hunting and the various cowboy contests he and Phillip loved.

I explained my father's involvement with the Mercantile and what the shipments to Carlton & Hodges meant to the craftsmen of Black Butte.

Whit got more and more silent.

Finally, Izzie said it was getting late and Whit could not stay the night here with us. Even though she was his aunt, it wasn't respectable with Ellen and me there. Whit said he would stay at the hotel if I would promise to take tomorrow afternoon off, starting with lunch at the Stew House, so that we could talk more.

"Only if Alta will bring Ginny Brewster or someone as a chaperone," Izzie stated firmly.

"Dag nab it, how can we talk, with some third party hearing every word?"

"Then, it will have to be here, again, tomorrow evening," Izzie pronounced. "Alta, you can cook us liver and onions."

Whit was quite agreeable to that.

I shot Izzie a look, but she gave me one right back, an "it's only fair" look. I had to admit she was right. The fuss was my fault. Anyone else would have just said "yes" and joyously married the man.

"All right," Whit agreed. "But I'm taking you to lunch, too. You and whoever."

"I'll see you then," I said shortly, exasperated.

As he went out the door, he muttered to me, "You never used to have to have a chaperone!"

"That's right," I snapped. "And that's how I got in all the trouble in the first place!"

On these terms we parted—neither very pleased with the other, and Izzie put out with us both.

Chapter Four

The next day at noon, as appointed, Whit did appear to take me to lunch. He walked into the Mercantile like a man looking for a fight. I thought he had been too well-brought-up to misbehave in front of a third party, so head high and armed with Ginny Brewster, I entered the fray.

He took us to O'Toole's. Ginny was only a little happier with this assignment than her last.

We left Lydia McKnight competently in charge, with Fred, for no longer than an hour and a half, as this was not one of Porphyria's days in the store.

Ginny tried hard to take a back seat and say nothing, but Whit perversely set out to include her in the conversation and would not be deterred: offering us each an arm, holding the door for both of us, seating her in O'Toole's before me, and asking her first what she wanted to order. Ginny was scarlet with embarrassment, and, consequently, it was a rather strange lunch conversation.

The specialty of the day was rabbit stew. Ginny and I both ordered it; I found it delicious, much like chicken. Whit scorned it in favor of his old favorite: chili.

Ginny seemed as unable to eat as she was to speak; all Whit was able to get her to talk about with any success was the hutch of rabbits she kept for her family as semi-but-edible pets—a fairly gruesome topic, considering the plates in front of us. After that, he teased her mercilessly about eating rabbit. It did not forward our personal discussion in any way, and none of us enjoyed it.

He walked us back to the Mercantile across the drying ruts of the central plaza, lifted his Stetson to us, said that he looked forward to seeing me at dinner, and walked away whistling with his hands in his pockets. I couldn't help it, I peeked until I saw him go into the Wagon Wheel. I swore if he came to dinner drunk, I would throw him out!

Our menu that night, curiously, was not the expected liver and onions. When I stopped at Jack Warden's on the way home, he had only rabbit to offer me. I served it fried with mashed potatoes, gravy, and coleslaw, using the last cabbage stored in our root cellar. I'm afraid I got the giggles when I served this meal, but Whit glowered at me.

"You promised liver and onions," he complained.

He refused to see the humor, so I dropped the subject; and since he was so grumpy, I did not even tell Izzie what was so funny to me. Still, I would love to have speculated about where Jack Warden got his rabbits to sell, and where O'Toole's got theirs!

Once again, Whit ate enormously while I giggled every time I asked him if he would like more rabbit and he took it—glaring at me.

Izzie remained put out with both of us.

Personally, I thought the dinner excellent. I hoped Whit was impressed by how much I was learning from Izzie about keeping house and cooking. More brides-to-be should live with a relative of the groom and be trained up to keep house in the way her future spouse is used to, which seems to make men happy.

I did want to marry Whit. It was the great point of my life. But now, that had to include the two things that had become essential in my life: Ellen and the store. Whit had not yet responded in any way to yesterday's passionate pleas. Perhaps his sullen face covered some process of thinking, but meanwhile, he wasn't letting anything show. We were supposed to be negotiating the terms of a marriage but it just was not happening.

Perhaps because no one was talking, and wanting to impress her old crush, Ellen rose to the occasion and began babbling on about how next year she and Millie would be in the first graduating class of the huge new high school. She told a silent Whit of her plans to attend the brand-new University of New Mexico in Albuquerque, expected to open in two years, and how she wanted to be a teacher. This was guaranteed to get a good response from Izzie, but Whit looked as if he were falling asleep over his coffee.

I suppose she felt she had to raise the ante to get his attention; I cannot think of any other reason why she would remark that she did not think Millie would be coming with her as they had planned, as Millie was all in love with the Baxter boy and probably would be getting married.

Both Izzie and Whit got quite upset on hearing this. Izzie said there was plenty of time to get married after; Millie needs several years at least of normal school, and Whit said Billy Baxter was just a kid and they couldn't possibly know their minds at such an early age.

Everyone stared at him, and he had the grace to blush and say he was the perfect example.

Izzie said we were here to talk about something more immediate than Millie's possible future choices, then looked at Ellen and changed the topic to the possibility of rain. Ellen tossed her head and said that we needn't think she was stupid; she knew what was going on—Alta and Whit were having a fight! She flounced upstairs in a huff to do her homework. We three just sat scowling at each other. It was all a mess.

Whit then got up and excused himself to go back to the ranch. "This is too upsetting. Sorry, but I have to go home and talk to Millie."

"I want to talk to her, too," agreed Izzie. "I'll keep her in tomorrow after school. We have to talk some sense into her."

"I'll be talking to the Baxter boy tomorrow, too," threatened Whit.

This effectively put an end to any discussion of the issues affecting my marriage to Whit, as no Whitaker could think of anything except Millie. I was quite annoyed. An actual marriage should take precedence over a sixteen year old's crush. But then, I was not (yet) a Whitaker.

Whit left, and I went to bed in a huff of my own. Everyone else was having a tantrum, why shouldn't I? I had no idea what Izzie did, nor did I care.

The next few days were all about Millie. It did give me time to think about my situation, what I wanted, and what was less important.

Millie and Ellen seemed to enjoy being the center of attention at first, but then, when Millie saw how upset her family was, she got furious at Ellen and yelled at her.

"Just because you never had a boyfriend, you have to go and spoil everything for me! It was just something we were talking about, not something to tell everyone!"

Then Ellen cried, and said, "I really thought you meant it!"

"You're an idiot!" Millie scolded.

Ellen was only a little contrite. "I never meant to set off such a to-do! You're all crazy!"

No one was talking to anyone—except Whit, who had an interesting conversation with Billy Baxter.

Billy was shocked by the very idea of getting married.

"I'm only sixteen!" he complained. "The girls all want to talk about getting married. I just wanted Millie to go to the school picnic with me. She said she would if I was willing to go steady. I didn't mind that, but then the next week Tom Drummond asked her to go to the big Drummond Ranch barbeque and she did, and I said, 'how can we be going steady if you go out with other boys,' and she broke up with me."

Interesting. The whole thing had been a kind of fantasy between two young girls in love with love.

Faced with the facts, Millie was forced to be completely honest.

"What was I supposed to do?" she asked plaintively. "I wanted to go to the Drummond barbeque, it's a big event! And then I met a boy from Bagnold at the barbeque and I thought he might ask me to their spring dance. I really wanted to go. The part about getting married was just a fun thing to talk about."

Millie was by now working up a full head of steam. She showed a remarkable talent in being able to talk with tears streaming down her face:

"This is all Ellen's fault! She went and talked about my private business! Just because she isn't interested in boys doesn't mean I can't handle a few admirers, and besides, it's mean to tell secrets!"

Everyone was now miffed at Ellen, which I did not think was fair. Ellen was furious with Millie, and Millie was livid in general and said everyone should just mind their own business.

I was quite miffed that my concerns were set aside over a storm in a soup bowl like this and was seriously growing angry with Whit—I suspected he had latched onto the matter as a way of avoiding me!

The whole thing blew over, except now the two girls were not speaking to each other. Billy Baxter asked Millie if she still wanted to go steady. She said no.

The Bagnold boy did not ask her to the dance, but another boy did. Because of the recent to-do, she was not allowed to go, but she did *go steady* with this new boy for the next several weeks—in a long-distance kind of way.

Whit came to the store on Friday and apologized rather sheepishly for all the fuss.

"Maybe you and I could talk now, just the two of us," he suggested.

"Yes," I agreed. "I'm certainly ready."

Porphyria was coming in that afternoon. Whit came back at one, and I left her in charge. Whit and I went to the house alone. Yet again, we ignored peering eyes and went into the empty house—also ignoring curtains that rustled in a next-door window. Izzie and Ellen were both at school. But we needed privacy for this discussion. I would repair my reputation all over again if I had to.

I made coffee and we sat at the kitchen table. I gave Whit the leftover cookies.

"I guess you've seen the Whitakers in a bit of a different light. Hope it hasn't scared you off," Whit said. "That Ellen is a blabbermouth!"

That remark offended me and was definitely not the way to my heart. I do believe he meant it humorously, but I answered him defensively: "She was wrong, certainly, but she's just a child. And we should have taken her more into our plans."

"I'm not saying anything against her," Whit protested piously, but of course, he had, and it rankled.

"The whole thing has made me think very hard about what I really want," I said, perhaps a bit righteously.

Whit now looked adamant, a man who did not want to give up his point. "If you mean about the store, I do see that everyone comes to you, Alta, to run it. But I don't see why someone else couldn't do that."

"I don't know if anyone could," I disagreed. "Most of what goes on at the store these days comes from my ideas. They need me to show them how." But I did remember what Myrtle had said when I was worried about going to New York to get Ellen. She had said that if the new systems were good, they would run without me. She had been right. The germ of an idea began to grow.

Whit frowned. "Isn't John ever going to take back over? It's his store."

I shrugged. "This is the way it's been since Myrtle died."

We sat there.

After a while, Whit said, "We could get a place here in town, just right at first. You could keep on going to the store, and I could ride out to the ranch every morning and come back at night."

"But you'd be spending all your time going back and forth! And, even if it did work in good weather, think what it would be like in winter. There would be times when you couldn't get home. Or, even worse, when you couldn't get out to the ranch for weeks. And them needing you so badly... that just wouldn't work."

"What, you're going to drive back and forth?"

"I could have a little buggy—"

"Same thing!"

Exasperated, we sat in stalemate.

Whit tried again, "It's been a year and a half now since Myrtle died. John just seems to get worse."

I sighed, "I'm always thinking any day now, John will get back to what he used to be."

Whit snorted, "Maybe he doesn't feel he has to!"

I started to object but stopped myself. Whit had a point. John did need to realize he couldn't just leave everything up to me forever.

"I think we ought to include John in this conversation," I said. "It affects him most, next to Ellen."

Whit agreed.

So, the next day, Whit came to the store and he and I went hand in hand to John, asking for a private talk over in his office. At first, John was just surprised. He knew Whit was back in town, everyone did, but he had not supposed this would in any way matter to me; that story was so old. Then, when he understood we really were discussing the possibility of marriage, he got very agitated.

"But, Alta, you can't go off and live on a ranch out in the country! What would happen to the store?"

"That's it exactly, John. What would happen?"

The staff was well-trained. The past week had proven that they could get through an ordinary day of business without me.

But there was so much more to it than just waiting on customers. All the paperwork that John used to do was now done by me: balancing the books, collecting accounts due, writing checks to pay our staff and vendors, keeping the inventory, and re-ordering as needed. I received new merchandise, marked it, and got it on the floor. It was all a big job and had somehow defaulted onto me.

Although I loved floor work, and my talent was obviously for waiting on customers, unaccountably I had become the business manager!

Add to this managing my three consignments.

All this had grown out of the responsibilities and obligations that had made me refuse Whit the first time—when he wanted me to run away with him. Was it possible I could manage the increased workload, yet still add in the demands of marriage and being a ranch wife, albeit one with a superior housekeeper? It sounded daunting.

Whit sat through this discussion so patiently, and asked such thoughtful questions, rather than offering annoying suggestions, that I was in danger of forgetting the petulant, sulking opponent of the last few days and falling in love with him all over again.

He now asked, in an offhand manner, "Could any part of all this paperwork business be done at home?"

Flowers bloomed in my heart, and even John looked up, intrigued. "Sure," he responded, thoughtfully. "Sure it could. Most of it, in fact."

The seed of an idea took root and sprouted joyously.

"What if I could find a 'General Manager,' a kind of ultra-Porphyria. John continues to make the bank deposits, but the new person keeps an eye on the store as a whole: handles the cash register, receives and manages the mail, takes inventory, and oversees shipping and presenting the new merchandise? Suppose I handle the paperwork from home... that is, the ranch... and still come into the store two full afternoons a week, weather permitting. Then, I could keep in touch with everything going on in the store, but it wouldn't be a tragedy if I couldn't get in for a few days. Could that possibly work?"

Whit gave me the sweetest smile—so full of love and hope that my heart nearly burst out of my chest.

John rubbed his whiskers and grunted. "I suppose Biggers could send his boy out to bring stuff to you. But where are you to find such a manager person?" I could see him rating and discarding our acquaintances in his mind.

I gave him a smile as sweet as the one I had just had from Whit.

"Leave that to me, John," I said. "I have an idea."

"Well," said John. "Do what you want to do," and he went back to the pot-bellied stove where a crony was waiting for him.

We borrowed Ginny as a brief chaperone and went immediately to the telegraph office, where I filled out a message and handed it over to Mr. Ignacio. He sent it off at once as a special courtesy to me. It was to Cora Bailey in New York City.

It read:

> *Would you come West to work store STOP.*
> *Need you STOP*
> *Alta STOP*

Exactly ten words.

Her answer was waiting for me the next morning when the telegraph office opened.

Six words, only. She didn't need ten!

> *How soon can I come? STOP*
> *Cora STOP*

Chapter Five

When Isobel heard our news, she immediately started a celebratory dinner. She sent Ellen to invite Paul and Jeremy to join us, to make it truly festive. I went back to work at the Mercantile, but she and Ellen spent all Saturday afternoon preparing us a lovely lamb roast with all the trimmings, with gingerbread and whipped cream for dessert. Ellen put out the best-stemmed glasses for the last of this year's fermented apple cider and laid the table with the best cloth and dishes. She even made a centerpiece out of candles and four early and carefully hoarded orange nasturtium blooms in a blue pot with lots of leaves.

The addition of Paul and Jeremy made for a riotous meal together—a great relief after days of arguments. Isobel was as excited as I was that Cora was coming to Black Butte and told the two men all about her and what an addition she would make to our dinner parties. Paul told hilarious, and no doubt libelous, stories of predicaments caused by illogical tangles of territorial law. Jeremy teased me relentlessly about the little pearl-handled gun I carried in my reticule. Whit was stunned to

444

discover I should feel the need to carry it and was even more appalled when Paul assured him I needed it.

The truth was, Whit and I had spent hardly any time together, only a few weeks in all—however intimate the circumstances—and we, neither one, knew the other very well. It seems you can fall in love on the spot, but it still takes time and experience to come to know the one you love.

We sat joking and laughing for several hours before Izzie and I rose to clear the table and wash the dishes. The three men made a show of helping but were such a hindrance we banished them to the parlor, with the promise of sherry to drink a toast when we were done.

We brought the sherry in on Izzie's silver tray, a long-ago wedding gift from Paul and Jeremy, and we all rose for the toast. Izzie allowed Ellen a half-glass, which set off fond memories of home and Father's Amontillado. Then, as people sat down again, I asked for their attention:

"I have something to say," I announced. I daresay I looked quite determined, but my heart was in my throat. I would have preferred a smaller audience but could no longer put off mentioning some new conditions to the marriage, which I had been pondering. I wasn't at all sure Whit was going to approve. But I had come to think it was as much an issue as Ellen or my working at the Mercantile.

"Lord love us, Alta, what could there possibly be left to talk about after the past week?" Whit rolled his eyes, but he did sit back down to listen to me.

"Whit, I love you with all my heart and I want to marry you, and Ellen and I want to live on the ranch with you."

Ellen agreed enthusiastically.

I went on, "It looks like things can be worked out about the store as well. But there is one more thing. I didn't mention it before because I didn't know if we were going to get this far."

Everyone looked at me in alarm and I blushed crimson.

"I want a courtship," I said.

"A what?" Whit didn't seem familiar with the word.

"A real courtship, Whit. What I didn't get to have before."

"But we don't need that now! We can get married in a week or two and start our new life. Surely we don't have to wait any longer!" Whit looked almost angry.

I could see I had a lot to explain:

"Whit, for three years I have lived in this town as a 'fallen woman' because of how we behaved those few weeks when I first came. You're not just going to waltz in here and marry me and confirm everything everyone already believes about us!"

Paul was nodding his head, and Jeremy said, "Hear, hear!"

"Alta, I'm sorry about that," Whit said, clearly thinking he had apologized enough.

"No, Whit, I don't reproach you. I was as much to blame, myself. I never asked you the questions I properly should have. I willingly went off with you alone, something I would never have done back East. I guess I thought there might be fewer rules out West. Turned out, I was wrong."

Whit put his hands over his face and moaned, "Lord love a duck, are we never going to get past that?"

I gave him my sweetest smile. "Yes, we are, and I'm going to tell you how. You are going to court me in a proper manner, as if I were someone you have just met at your Aunt Isobel's house."

"Brilliant!" Paul said.

Isobel clapped her hands and sat up. "Alta is right, Whit. You must show the town that to you she is, and always was, a *decent woman*. That's the only thing that will really make them change their opinions."

"But everyone in town loves her!" Whit protested.

"Yes, but they also have a wrong idea about her character

that will always keep her from being well-thought-of," Paul scolded. "You have this one chance to correct a wrong opinion, which *you* caused."

Whit could not protest after that, so I lined it out for him:

"You can call on me Wednesday evenings, which I am told is 'Courting Night' around here. We'll give you dinner and Izzie and Ellen can chaperone us. On Saturdays, you may come to dinner again, as a formal suitor, with flowers and possibly candy. On Sundays, you should take us all to church. Sunday afternoons, we can go for a buggy ride. With Ellen along, of course. We can call at the ranch. If there are any social events in town this summer, such as church socials or the cakewalk in August, you will want to escort me, with a chaperone."

Ellen said, "Can Millie be a chaperone, too?"

Isobel said, "Of course she can."

"This all sounds undeniably proper," Jeremy pronounced, with a twinkle in his eyes.

Isobel said, "I hear there may be a Chautauqua lecture in July, a Professor from the South who knows all about birds. I want to go, too."

Wonderful. Everyone was on board with my plan except the most important passenger!

Whit made a temple of his hands and looked at me over them with some steel in his eyes.

"How long does a *proper* courtship have to last?" he asked. "When will the townspeople decide we are virtuous enough to get married?"

Everyone looked at me; it *was* my idea.

I considered. "Maybe early September, if my parents can come by then."

"Well, that's a relief," Whit said wryly. "I was afraid you'd say a couple of years."

"That might be ideal," I gave him the overly sweet smile

again. "But I don't think we sinned enough to have to wait that long. Just long enough time to plan a really nice wedding."

"Um..." Whit objected. "I was thinking, just stand up with Reverend Michaels..."

"I want the whole thing," I said firmly, hoping I wasn't going too far. "A wedding dress and bridesmaids and a cake and everything."

"And you shall have it," Isobel stated firmly, almost glaring at Whit.

"And a honeymoon, too, I suppose?" Whit asked, getting everything straight.

"Absolutely. Albuquerque would be fine," I allowed, lowering my eyes demurely. I was done with my harangue.

"I've been thinking about that, myself," Whit said slyly, with the air of a man who was getting even. "If I have to go through a fancy wedding and all that stuff, I don't want even more fuss at some fancy hotel." His eyes flashed at me. "I'd rather take you camping up in the piney woods."

If he thought that was going to put me off, he didn't really know me very well, either. Then, again, I suppose that's part of what a honeymoon is for—to get *acquainted.*

"Really?" I purred, letting him see my delight. "I would like that better than anything!"

He looked surprised but pleased. "All right, then. I agree. A real courtship for the summer. A fancy wedding and we go camping for the honeymoon."

"For a few days," I agreed, "while Cora manages the store."

"I was thinking more like two or three weeks. I can tell you now, it's going to take a while to get over all that fancy." Whit gave me a severe look, but I knew he was laughing at me.

Izzie said, "Whit's right, Alta. You aren't likely to have a better chance to take a real vacation. Get off to a good start. When you come back, there'll be a million things to do."

Ellen couldn't stand aside any longer and broke in with the truly important question, clapping her hands to implore, "Can Millie and I be bridesmaids, Alta?"

"Yes!" I said, capitulating to everything. "Isobel, will you be my matron of honor?"

"Yes, I will," she said soothingly.

I felt dizzy. I had put my dreams on the line and won. I had done it before when I bargained with Father to work at the store, and again when I told my family I was coming West, and finally when I told John what I wanted for the Mercantile. But never had the outcome mattered so much.

"Is everything really all right with you, Whit?" I asked, almost fearfully. "Put all together like this, it seems I'm asking a lot of you."

Whit looked thoughtful for a moment, and then I could see he was grinning.

"It does beat all," he remarked to the room in general. "Here I thought I had me a feisty, rule-breaking, modern woman, and instead, I'm marrying the girl next door!"

Isobel laughed and agreed, "Just as it should be!"

Whit came to me and took me in his arms, looking seriously into my eyes—then his blazed at me in the thrilling way I loved, and he said, gently, "Alta Belle, I would do much more than that for the privilege of marrying you."

He gave me a *chaste* kiss. After all, everyone in the room was watching us with interest—especially Ellen.

That was Whit's gift to me; with his kiss, he showed me that he understood what I had been saying, and he started as we meant to go on: properly.

Chapter Six

The next day being Sunday, Whit escorted us all to church, where we were joined by Paul and Jeremy. We caused quite a stir in the small congregation.

After the service, we all filed out row by row, the front rows first. Everyone wanted to talk to Whit and ask about his adventures. Shaking hands with Reverend Michaels, Whit asked for an appointment on Monday, which was willingly given.

Whit helped us all up into his buggy and drove us out of town, leaving the churchyard abuzz. I blushed and blushed. Izzie patted my hand in sympathy, but I was finding it was just impossible to escape being the main topic of Black Butte's conversation!

Whit drove us out to the ranch to make an official announcement to the rest of the family. Paul and Jeremy followed along behind us as soon as they could get Dandy and the gig out of the livery stable.

Of course, I had met Desmond Whitaker several times, since I lived with his sister-in-law and his daughter Millie was Ellen's best friend. Although I had always felt guilty of driving his son and heir away from the ranch, he had never mentioned that unfortunate connection and had always been unfailingly polite.

Although Ellen had been out to the ranch many times, I had never seen it. About ten miles outside town to the west, a private road passed through a gated wooden arch marked with the Whitaker brand—the lazy W—a circle enclosing a sideways W. The red dirt road ran north about two miles across Whitaker land: barren sage flats with the occasional clump of piñon pine, going always slightly uphill toward the towering mesa and red bluffs. We passed two paddocks full of sheep, but Whit explained most of the stock was in flocks grazing up in the hills, under the care of shepherds who lived up there in little shacks called "crofts" to watch over them.

We came at last to the top of a hill and looked down at the sprawling ranch: many buildings, corrals, and paddocks, with a wide courtyard, groves of cottonwood trees, and a rambling three-storied wooden house surrounded with verandas.

Beside the front entrance was a spouting fountain—the artesian well with "the sweetest water in the West," as Whit had promised.

I was greeted by Whit's father and introduced to the younger brother, Phillip. He was a true Whitaker, although the shortest and squarest of the brothers, and although he seemed too shy and ill at ease to speak to me, he did give me a sweet smile much like Whit's.

Then I was introduced to the longtime housekeeper, señora Juana Rojas. Everyone was welcoming and warm.

Millie and Ellen decided to make up from their quarrel and be best friends again.

We were all seated at a huge dining table, presided over by señora Rojas, for a formal Sunday dinner of roast chicken with all the trimmings, served by various Rojas daughters, each introduced to me like a family member. Young Joaquim waved to me from the kitchen, where he appeared to be washing up pots and pans.

Before the dessert of apple pie, we were all served sparkling wine, to my surprise, and Demont Whitaker rose to make a toast acknowledging my engagement to Whit.

"Alta, we are very happy to welcome you into our family, and Ellen, too. We are all pleased that things have worked out so that you two can be married, and are counting on you, Alta, to be a good influence on this rapscallion, so he can settle down and be a sheep rancher like he's meant to be. Let's all drink to the happy couple."

Millie and Ellen could talk about nothing but the prospect of being bridesmaids. They were just beginning to realize that at some point we would all be living together out at the ranch. Millie teased Ellen by telling everyone that she should be the senior bridesmaid since she would now be Ellen's "Step Aunt," which we guessed was technically true.

After dinner, señora Rojas made a point of speaking to me.

"You are welcome here, señorita. It is too long since there was a *Lady of the House*. A good omen for the future."

It was easy to see that Whit was a great favorite with her. Also, easy to see why Minnie Scruggs might have been dismayed by what was expected of her.

I wondered privately how Juana Rojas really felt. *She* had been the lady of the house since the death of Whit's mother. It would be expected that I would want to make changes and she could not like that. It sounded like a lot of future problems to me.

I did want to make changes. Looking around the large old common room of the ranch house, I felt a surge of excitement. How easy it would be to make this part of the house more impressive, more indicative of the status of this family: a few of Ruth Yazzie's larger Navajo rugs, some heavy wood and leather sofas, such as I had seen in the La Fonda lobby in Santa Fe, a few Zuni pots, some large paintings of Western scenes, perhaps buffalo—I was running away with myself! In its own way, it was a challenge to match remodeling Burke's Mercantile. I was no longer the naive newcomer I had been; for some time now, I had been aware that the Whitaker family was considered something like aristocracy in Black Butte. Whatever kind of woman I might be, I had fallen in the briar patch.

Now that we had the Whitaker family approval, our next visit was to Reverend Michaels. Monday, on an extended noon-hour, we visited the parsonage, accompanied for moral support by Izzie and Paul. Paul gave a brief account of his effective investigation, assuming the Reverend would not have heard the bar talk and produced the magic legal papers. Reverend Michaels may or may not have heard, but he read the papers thoroughly with a good deal of *harrumphing*, and then gave Whit a stern frown.

"Well, son, it looks as if you got out of that a lot better than you deserved!" he remarked.

"Yes, sir," Whit agreed, pulling out the sheepish look, which always served him so well. "I was sure stupid, but I mean to do better this second time."

We then explained our desire to marry, and the interview moved into the congratulatory phase: with handshakes and compliments all around.

"You plan to stay put, then?" Reverend Michaels was not interested in being tactful, he got to the heart of the matter.

"Yes, sir. I'll work with Father at the ranch, and eventually take over. We're cutting out a section on the north, up close to the hills, for my younger brother to set up an Appaloosa stud farm. We're planning to turn it all into quite a spread."

"That's good news for the town as well as for your father.

And I'm glad to see you have the support of your family in this marriage."

Turning to me, the Reverend asked, "Your family is in New York City, I believe?"

"Yes, and I'm very much hoping they will be able to make the trip west for the wedding." Indeed, I would be devastated if they didn't.

We then turned to the delightful business of reserving the church for a wedding on the first Saturday in September—the 3rd. We requested the choir be asked to sing, and it was agreed I would work with the church ladies to plan a reception in the basement hall, which they would implement, all for agreed-upon fees, which would go to the benefit of the church. Mr. Ignacio's band would be engaged to provide music for the reception and dancing. Miss Frey would play the organ for the ceremony in the church.

These important arrangements made, we four went immediately to the telegraph office where Mr. Ignacio made jokes about how often he was seeing us lately, and smilingly accepted from me yet another wire, this one to my parents:

Marrying Isobel's nephew September 3 STOP
Please come STOP
letter follows STOP
Alta STOP

I was getting pretty good at making important announcements in ten words or less!

"Well, Alta," said Izzie as we left with Mr. Ignacio's congratulations. "It's official now. It will be all over town by supper time!"

"I guess that means we're engaged!" I mused happily.

"I guess so," Whit agreed, but he looked thoughtful.

Father's answer came quickly on Tuesday:

Be there with Bells on STOP
Bringing Adah, Edgar, Cora STOP
Dad STOP

Ten words, exactly! My heart brimmed over with love for my "Dad."

On Wednesday, official courting day in Black Butte, Whit arrived with more than the usual ceremony: he brought a large bouquet of Queen Anne's lace, harvested from some field, which looked magnificent in Izzie's blue jug. He handed me a pretty box of chocolate walnut fudge made by señora Rojas's daughter, Delores. Then, in the presence of both Izzie and Ellen, he produced a small blue velvet case and handed it to me.

"This was my mother's ring. It would please me very much if you would wear it as an engagement ring."

I opened the case to find a thin gold band set with an Irish pearl, very delicate and completely appropriate. I thought of the garish Bufford Sapphire now worn by Aggie. The contrast between the two rings was as great as that between the two Charleses.

To me, the pearl was beyond price. The ring fit very well, and I was flushed with pleasure; I was so moved, it was hard to find the words to tell Whit how much I liked it and how honored I felt. But it was all right. From the emotion on his own face, I could see that Whit understood.

Izzie gave him a big hug. "Well done, nephew. I remember that ring. Your mother wore it always. She would, I know, be very proud to pass it on to Alta."

So, we were officially engaged, and Izzie was right. The whole town knew it.

The next day, Thursday, Whit made an extra trip into town

to take me to lunch, chaperoned by Ginny, followed by a formal call on Lavinia Hoaglund, who had done so much to help me, so that she could be the first to see the ring. If not always a perfect judge of the character of the men who had approached me, she had been unerringly correct in her opinion that the church women of the town were the ones who really mattered and had staunchly faced them down at my side.

Actually, she was not really the first; I suppose that was Izzie and Ellen.

And then, as I left the house to go to work that morning, I had noticed our neighbor, Mrs. Kelly, shaking rugs off the front porch. She had been frostier every time I had seen her the past week. Without question, it was her eyes I had felt peering through the drapes on both the occasions I had brought Whit into the house, when we all knew Izzie and Ellen were not at home. I immediately ran to the fence between our houses to make repairs.

"Mrs. Kelly, come see my engagement ring!" I called.

At first, she did not deign to respond, but I kept calling her and waving my hand about. Finally, curiosity snagged the cat, and she came over, still quite aloof.

"Mrs. Kelly, I am engaged to Mr. Whitaker. See the ring he gave me? Isn't it lovely?"

Ice began to melt at the mere sight of the pretty thing.

"It belonged to his mother, Mrs. Kelly! I feel so honored to wear it."

"Very nice," she had to agree, taking my hand, the better to see.

"We will be married in September. I do hope you and Mr. Kelly can come."

"Well, aren't you sweet to ask," she smiled, completely won over. Who can resist a wedding?

I was quite relieved. I had worked too hard to recapture my

reputation to lose it a second time over two little unchaperoned house calls! That had been a dreadful risk.

So, Mrs. Kelly was third to see my ring, and then, everyone at the Mercantile, of course, and every customer who had come in. It had been quite disruptive all morning.

Still, I could tell Mrs. Hoaglund, who had become "Lavinia" to me by now, that she was the first to *officially* see it.

She welcomed us warmly and sent Ginny to the kitchen to enjoy cocoa and cookies with Lupe, while she entertained us with sherry and congratulations in the parlor.

I could see she had intended to be rather severe to Whit, but he was so charming and thanked her for her goodness to me so warmly that she melted before my eyes. No backbone at all, a complete push-over for a good-looking, sweet-talking man—no better than myself! I wondered how in the world she had managed to retain her own good reputation all these years! Had there ever been a Mr. Hoaglund? I had never heard anything about him!

I told her the arrangements we had made with Reverend Michaels, and she immediately insisted that I must let her act as "assistant mother," since mine was in New York City.

"Who better to oversee your arrangements with the church ladies! You must let me. I think I have earned the right!"

I was delighted because truly, I know little about weddings. Whit thanked her, too, very sweetly.

"You must come to me on your noon hours, Alta," she instructed. "We will plan what you want, and then I will keep you informed on how arrangements are going."

We left with a great many hugs, a few tears, and mutual affection.

As Whit and I walked along the street back up to the Mercantile, I looked back and thought I saw a man I recognized going through the gate and up the stairs to the boarding house.

It looked like Lawyer Stevens. But, surely, I was wrong. What business could he possibly have with Lavinia Hoaglund? I dismissed the thought, none of my business.

But if it had been Mr. Spencer, I was glad we had not met him face-to-face at the gate. I didn't know if Paul had told Whit that story and would much prefer that he not hear of it. Men get so predictably territorial over things like that.

Whit had heard my stories about Mrs. Farrogot, and they had made him angry enough. I was afraid he would say or do something rude at church, but I should have known better. When he finally saw her, what Whit did was so outrageous I could hardly keep from laughing out loud. It was after the service when everyone was coming out. When the time came to pass her, and I made my usual cool nod, Whit stopped us right in front of her, smiled broadly, removed his hat, and made her an elaborate bow.

"Mrs. Farrogot! I haven't seen you since I got back from Alaska. What a lovely hat, did you make it yourself?"

The poor woman was so flabbergasted by this tactless remark, made right in front of me, that she didn't know what to say; she just rather sputtered for a moment or two, and then hurried away with her friend, Mrs. Goring. I'm sure it didn't help that I was red in the face from trying not to chortle.

Thereafter, whenever she was unable to avoid us, Whit always did the same with some new personal remark, such as, "Ladies, you look like three sisters in your lovely summer dresses; did Mrs. Farrogot make them?" or, "Mrs. Farrogot, what a splendid color you are wearing. Where did you find the fabric?" This never failed to enrage her, and it is no wonder she came to church less often.

Although I thought it hilarious, I did not think it useful in mending the bad feelings between us. Izzie, trying not to laugh herself, scolded Whit roundly, and remarked that a church was supposed to be a place of sanctuary.

Whit gave her a look. "Not stopping, Aunt Izzie! It's for Uma Deetz, too." We did not object further.

I was beginning to see Whit in a new and favorable light that seemed to increase my love for him every day. I caught glimpses of the man I had first admired during the stagecoach accident, and only rarely since. But that man was always there, I thought, the man Whit truly was. The lazy, teasing cowboy sulking on the divan when I made him stop kissing me was a mask he habitually wore. It hid the man beneath, whom he did not intend us to see; a junior version of stubborn stonewall Demont, his father, and of his steely brother Paul, who could sling a gun with the best of them. Whit was far from being the petulant boy he liked to pretend to be.

He made me feel safe. If he chose to pose as a lazy livery lout, let him. The man beneath the mask thrilled me to the core.

Chapter Seven

I zzie agreed, as my matron of honor, to see me through the amazing number of appointments Lavinia was arranging for me. She was a much-needed voice of calm and reason amid the growing chaos. Thank goodness for Izzie, since Ellen and Millie seemed always to be out at the ranch and were no good to me.

Many things were quickly decided. Paul would be Whit's best man, and Jeremy and Phillip would be the ushers at the church. Lavinia told me not to worry about what they were to wear. She, herself, would see to it that they were appropriately attired.

Isobel and I were waiting at the Mercantile with Lavinia for an appointment with Consuelo Martinez to discuss my wardrobe when Uma Deetz came into the store. She brought a new consignment of hats and an interesting proposal.

I was getting better at reading her reactions despite the heavy veil, and I could see the effort it cost her, but she did come up to us and spoke to me. Clearly she would have preferred to speak to me privately. I assumed she must have something important to tell me to break through so much discomfort, but when I heard what she had to say, I was floored.

"Alta, will you let me make your wedding dress?"

"But, Uma, I thought you made only hats!" I exclaimed, dumbfounded.

"Let me at least show you a design," she begged, producing a roll of parchment.

How I had congratulated myself on "discovering" Uma's talent, and how pleased with myself I was to winkle her out of her self-imposed isolation and into my hat salon, all for her own good, of course. I guess I thought hats were the peak of ambition. Such arrogance. Apparently, I needed a lesson for *my* own good.

The drawing she showed us took our combined breath away! All three of us saw at once that it was the perfect wedding gown for me: it was a simple A-line with a high-necked, long-sleeved bodice of cotton lace, ending at an empire waist. The skirt below was unconventionally made of fine batiste, starched stiff. Another surprise—gores were set in at each seam that doubled the flare of the skirt. Worn over a horsehair petticoat, the skirt belled out like a ballgown, a hoop skirt without the hoop! It was a triumph, a truly original concept. And I would have condemned its designer to a life confined to millinery!

Uma earnestly explained that, after the wedding, worn with a regular petticoat, the dress became a simpler gown, just with extra flare at the bottom, a style especially becoming to my figure and perfect for years of wear as a "best dress," ideal for dancing at the Harvest Ball, for example. Because it was cotton, it could easily be dyed any color I liked. A true *Western Wedding Dress.*

Except for one thing:

"Uma," I pointed out, "It buttons in back. So many buttons! And eight more on each wrist!"

"Twenty in the back. All the better for the wedding *night*," she murmured. Of course, I couldn't see for sure, but I could have sworn she blushed.

Lavinia and Izzie burst out laughing, and now it was I who blushed, easily painting a scene in which each button was unloosed with a kiss to the wrist, to the back of the neck, and so on...

My goodness, Uma Deetz! I would have to revise all my opinions of her still more. She must be as great a romantic as Miss Frey who played the organ at church!

Uma unrolled a second parchment: to go with the elegant gown was a stunning floor-length veil, descending from a wreath of flowers, edged in lace and with a two-foot train, the full length of it was studded with a scattering of small, free-standing appliqué flowers, sewn on with a seed pearl center. It was everything I could have wished, had I spent years dreaming of my wedding day, as some girls do.

"Well, what do you think?" Uma asked us.

There was no question, of course. It was the dress. We were all in agreement.

There was just one thing. A brilliant thought had occurred to me:

"Uma, the dress is wonderful, as you very well know," I said seriously, taking her hand. "Please make it for me. You are doing me the greatest favor to offer. But, only on one condition."

Uma was alarmed and tried to pull her hands away, but I held on.

"Uma, you make the dress only if you will attend the wedding. Otherwise, we'll ask señora Martinez."

That was a flagrant lie; there was no way I could forgo this dress now that I had seen Uma's design. But I wanted her to have the pleasure of seeing me wearing it to walk down the aisle. I don't think Uma understood how personally involved I had become in her situation, how responsible I felt for her. I didn't want to cause her pain; I saw her struggle and felt cruel, but I wanted her there and thought it was important for her, too. Here I was again, I suppose, deciding what was best for her, but I think I was in the right on this one.

Neither Isobel nor Lavinia said a word, but I could tell they thought I was a bully.

Finally, Uma gave in. "Okay," she whispered. "But sitting in the back."

"Fine," I bargained, "If you will also come to the reception, afterward."

She drew in a great breath to refuse, but I stopped her with a stern gesture. "At least, an appearance."

"Just a bit, then," Uma promised unhappily. "Five minutes."

"Agreed."

I dropped her hands so that we could shake on our contract. The important things confirmed, we settled lesser matters such as price and appointments for fittings. I can be kind; I agreed the fittings be held at Uma's house, a concession which I believe greatly relieved her.

I made secret plans. Someone, Aunt Adah perhaps, or Virginia or even Sally, would be appointed to take her under their wing at the reception—for a great deal longer than five minutes. She should have refreshments, certainly, possibly even be detained until the cake was cut. It would be so good for her.

Señora Martinez arrived toward the end of this exchange and we showed her Uma's design—more public stress for Uma. But she handled it well, as it seemed she knew Consuelo from the old days when she had made a scant living doing mending as inconspicuously as possible to avoid meeting customers face-to-face. Consuelo, out of compassion, had been collecting jobs for her around the time I met Uma and so was another concerned person. We were just not going to allow Uma Deetz to isolate herself anymore!

Consuelo praised the design for the wedding dress and especially liked the skirt. She readily agreed that she and the *Modistes* would make the rest of the wedding clothes and all my trousseau. This was a relief. I had worried that there might be resentment about my going "out of house" for the most important garment, but it seemed they already considered Uma to be a member of the Mercantile family, and therefore qualified.

Another lesson for me.

It was settled. Uma would make my dress and veil. The Mercantile *Modistes* would make the rest. My father would send money!

I heaved a great sigh of relief. The arrangements were made. Now, I would have time for courting. But no! It seemed we were only beginning. Suddenly I was busier than ever!

A conference was held at the Martinez *casa* with all the *Modistes* and my attendants. Consuelo included Clara Gutierrez as well, since starting July 1st, she would be Head of Consignments.

"So that you two can be better acquainted," Consuelo explained, and I was glad of the chance.

The committee went wild over Uma's design for the dress and veil. How I wished Uma had been willing to be present to hear their praise. Although she had made strides, this was just too public for her, and she begged not to come.

"Bad enough at the store, so many people! Maybe later I will bring the dress to show them. But, I have to get over last week first."

I let her off the hook; I had already pushed her farther than I had meant to. She would at least, however, need to get to know Clara. I hoped that would not be a problem.

It was quickly agreed that the two bridesmaids would wear

white batiste summer gowns to match my dress, with short, belled sleeves and square necklines, trimmed in blue satin ribbons and with long blue satin sashes.

Ellen and Millie had been hoping for something more extravagant and complained. Consuelo suggested that these gowns should have a special chemise and petticoat, trimmed in white eyelet threaded with blue silk ribbons. The fancy undergarments satisfied the girls' need for glamour. They would wear flower wreaths, with hanging blue ribbons, and carry bouquets. They would need new white slippers. Both girls were ecstatic.

Izzie was to have a medium-blue silk sheath, practical for a widow to wear afterward, with a high neck and long sleeves.

Clara proved her usefulness by suggesting that we ask Uma Deetz to make Izzie a very special blue silk hat to match, adding that she, Clara, would offer to work with Uma at her house on the whole project since there would be too much for one person to do. She could sew the long seams, hems, and such lesser work, like an apprentice, bowing to Uma's expertise. The clever thing was that Uma could not refuse since Clara was soon to be her connection to the Mercantile. They would learn to work together comfortably. I saw that Clara was going to be quite an asset.

We all enjoyed ourselves for another hour after that, drawing pictures of gowns, looking at fabric samples, and exhausting Consuelo's generous supply of sweet, cold tea and sugary, Mexican wedding cookies.

They had become my new favorites. I liked them even more than sugar babies, probably because of the nuts and powdered sugar.

Seeing me help myself to yet another, Clara said, "Miss Carlton, do you know why they are called wedding cookies?"

"No idea," I confessed, as sugar dusted my lap.

"It is old Mexican tradition," she told me. "Piled up high in a pyramid on a silver tray just like this, it serve the same purpose as a cake at Anglo weddings. Delicious, yes?" She offered me a napkin.

I gratefully took it.

"What an interesting idea. I'm almost tempted. But can you imagine how that would be received by the Ecumenical ladies?"

We shared a slightly hysterical laugh. It was not possible to imagine such a thing on my reception table. Not even as an "extra," really.

Biggers came in the wagon to take us back to the Mercantile, and as we were jouncing slowly along lower Main Street, Isobel asked Lavinia what flowers we would all be carrying, and how the church was to be decorated. I had so thoroughly taken Lavinia at her word, I had not even given these matters a thought, except for a sort of daydream of Queen Anne's lace everywhere, which I knew could not be.

Lavinia sighed. "Probably a lot of blue and white satin ribbons. You all can carry silk roses. That's what most people do."

Isobel asked, "What would your flowers have been if you were getting married back in New York City, Alta?"

I did not even have to consider. "Roses from Mother's garden," I said dreamily. "Pink cabbage roses. They would be at the peak of their second bloom. The whole church would reek of them."

I was lost in dreams of home, heavily influenced, I admit, by memories of Aggie's wedding.

"What flowers did you have, Izzie?" Lavinia asked.

"No flowers. John Quimby and I stood up in front of a Justice of the Peace. No flowers and I just wore my Sunday dress. All our money went to buy the farm. We didn't mind. We were in love."

Two tears ran down my face. That was the saddest—and at

the same time, the sweetest—thing I had ever heard. My emotions were becoming completely unhinged. I really was trying to do too much!

Lavinia had a strange expression on her face. Nobody said anything more on the subject, but I believe that was when she first began to foster a scheme that put most of mine in the shade.

Chapter Eight

That poignant conversation with Isobel had a deep effect on Lavinia. She determined that my marriage to Whit would have flowers to remember, and although this was arid New Mexico Territory, those flowers would be roses.

Impractical, to say the least.

Jeremy Wells had once amused us after dinner with a rant about roses and the perverseness of human nature. In his many travels, he had noticed that people living in the most inappropriate climates—for example, in the steaming tropic—felt compelled to try to grow roses. They battled heat, pouring rains, devouring insects, and damp molds, fighting for each flower, dismissing the exotic native blooms that flourished with no effort all around them. Nothing would do but roses.

"I blame the English diaspora," Jeremy had drolly claimed. "Roses reminded them of home."

He was not wrong. Even here in Black Butte, where anything other than native sagebrush and coarse grasses had to be hand-watered and covered with canvas during the coldest times in winter, Lavinia knew that two of the church ladies labored to bring a few rosebushes to bloom: Daisy Goring and

Marva Dooley. Neither of those ladies seemed the type to care so much about a flower, but one should never presume to know another's heart.

Even though I did not think of either lady as a friend, both were happy to contribute whatever might be blooming in early September to my wedding. Their roses were red and pink.

"Those two ladies are such good friends of Mrs. Farrogot," I remarked to Lavinia in surprise. "I wouldn't have thought they would do anything nice for my wedding."

"Lord love you, Alta! Do you think either Daisy or Marva would miss the wedding of the year? They're both on the reception committee to make sure of getting seats!"

While I pondered this strange facet of human nature, word of her search for roses spread and Lavinia was approached with offerings from several people even she didn't know. It was amazing how many townspeople were feeling personally involved in my coming nuptials.

Isobel, finally hearing of the great search at sewing circle, promised the whole wildly-blooming, pink Cecile Brunner vine from the back veranda of the Whitaker ranch house.

"They are tiny but very fragrant, and they come with a lot of greenery," she pointed out. "They would make sweet bouquets for the bridesmaids, and very nice wreaths."

I was surprised at how freely Isobel dispensed Whitaker property without asking first. Personally, I wondered if Juana Rojas, who must consider those roses her own, would have been quite so generous.

Lavinia accepted them gladly. Clearly, there would be enough roses for arrangements to stand on pedestals to either side of the altar, especially if she could find some greens. The tiny pink vine roses could adorn the bride as well as her attendants.

Anyone else would have stopped there, job well done. But

not Lavinia. Her vision had been all-white roses and white satin ribbons decking the church and hall. Clearly, that was not to happen. None of the promised roses were white. Tradition said a bride's flowers should be white, signaling virtue.

Lavinia's resolve stiffened. She was determined to present me as a virtuous bride, and she did know where there were some white roses. Years ago, she had gone with a friend to attend Mass at the Catholic church in Beantown. She knew there was a rather large, sheltered garden behind the church, containing several white rose bushes, grown to bedeck the altar.

Lavinia rented a horse and gig from the livery stable and drove to Saint Bartholomew's Catholic Church in East Butte, calling at the rectory. It wasn't necessary to bother the priest. His housekeeper sent her to señora Fernando, head of the Altar Guild, who was happy to pledge assistance to her counterpart in Black Butte. On the basis of a reciprocal agreement, of course. She was sure she could provide several dozen stems of white roses from the church garden, plus several more dozen assorted from personal gardens. Some of them would be white as well.

Lavinia swore without a quiver that her ladies of the Sewing Circle would return the favor next year, upon request. They shook hands, and Lavinia accepted a cup of Catholic tea.

Señora Fernando made the helpful suggestion that blown rose petals should be saved so that a flower girl could lead the wedding procession strewing petals down the church aisle.

Lavinia had heard of the practice, and immediately determined we would add this touch. She knew just who the flower girl should be: four-year-old Maria Luz, the youngest granddaughter of señora Rojas. She was adorable and mature for her age. It was the perfect inclusive gesture to the family.

On her triumphant drive home, Lavinia detoured up the hill to Uma Deetz's small house to tell her she would no longer have to make silk roses after all. This lifted a great burden from her shoulders and would allow her to concentrate on the dress and veil. I can only guess Uma had been staying up late at night making roses, she had so much else to do.

Uma was pleased to hear I was to have real flowers, instead, but shocked to hear Lavinia had been able to find so many. Lavinia explained.

"Catholic roses?" Uma questioned, hesitant. "How did you get all those church ladies to agree to that?"

"Oh, they don't know yet. But I'm sure it won't be a problem. I'll explain it to them later. I know they're snobby, but I can be very persuasive."

"Okay." Uma seemed unconvinced. "But that's a lot to ask."

"Don't worry about it," Lavinia waved her off breezily. "It'll be fine."

"Hope so." Uma had, perhaps, had less than pleasant experiences with some of those ladies, herself.

Lavinia drove home, enjoying the complete satisfaction of a job well done.

This was how it came to be that every rose in Black Butte bold enough to present bud or bloom close to the date of September 3rd was enlisted to celebrate my wedding.

The truth was, I had no idea how many people were now involved in preparing my coming nuptials and getting personally involved. They would all be expecting to attend.

When I first heard of all the people contributing flowers and put that together with all the church congregation decorating and providing food, I began to get overwhelmed. It quite took my breath away to realize how many people were now looking forward to what I had been thinking of as my own small, intimate event. I had to sit down for a few minutes to compose myself. In fact, I was wearing my blue gabardine, which I thought looked better with a corset, so I literally could not get my breath for a while.

I had given up stays long ago, but that was the day I decided I was giving up corsets as well. It was ridiculous that a healthy young woman should have to take time out of a busy life just to catch her breath! I took my corset off that night and never put one on again. I might lose my hourglass shape but at least I could fully inflate my lungs!

I got no argument from Uma regarding the wedding gown, nor from señora Martinez. I don't think either lady wore a corset herself! Whatever my life might be going to hold, at least I was going to have the breath to deal with it!

However, being able to breathe did not make me feel any easier about my wedding. In fact, it possibly cleared my head enough to notice all the signs that arrangements were getting well out of hand.

It was courting night and I could take my concern to Whit and Isobel.

"Just how big is this wedding going to have to be, Izzie?" I asked.

"Well, dear," she consoled me, "you can easily limit those who attend the ceremony, as the church will only hold about fifty. But, the reception, well, it needs to be pretty much... open invitation."

I gasped.

"Shucks, Alta," Whit seemed surprised at my reaction. "That's usually the way we do weddings out here. Is it different back East?"

"But how will we afford—"

"Don't worry about that," Whit dismissed it all airily. "We Whitakers are planning to provide the alcohol. That's the main thing."

Only slightly reassured, I said tentatively, "All right. And the rest of it? I have no idea how to plan—"

"Alta, don't worry about it. The church ladies know all

about weddings. They will know by now how much is usually needed. And Lavinia will schedule a planning meeting with you soon about the menu."

Izzie was right, everything was made easy for me. And, yes, the whole town was, more or less, invited. Whoever wanted to come.

The menu was quickly decided. Lavinia advised me to expect a mountain of sandwiches: chicken, beef, and a delicious cheese concoction, grated and mixed with sweet pickle relish, which she provided samples of for my lunch that day. There would be many salads: including potato, macaroni, cabbage, Waldorf, and aspics, and platters of deviled eggs. Cider, coffee, and tea would be served, besides the punch—which would be the basis for Whit and Phillip's contribution —as well as what was traditionally out back behind the church.

It seemed that many of the guests would bring supplementary dishes, almost like a potluck. I should plan for about one hundred guests, and "the Lord will provide the rest," as Lavinia said. How sensible! Why had I been worried? Well, now I was worried about the wedding cake.

They were all astonished I would give that a second thought. Lavinia was apologetic. "Sorry, Alta, I meant to tell you sooner. Mrs. Nettleton does that cake for all the Protestant weddings. Mrs. Corrigan used to do it for the Catholics, but she moved away. I have no idea who does it now. We'll make an appointment and go see her next week. She charges only a little more than her costs and the profit goes to the church. It's very reasonable."

Mrs. Nettleton felt strongly that I would like a four-tier white cake on pedestals, to form a tower, for such a big wedding, and that given the rose-gathering project, it should be decorated with white fondant roses set off by pale green candy leaves, and, in a nod to Uma Deetz's wedding veil, which I found was discussed all over town: candy pearls.

Uma Deetz returned the compliment: whatever flower she may have been thinking of when she designed the veil, they were roses now. Anything else would have been sacrilege.

"They are roses," Miss Deetz declared, tartly. "Full-blown wild roses with a pearl center." She already had Clara spending all her time making flowers for the veil, whatever they were.

Mrs. Nettleton was quite surprised when I mentioned a groom's cake.

"We don't do that back East nonsense, here," she stated firmly.

That was that.

However, she did plan to bake five huge white sheet cakes, each capable of serving twenty, with each serving marked by a fondant rosebud and leaf. Hopefully, we would not run out.

It seemed that at what I had thought of as a simple ceremony for thirty or forty, there would be real roses, plenty of cake, and more people than could be imagined!

Chapter Nine

In due course, letters came from New York. Father and Mother were as thrilled as I had hoped, apparently on the basis that my groom must be acceptable if he was Isobel's relative.

They had already been discussing a fall trip west, eager to see all the things I had been writing about, especially the Mercantile and the Indians. Now they would come for a wedding.

Charles must remain behind to keep an eye on Carlton & Hodges, alas, but of course, he and Agnes could not have come anyway, due to her "condition." Aunt Adah and Cousin Edgar would represent the family and make the journey even more delightful. They would all arrive two weeks before the wedding and start their journey home several days afterward.

They were also pleased to escort Miss Bailey and amazed that I should be the instrument of offering her such advancement. Father held her in the highest regard and thought two weeks would be just the right amount of time to familiarize her with the workings of the Mercantile so that she could take over while I was gone. They would miss her in Findings at Carlton & Hodges.

I was flattered that Father would consider what I offered Cora to be an *advancement*. To myself, I thought: *if he regarded her so highly, he should have promoted her to head of Dry Goods!*

Father wrote that this year's Roundup, just over, had once again been a great success, perhaps even more so than last year. The final tally would not, of course, be in for several months, but once again, they were nearly sold out. Customers were clamoring that it should be a yearly event. Young Mr. Hodges was pleased; old Mr. Hodges was silent.

Mother had been mentioned in the *New York Times* at a charity event for Presbyterian Hospital as:

> *Prominent among the many*
> *well-dressed ladies was Mrs.*
> *Horace Carlton, wearing only*
> *a small part of her extensive*
> *collection of the beautiful Native*
> *American jewelry currently being*
> *touted by her charming*
> *husband (dashing entre-*
> *peneur of Carlton &Hodges's*
> *Western Roundup fame) who*
> *has personally created the*
> *the rage for turquoise that is*
> *taking New York by storm.*

It would seem Father was succeeding beyond his dearest dreams.

I was counting on him to see past the rough exterior of the Mercantile, with its Western atmosphere, to see the Western miracle I thought it was. I hoped John would at least talk to him. I wondered how to produce some Indians.

As to Cora, John had nothing to say when I told him the date she would be coming to work. He *harrumphed* and went away to his office. I was not worried on that account; I believed Miss Cora Bailey would be more than equal to the task. At the very least, he would soon be saying, "Do what you want," to her, just as he did to me.

Cora wrote me, expressing her confidence that between us we could work everything out. She confessed that I had saved her from the well of despair. She had been deeply depressed at Carlton & Hodges since being passed over for promotion several years ago. She was eager for a new start and could hardly wait to get on the train. I was counting on her to see the Mercantile as an *advancement* when she got here.

I never thought I would leave New York City. But my excitement in coming to you knows no bounds. I will love Black Butte even if there is never a leaf nor a blade of grass in sight, as you have warned me!

Lavinia was preparing her best rooms for Cora: the second-floor front suite, a small bedroom, tiny dressing room, and a very pleasant sitting room with windows looking out southeast onto the street behind the hotel, allowing plenty of light.

Compared to the single room at the back, which had been mine, it was luxury accommodation.

Izzie and I were making new curtains and braiding a large, oval rag rug for her sitting room. We made every casual visitor who came to see us take a hand in braiding coils, even Whit and

Paul. I oversaw the braiding, and Izzie stitched the coils together. It was great fun.

I loved seeing grown men trying to do a woman's handwork, but neither of these men had clumsy hands. Paul's fingers were strong as the steel in his eyes, and I vividly remembered the grace with which he held his pistol cocked and ready.

As to Whit, I had reason to know that his beautiful square hands, scarred from work on his claim, were more than agile. Thinking about his hands made me flush—better to think of Cora's room.

Isobel and I wanted to add a few more *creature comforts* to the rooms than Lavinia could be expected to provide. I had already found several framed oil paintings of Western scenery from a catalog. One was of a grove of golden cottonwood trees and the other was a view of several cows grazing in a field. Not great art—they must churn copies of them out by the hundreds—but nice to look at. Isobel contributed a few pillows and an attractive green vase; I was looking around for something to fill it. All I had found so far was a peacock feather on a back shelf in the Mercantile storage room. How I wished for the *White Elephant* booth at the bazaar! But it was months away.

Whit's Uncle Brendon wrote that he and his wife, Fitzi, were coming down from San Francisco! They would stay out at the ranch. Whit was delighted.

Clara Gutiérrez had proven adept at handling the *Modiste*s, which took a great deal of work off my shoulders, but as so often happens in life, I had not realized how much my regular work would increase with the definite expansion of business we were experiencing. I kept falling behind with the account books, inventory, and reorders.

I started taking reorders and catalogs home to work on in the evenings. In addition, all the lovely letters I had received needed to be answered. Writing letters takes time—something I did not have much of.

I wanted Father and Mother to be fully in the picture when they came, and there was so much more I needed to tell Cora. Besides, I really should write to Aunt Adah and tell her how pleased I was that she and Edgar were coming. Margaret had responded with a brief, cool note; I certainly wanted to answer her more fully and try to open a better correspondence with her. These letters could only be written late at night after my other work was done. For the first time in my life, I found myself suffering from a lack of sleep.

Whit began to complain I wasn't much fun these days.

"You don't have time for me during the day, and now you're acting like you want me to go home early tonight. I thought you were the one who wanted the courtship. What for if we aren't enjoying it?"

He wasn't wrong.

"It's only for a little while, just until I can catch up on orders and answer all these letters. You'll see Whit, we'll have more time soon."

"How about more time now?" Whit demanded and began trying to tickle my waist to distract me.

Far from being amused, that made me angry. I batted his hands away.

"You ought to understand my responsibilities by now. And you're not funny. You're not very attractive when you act like this!"

Whit backed off, looking a bit shocked. I suppose my behavior wasn't attractive either.

"All right, Alta. We'll do it your way," he said and left a few minutes later.

Izzie scolded me. "That's not very smart, Alta. He cares for you so much. You shouldn't rebuff him like that."

"I have too much work to do," I wailed and ran up to my room. A large stack of inventory sheets cluttered my little desk. Firmly, I put guilt and remorse out of my mind, and I took up the first sheet. Soon, I was lost in my work compiling an order to a San Francisco factory for heavy-duty work pants and jackets, ready-made. If only women's clothes came that way! I believe it was after two when I finally went to bed; I only quit then because the oil in my lamp was running out.

I assumed the thoughtful manner Whit adopted after that night was just a natural reaction to my request. I did know him better than that by now, but I wasn't really paying attention.

When Whit proposed to get out of my way for a while by going on a camping trip, I gave him my relieved blessing, remembering his trip with Phillip hunting Appaloosas.

"Just don't stay away as long as you did last time," I jokingly admonished. "I'll be all caught up soon."

Then I learned he had invited Ellen, Millie, and Izzie to go along, not Phillip! It was to be a five-day, four-night trek up into the canyon country to visit the small settlement at Antler Springs—where the Yazzie family lived amid a sprawl of hogans and flocks of grazing sheep. He even managed to recruit Paul, who was glooming around town with time on his hands because Jeremy had gone off to Boston to visit his mother.

On the next courting night, Whit assured me he would leave Izzie's house right after dinner so I could work. While we enjoyed her excellent meatloaf dinner with potatoes and gravy, he regaled us with such delightful details of the planned trip that I began to feel left out.

He was stocking his beloved covered wagon for this trip: loading up with tents, blankets, and awnings, and was bringing fishing gear so everyone could catch their own dinner—trout fresh from canyon streams to grill over the campfire.

I began to feel even more envious and then *offended* at not being part of it. Whit must have seen my feelings on my face, he always teases me that I cannot hide them. But he only talked on.

"Too bad it's the wrong season for piñon nuts. It would have been fun to gather them. Still, we ought to see wildflowers. Mariposa lilies should be in bloom and Indian paintbrush. The Yazzies will give us a feast. I bet they make fry bread."

"That's not fair!" I burst out. "You're all going to have so much fun, and you're not including me!"

"But, Alta," Whit countered with maddening logic, "it's all been planned to get us out of your hair so that you can work. That's what you said you wanted."

"I didn't mean for you all to go off and have a wonderful time doing just what I would love to do, while I have to stay home alone doing stupid orders!"

"Bless my boots, Alta! There's no pleasing you," Whit smiled ruefully at me and shook his head. "You know you and I'll be going camping after the wedding. That's not so long to wait."

His tone was infuriatingly patronizing.

"I want to go now!" I lashed out and burst into tears, like a child.

Such an embarrassing lack of self-control.

Whit took me in his arms and gently comforted me.

"Well, then, Alta, you shall go. Don't cry, Darlin'."

"But... how?"

"Alta, I did sort of wonder if you might change your mind, so I asked John if you could take a week off. He said it should be fine if Porphyria could handle things while you were gone. She's all set. They both wondered why you weren't asking for more time off. Planning a wedding is lots of hard work. Did I do wrong?"

I caved in completely, knowing I had just been hustled by "the man inside." And so easily! I had not expected it.

"No, no," I sniffled. "I want to go. I'm glad you did."

He gave me his sweetest smile. I thought it made him look a bit like a sheepdog—he had rounded me up like one.

I might as well enjoy his victory, especially since going camping had suddenly become the thing I most wanted to do. Also, I admit, I loved knowing he could take charge if he stirred himself.

I had no intention of letting that happen very often.

Chapter Ten

AUGUST 1892

A safari to darkest Africa could not have been better planned than Whit's camping trip.

We left at dawn on a perfect day in early August. The hot, blue sky held no clouds, only the golden sun. Balmy breezes cooled our cheeks. The countryside was ablaze with color.

We headed northeast from the ranch on red dirt backroads that wandered through the foothills, past intriguing canyons and rock formations, with sudden vistas of rust- and ocher-stained bluffs and table mesas. It was a country of astounding beauty. The clear sunlight made your eyes hurt.

Whit showed us how the cowboys covered their faces with bandannas, cutting little slits for eyeholes. I preferred to squint and enjoy the breeze on my face. It was too stuffy inside a bandanna.

Whit and Paul took turns driving the wagon, which was a lovingly restored antique Conestoga pulled by a yoke of oxen. The brothers had spent years working together on this project and used it for camping trips as often as they could.

The oxen were named Mo and Slow, and it was impossible to get them to move faster than molasses.

Whit told us that this made our journey historically realistic and was exactly how the pioneers had traveled.

"That's very educational," Isobel commented tartly, "And I appreciate it as a teacher, but I wouldn't mind going faster. I don't have to relive history to appreciate it."

Whit laughed. "Sorry, this is the best I can do, Aunt Iz. Consider it me getting even for you making me sit in the corner!"

The girls seemed to think that was very funny, but Isobel did not.

"You always had such a smart mouth," she commented.

But that did not make Mo and Slow go any faster.

Our slow progress made it easy to jump out and walk alongside when one got tired of being jostled and jounced on the rough road. It was worse than the stagecoach. Besides, walking was good exercise.

Two hands from the ranch came with us. Benny drove a fully-stocked chuck wagon and would be our cook. Slats wrangled a small remuda of riding horses for our pleasure, should we tire of walking.

The Conestoga led our miniature wagon train, with the others trailing along behind us, far enough back to let our dust settle before they stirred up even more.

The cowboys were a brilliant addition to our party. They would set up the tents, build fires, cook, care for the livestock, and, in fact, do all the work while we enjoyed ourselves. I was so happy to be coming along, I didn't even feel guilty!

I could ride, of course, but was used to a side-saddle on the packed-dirt lanes of Central Park. I was not comfortable yet with the Western style of riding astride, as the girls did so easily.

Isobel was an excellent horsewoman and chose to travel in a split riding skirt. Even I could see how convenient that garment was for physical activities such as climbing in and out of the wagon, but it seemed inelegant and unfeminine to me. Ruefully, I acknowledged I was not yet completely Westernized, whatever I thought of myself.

Despite being dressed to ride, Isobel chose to walk with me.

"Izzie, you and I would have been good pioneer women," I welcomed her. Whit had started a fantasy, playing in my head as I walked along. "Picture us in sunbonnets, trudging along beside our wagons, conquering the West, and dreaming of bringing civilization to the wilderness!"

She laughed at my fancy. "I'll bet you a buffalo nickel it was more like barefoot and pregnant, with splinters in our toes, thinking: *The beans are all gone, guess I'll have to make mush and molasses for dinner again.*"

"Izzie, you aren't the least bit romantic," I complained.

"Just historically realistic," she replied, complacently. "I should hope all that romantic nonsense ought to be pretty well pounded out of me by now."

I thought that sorrowful. If I had been a pioneer woman, I'm sure I could have walked all the way to Oregon.

The two girls were in horse heaven and chose mainly to ride. Millie's pony, Beauty, was included in our remuda, along with Dandy, on vacation from the livery stable, and Whit's favorite bay, Spirit. Whit had even thought to include the horse reserved for Ellen to use when she came out to the ranch: Rusty.

All the rest rode like centaurs. Millie had ridden since she could walk but, to my prejudiced mind, Ellen was her equal. You would never have guessed she had been born in a New York slum and had never sat on a horse before she came West at fourteen, no more than you could believe she had once been ill with tuberculosis. She sat tall in her saddle, sun-bleached hair in pigtails, wearing an old leather hat with her patched old riding skirt. She never bounced up and down as I did. She was the picture of health, exactly as promised in the newspaper advertisements praising our hot, dry climate and urging convalescents to *come West for your health!*

Whit on a horse was a sight to see, and I must confess I could hardly take my eyes off his lean hips and muscled thighs, but that way lay folly. I had a flashing memory of visiting the Museum of Art with Margaret and of the revelations it contained. It made me flush to realize I was now comparing Whit to the Greek and Roman statues we had seen there. Whit was leaner and harder, and he rode fully clothed, but thinking of him in the museum context unnerved me to the point that I had to climb back into the wagon and hide myself away for a time. For goodness sakes! I was becoming completely unhinged!

Not surprisingly, that subject stayed on my mind. I had dealt with my more immediate concerns so firmly and successfully, I suppose it cleared my mind for the deep, dark worries to creep in.

Worries about the day... or night... coming so soon—when all mysteries would be revealed.

Paul was driving the wagon, and Whit, all too magnificent on Spirit, rode circles around the girls, teasing them. Then he put himself out to entertain them, leading them off on little explorations up box canyons and around curious rock formations.

The rest of us plodded on at our Slow and Mo pace, steadily marking off the miles.

At noon, we stopped for bread and cheese at a sandy creek in the mouth of a wide canyon. It was just too tempting. I stripped off my shoes and stockings, hoisted my skirts, and waded in the water, remembering another time I had done the same. The two girls followed me at once, shrieking at the cold water, so icy it must have just melted. Even Isobel joined in, complaining of the pebbles hurting their tender feet.

Whit and Paul accused us of spoiling their fishing hole.

They gathered up their gear to walk higher up the stream to find a better place. The girls immediately abandoned wading and clamored for permission to go along.

Whit was skeptical. "You two are always talking and giggling. You'll scare off all the fish," he objected.

"We won't make a sound," Milly promised.

Ellen nodded with her hands clasped over her mouth to show how silent she could be.

"We'll be sorry," Paul forewarned, but they let the girls come and started up the canyon, leaving Isobel and me to sunbathe on a big rock under the watchful eyes of Benny and Slats.

They had barely gone out of sight around a bend when we heard gales of laughter floating back.

"Oh, well, no fish," Izzie predicted. "Doesn't matter. Benny will have more steaks."

We chatted about this and that, sunning ourselves on our rock. Then, Slats put up an awning so that we wouldn't burn, and all four of us fell asleep in the drowsy, bee-buzzing, lazy afternoon. It must have been two hours later when we awoke to hear our fishing party coming back. They were all four making enough noise to stampede a herd of steers and eager to show off creels full of the fat trout they had caught.

"I caught three!" Millie shrieked. "Ellen only got two!"

"I would have got more, but you screamed and made me drop my pole in the deep water," Ellen complained, righteously.

"Never mind," said Whit, the peacemaker. "We have plenty of fish for dinner tonight."

"A feast!" cried Millie in raptures.

Whit had found a small, flat piece of red jasper and brought it to me, making my heart bump as we both remembered our illicit picnic from years before. It pleased me that he remembered it as well as I did. I carefully put the rock in my pocket, to add to the ones I still treasured in my jewelry box.

Regretfully, we left this idyllic spot and got back on the trail. In the late afternoon, we stopped in a tiny box canyon still carpeted with grass. The men put up our tents and made a campfire. We put on shawls and spread blankets to sit around the fire. We ate grilled trout glazed with butter, accompanied by skillet biscuits and potatoes baked in the coals. I had never eaten any fish so fresh as this, not even oysters in New York City, and could hardly believe how good it tasted, large pink flakes coming off on my fork. Even having to be careful of small (almost invisible) bones did not spoil the feast. It was quite possibly the best meal I had ever eaten, although I will always remember Mrs. Croft with reverence.

When the stars came out, Slats produced a guitar and taught us mournful cowboy laments. Then, we lingered over the dying embers until long after the new moon had set.

Chapter Eleven

We slept late the next morning, not surprisingly. This was, after all, a vacation. Even so, we were back on the road well before noon.

To make up for the late start, we made no stops to explore or fish. We reached the Navajo compound by mid-afternoon.

The Yazzies, forewarned last week by a rider from the ranch, welcomed us graciously, greeting both Whit and me as trusted friends.

I could tell this astonished Whit. Despite all I had told him, it had been hard for him to believe I actually knew these people and had a business arrangement of my own with them. They had been his friends since he was a child.

Ruth seemed bulkier than I remembered her. I realized she was wearing a carrier on her back. She saw me looking and turned so that I could see more clearly.

"This is our son," she grinned modestly.

Two obsidian eyes regarded me solemnly from the carrier. I waggled my fingers at the infant and made nonsense noises, as one does. The child crowed with laughter, his eyes turning merry as blackberries.

"He has other names, but we call him Josito, for Tom's brother," Ruth said.

I would have liked to talk to her longer, but for now, it was obvious I must first attend to business.

The shadows were fading as the sun sank lower, and the air grew cooler by the time we were served a wonderful dinner of lamb stew, fry bread, and coffee. Everyone fell on the feast like polite wolves. I had not been so hungry in weeks. The bread—a dough made of gluten flour, patted flat, and fried in deep oil—was so good, I stuffed myself. I could have lived on it entirely, although I fear, in a short time, I would have gotten as round as a pumpkin.

As we finished eating, the sunset put on a show that the people in New York City would have paid to see! Maybe accompanied by an orchestra. It was as thrilling as any revue I had ever watched.

Suddenly the horizon was piled with fluffy clouds turning red, orange, and yellow. The sky seemed to blaze up and for a brief, magical while, the world exuberant in the fiery glow. Slowly the colors dimmed and receded, violet and purples crept in, the red and orange mellowed to pink and blue, and the hot sun sank below the horizon. A reflection of the glory lingered, then was gone. Everything cooled down, then dark blue velvet night fell, and the diamond stars came out.

It took a while for conversation to resume. We had to recover from all that splendor.

Dessert was peaches so sweet and juicy we all had to go down to the stream to wash off.

There was quite a bit of moonlight frolicking in the water. Whoever said Indians were stoic and inscrutable should have seen us that night!

Whit and I sat up late under the stars before I retired to the tent I shared with Izzie. She was still awake reading by the light of a kerosene lantern. We turned out the light and got into our cots, intending to have a good chat, but our day had been so full I fell asleep at once. I wouldn't know, but I imagine Izzie did, too.

Chapter Twelve

With no crowing roosters to wake us, we slept in late the next morning. I believe our gracious hosts were up and about their regular duties at dawn.

I vaguely remember Whit sticking his head inside the flap of the tent to announce that he and Paul were taking the girls off on another expedition. Sam knew of a trail leading to the top of nearby Table Mesa. If the horses couldn't manage it, they would go up on foot.

Isobel raised her head crossly.

"For Goodness sakes, just go!" she complained, turned over, and went back to sleep. I didn't even bother to respond.

When we finally did emerge, slept out but feeling a tiny bit guilty, no one seemed to be paying us any attention. Slats gave us coffee and Ruth left her loom long enough to give us fresh fry bread. I ate two and was sorry for it.

"I'm eating like a pig," I complained.

"For goodness' sake," Isobel scolded me. "You're as thin as a pin, Alta! Have three if you want. I'm the one who will gain ten pounds if I even look at them!"

Nevertheless, she ate two, herself.

She and I established ourselves on a beautiful rug in the shade with our pillows and our books, not far from the weavers. Isobel was still deep in *Jane Eyre*. I was once more trying to read *Moby Dick* and finding it harder to get a foothold than ever. I put it down in favor of savoring the beautiful, sage-scented morning.

"Isobel," I interrupted her without a qualm. "Wouldn't it be Heaven to live in a place like this?"

"Um..." she responded.

I smiled at her fondly and let her go back to reading. Instead of idle chat, I should use this peaceful time for introspection. There were just a few little things that were driving me crazy.

It had to be acknowledged I had let myself fall into a state. Everyone around me knew as much; it must have been a bit of a mystery to them as to why. Clearly, I had gotten everything for which I had asked. I was marrying the man of my dreams. My beloved had granted what many would have considered outrageous demands: the courtship, the ward, the Mercantile. He had amazingly acknowledged that I had obligations and business of my own. My friends were arranging a dream wedding for me. My parents were coming. I should be sublimely happy.

Yet, I had become a cocklebur of nerves. The very idea of marriage was alarming me. Especially that one nagging question that would give me no peace. And here was Izzie beside me, the one person I might ask for advice, with all the privacy I could desire. I wasn't sure I had the nerve, but time was running out.

Benny interrupted my reverie with the coffee pot to refill our mugs. Tonight, our last, we were returning hospitality with a chuck-wagon barbeque.

"Benny," I said, "you have all that food to prepare. Can Isobel and I help?"

"Bless you, no!" Benny was shocked. "Don't I got Slats to help me? Besides, this is our special thing, and I don't want no other great cook like Miss Isobel, here snooping around my secret barbeque sauce!"

Isobel chuckled and turned a page. I'm sure she had not the slightest intention of helping, even if I did.

"You two fine ladies just enjoy yourself here in the shade, and if you want more coffee or any little thing, just give us a wave," he offered, and went back to his pots, whistling.

We took him at his word. We were in a unique position that both of us were prepared to enjoy to the lull, as it was unlikely to happen again any time soon. We had nothing to do but watch other people work.

We reclined in our bit of shade like two queens, taking our ease on a Navajo rug that was probably worth one hundred silver dollars in New York City. The sky was so blue it could break your heart. A soft, dry breeze brought us all the delicious scents of a lazy July afternoon: sage and piñon pine, and red dust with just a dash of barbeque sauce.

It was now or never.

Taking a deep breath, I finally spoke:

"Izzie, I've been wanting to ask you something."

"Lord love us, Alta, you're jumpy as a barn cat!" she objected, but she must have seen something in my face.

She put down her book and sat up, reaching under the rug to remove a small stone on which she was now sitting. Then, half reclining in her little nest of pillows, she gave me her full attention.

"Ask away, Alta. I'm listening."

"Well, it's very rude and improper of me, but I have no one else to ask, and—"

"Heavens to Betsy, Alta, just say it!"

"Well, it's about the man-woman part of marriage. That is, I know what it is that men and women are supposed to do, but it seems women often find it difficult to comply. Mother referred to it as 'a wife's duty'—Izzie, don't you dare laugh at me!"

She laughed anyway.

"Oh, Alta, I love you! My mother called it 'a woman's burden,' but promised that children would be a great compensation. What, exactly, was it you wanted to know?"

"I guess—well, to be specific—you seem to look back on the time you were married as a happy time. Did you find that particular thing awful?"

Izzie sat upright and took both my hands in hers, a teacher to the end—her true calling.

"What a lot of distress we cause young women by cloaking this matter in so much ominous mystery! You deserve a direct answer. It was not awful at all. Perhaps a little awkward at first, but then, wonderful. It made a secret bond between us, which kept growing. I know it would have lasted all our lives, had he lived, which made it even harder to lose him. That is why I don't expect to remarry. How could I ever meet another man so perfect for me?"

"Oh, that is exactly my question!" I cried. "How would you know if you did? Meet another such, I mean?"

"You would know," she assured me complacently.

That was no answer at all!

"Um," I demurred, not willing to accept this blanket certainty. "The thing is, lately, I have been thinking so much of my sister Aggie, and the misery of her marriage. Before the wedding, she and Charles seemed so certain they had each found the right one. He never left her side and she hung onto him like a vine. They were always sneaking away into the rose garden or hiding in the darkest corner of the parlor behind the palm tree, holding hands and kissing. You never saw a couple so much in love," I shrugged at the memory.

"Rather like you and Whit," Izzie observed wryly.

"Exactly the point," I agreed again. "Then, they came home from their honeymoon like enemies! She wouldn't let him touch her and criticized everything he did. Mother said she wasn't taking to marriage, and that some women needed a while to adjust. Aggie was awful; and with his big, sad brown eyes, Charles looked like a scolded cocker spaniel. Yet, Aggie has two babies already, and Father writes she is now expecting a third! I could not bear to live like that."

Izzie thought hard for a moment

"Alta," she said, finally, "women are so constructed as to enjoy the joining as much as a man. In fact, we should insist on enjoying it. But I fear not many women know that beforehand, and even fewer men. We all see couples who do not form that bond. How sad that they must muddle on in marriages so lacking in accord. They must find other ways to fill their lives: a woman dotes on her children; the man lives through his work. But, Alta, I ask you to look around for the other couples, the ones who do bond. How often I have been talking to a woman and suddenly seen her eyes light up; I turn and see her husband has come into the room."

Now, it was my turn to be thoughtful. "I believe you are right. My parents are like that. Mother has such a fond, indulgent little smile when she sees Father, and no matter how hard he is supposed to be working in his library, he must come into the parlor every half hour or so and stand close to her and talk for a few minutes. Yes, I do see."

"Alta, I know a little of your life in New York, and I must say from what I saw of your first Charles, I do not like him very much, although I am sorry for his situation. Being Whit's aunt, I suppose I am partial to him, but I do see in him good qualities. He is gentle and aware of other people's feelings. And don't forget, Alta—Whit was married once before. He is not without experience. I do have high hopes for the two of you."

That was nice, so I thanked her, we hugged, and she went back to *Jane Eyre*.

Parts of what she said had been very informative, indeed. Yes, she had not, in the end, really answered my question. She had identified the "mystery," but it seemed all she could advise me was to marry and hope for the best! I couldn't accept it.

That night, the barbeque was a grand success. Benny produced a great vat of barbequed spareribs so tender the meat was falling off the bones, along with two huge pots of beans cooked with molasses, chilis, and onions.

Slats magically produced a continuing supply of pan after pan of perfect cornbread, baked over the fire in cast-iron skillets. Everyone stuffed themselves, but my stomach had turned queasy again. Despite my loss of appetite, I don't think there was one bean left over. The poor camp dogs got only bare bones, picked clean even of gristle.

During dinner, Whit said to me, "Alta, I sure can see why you think so much of your Ellen. She's a great girl, isn't she?"

"I think so," I agreed. "I'm so glad if you see it, too."

"She's a good sport and doesn't have to have things all her own way. She doesn't whine or complain and sticks to the end. She follows instructions, but not so far as to be stupid. She's fun to have along."

"That's high praise," I beamed at him.

"You've told me all the trouble she's had in her life, but a person would never know it. She's always smiling and happy, and she makes everyone around her feel the same. Alta, I'm getting pretty fond of her."

"I'm so glad," was all I could manage over the lump in my throat. I had not been sure I would ever hear words such as this.

"Besides," he concluded, draining his coffee, and looking around for more, "she's twice as smart as Millie."

I defended Millie valiantly, but inside I was filled with pride.

What he had observed was true, but not all men would have been willing to take on a sixteen-year-old girl at the beginning of their marriage.

Benny's cowboy meals did not usually feature dessert, but tonight he produced a great sack of toffee candies wrapped in paper twists. Somehow, it was the perfect end to a blissful meal.

Afterward, we sat around the fire and drank yet more coffee.

Tom rose and made a rather formal speech, thanking Benny and Slats for the enormous meal, and then thanking us once more for the new prosperity in the enclave.

He concluded, "I would like to meet the great Horace Carlton to thank him in person for all this business he brings us. Do you think he will ever come West to see us?"

"Easiest thing in the world," Whit said at once. "He *is* coming West! In fact, he'll be here in a couple weeks, and he wants to meet all of you."

The Yazzies were amazed and whispered among themselves.

"The Great Carlton comes here? On the train?" Joe Nez asked.

"Yes," Whit answered easily. "He is coming for our wedding."

A great silence fell. Everyone looked at us.

"Your wedding?" asked Sam, Whit's good friend.

Whit and I looked at each other in consternation. Somehow, in all the excitement of the bliss, we had neglected to share one important piece of information with our friends.

"Not married," said Tom, his face a mask.

"We thought you *were* married," Sam commented.

Oh, dear! They had been too polite to comment on the strange fact of our knowing each other and traveling together. Even being as well chaperoned as we were, it must now seem improper to them, aware as they were of Anglo customs.

"That explains why you don't sleep in his tent," Ruth spoke

to the heat of it, a mystery solved, which had apparently caused a great deal of discussion among them. "And why you do not yet have a baby, like me," Ruth concluded.

All the women were nodding and whispering to each other.

I was dying of embarrassment and wishing we could have the shy, silent Ruth back; the one I had first met. These people were as bad as Black Butte!

Whit spoke with what dignity he could dredge up. "You must come to the wedding. It is September 3rd," he urged, helplessly. I almost gasped, but I could see he felt he had to invite them. It was all very awkward.

A host of complications reared up in my mind, and I saw Isobel pale. The church was already full; how in the world would the Yazzies fit into the reception hall? Where could they stay, out at the ranch? What would Black Butte think of them? But I hastened to add my warm second to the invitation. They were my friends, too.

There was a brief lapse of perfect Navajo manners. Tom, Sam, and Joe almost collapsed with laughter, pounding each other on the back and arms and staggering about the campfire. The ladies tittered into their hands.

When decorum was restored, Tom spoke to us kindly:

"You are good to invite, but it is not our way." He was still having a little trouble restraining his laughter. Perhaps he was imagining some of the same scenes that had horrified me.

When he had control of himself, Tom went on. "Tell me this; would you come to us afterward? Bringing the Great Carlton with you? We, too, have much to celebrate. We will marry you in the old way—a cleansing, a blessing, a dance, a great feast. Then you will be one before the Great Spirit as well as your own white God. It will be a double strong joining; nothing will break it!"

I looked at Whit with stars in my eyes. He nodded his agreement and hugged me. What a generous invitation! What a wonderful wedding trip that would be!

"We'll take a week for ourselves and then gladly come to you, if you really mean it," Whit accepted.

We both knew they meant every word.

Whit bargained, "But I will bring Horace Carlton to meet you the week before the wedding if that is okay for you. He must return East right after the ceremony." He turned to me for my approval.

"Perhaps your Cousin Edgar would like to come, too. All you ladies will be busy with your grand wedding."

Isobel and I both agreed, nothing could be better. I knew Father and Edgar would be delighted.

We were all agreed. Even better, Tom thought that with help from Joe and his store, there was enough time to gather Father's new order and deliver it to him personally. Nothing could be better.

We were all pleased with one another, which is the perfect end to a visit. We prepared to retire early in anticipation of a good start the next morning.

Ellen and Millie had spent the evening sitting with the group of girls their age. There had been a great deal of giggling, and much unnecessary sauntering past the group of older boys. It had been a most satisfactory evening for all the young people, too.

Ellen stopped me on the way to my tent, hugging me around the waist and wishing me goodnight.

"Alta, I am so glad you and Whit are getting married. You know I was always a little in love with him, from the first letter you wrote, along with all the other girls at the Sanatorium. But now that I really know him—it is even better! We had such a good time today. And he's going to belong to us both, isn't he?"

I hugged her back, assuring her it was true, and she ran happily off to the tent she shared with Millie.

I was moved by what she had said. It meant a great deal to me that the two people I most loved should love each other.

I believe I might have married Whit, despite my concerns, even if everyone I knew spoke against him, but to see him so universally admired wherever we went was a great joy.

So, that was one of my nagging problems solved—even if the larger concern was not.

We returned to Black Butte sunburned, covered in dust, and telling each other that camping was the best vacation in the world.

Even though it had been my first time, I couldn't help but agree. No one I knew in New York had ever done such a thing. I could hardly wait to do it again.

Then, I had a thought that left me covered in goosebumps. The next time I went camping, it would be my honeymoon.

Chapter Thirteen

"Alta, come see what I found!" Whit grabbed my hand to pull me to my feet.

Most of us were on the ranch's back veranda, recovering from a massive Sunday dinner of *pollo con arroz,* cooked for us by Delores Rojas to celebrate our return from the camping trip. We were digesting and watching the colors change on the foothills and red bluffs to the north as the sun sank lower in the afternoon sky.

I laughed. Whit was starting something new since we came back from the camping trip. He would lure me off to some private place and then he resumed ravishing me with his tongue and his hands—as he had done when he first came back in the spring.

I loved his simple kisses and embraces, but I didn't know what to do with his more demanding intrusions. He had behaved so well once we officially started courting, that I was at a loss how to handle this new development.

In the few days since we had returned from our camping trip, all during which his behavior had been angelic, he had turned into the very devil. I went from nervous wreck to angry and distrusting. It seemed the more I protested the more he intruded on my person.

So, today, my laughter was wary as I asked him what he had found. He bent to whisper into my ear, sneaking a little kiss to my neck that no one could see. It made alarming shivers run up my spine.

"There's a litter of kittens in the barn. Come and see; they're real cute; I want to show you," he whispered.

Whit knew perfectly well I would want to go. Nothing was as much fun as new kittens, and of course, I would want to see them. But—the barn! Oh, dear, what dreadful new liberty would he attempt in such an isolated place?

Two could play this game. I exclaimed loudly, as if in innocent pleasure, "New kittens! What fun! Ellen, Millie, did you hear? In the barn. Let's all go see them!"

The girls needed no urging. They jumped out of the veranda swing where they had been whispering secrets to each other, ready to go. Whit stuck his tongue out at me in disgust. I gave him a sweet smile. I had foiled him this time. He had no choice but to escort all of us to see his "big discovery."

Once we reached the barn, it turned out we had to climb a ladder up to the haymow. We made him go first; it was hard enough to manage skirts modestly while climbing a ladder without some man below gawking at our legs.

The haymow was nearly empty; the new crop would be baled and stored in late August. There were still a dozen bales stacked up, forming a sort of cave, and several had burst open to strew hay out on the floor. There the kittens were—five of them —playing and tumbling over each other in the motes of dust floating in sunbeams that came streaming through cracks in the wooden walls.

I had half expected there to be no kittens at all—just a ploy in Whit's new kissing game.

They belonged to a black-and-white barn cat named Matilda. It was late to have a litter; they must have been born at the end of June, when most came in May or earlier, and were old enough by now to be utterly adorable. They were also surprising because they were all mostly gray, whereas Matilda was mostly white. All the cats I had seen on the ranch were black or calicos.

One kitten was entirely gray, and Millie picked it up at once. Matilda seemed resigned to her babies being handled now that her hiding place had been found.

"Oh, I love you!" Millie purred to the kitten. "This one is mine," she informed us. "I'm naming her Muffy. She's just the same color as my rabbit-skin muff."

"Will señora Rojas let you have it in the house?" Ellen asked, surprised. We all knew Isobel would not, she had said no often enough already: no to a puppy, no to a previous kitten, and no to a baby duck.

"It's my house," Millie responded, loftily. "Of course, she will. You should pick one out for yourself. I'll keep it for you in my room until you move out to the ranch house."

"If you're sure it's all right," Ellen hesitated. But she couldn't resist and picked up one with black streaks on its two front legs. "This is Boots. If ever there was a 'Puss in Boots,' this is him," she exclaimed. We all agreed, there was no other possible name for a kitten marked in that way.

Only Whit scoffed. "Are you so sure it's a he? And, Millie, can you tell it's a girl?"

Of course, neither could answer. In my opinion, it is not possible to tell the sex of a kitten until it is nearly fully grown.

Whit had given up his sulk and was laughing at us now.

"Well, Alta, aren't you going to pick one, too? I'm sure Millie will keep it for you as well." He innocently slipped his hand around my waist, gently stroking my back.

"Oh, I will," Millie was quick to agree.

"Thank you, Millie, but I don't think so. I have enough trouble taking care of this tomcat," I demurred, shrugging off Whit who was letting his hand slip down much too low.

Whit made another face at me. He didn't find my remark funny, but the girls thought it was hilarious.

"How can you tell he's a tomcat?" Ellen quipped, nearly collapsing with laughter at her own joke. She was always a great one for puns and *bon mots*. Millie thought it was funny, too.

I could tell, but I passed that off. It was definitely not a suitable joke for further discussion with my young ward and her friend, despite what Isobel had said about educating young girls. At least, not in front of an actual man.

We did not stay in the haymow much longer, but went back to the house, the girls cuddling their new pets which were obviously old enough to leave their mother. Matilda had chosen a good hiding place.

As Millie had predicted, señora Rojas did not object, although I thought I heard her muttering "*pulgas*" under her breath as she went off, a Spanish word I did happen to know.

I returned to work on Monday morning with renewed energy, planning to attack the reorders once and for all and get them out of the way. Things seemed to have gone on well enough without me, and I visited each department for a quick check before I retired to desk work.

I started with Porphyria, who gave me a good report but added a suggestion:

"Miss Carlton, I think you should fire Lydia McKnight," she said, lips tight in disapproval.

"Lydia?" I was astonished. "What has she done?"

"She doesn't follow orders," Porphyria said, primly.

"In what way?" I asked since nothing more seemed to be forthcoming.

Porphyria looked pained. "I asked her to help us out in Dry Goods in her spare time by taking an inventory of trimmings to have ready for you. Yet, she stops every time a customer comes in and rushes over to help them as if Ginny or I would not."

Light began to dawn. "What kind of customers?" I asked, reining in my exasperation. Of all my employees, Porphyria was the one who took the most patience to deal with.

She shrugged.

"Porphyria, was it Hispanic customers?"

All I got was another shrug.

"Lydia is following my instructions in that," I said, hearing my voice take on *manager's* tone. I didn't in the least try to soften it. "I have asked her to deal with Hispanic customers, if possible, since she can speak Spanish, which makes them feel more comfortable. I told you that."

Porphyria tucked in her chin, the picture of injured self-importance. "When you are gone, it's my orders she should be following."

I stuck my own chin out and tried to appear taller than her. "Not if they contradict orders of mine."

She did not choose to answer that but stared at the floor. I nodded sharply.

"I do not intend to fire Miss McKnight," I said firmly. "I consider her one of our best employees."

Porphyria turned quite red. I'm sure she believed that description should be hers, not Lydia's.

I went on in a calm voice, "I do thank you for starting the inventory. Please bring it to me as soon as it's finished. I'll be working on orders all day."

I left her staring at her feet without further discussion. I'm sure Porphyria thought the less of me, but I thought I could live with that.

Next, I talked briefly to Clara, who had certainly overheard us and looked slightly amused. All was well with Consignments. I was very pleased with her work and told her so.

In Housewares, I found Lydia in a high state of agitation, ready to hand in her resignation.

"That woman is impossible to work with," she complained in a harsh whisper. "I know she asked you to fire me!"

It took me a while to smooth down Lydia's feathers, but I gently begged her to be patient a little longer.

"Everything will be quite different once Miss Bailey comes," I promised her. "And Porphyria will go back to half-days."

Lydia was doubtful, but I was certain Cora would be the answer to all the problems I might have at the store.

I couldn't help wondering how "Miss Efficiency," as I thought of her, would handle a problem like Whit.

The rest of my crew seemed to be fine. Fred reported that John had been the same as always while I was gone, seemingly unaffected.

Going back to my desk, I reflected wryly that as far as John was concerned, Cora wasn't needed at all. Just put Porphyria in charge. But I knew that would lead to disaster. Everything would slowly slip back into the old ways, and soon enough, that would be the end of an obsolete haberdashery that did not meet the needs of a growing community.

That was not going to happen while I was in charge. I might be getting married, but I was still in charge of the store. At least, until John decided to take it back.

I was just opening my folder of inventory reports when Whit came wandering in, completely unexpected and the picture of an idle cowboy. His spurs jangled down the full length of the store to my desk, where he proceeded to greet me with a smacking kiss in front of the entire store!

"What is the matter with you?" I hissed, struggling out of this inappropriate embrace. "Don't do that again!"

"Can't I say good morning to my girl?" he pouted. "I had to come into the grange; thought I would ask you out for a cup of coffee at the Hotel."

"Not today," I retorted, primly. "I absolutely have to do orders all day." I was not pleased with him. He had not been careful of my hair, and I was trying to reset several dislodged hairpins that threatened to let down the pile of curls on top of my head.

"I don't see why you can't give me half an hour. What would that hurt?" Whit complained, trying the sad sheep eyes for effect. "I miss you."

"For goodness sakes, we just spent a whole week together," I exclaimed, exasperated.

"Okay, Alta. Have it your way."

He made a face and left, jangling his spurs as loudly as possible all the way out. I'd bet my own boots he went to the Wagon Wheel, not to the grange. From that day on, he began to show me a whole new style of courting.

We no longer sat close together sharing delightful gossip about our friends, trying to stifle our laughter. No more long, deep conversations about our hopes and dreams for the future. He no longer held my hand or gently hugged me around my shoulders, which I had loved. Now, he seemed determined to attack my person by fondling me through my clothes or trying to slip a hand down my front, despite my protests. I tried to keep some distance between us, as every encounter turned into a wrestling match.

In a scientific magazine, I had read of a strange sea creature with eight arms called an octopus. That sounded about right.

On Wednesday, Whit appeared bearing tiny pink roses and chocolate nut cookies from Delores to appease Isobel; he promptly pulled me into the coat closet in the parlor and shut the door. It was dark, there wasn't a speck of light.

With one arm, Whit pulled me tightly against him. With the other, he twined his fingers through the hair on the back of my head to hold me still while he kissed me. He forced my lips open with his own. He had done this before and I found it thrilling, but this time, he shocked me out of feeling anything but dismay.

He began to ravish my mouth with his tongue. I had never imagined such a thing and struggled to be free, but he held me captive. I stopped fighting. There was no sense in resisting, he was too strong.

Then, what he was doing became exciting. I found I was tingling everywhere and trying to press even closer against him. My knees had absolutely turned to water, and he was holding my entire weight. I'm embarrassed to have to report I moaned out loud.

That was when he stopped, holding me away from him with the same strength he had used to subdue me.

"Remember that, Alta," he whispered.

As if I would ever forget!

Then he opened the closet door and pushed us both out just as Isobel was opening the front door to Paul, who was coming to dinner. Ellen was right there to greet him. Everyone looked at us with shock.

"Really, Alta," Izzie scolded.

"Do we need to push up the wedding date?" Paul asked disapprovingly. "You were brought up better than that, Whit."

Ellen stared at us with huge eyes.

I was deeply embarrassed and couldn't speak because I was lost between humiliation and the feelings Whit had aroused.

Whit made no apology. He just looked pleased with himself and had nothing to say. He steered me to the satin settee and sat me down. I promptly nearly slid off. I know he did it on purpose.

The others stalked off to the kitchen and Whit sat down beside me. He folded his arms across his chest and beamed at me.

"Why are you acting like this?" I hissed. He was causing me so much distress.

"It's my job," he informed me. When I looked blank, he enlarged on his remark. "As the groom."

"What job?" I was still mystified.

"All the fellows are telling me the last weeks before the wedding, the groom has to begin warming up the bride so that the wedding night can go well."

"I never heard of such a thing!" I disclaimed, with some heat. "It's ridiculous!"

He shrugged.

"What 'fellows' are saying that?"

He shrugged again. "The hands out at the ranch. In the saloon."

"Really, Whit!" I was so disgusted now, I found myself echoing Isobel's remark.

"Even Tom and Sam told me that, up at Antler Springs," Whit defended himself. "All the Nez boys said it."

"They have to be teasing you," I protested. "I bet they all thought you were hilarious believing it!"

Whit couldn't deny that, but he wasn't backing down, either.

"You're coming along real well," he assured me.

"Well, you're not!" I snapped. "You're moving toward a bride calling off the wedding night altogether!"

It was true I found the whole thing slightly amusing, but more infuriating. He didn't take me seriously at all, just waggled his tongue at me and went off to the kitchen, leaving me there slipping off the settee and furious.

Infuriating!

The job of chaperone now became something to complain about. Nobody wanted to do it anymore and no one would let the children come with us. That left Paul and Jeremy, who put up with no nonsense; our outings became like taking a buggy ride with the sheriff.

Whit had no remorse, looking smug, while I blushed upon blushes and searched the floor in vain for any kind of composure.

His embraces had become so thrilling I didn't really want to stop him anymore, even if I could. I was addicted to his game, getting as bad as he was, clinging to him and stroking his arm, smoothing his sleeve. It reminded me of the way Aggie had used to be with Charles.

That was a sobering thought! It forced me to think about what I was doing. It was then I determined to stop this at once. If there was the slightest chance I was heading for a marriage like Aggie's, drastic measures were called for.

Besides, Whit may not have noticed that I am quite competitive. I decided not to let him win this game.

What a relief to take charge again! But, before I could decide just which drastic measures to take, everything got complicated again. We were now only weeks from the wedding and once again, I had no time for Whit. Every minute I was not working at the store, was taken up by conferring with one of my wedding planners.

I had no time for lunch. Breakfast became coffee and a piece of toast as I rushed to get to work just fifteen minutes earlier. At dinner, I was so exhausted all I wanted to do was retire for the night.

"Just when things were going so good," Whit complained. He could sulk all he wanted, I barely had time to notice.

My Mercantile *Modistes* had finished the wedding clothes and were now turning out my trousseau at a great rate. Lavinia and Consuelo had conspired together as to what I should have, and I must say, it was a great deal more than I would have asked for. I had thought perhaps several housedresses for evenings at the ranch, maybe a party dress for the dinners that we might be invited to. I would like to have a new nightgown. That should be enough.

But not those two ladies! To my mind, they were putting me into my sister Aggie's class. I hoped Father would not mind.

I was to have two cotton day dresses for the ranch, and for chores a colorful calico to be worn with a pinafore apron. Then, two dinner dresses for evenings at home. We would certainly be asked out to dinners and small parties, and for that, I would have a choice of a rose lace and taffeta gown, which I quite liked, or a dark blue velvet skirt to be worn with a lovely lace blouse. All very suitable for the ranch wife I was soon to become.

They agreed I should wait at least a year before wearing my wedding gown as a party dress, and certainly should dye it whatever color I might then prefer.

Consuelo, herself, was making a tailored burgundy gabardine suit, that would see me to church through the fall.

Hard as it was to believe, winter was coming; I must have several heavier gowns of wool or light worsted for the ranch, and a new black wool suit for work, with four new white cotton blouses, each lovelier than the last, with pleated frills and lace. Lydia would love them! The fourth blouse was my favorite, tailored and starched with white soutache trim.

Uma was to make me a hat to go with each suit—the burgundy and the black.

All this bounty was supported by the appropriate petticoats in varying thicknesses.

What truly astounded me was the huge pile of intimate clothes Consuelo and her ladies had created for me. I had three new cotton nightgowns and three more flannel, all embroidered and trimmed with lace, two appropriate wrappers, plus one special set made of the thinnest broadcloth. The wrapper was elegantly full, really a *peignoir*. Both were beautifully embroidered with white satin-stitch hearts and sprays of roses, trimmed with the most delicate lace.

"For the wedding night," whispered Consuelo, politely concealing her blush behind her hand.

There was an astonishing pile of chemises and unmentionables: eight matching sets, every one delicately adorned with lace, tiny ruffles, or eyelet threaded with silk ribbon. Usually, there was embroidery as well. One set was trimmed with wreaths of dainty embroidered rosebuds that must have added days onto the making.

"For the Wedding Dress," Consuelo once more confided in a whisper, but all the ladies heard her and giggled.

"Oh, señora Martinez," I protested, "These are so beautiful, but there are far too many of them, and what I need are plain ones to wear every day!"

"Nonsense," she replied in surprisingly improved English. "You must wear these pretty ones every day. *Esposo* must see you always fresh and dainty, a woman to be adored. *Es cierto.*"

"*Que verdad,*" the other ladies agreed.

"Señora Martinez," I accused her with mock-severity, disbelieving. "Nobody goes that far. Do you wear such undergarments, yourself?"

"*Claro, que si,*" she responded, modestly lifting her skirt just enough for me to see a hint of a petticoat, and just a peek at calf-length pantaloons, both edged in beautiful lace. She smiled at me complacently.

Several other ladies showed me the same, blushing and laughing.

"*Gracias,* señora," I said, meekly, using almost my entire vocabulary of *español* to thank her.

It would increase my washing chore, but I hoped I knew good advice when I heard it. From the level of tittering from the other *Modistes* who were there that day, I had just been given a *universal truth*.

It seemed carping to have any complaints amid such bounty, but nothing in my trousseau was suitable for a camping honeymoon. What Whit had told me of his plans for us made our visit to the Yazzies sound luxurious. There would be no chuck wagon with Benny to cook for us. No one would intrude on our privacy to put up our tent. We would be doing that ourselves and gathering our own firewood.

I didn't have a thing to wear.

"Don't worry about that," Izzie soothed me. "We'll get you a couple pair of boys' work pants and flannel shirts at the Mercantile. I've got an old pair of boots that ought to fit you. Whit can get you a fleece-lined jacket from the ranch. You'll be fine."

"Maybe we should get some long johns, too," I joked, thinking of my beribboned nightgowns and lacy unmentionables. I was astonished when Izzie took it seriously.

"Not a bad idea," she said thoughtfully, then started to make a list.

"Get red ones. Then you'll match Whit," Ellen commented, very interested in this conversation about underclothes.

"What in the world?" I asked.

"Millie says Whit sleeps in red long johns all the time," Ellen reported.

"If that's true, I'll be calling the wedding off," I joked, the second time I had made that joke—but there was a grain of truth in it. The picture that I summoned of getting into a bed with a man in red long johns was just too off-putting to contemplate.

"Heaven's sakes, Alta. If everyone objected to that, there

wouldn't be a single married couple in Black Butte," Isobel retorted. I don't think she was joking at all.

I pushed aside the slice of apple pie Izzie had just served me. Who could eat with things like this on their mind?

I worried that I was running out of time, and if I didn't implement my plan soon I would lose my chance.

The Sunday before my parents were to arrive, we were all asked out to the ranch. Señora Rojas gave us a suitably light hot-weather dinner of cold fried chicken, chopped cabbage salad, and bowls of vine-ripe tomatoes and cucumbers, swimming in sugar and vinegar, with hot rolls. I must say, I had no room for the four-layer chocolate cake that followed, but no one else refused it. I had such a nervous stomach that all I managed was a wing of chicken and a few cucumber slices.

Afterward, most of us sank blissfully into a drowsy after-noon; the two girls went out riding despite the heat. Father Desmond was officially reading newspapers in his office but was really enjoying a pleasant Sunday afternoon nap. The other men and some of the hands wandered out to the corral, lazily observing Phillip's new Appaloosas, less wild now than they had been.

Leaving the cleaning to her daughters, señora Rojas lounged contentedly on the back veranda, chatting to Izzie as they worked together to stitch the final coils onto our rug for Cora.

I should have joined them, but, instead, I walked out in the heat and dust to the corral and enticed Whit to go for a little walk with me, whispering that I wanted to see the kittens again. He looked rather surprised and dubious but escorted me as asked, despite some quite unnecessary teasing from the hands. We walked around the corner of the stables to the barn, and he led me in. I was hoping no one noticed where we went.

We strolled past the stalls, each one containing an observant animal friend interested in what we might be doing on such a lazy afternoon. Whit told me their names, stopping to speak to each one, rub their head, and twist their ears. They all responded to him with pleasure.

He took his time and I was hard put not to show my impatience; I know he was dawdling just to tease me. At last, we reached the ladder to the hayloft.

"Ladies first," Whit offered, grinning. Not a trace of the gentleman who had brought us here the first time.

"You go first, Whit," I responded sweetly, "to help me up the last few rungs."

He made a face at me but scrambled up as agilely as a squirrel in Central Park. I had no trouble following him.

Whit helped me off the ladder and safely onto the wooden floor. The loft was not yet completely empty. A small wall of bales still stood toward the back. It was killingly hot and dusty, but I hardly noticed.

We looked around for the kittens and Whit shrugged.

"They're gone, Alta. I thought they would be out and about by now."

"Oh, too bad," I responded.

He looked at me askance for a bit, and then threw himself down to lounge amid the loose hay; propped up against one of the remaining bales, he was a perfect picture of idle carelessness. He stuck a piece of straw between his teeth and regarded me rather challengingly, waiting to see what I would do next. There was hardly a breath of air.

"Well, Alta?" he said.

"Well, Whit. Here we are in the haymow," I responded with some acerbity. "You've been trying to get me here all summer. Here I am."

He chewed on his straw, looking amused. "So, what did you have in mind?" he inquired.

He sprawled in complete relaxation, one knee up, his shirt

unbuttoned rather more than was necessary, exposing an expanse of manly chest. A wayward shaft of sunlight fell across him and lit him like a fallen angel. Although the hot air did not move, motes of glittering dust drifted all around us.

I regarded him steadily. "About the same as you, I reckon."

He looked at me skeptically. I put one hand to the neckline of my gown and unbuttoned the top button. I had the satisfaction of seeing his eyes go dark.

The gown was from my trousseau: a printed challis of light blue flowers. Nine blue buttons opened it to the waist. One by one, I undid them, and then shrugged off the gown. It pooled around my ankles.

Contrary to the instructions of señora Martinez, I was not wearing my pretty undergarments. I wore nothing at all.

I will cherish the memory of the expression on Whit's face for the rest of my life. His eyes blazed, he said only "Alta," and then rose to remove his own clothes. We stood before each other as equals.

Then, he took me down into the hay.

I was mad to see him, but I had to wait until Wednesday. They were branding at the ranch and he couldn't be spared. It was a cruel ordeal I hope never to have to repeat. But we had to wait for courting night.

There were so many things I needed to talk to him about. I had dozens of questions to ask him about this and what we had done—and especially how he knew what to do.

I was covered in stickers and prickles from lying in the hay. I desperately wanted to know if he was, too. Or maybe not since he had been mostly on top. More than anything, I wanted to do it again.

I was in soap suds up to my elbows, washing up Isobel's cooking pots, when we finally heard his boots on the porch and his longed-for knock on the front door.

Izzie answered it from the parlor where she was tidying up, but I ran the length of the hall and flung myself into Whit's arms for a passionate kiss.

"Whoa, Nelly!" he exclaimed, steadying us against the door. He kissed me back as fervently as I could ever have desired. Then he held me off a bit. "Alta, you're all sudsy," he remarked.

"Sorry, I just couldn't wait to see you," I apologized, pulling off my apron to use as a towel for us both, while at the same time pulling him to the settee in the parlor, where I anticipated another round of embracing.

"Alta, really!" Izzie said, surprising me, and stalked off to the kitchen, presumably to finish my chore.

I raised eager lips to Whit but was surprised to find him red in the face.

"Alta, you can't be greeting me like that. Everyone will figure out we jumped the gun!"

"But it's just Izzie—" I protested.

"Dearest girl, I bet Izzie guessed Sunday. But we don't want the whole town speculating. Not after all your hard work to get this town to forget how you came in."

A tear rolled down my cheek, "But the whole town isn't seeing us right now."

"Alta, remind me to never let you play poker. Every feeling you ever have is always right there on your face!"

Two more tears dripped down. "Is it so wrong to show I love you?" I asked.

He took me in his arms again, to my satisfaction, and held me close.

"Girl, we've struck gold here. We're going to have a long and happy marriage."

We glowed at each other for a while. I thought longingly of the cozy bed in my room.

"Could we not just slip upstairs for half an hour?" I suggested.

Whit sighed. "Alta Belle, we have to pull back on the reins until the wedding."

"But that's more than two weeks away!" I protested.

"Your parents ought to be here Saturday. We have to be real proper. We'll hold hands, that's all. Maybe a peck for a kiss. Think of it as a build-up to our wedding night, sweetheart."

I contemplated that. I had no questions now. There would be a wedding night.

Whit stroked my hair very gently. "We owe it to Izzie not to embarrass her. And we sure don't want to offend your parents!"

I could understand that. He was right.

"So, we should start right now," Whit decreed.

"Merciful Heavens," I breathed.

Whit leaned in and whispered in my ear several things he planned for our wedding night. I blushed, then blushed again, and then settled down to a steady glow.

He went on, "You can't imagine how much better it's going to be than in the haymow." I couldn't help giggling. I did not regret the haymow in the least, it had been the only possible place, but it had left quite a bit to be desired as a bed.

Whit and I then made a pact to immediately become the most decorous engaged couple Black Butte had ever seen. We presented ourselves to Izzie in the kitchen, modestly holding hands but otherwise not touching.

"Aunt Isobel," Whit began, which made me giggle; he never called her that. "Thank you for giving us the privacy. We did need to have a little talk."

Izzie looked at us rather severely. She said something that sounded rather like my father's *harrumph*.

But she did give us supper, and soon enough we were happily reminiscing about the camping trip and planning for my parents' arrival. That lasted until Whit departed, giving me only a chaste kiss. Then Izzie subjected me to a lengthy lecture on much the same subject as Whit's, but not so nicely. I accepted it quietly and promised to be a model of virtue, trying to look as meek as possible.

I must have overdone it, because she finally laughed and stopped scolding me. She offered me a glass of sherry and we sat in the kitchen, chatting into the wee hours about all the exciting things to come.

At last, we climbed the stairs together to go to bed. She opened her bedroom door and turned back, smiling broadly, to have the last word.

"I told you so," she smugly reminded me, and then went to bed.

Chapter Fourteen

"Here it comes!" cried Ellen, pointing up Main Street to where the coach was coming down Cemetery Hill. She and Millie began to jump up and down cheering and waving.

Isobel and I were waiting on the boardwalk in front of the Butterfield Stage Office. Whit was there, with the support of Paul and Jeremy, and Lavinia had come to meet Cora Bailey.

However, quite a few others had joined us. Sheriff Higgins had strolled across the street from his office; he made it a practice to meet every stage. Several leatherworkers from the co-op, who were prospering from Father's orders, had come to meet their benefactor in person. Will Finnegan from the hotel was there to welcome his prominent guests. Hick Wagoner stepped out of his saloon to see what was going on and was inevitably followed by several of his curious customers. Mrs. Goring and her friend Marva Dooley had just been passing by.

The dusty coach pulled up, the door opened, and Cousin Edgar was first to jump out. He enveloped me in a bear hug.

"Alta, here you are! End of the earth, ha, ha! By Jove, it's good to be here!" He stretched and flung out his arms to enfold the whole town. "Wonderful place!" he exclaimed. He turned to help the ladies step out.

Mother and Adah were rumpled and dusty, but eager to embrace me. Cora emerged positively beaming. Father came out last, wearing a Stetson and "raring to go."

None of them seemed at all surprised by the large crowd that had turned out to greet them. I should have known Black Butte by now. The arrival of the great Horace Carlton was a civic event. Dewey Hughes was late, running up the street from the newspaper office—such a roving reporter for the *Black Butte Beacon*.

After the first excited embraces, I introduced Whit to my family. He met them with respectful dignity. He looked smashing: for once wearing a dark blazer, suitable for a young rancher, with his boots and Stetson. Today there was not a sign of the lazy cowboy or the demanding lover. I was proud to say he was my fiancé.

He introduced the rest of his family and said his father hoped to see them at the ranch tomorrow after church, for Sunday dinner.

Isobel introduced Lavinia, and then we took turns introducing the various dignitaries among the growing crowd.

My family is always admirable on public occasions. Mother was the perfect gracious lady, and Father made a great impression by remembering the names of some of his vendors and praising their goods. Edgar pleased everyone with his enthusiastic praise of the beauties of our scenic red hills.

As for Aunt Adah, you can always count on her for pithy remarks or an appropriate joke.

Mr. Finnegan led us to the hotel, promising that Butter-field's would have the bags delivered at once and he would provide baths for all as soon as they wished. The ladies claimed the privilege to be first, and as soon as possible, as they went to the rooms to await the luggage.

The men settled in the hotel bar, promising Father and Edgar a drink while they awaited their turns.

The family would meet again at six at Izzie's for dinner.

Lavinia took Cora in hand and headed for the boarding house. Izzie and I tagged along with them. We didn't want to miss Cora's first sight of the front parlor rooms.

I don't know what Cora had expected, but she praised everything Izzie and I had done to make her comfortable.

We wanted Cora to come with us to Izzie's, but Lavinia wouldn't hear of it.

"Absolutely not!" she objected. "I've prepared a special dinner tonight to introduce Miss Bailey to all the others. We must begin as we mean to carry on."

This seemed to be a general motto in Back Butte. We didn't argue.

I hugged Cora goodbye. "We'll see each other tomorrow," I promised.

Cora looked disappointed. She whispered in my ear, "Alta, I had so hoped we could have a private little talk tonight, just the two of us. There are so many things..." she left off, looking slightly embarrassed.

"Cora, you're not worried about the Mercantile, are you?" I was surprised.

"Well, I am, a little," she confessed. "But more worried about meeting Mr. Burke. Will he be at church?"

"It's possible," I allowed. "But I'll take you and Father to the Mercantile on Monday. You will certainly meet him then. Don't worry, Cora. Everything is going to be fine."

She did not look convinced, so I promised I would try to drop by later tonight. Perhaps I could ride along in the buggy bringing the family back to the hotel after dinner.

The gratitude she expressed made me feel a little guilty—so many people wanted a bit of my time, and I was starting to feel like a *piñata* with everyone swinging bats at me!

At dinner that night, we made quite a party gathered around Isobel's huge kitchen table, at full extension. I found myself comparing it with one of Mother's sparkling dinners. I thought we held up very well. We had flowers and candles on the table, even if only geraniums, and a lace cloth. Maybe we didn't have French wine, but the fermented apple cider was potent, the conversation lively, and the guests were all important people in my life.

Izzie served us pot roast stewed with root vegetables, a tossed green salad, and her wonderful biscuits, with a three-layer chocolate cake for dessert. In my opinion, she was easily as good a cook as Mrs. Croft.

Mother gave me all the news from home. My old friend Hortense had married her restaurant-bound second cousin in an elegant July wedding, and in lieu of a honeymoon, they were now both apprenticing at Éclair, which they would mutually inherit in due course of time. Imagine Hortense and I getting married almost at the same time!

Percy Ward's cousin had run off to Australia with a sailor from her father's yacht; people were saying Percy would never marry, now.

My sister Adelle sent her love and promised to visit me by the turn of the century. That made me laugh, as it was meant to do, but it was probably accurate. I could not imagine either her or John traveling anywhere until their family of boys was much older.

Charles sent congratulations—but Agnes did not.

"You must excuse her, Alta. She is expecting again. You know how she is when she is in that condition."

I did, indeed. Mother confirmed this would make three. It

was sad but thoughts of that marriage no longer worried me. I knew for a fact mine would be nothing like theirs.

By nine-thirty, everyone began falling asleep at the table, so Whit and Jeremy walked down to the livery and brought back the buggy. I rode along to drive my family to the hotel and then Whit dropped me off for my promised visit with Cora.

"I'll be back to get you in half an hour," he promised me, and then drove off to return the carriage to the livery stable.

It was late, and Cora was tired, too. She welcomed me eagerly, but with a yawn. I told her a few amusing tales of Porphyria's style of management and what a relief it would be to the staff when she took over. We talked a bit more about John. I think she was feeling more confident by the time we heard Whit's whistle from the street and looked out to see that he had exchanged the buggy for Paul's gig.

I kissed her goodnight, promised to sit with her at church in the morning, and ran down to join Whit.

August was nearly over, and it was a lovely, warm night with a nearly-full moon. We couldn't resist. Whit drove us eastward out of town on the road toward Bagnold, and it was wonderful to be alone, just the two of us. At this late date, we simply didn't care if anyone saw us or not. Surely, we were close enough to the wedding now to be allowed this one quiet escape.

We let Dandy dawdle at the pace he preferred until we were halfway there, and then we turned around and started back. We did nothing any chaperone could have objected to. We cuddled under Paul's Hudson Bay blanket to keep warm and enjoyed being close to each other. We had so much to talk about we could have gone on until dawn.

If Isobel heard me coming home so late that night, creeping up the stairs to my room, she was kind enough not to mention it the next morning.

At Church, our party made quite a stir among the congregation, easily taking up an entire pew. After the service, the number of people wanting to meet Father delayed our departure for the ranch.

Reverend Michaels shook Father's hand, saying, "It is an honor to meet the benefactor of Black Butte. Your orders from so many of our craftsmen have made quite a difference in this town."

Father was delighted. After years of negatives from old Mr. Hodges, he was blossoming under all this praise. He had begun to develop a rather hawk-like look in his eyes that made me guess he might be broadening his ideas of expansion.

John Burke was at church and did his best to avoid us. It was easy to escape Father, circled by admirers, but I managed to corral him long enough to introduce Cora.

John had little to say, as was to be expected, and beat a hasty retreat. Cora looked crestfallen, but I assured her that was just John's way and promised her that they would be easier together soon enough once she was working at the Mercantile.

Finally, we were able to make our escape and boarded the various carriages and buggies waiting to take us all out to the ranch. My relatives seemed to have rebounded from their exhausting journey to a remarkable degree. I would have expected Aunt Adah to have stamina, but a delicately-bred woman like my mother could have been excused, needing a week in bed to recover. Mother had roses in her cheeks and required a running travelogue from Whit the entire way. By the time we approached the ranch house, Cousin Edgar had become a cowboy and begun talking like my fiancé!

I had become fond of Mr. Whitaker by now. Father Demont, as I now thought of him, had always been courteous and warm to me. To my mind, he would have been in the right to blame me for driving off his heir, but he never discussed the past and made it clear our marriage was his hope for the future of the ranch.

He always took me seriously and talked to me about running the Mercantile, which no one else ever did.

We were received graciously by señora Rojas, very much our hostess. Everyone sampled the amazing artesian water and exclaimed over its purity and coldness. Then we were all seated at the truly enormous table in the dining room. It was set with a damask cloth and colorful Mexican pottery. We were served a French red wine and a fiesta of spicy Mexican dishes by various Rojas daughters, who brought heaping platters to the table and left it to us to pass them around—family-style.

Father Demont described each dish as it was passed—urging us to sample at least a little, accompanied by warm tortillas.

We were offered both chicken and beef enchiladas in a spicy red sauce, stewed chicken in a very spicy chocolate sauce called *mole*, platters of shredded beef called *carnitas*, and a dish of green chilis dipped in batter and fried, called *chili rellenos*. These dishes were all very spicy, but complemented by two that were not spicy at all: rice cooked in a red sauce and red beans, mashed and served hot and steaming.

My family made valiant efforts not to show consternation at the spicy food and forged ahead as best they could. The ladies sampled and praised each dish, but politely refused any large serving. It immediately became apparent that the wine was not nearly as effective at quenching the fire as the artesian water, and young Pepe was kept busy refilling our glasses.

Both Father and Edgar were determined to have the full experience and ate copious amounts of everything. Father was soon quite red in the face, and by the time the beef *tamales* came around, wrapped in corn husks, Edgar had actual drops of perspiration rolling down his brow.

Aunt Adah was disappointed by her inability to adjust but

discovered, with pleasure, that a fine meal could be made from the rice and *refritos*, and the tacos were quite delicious with the shredded meat. At her urging, we ladies found she was right. No one could be in danger of starving at that table.

Everyone enjoyed the desert: delicious *flan* with a caramel glaze.

I was the only one who scarcely ate. Whit and I had been able to sit together at the table, to my joy, and while we both behaved with perfect decorum, underneath the draped table-cloth, he kept a tight hold of my right hand, holding it on his knee.

I was not about to pull free just to eat even if I wanted to, which I did not. My heart was in my throat the entire meal. Mere food could not penetrate.

Before the flan was served, Father Demont asked for the wine glasses to be refilled and stood to make a formal toast.

"First, let me welcome the Carltons and the Abbots. We deeply appreciate your coming so far to support this marriage. The people of Black Butte already know that Alta comes from a substantial family. You will find a warm welcome here, and I imagine most people already claim you to be part of our town, as well as New Yorkers." He raised his glass: "To the new Black Butters."

"Well, that's a relief," quipped Aunt Adah. "I feared it might be Black Buttians, or worse, Black Buttites. 'Butters' is better."

Everyone laughed and raised their glasses to my aunt.

Father Demont continued, "Secondly, may I welcome the lovely Miss Cora Bailey to Black Butte, her new home. A charming addition to our town."

He bowed to Cora, and we drank to her health.

Mother sat at his right, but I realized he had made sure Cora sat to the left, and he had been talking to her frequently during dinner. If I didn't know better, I would almost think he was flirting with her!

The toasts were not done: Father Demont had just a little wine left in his glass, but he raised it once more.

"And now, let us drink the final toast to the young couple, the future of Whitaker Ranch, and I dare say, Black Butte as well. To Alta Belle and Charles Demont, whom most of you know as Whit."

That was charming. Whit and I beamed at each other. Whit raised his glass back to his father.

My father stood, formally, and turned toward Father Demont. "Let me return the toast, and thank you, not just for your wonderful hospitality tonight, but for all your family has done to help Alta since she first came here."

He drank off his glass, and there was a flurry of laughter and awkwardness since many had already emptied their glasses. Also, because it was obvious that Father didn't know the whole story. Some raised their water glasses, and conversation sprang up loudly. We were all friends now.

Monday morning, I took Father and Cora to the Mercantile. John saw her and only grunted as a greeting, turning away to meet Father. He was certainly planning to slip away, but Father, skilled from handling negative old Mr. Hodges, was easily John's match. He was so interested in everything about the store and asked so many pertinent questions that John was pulled in despite himself. It wasn't long before he took Father off into the Hinterland.

I know Cora was upset again, despite my constantly explaining the situation to her, but it was all right. Porphyria took her off for an animated tour of the store and introduced her to everyone.

By the time John brought Father back, he had been promoted to a crony—entitled to a cigar and coffee in front of the stove. Father decided to stay the afternoon here. He was loving the Mercantile and eager to meet townspeople.

Cora wanted to begin work at once, so I installed her at my desk and gave her the books so she could begin familiarizing herself. I had to hurry off to meet Mother and go to a fitting with señora Alvarez who was making my blouses.

Two days later, Whit and Phillip took our men off on the promised trail ride to Antler Springs.

"Whit, they are greenhorns! They can't possibly ride so far," I protested.

"Not so far," Whit explained. "We'll take a wagon to just south of Bagnold. It's only about a four-hour trek into the compound from there. We went the long way before. We'll ride two hours and then stop and camp for the night, go the rest of the way in the morning. They'll be fine."

John outfitted them both with heavy, duck work pants, jackets, and flannel shirts. Old work boots were found at the ranch, so as not to ruin their fancy etched ones. They even had bandannas around their necks to cover their faces if the dust or wind-blown sand got too bad.

An amazing fuss was made over this outfitting. Father and Edgar went stomping around, making as much noise with their spurs as possible. I believe Father was more excited about this visit to the Yazzies than he was about the wedding!

"Please bring them home safe," I begged Whit.

"Alta, they'll be fine. This will be like Sunday School," Whit reassured me.

Phillip was a bit more thoughtful. "They might come home having to ride side-saddle, though!" he gibed.

Everyone but me thought this remark hilarious. I thought it might likely be true. But it was the first time I had known Phillip to say much of anything, much less make a joke. He always seemed very shy around me and said little. Now, I noticed he was more grown-up than I had thought. The shortest and stockiest of the brothers, he nonetheless had the Whitaker eyes and all the Whitaker charm. He was actually rather attractive.

Lavinia took charge of Mother, and to my surprise, they became great friends. I'm sure this was due to Lavinia's beguiling deference. She never once referred to herself as "erstwhile Mother of the Bride," but incorporated Mother fully into the wedding plans, taking her around to meet everyone: the church ladies of the Sewing Circle, Mrs. Nettleton, even to visit Reverend and Mrs. Michaels. Aunt Adah was enthusiastically included in it all. Such a hustle and bustle. I seemed to move without a will—like a puppet in a dream play called "The Wedding."

Consuelo Martinez gave Mother a lovely tea to meet the Mercantile *Modistes* and observe the final fitting for the last of my trousseau.

Isobel came with us, and Cora took time off from the Mercantile to come, too. Clara Gutiérrez had urged her to take the opportunity to meet the members of this consignment, which was contributing so much to the success of the store.

As the highlight of the occasion, I was to model the wedding dress, which everyone was dying to see. It was finished and Uma had sent it over to Consuelo especially for a viewing at the tea. Uma steadfastly refused to attend, to my disappointment. I wanted her to meet my family.

Rosalie Alvarez helped me into the gown.

"Alta, is it supposed to hang loose like that?" she asked. "I suppose it must, or Miss Uma wouldn't have sent it over."

I surveyed myself in the small dresser mirror in señora Martinez's bedroom. All I could see were puffs of veil and lace. It looked fine to me.

She led me out to stand before the ladies, straightening out the skirt and veil to the best advantage.

At first, there were the expected exclamations of delight, then silence. Finally, elderly señora Gomez said the obvious:

"It's hanging on her like a bag! The girl's a scarecrow!"

A hiss of agreement ran around the room.

Mother got up and came to me, brushing aside the veil and pulling the gown tight at the waist behind my back. Now, there were satisfied murmurs.

"That's the way it ought to look. It doesn't fit," commented señora Martinez. "When was your last fitting, Miss Alta?"

It was all like bees buzzing in the sagebrush, but I tried to connect with what was going on.

"Two weeks last Tuesday?" I guessed.

Lavinia thought it was longer than that.

"Alta, you've lost too much weight!" Mother scolded. "You'll get sick!"

"Don't worry," Aunt Adah remarked in her dry voice. "Once they're married, she'll gain it all back and more."

At that, the ladies burst into laughter and chatter, and I believe a few rather ribald jokes were passed around at my expense. Sometimes it is a good thing *not* to know a language.

Mother and Consuelo paid no attention but were consulting together.

"She cannot wear it like this."

"You are quite right; we must get Uma at once to come down here and fix it."

Consuelo left the room, and shortly we all saw her daughter, Amanda, running off up the street. Consuelo came back to us, entirely composed.

"Uma will come shortly. While we are waiting, I suggest we all have another cup of tea, and I will get more cookies. Mrs. Carlton, will you pour?"

Mother, herself, could not have handled the crisis more smoothly. While we waited, everyone drank tea and ate Mexican wedding cookies, chattering happily. Mother sat me down in a straight chair and brought me tea and a small plate of cookies.

"Eat," she instructed.

"I'll get powdered sugar all over the dress," I objected.

"It'll brush off. Eat up, girl," Aunt Adah commanded. She leaned over and whispered in my ear, "Nobody wants a stick in their wedding bed. He'll be needing something he can get ahold of."

I was too shocked to eat hearing that, but after consideration, I decided it was good advice. I took a cookie and managed to eat most of it, but powdered sugar did shower down on my lap, and I was brushing at it in distress when Uma finally arrived.

She came in heavily veiled, as always, and muttering to herself in disgust.

"You told me you would stop losing weight!" she barked at me.

I had no answer.

She *tut-tutted* over the powdered sugar and made me stand up while she ripped out seams in the middle of my back and hand-stitched new darts to take in the extra material.

"Nobody wants a skinny malink!" she muttered, re-stitching the waist seam.

Whit does—I thought rebelliously to myself. How could I help it if food stuck in my throat, and I couldn't swallow?

When Uma was done, the lovely dress fit me again as it was supposed to do. All the ladies clapped and praised Uma for her design and sewing skill.

For once she was forced to endure public approval. I hoped it would do her good.

It must have had some good effect; she was persuaded to sit

down and take a cup of tea! I was distracted by people closely examining details of my gown, but I did notice that Cora moved to sit beside Uma—talking in that informed and genuinely interested way she had about her. I could see Uma warming to her.

So, now the dress fit, and at least one good thing had come out of it all.

The Brandon Whitakers from San Francisco arrived. We went out to the ranch to meet them; they were very nice, but everything was a blur to me.

I missed Whit.

Finally, the travelers returned. It had only been three days, but it had seemed like a fortnight. Each rider carried a large, rolled bundle behind their saddles: the jewelry consignment.

Father and Edgar were still riding astride, but when they dismounted they walked with discomfort.

"I have blisters in places you couldn't possibly imagine," Edgar confided to me.

He'd be surprised!

Father was stoic but pleased with the trip. The Yazzies had been great hosts. The new jewelry was fantastic.

Edgar sported a large silver bracelet, which he rarely took off. Father wore a ceremonial necklace, of a design I didn't recognize, featuring a large bird. He also stood in a strange, new stance: one hip stuck out as his hand casually brushed back his jacket. I realized he was wearing a pistol in a holster on his right side, strapped to his leg, Western style!

"What in the world?" I exclaimed.

"I have to protect the jewelry, Alta," he explained. I could see he was delighted. "I'll be wearing this all the way home until we get it safely into Carlton & Hodges."

"I certainly hope you are not planning to wear it when you walk me down the aisle," I protested.

He shrugged.

"If you do, I'm calling off the wedding!" I huffed—for the third time. Even as I said it, I realized what an empty threat that had become!

He laughed and gave me a hug. "We'll see," he teased, good-naturedly.

I guess he knew I didn't mean it anymore.

Chapter Fifteen

"Wake up, wake up!"

Someone was too loud!

It had been so hard to get to sleep last night. It seemed only minutes since I had finally managed to drift off, and now someone was shaking me and opening the curtains of my east window so that the sun was streaming in right onto my face!

"Go 'way," I muttered, raising my arm to shade my eyes.

"Alta, wake up! Look, we brought you your wedding breakfast to eat in bed!"

It was Ellen's piercing voice. I opened a reluctant eye, and there was Millie, too. They were both beaming with pride.

"Sit up, lazy bones, or you'll make us spill it," ordered Millie, in a schoolteacher's voice she must have learned from Isobel.

Wearily, I struggled to sit up against the headboard. A laden tray was plunked over my lap. I was staring at a great bowl of steaming oatmeal, swimming in melting butter and brown sugar. There were two hot biscuits smothered in strawberry jam beside a cup and saucer, and the small teapot was covered with a pink crochet cozy. There was barely room for the tiny plate bearing three crispy pieces of bacon.

Lord love us, it was enough food to feed the whole family! My breakfast was usually a leftover biscuit and two cups of tea.

My throat closed so tightly, it was lucky I could breathe through my nose.

They had even picked a precious geranium bloom and stuck it in a little green medicine bottle someone had kept due to its pretty color.

Everything was perfect, right down to the linen napkin. I should be thrilled to be given such a treat. Instead, I wanted it gone. Off my lap and out of my sight!

Isobel hovered outside my door, staring in to see how much I enjoyed my surprise. All three were standing over me—crowding me. No wonder I couldn't breathe.

I wanted to scream: *Let me be alone, I'm not ready yet!*

My ears were ringing; it was unpleasant. My head began to ache so badly I had to put my two hands up to my temple to try and hold it together. I don't know which was worse: the staring or the smell of the bacon.

I began to cry.

Consternation reigned until Isobel took charge. She shooed the girls out and removed the offending tray. She brought me back a cup of tea in its place. She gave me a wet washcloth to cool my face; that helped a lot. She sat and listened patiently while I sobbed about how tired I was and how too much was expected of me.

She coaxed me to get out of bed and sit at my vanity while she brushed my hair. That was so soothing, I did begin to feel I could drink the cup of lukewarm tea.

She did up my hair into a low bun at my neck, as we had planned I would wear it, for the veil. I examined myself in the mirror and felt better. My headache went away. I could tell the girls were out in the hall trying to peek in, but I was able to ignore them now.

Isobel persuaded me to put on my fancy small clothes and petticoats, just before Mother and Aunt Adah arrived to help dress the bride.

Isobel went down to greet them and bring them up to my room. Hearing their feet on the stairs made my chest cramp up and I began to feel jittery. It had been so calm and soothing with just Isobel.

Mother and Aunt Adah came in laughing and talking—wide awake and so full of energy it made me want to crawl back into bed. Mother was immediately concerned to find me pale-faced and fidgeting.

"Alta, you aren't nervous, are you?" she asked.

I burst into tears again.

She pulled up a chair to the vanity, sat down, took my hands, and stroked them to calm me.

"What is the matter, dear? Are you regretting the marriage?"

"No, no! I want to marry Whit." I wanted people to understand but that was hard when I wasn't sure I understood myself. "I guess it's the wedding I regret!" I sobbed. "We should have done what Whit wanted and just got married in the preacher's parlor and sent you a telegram!"

My mother put a restraining hand on my knee, as it was shaking up and down.

"Don't do that, Alta. It isn't lady-like, and it just makes everyone else nervous, too."

All these people were crowding around my vanity. I knew they were full of concern, but it was irritating.

"This is nothing," Mother reassured the others. "Only to be expected. A case of last-minute wedding nerves. All my girls had it. She'll be fine in a bit."

More tea was produced for me, and I drank it while the girls and Isobel got dressed. Millie and Ellen were helped into their finery, shooting sideways glances at me in case I was going to scold them.

I should have apologized for spoiling their treat, but in some mean way, it made me feel slightly better to let them stew. I was ashamed of myself, and that made me cry again.

Mother did the girls' hair while Isobel did up her own. She put on her blue suit and hat. Aunt Adah sat in a chair and made suggestions.

They put me into my dress and did up the eighteen buttons in the back.

Mother bunched a handful of fabric at my waist. "It's still too loose. Alta, you've lost weight again. What in the world!"

Isobel took a handful of fabric herself and agreed. "You were supposed to eat," she scolded.

Two hot tears rolled down my cheeks.

"Nobody will notice on a galloping goose," Aunt Adah consoled us. The veil will hide it."

Mother decided to make the best of it.

"It's a truly beautiful dress," she observed.

"She's still a beautiful bride," Isobel said.

"She's the best of your three," Aunt Adah contributed.

Mother and Aunt Adah were searching for handkerchiefs to dry their own eyes. Such a fuss and to-do. I began to tremble slightly and felt cold as ice.

Then they put on the veil, and we all cried.

Larry arrived, the official wedding coach driver for the day, to take us to the church. It was decorated with white satin ribbons, as were the horses. We went downstairs, careful of our finery, and crowded into the coach. I was glad for a breath of fresh air, but the movement of the coach made me feel dizzy.

My petticoats and veil took up so much room, I couldn't see out.

Larry drove around the back of the church to the door of the reception hall. He wrapped the reins around the brake and jumped down to place the steps and help us out.

Inside, Lavinia and Cora were waiting for us with the flowers, along with Delores Rojas bringing Maria Luz, our little flower girl.

A draft was blowing through the hall. I began to shiver. Aunt Adah hurried to shut the door as Larry drove the coach away. Almost at once, I felt a flush of heat and broke out in perspiration.

"You look a bit feverish, Dear," Mother remarked, feeling my brow. "Do try to relax."

Lavinia had used cuttings from the pink Cecil Bruner vine at the ranch to make lovely wreaths for the girls and bouquets with long white satin streamers. The flowers were quite fresh and fragrant, smelling slightly of cinnamon.

Millie and Ellen were suddenly young ladies; I had never seen them look so pretty. They were still wary of me, which made me feel even worse. I went over to them and made my overdue apology:

"Sorry I was so awful about the breakfast. You worked so hard to make it and you even picked a geranium for me. And I didn't want it!"

"It's okay," Millie told me so sweetly.

"Yes, we ate it ourselves," Ellen added.

"Look at you two! You're all grown-up and so pretty!" I meant it, too.

They were eager to make friends again and threw their arms around me for kisses and hugs, so it was all right. I wasn't sure I deserved it. Grown-ups might not have been so forgiving.

Isobel looked like a queen in her blue silk suit. The hat Uma had made for her was of tailored blue silk with a high crown, swathed in a cloud of blue polka dot veiling. It gave her a regal air. Of course, Isobel could make a house dress and apron look stylish.

Then, Lavinia produced my flowers, and they were so utterly bridal everyone started wiping their eyes again. Both the wreath that fitted over my veil and my large bouquet were made of the purest white roses. Their fragrance filled the room.

"White roses!" Isobel exclaimed in wonder. "Wherever did you find them?"

"Behind Saint Bartholomew's Catholic Church, Isobel," Lavinia said calmly, staring Izzie right in the eye.

"But, Lavinia," Izzie protested.

"Don't worry about it," Lavinia insisted. "It will be fine."

Isobel seemed doubtful, but just then we began to hear organ music overhead, and Cousin Edgar came bounding down the inside stairs to give us the latest bulletin.

"Here you are!" He exclaimed. "Whit and Paul are waiting in the vestry with Reverend Michaels. Gad is Whit nervous! You wouldn't believe it, he's white as a sheet!" He beamed at us with satisfaction. "People are starting to come in. Won't be long now."

He gave me a close inspection. "Alta, you are a stunner! I always knew you would be." He gave me a smacking kiss on the cheek and rushed off, back upstairs.

I took a deep breath—wishing my knees didn't feel as if they would buckle under me at any moment now. I couldn't fall, it would ruin my dress. It was bad enough that I couldn't seem to keep the satin streamers of my bouquet from pooling on the floor. I held on tight to my bouquet and tried to stop the way it was trembling in my hands.

For the first time, I noticed the reception hall.

The church ladies had done us proud. White streamers with

great white ribbon rosettes looped the walls and the five refreshment tables: three tables for the various sandwiches and salads —all attractively laid out ready-to-go and covered with white napkins—the punch table, stacked with cups and featuring a great bowl, sat cooling itself with a chunk of precious ice, and the cake table.

Mrs. Nettleton was fussing with the cake table, positioning the three-tier cake just so. It was a real wedding cake, just like in New York! Why had I expected anything else? In the kitchen, silver trays of decorated squares from the flat-sheet cakes waited to be brought out as needed.

Each table was enhanced by a scattering of rose petals and a vase of roses, made as huge as possible with cuttings from the few hedges and fir trees around town. One seemed to have decorative greens from someone's vegetable garden—I was sure I saw dill and carrot tops! It was lovely.

The cake table was entirely bridal with white roses. The only color was the bits of green frosting leaves.

Marva Dooley came out of the kitchen and she and Mrs. Nettleton came to admire my dress and veil, before hurrying upstairs to claim the seats being held for them. Aunt Adah and Cora followed, with Cora pausing to touch foreheads with me through the veil.

"Courage, Alta. I'll see you up there."

Thinking of the church filled with people made me perspire all over.

I was surprised to see Uma slipping in the outside door. I'd been afraid she wouldn't come after all and was pleased to see her.

"Good," I said. "You came."

"Not good," she snapped at me, grabbing a fold of material around my waist. "I told you to start eating. Here you are baggy again!"

Muttering under her breath, she got Isobel to hold my veil aside, gathered the extra fabric, produced a needle and thread, which I swear was stuck in her hatband, and tacked the offending material in a clump at the back of my waist.

Mother *tut-tutted*. Such a shame, after all the fittings.

"There," Uma muttered, snapping her thread, and returning the needle to her hatband. Isobel rearranged the veil.

Uma stared down the circle of watchers who were somewhat surprised by her temper.

"What? Nobody will notice but Whit!" she huffed. "Just don't take off the veil."

No one could object to that!

Uma scuttled away up the stairs, to squeeze into the back pew, I presume, leaving me to feel like an idiot. Mother and Izzie were now using their hankies to smother laughter.

I didn't think it was funny at all. I had disappointed my friend and was a wretched model for her stunning dress. Whit was getting skin and bones tonight. I wondered just how much weight I had lost in the last few months. So stupid of me. Why was it so cold in here? I was shivering again so hard I had bitten my tongue!

Phillip came briskly down the stairs.

"Time to come up. The church is full, and Mr. Carlton is waiting for you in the vestibule."

He took a good look at me.

"What's the matter, Alta? You look worse than Whit, and he's looking rattlesnake-bit."

"Just nervous," I waved off his concern. "I wasn't expecting it all to be so *big*."

"Take it easy," he urged me. "See you upstairs." And he was gone out into the reception hall.

I wasn't sure I could make it, but we started up the stairs: the girls first, Mother supporting me as well as she could in the narrow stairwell, and Isobel coming behind, holding the train of my veil.

Phillip came last. Looking back, I thought he lingered by the punch bowl. But that was silly. I must have been wrong; he was right there with us.

As we came out into the vestibule, warm August sunshine was streaming in through the open front door. I stepped into it to get warm and was greeted by clapping. Startled, I saw a crowd waiting outside. Father pulled me away, waving and smiling at the waiting people, and pulled the door shut.

"The church is full. They are waiting for the reception to start," he explained.

Although the door had just been open, it was very stuffy in here. I was breathing too fast, trying to catch my breath. Must stop that—I had read somewhere that could make you faint!

Father looked at me with concern. "Alta, are you quite well?"

Mother hastened to reassure him, "She has a massive case of the vapors, Horace, that's all. She'll be fine. Remember Adelle on her wedding day?"

I didn't remember anything like that, but I had been a child. I remembered very well Aggie had been a pain. I wished Mother were a little more worried about me; but no, she was smiling mistily and took Jeremy's arm to be escorted down to the front pew to join Aunt Adah.

When Mother was seated, Miss Frey brought the piece she was playing to an unwritten final chord and after a pause, filled with rustling as the choir of eight singers rose to its feet, began the introduction to their hymn.

At that point, my knees did buckle. Father caught my arm and held me up.

"Good God, Alta, what's wrong?" he asked in a loud whisper, as the choir began to sing.

"It's nothing, Father. I'm just nervous, I guess. You heard Mother."

"Alta, do you want to call this off? We can, you know. You don't have to go through with this if you feel you are making a mistake!"

"No, no!" I hissed in horror. "I want to get married. I'm just nervous." I hung on tight to his arm.

Father, at least, was suitably concerned!

"Here, sir. Let me," Phillip said, stepping forward. He lifted my veil and threw it back over my head. He produced a silver flask from his back pocket, uncapped it, and handed it to me.

"Take a good swig of this, Alta. It will brace you up a bit. I'm betting you'll be fine once we get started."

I looked at Father.

"It couldn't hurt," he agreed.

I looked at Isobel. She shrugged.

So, I did as I was told. I handed my bouquet to Isobel, took the flask, and tilted my head back to take a mouthful. The liquid seared my mouth and throat and burned all the way down, making me truly gasp for air—I presume it was whiskey. Yet, even as I opened my mouth to protest, sweet warmth began to spread up from my stomach.

"One more," Phillip urged. "Maybe not so big."

I obeyed, and it was the same as before, but the warm rush was even better. I sighed and smiled, feeling myself relax for the first time on this momentous day.

"That should do it," Phillip took the flask back and offered it to Father. Father took a big swallow and sighed with pleasure. Phillip had one, too. Isobel declined. Phillip twisted the cap back on and restored the flask to his pocket. It must be empty now.

We all stood smiling at each other as the choir launched into their final chorus.

"That hit the spot," Father remarked.

"Thank you, Philip," I said. "You're going to be the world's best brother-in-law."

His face was rather fuzzy, and my tongue had trouble forming the words, but my regard for my remarkable new relative was sincere.

Phillip leaned forward and kissed me on the forehead.

"Whit's a lucky man," he said.

Then he gave me a round lozenge. "Eat this," he said.

I obediently put it in my mouth. It was licorice.

Phillip gave one to Father and took one, himself.

"For our breath."

"Good thinking, young man," Father complimented.

Phillip pulled my veil back down and Isobel gave me back my bouquet. She was grinning at me.

"Feeling better, are you?" she asked.

"Much," I agreed.

The choir was finished. We heard the rustle of them sitting back down.

"Are you ready?" Phillip asked, looking around.

Everyone was. He went through, leaving the door open, and walked down the aisle in a stately manner, nodding to Miss Frey and turning to take his place beside Whit and the other groomsmen to the right of the altar.

Miss Frey began "The Bridal Processional," with greater emotion than I had ever heard her play before.

Isobel brought Maria Luz forward and started her off down the aisle with a little push. The child seemed to relish everyone looking at her and scattered petals with a will. It was only when she reached the altar that she seemed to falter. Then there was a burst of laughter.

"What happened?" Ellen asked, craning to try to see.

"Oh," whispered Millie, in distress, "She didn't go to the

left like we practiced, she ran to Whit and is hanging onto his leg!"

"Drat!" exclaimed Ellen.

Father was chuckling. Isobel hissed at Millie, and she started down next, suddenly poised as if nothing had happened. Ellen started on her turn. Then, there were more ripples of laughter.

"What is it?" Now I was craning to see.

"Those silly girls," Isobel was disgusted. "First, Millie made faces and tried to get Maria Luz to come over to her, and then Ellen just picked her up and took her there." What did it matter where the child stood? Isobel composed herself and began her journey. We were next!

"Last chance to call the whole thing off," Father offered jovially, teasing me.

"No, let's do it," I insisted, taking his right arm, and smiling at him with all the love I was feeling.

"Alta, you are a beautiful bride," he smiled back.

I couldn't stop smiling at him. "At least you're not toting your gun," I said.

Father laughed and took me through the door. We were assaulted by the scent of roses.

Along the aisle, the pews were draped with white rosettes like downstairs. Great urns of pink cabbage roses graced either side of the altar. The church smelled like a bower.

My eyes were sharp even if my tongue was not, and I caught Whit's eyes at once. They blazed at me in the way I had always loved. I was ready to be married now.

Miss Frey burst triumphantly into the familiar processional from "Aida."

I was warm and fuzzy now and felt I was floating down the aisle on Father's arm, supremely happy, all nerves forgotten, going toward the future I had always wanted.

We reached the altar and paused before the Reverend

Michaels. Whit stepped forward and joined us. He looked full of joy.

The dearly beloved ceremony began.

"Who gives this woman?" the Reverend asked.

"I do," Father said. He kissed my forehead through the veil.

Isobel stepped forward and I handed off my bouquet to her.

Father took that hand and, with ceremony, gave it to Whit.

Whit broke with tradition in a way we had not rehearsed. Taking my hand in his left, he turned and offered the right to vigorously shake Father's hand.

The congregation rustled. They liked that.

"Thank you, Sir. You are giving me an angel," Whit said, loudly so everyone could hear.

A great sigh drifted through the ranks of watching ladies. Noses were blown; I think the men were affected, too. I thought it was very romantic, myself, and felt all misty as Whit leaned close to me to peer through the veil.

"Licorice?" he remarked with surprise, in a rather loud whisper.

Father whispered back, no doubt sharing more scented breath. "Yes, Phillip gave it to us. To cover the whiskey."

"Ahh," Whit replied, perfectly understanding. In fact, he smelled of licorice, himself!

He turned us to face the reverend—who was frowning —expectantly.

"Are you quite sure you are ready now?" he asked crossly.

"Carry on, Sir!" Father gave him a smart military salute and briskly marched the few steps to the front pew to join Mother.

Her whisper was loud enough for both Whit and I to hear: "Really Horace!" I had never heard her scold him before.

Considerable tittering was coming from the pews.

However, the reverend now smiled forgivingly and began his traditional remarks about the state of marriage.

I couldn't stop looking at Whit's beloved face. I was so happy to be there. I could tell he didn't really mind so much that I was all skin and bones. We were both where we wanted to be.

The reverend was approaching the vows. Even that did not make me nervous anymore. I had planned exactly how to handle this last problem.

I knew beyond any question of a doubt that my marriage would be like Adelle's—not Aggie's. Whit understood that I would always be working at the Mercantile. He had willingly given me the courtship I had wanted. There was only this one hurdle left.

When Reverend Michaels asked me if I would love, honor, and "obey," I gave my "I do" in a clear, firm voice. Whit looked over at me and laughed out loud. He raised our entwined hands to kiss mine.

If the congregation did not understand why the groom laughed when the bride made her vows, it was because they could not see what he could *clearly* see, standing beside me. The glamorous, flowing veil, with its fluttering roses, hid from all eyes but his that I held my left arm behind my back—with two fingers firmly crossed.

He understood me perfectly.

Acknowledgments

Rose Walker would like to thank Breanna Bean for early copy editing.

About the Author

After a career in university press publishing, Rose Walker has retired to live up a mountain in the El Dorado Hills of Northern California's Sierra Nevada, where she writes her romances. As a child, she lived in Gallup, New Mexico during World War II. Although her family moved to the Pacific Northwest, she never forgot her love for the land of enchantment.

Made in the USA
Las Vegas, NV
06 August 2023

75726853R00329